"One
HELL
of a book!"

—Robert Bloch, author of *Psycho*

"If they don't manage to 'zap' you (as they did me) at least once, then you're probably not living in the twentieth century."

—Thomas N. Scortia, author of *The Glass Inferno*

"*Inferno* is quite literally a cakewalk through hell. . . . I kid you not, Larry Niven and Jerry Pournelle have had the chutzpah to rewrite Dante's *Inferno* as if they were some unholy hybrid of Roger Zelazny, Robert Heinlein, and Philip José Farmer. You are right there in the nether-reaches of the ultimate Sam Peckinpah movie with all the matter-of-fact solidity of a Hal Clement novel. It gets to you, it really does, this being lunacy of a transcendent order."

—Norman Spinrad, author of *No Direction Home*

Books by Larry Niven and Jerry Pournelle

Inferno
The Mote in God's Eye
Oath of Fealty

Books by Jerry Pournelle

Birth of Fire
High Justice
King David's Spaceship
The Mercenary
West of Honor

Published by POCKET BOOKS

INFERNO

LARRY NIVEN
AND
JERRY POURNELLE

POCKET BOOKS

New York   London   Toronto   Sydney   Tokyo

Another *Original* publication of POCKET BOOKS

POCKET BOOKS, a division of Simon & Schuster, Inc.
1230 Avenue of the Americas, New York, N.Y. 10020

ISBN: 0-671-67055-7

First Pocket Books printing May 1976

24   23   22   21   20   19   18   17   16   15

POCKET and colophon are trademarks of
Simon & Schuster, Inc.

Printed in the U.S.A.

For Dante Alighieri

WALL

HILLS

PLAIN OF JARS

VESTIBULE

ACHERON

FIRST CIRCLE: VIRTUOUS PAGANS

FERRY

VILLAS

OBSERVATORY

PALACE OF MINOS

VILLAS

CLIFF

SECOND CIRCLE: THE WINDS

CLIFF

THIRD CIRCLE: THE GLUTTONS

CLIFF

FOURTH CIRCLE: HOARDERS & WASTERS

CHASM

BRIDGE BUILDERS

CLIFF

SWAMP

FIFTH CIRCLE: WRATHFUL & SULLEN

ADMINISTRATIVE CENTER OF HELL

WALLS OF DIS

TOMBS

GREAT MAUSOLEUM

SIXTH CIRCLE: HERETICS

THE GYAS: LAKE OF BOILING BLOOD

ISLAND: SEVENTH CIRCLE

ROUND ONE

ROUND TWO: WOOD OF SUICIDES

ROUND THREE: FIERY DESERT

WOOD OF SUICIDES

GREAT CLIFF

EDGE OF LOWER HELL

LOWER HELL

WATERFALL

PART I

1

I THOUGHT ABOUT BEING DEAD.

I could remember every silly detail of that silly last performance. I was dead at the end of it. But how could I think about being dead if I had died?

I thought about that, too, after I stopped having hysterics. There was plenty of time to think.

Call me Allen Carpentier. It's the name I wrote under, and someone will remember it. I was one of the best-known science-fiction writers in the world, and I had a lot of fans. My stories weren't the kind that win awards, but they entertained, and I had written a lot of them. The fans all knew me. Someone ought to remember me.

It was the fans who killed me. At least, they let me do it. It's an old game. At science-fiction conventions the fans try to get their favorite author washed-out stinking drunk. Then they can go home and tell stories about how Allen Carpentier really tied one on and they were right there to see it. They add to the stories until legends are built around what writers do at conventions. It's all in fun. They really like me, and I like them.

I think I do. But the fans vote the Hugo awards, and you have to be popular to win. I'd been nominated five times for awards and never won one, and I was out to make friends that year. Instead of hiding in a back booth with other writers I was at a fan party, drinking with a roomful of short ugly kids with pimples, tall serious Harvard types, girls with long stringy hair, half-pretty girls half-dressed to show it, and damn few people with good manners.

Remember the drinking party in *War and Peace?* Where one of the characters bets he can sit on a window ledge and drink a whole bottle of rum without touching the sides? I made the same bet.

The convention hotel was a big one, and the room was eight stories up. I climbed out and sat with my feet dangling against the smooth stone building. The smog had blown away, and Los Angeles was beautiful. Even with the energy shortage there were lights everywhere, moving rivers of lights on the freeways, blue glows from swimming pools near the hotel, a grid of light stretching out as far as I could see. Somewhere out there were fireworks, but I don't know what they were celebrating.

They handed me the rum. "You're a real sport, Allen," said a middle-aged adolescent. He had acne and halitosis, but he published one of the biggest science-fiction newsletters around. He wouldn't have known a literary reference if it bit him on the nose. "Hey, that's a long way down."

"Right. Beautiful night, isn't it? Arcturus up there, see it? Star with the largest proper motion. Moved a couple of degrees in the last three thousand years. Almost races along."

Carpentier's trivial last words: a meaningless lecture

to people who not only knew it already, but had read it in my own work. I took the rum and tilted my head back to drink.

It was like drinking flaming battery acid. There was no pleasure in it. I'd regret this tomorrow. But the fans began to shout behind me, and that made me feel good until I saw why. Asimov had come in. Asimov wrote science articles and histories and straight novels and commentaries on the Bible and Byron and Shakespeare, and he turned out more material in a year than anyone else writes in a lifetime. I used to steal data and ideas from his columns. The fans were shouting for him, while I risked my neck to give them the biggest performance of all the drunken conventions of Allen Carpentier.

With nobody watching.

The bottle was half empty when my gag reflex cut in and spilled used rum into my nose and sinuses. I jackknifed forward to cough it out of my lungs and pitched right on over.

I don't think anyone saw me fall.

It was an accident, a stupid accident caused by stupid drunkenness, and it was all the fans' fault anyway. They had no business letting me do it! And it was an accident, I know it was. I wasn't feeling *that* sorry for myself.

The city was still alive with lights. A big Roman candle burst with brilliant pinpoints of yellows and greens against the starry skies. The view was pleasant as I floated down the side of the hotel.

It seemed to take a long time to get to the bottom.

2

THE BIG SURPRISE WAS THAT I COULD BE SURPRISED. That I could be anything. That I could be.

I was, but I wasn't. I thought I could see, but there was only a bright uniform metallic color of bronze. Sometimes there were faint sounds, but they didn't mean anything. And when I looked down, I couldn't see myself.

When I tried to move, nothing happened. It felt as if I had moved. My muscles sent the right position signals. But nothing happened, nothing at all.

I couldn't touch anything, not even myself. I couldn't feel anything, or see anything, or sense anything except my own posture. I knew when I was sitting, or standing, or walking, or running, or doubled up like a contortionist, but I felt nothing at all.

I screamed. I could hear the scream, and I shouted for help. Nothing answered.

Dead. I had to be dead. But dead men don't think about death. What do dead men think about? Dead men don't think. I was thinking, but I was dead. That struck me as funny and set off hysterics, and then I'd

get myself under control and go round and round with
it again.

Dead. This was like nothing any religion had ever
taught. Not that I'd ever caught any of the religions
going around, but none had warned of this. I certainly
wasn't in Heaven, and it was too lonely to be Hell.

*It's like this, Carpentier: this is Heaven, but you're
the only one who ever made it.* Hah!

I couldn't be dead. What, then? Frozen? Frozen!
That's it, they've made me a corpsicle! The convention was in Los Angeles, where the frozen-dead movement started and where it has the most supporters.
They must have frozen me, put me in a double-walled
coffin with liquid nitrogen all around me, and when
they tried to revive me the revival didn't work. What am
I now? A brain in a bottle, fed by color-coded tubes?
Why don't they try to talk to me?

Why don't they kill me?

Maybe they still have hopes of waking me. Hope.
Maybe there's hope after all.

It was flattering, at first, to think of teams of special-
ists working to make me human again. The fans!
They'd realized it was their fault, and they'd paid for
this! How far in the future would I wake up? What
would it be like? Even the definition of *human* might
have changed.

Would they have immortality? Stimulation of psy-
chic power centers in the brain? Empires of thousands
of worlds? I'd written about all of these, and my books
would still be around! I'd be famous. I'd written
about—

I'd written stories about future cultures raiding corp-
sicles for spare parts, transplants. Had that happened
to me? My body broken up for spares? Then why was
I still alive?

Because they couldn't use my brain.

Then let them throw it out!

Maybe they just couldn't use it yet.

I couldn't tell how long I was there. There was no sense of time passing. I screamed a lot. I ran nowhere forever, to no purpose: I couldn't run out of breath, I never reached a wall. I wrote novels, dozens of them, in my head, with no way to write them down. I relived that last convention party a thousand times. I played games with myself. I remembered every detail of my life, with a brutal honesty I'd never had before; what else could I do? All through it, I was terrified of going mad, and then I'd fight the terror, because that could drive me mad—

I think I did not go mad. But it went on, and on, and on, until I was screaming again.

Get me out of here! Please, anyone, someone, get me out of here!

Nothing happened, of course.

Pull the plug and let me die! Make it stop! Get me out of here!

Nothing.

Hey, Carpentier. Remember "The Chill"? Your hero was a corpsicle, and they'd let his temperature drop too low. His nervous system had become a superconductor. Nobody knew he was alive in there, frozen solid but thinking, screaming in his head, feeling the awful cold—

No! For the love of God, get me out of here!

I was lying on my left side in a field, with dirt under me and warm light all around me. I was staring at my navel, and I could see it! It was the most beautiful sight I'd ever imagined. I was afraid to move; my navel and I might pop like a soap bubble. It took a long time to get the nerve to lift my head.

I could see my hands and feet and the rest of me. When I moved my fingers I could see them wriggle.

There wasn't a thing wrong with me. It was as if I had never fallen eight stories to be smashed into jelly.

I was clothed in a loose white gown partly open down the front. Not very surprising, but where was the hospital? Surely they didn't waken Sleepers in the middle of a field?

They? I couldn't see anyone else. There was a field of dirt, trampled here and there, sloping downhill to become a shiny mud flat. I raised my head, and he was standing behind me. A fat man, tall but dumpy and chunky enough that at first I didn't notice his height. His jaw was massively square and jutted out, the first thing I noticed about his face. He had wide lips and a high forehead, and short, blunt, powerful fingers. He wore a hospital gown something like mine.

He was beautiful. Everything was beautiful. But my navel? *Magnifique!*

"You are well?" he asked.

He spoke with an accent: Mediterranean; Spanish, perhaps, or Italian. He was looking closely at me, and he asked again, "You are well?"

"Yes. I think so. Where am I?"

He shrugged. "Always they ask that question first. Where do you think you are?"

I shook my head and grinned for the pleasure of it. It was pleasure to move, to see myself move, to feel my buttocks press against the dirt and know something would oppose my movements. It was ecstasy to see myself in the bright light around me. I looked up at the sky.

There wasn't any sky.

Okay, there has to be a sky. I know that. But I saw nothing. Thick clouds? But there was no detail to the clouds, just a uniform gray above me. Even in my sensation-starved condition it was ugly.

I was in the middle of a field of dirt that stretched a couple of miles to some low brown hills. There were people on the hills, a lot of them, running after something I couldn't make out. I sat up to scan the horizon.

The hills ran up against a high wall that stretched in both directions as far as I could see. It seemed straight as a mathematician's line, but I sensed the slightest of inward curves just before it vanished into deep gloom. There was something wrong with the perspective, but I can't describe precisely what, just that it didn't seem right.

The hills and the mud flats formed a wide strip between the wall and a fast-moving river of water black as ink. The river was a mile away and didn't seem very wide at that distance. I could see it perfectly, another perceptual distortion because it was too far away for the details I could make out.

Beyond the river were green fields and white Mediterranean villas, walled complexes with the squat classical look to them, some quite large. They weren't arranged in any order, and the effect was very pleasing. I turned back to the wall.

Not very high, I thought. High enough to be trouble climbing, perhaps two or three times my six-foot height. I was hampered by the perspective problem. The nearest point of the wall might have been a mile away or ten, though ten seemed ridiculous.

I took a deep breath and didn't like the smells. Fetid, with an acrid tinge, decay and sickly sweet perfume to cover the smells of death, orange blossoms mingled with hospital smells, all subtle enough that I hadn't noticed them before, but sickening all the same. I won't mention the smells often, but they were always there. Most stinks you get used to and soon don't notice, but this had too much in the blend and the blend changed too often. You'd just get used to one and there'd be another.

Beside me on the ground was a small bronze bottle with a classical beaker shape. I figured it would hold maybe a quart. Except for the man standing above me there wasn't another blessed thing.

"Never mind where I am," I said. "Where have I been? I don't remember passing out. I was screaming, and here I am. Where was I?"

"First you ask where you are. Then where you were. Do you think of nothing else you should say?" He was frowning disapproval, as if he didn't like me at all. So what the hell was he doing here?

Breaking me out of wherever I'd been, of course. "Yeah. Thanks."

"You should thank the One who sent me to you."

"Who was that?"

"You asked Him for help—"

"I don't remember asking anyone for help." But this time I'd heard him pronounce the capital letter. "Yeah. 'For the love of God,' I said. Well?"

The fat meaty lips twitched, and his eyes filled with concern. When he looked at me it wasn't in distaste, but in sympathy. "Very well. You will have a great deal to learn. First, I answer your questions. Where are you? You are dead, and you lie on the ground of the Vestibule to Hell. Where were you?" He kicked the bronze bottle with a sandaled foot. "In there."

Hot diggity damn, I'm in the nut hatch and the head loony's come to talk to me.

Carpentier wakes up a thousand years after his last flight and sloppy landing, and already he's in trouble. Spoons and forks and chopsticks, traffic lights, the way a man puts his pants on, all may have to be relearned.

Law and customs change in a thousand years. Society may not even recognize Carpentier as sane.

But wake him in a thirtieth-century loony bin among thirtieth-century twitchies, and now what? How can he adjust to anything?

There were other bottles sitting unattended on the dirt, some larger than mine, some smaller. I don't know why I hadn't noticed them before. I picked one up and dropped it quick. It burned my fingers, and there were faint sounds coming from inside it.

It sounded like human speech in a foreign language, a voice screaming curses. That tone couldn't be anything else. Endless curses screamed—

Why would they put radios in old bronze bottles and scatter them through the loony bin? My hypothesis needed more work.

The people up on the hills were still running. They'd looped back to about where I'd first seen them, and whatever it was they chased, they hadn't caught it yet. Do they let the nuts run in circles in futuristic loony bins?

Where had I been? Where? There wasn't any hospital around here, no facilities for keeping all or part of a corpsicle, nothing but this crazy man and a lot of bronze bottles and people running in circles and—and insects of some kind. Something whined and did a kamikaze into my ear. Something else stung me on the back of the neck. I slapped frantically, but there wasn't anything to see.

It felt good even to hurt myself slapping.

My "rescuer" was patiently waiting for me to make some response. It wouldn't hurt to humor him until I had more information.

"Okay, I'm in the Vestibule of Hell and I was in a bottle. A djinn bottle. How long?" I told him the date on which I'd fallen from the window.

He shrugged. "You will find that time has not the same meaning here as you are accustomed to. We have all the time we will ever need. Eternity lies before us. I am unable to tell you how long you were in that beaker, but I can assure you it is not important."

Not important? I almost went mad in there! The realization made me start to shiver, and he dropped to his knees beside me, all concern, to put a hand on my shoulder.

"It is over now. God will not allow you back into the bottle. I cannot assure you that there will be nothing worse before you leave Hell. There will be much worse. But with faith and hope you will endure it, and you will be able to leave."

"That's a lot of comfort."

"It is infinite comfort. Did you not understand? I know a way out of here!"

"Yeah? So do I. Right over that wall."

He laughed. I listened for a while, and it got irritating. Finally he choked it down to a chuckle. "I'm sorry, but they all say that, too. I suppose there is nothing for it but to let you try. After all—we have plenty of time." He laughed again.

Now what? Would he turn me in if I tried to climb the wall? I got up, surprised at how good I felt except for the gnats and the smell. My imaginary exercises in the bottle—

Look, wherever I really spent all that time, effectively I was in a bottle, right? It's a convenient figure of speech. Anyway, my exercises in the bottle had paid off. I started briskly toward the wall.

Wherever the ground dipped low it became squishy mud, ankle-deep, with small live things in it. I tried to stick to the high ground. The fat man kept right alongside me. There was no chucking him. After a while I said, "If we're going to walk together I might as well know your name."

"Benito. Call me Benny if you like."

"Okay. Benito." *Benny* sounded much too friendly. "Look, Benito, don't you want out of here?"

I hit a nerve. He stopped short, his wide face a gamut of emotions unlike anything I'd even seen. After a long time he said, "Yes."

"Then come over the wall with me."

"I can't. You can't. You'll see." He wouldn't say anything else, just kept pace with me as I walked on.

And on.

And on, and on, and on. The wall was a *long* way off. I was right about the perspective. We'd been walking for over an hour as far as I could tell, and the wall looked no closer.

We walked until we were exhausted, and it was still a long way off. I sat down in the mud to slap gnats. "Didn't seem that far. How high is that thing, anyway? Must be colossal."

"It is no more than three meters high."

"Don't be silly."

"Look behind you."

That was the shock of my life. The river was now maybe three miles away instead of one. And we'd walked for *hours*. But—

Benito nodded. "We could walk for eternity and never reach the wall. And we *have* eternity. No, you don't believe me. Very well, convince yourself. Continue toward the wall. Continue until even you are certain it can never be reached, and then I will tell you how you can escape."

It took me several hours, but I finally believed him.

The wall was like light speed. We could get arbitrarily close, but we couldn't ever reach it. Like light speed, or the bottom of a black hole, but like nothing else in the universe I knew.

We weren't going out this way.

And—and just where were we?

3

I sat in the dirt and slapped gnats while Benito explained it again.

"We are dead and in Hell. This is the Vestibule to Hell, where those who would make no choices in life are condemned. Neither warm nor cold, believers nor blasphemers—you see them in the hills. They chase a banner they will never catch."

I remembered then. "Dante's *Inferno?*"

Benito nodded, his big square jaw heaving like a broaching whale. "You have read the *Inferno*, then. Good. That was the first clue I had to the way out of here. We must go down—"

"Sure, all the way." Something about a lake of ice, and a hole in the center of it. It had been a long time since I had read Dante. I couldn't see that remembering a thirteenth-century book would do me any good to begin with. This couldn't possibly be the real Hell. Dante's cosmology had been ludicrous, for one thing.

So where was I? "How come you're so sure this is the place Dante described?"

"Where else could it be? All of the features are here. All of the details."

And I'd been dead a long time. Centuries? What kind of civilization would build an exact copy of Dante's Inferno? An Infernoland. Was it part of a larger amusement park, like Frontierland in the Disneyland complex? Or was Infernoland all there was to it?

Who was Benito? A stooge, or a revived corpsicle like me?

The wall. How had they managed that trick? The wall hadn't moved, and I certainly had. Some kind of local field effect? A time slip? Bent space? Come on, Carpentier, you *wrote* the stuff. What's the explanation? Not *the* way they did it, just a plausible way!

"First, we must cross the river," Benito was saying. "Do you believe me now when I tell you that you must not attempt to swim it, or even get wet from it, or must you try that too?"

"What happens if I just dive in?"

"Then you will be as you were in the bottle. Aware and unable to move. But it will be very cold, and very uncomfortable, and you will be there for all eternity knowing you put yourself there."

I shuddered and slapped a gnat. He might be lying. I wasn't going to try it.

It looked very nice across the river, and that was where we had to get before we could find Dante Alighieri's escape hole in the center of Infernoland. The hell with getting to the center! Let me get to those villas over there and I'd be happy enough. "Who's on the other side of the river?"

"Virtuous pagans," Benito answered. "Those who never knew the Word of God, but kept the Commandments. They are not persecuted. Their fate may be the most cruel of all those in this place."

"Because they aren't tortured?"

"Because they think they are happy. You'll find out, let us go and see them."

"How?"

"There is a ferryboat. Once it was a rowing boat, but—"

"Got overcrowded in Hell. Too many arrivals. Sure." And in Disneyland I'd been on a Mississippi riverboat big enough for fifty or sixty people to walk around on. It chugged around on a little pond it shared with a miniature clipper ship. The Builders of Infernoland had a sense of humor, putting a ferryboat in place of Charon's old rowboat.

Maybe we'd meet some of the paying customers on the ferry. I didn't think Benito was one. He behaved more like a fanatical Catholic.

And what was I? Nobody had given me any role to play. Who inhabits Infernoland?

Who inhabits the Inferno?

Damned souls. Could that be my job now—to play damned soul for the amusement of tourists? It wasn't a role I liked very much.

It took as long to leave the wall as it had to go toward it. At least things were consistent. There were laws to this place, if only I could discover them.

When we passed the bottle that had been beside me when I woke up, we turned left and angled toward the river. An old drinking song from science-fiction conventions kept running through my head. "If hosen and shoon thou never gavest men, *every night and all*, the fire will burn thee to the bare bone, *and Christ receive thy soul.*" Was that really where I was, in a real Hell, where justice was meted out to the ungodly?

Scary. It would mean that there was a real God, and maybe Jonah was swallowed by a whale in the

Mediterranean Sea, and Joshua ben Nun really did
stop the Earth's rotation for trivial purposes . . .

There was something leaning against a rock. At
first I couldn't make it out: a pink mound with hair
trailing down one side. We got closer and the mound
became five-hundred-odd pounds of woman sitting
cross-legged in stinking mud. A swarm of gnats
hummed around her. She didn't bother to swat them.

She looked up at us with lifeless eyes. Benito took
my arm to hurry me on past her, but I shook him
off. She couldn't be quite sane either, but she might
be able to tell me something straight. It was more
than he would do, and I needed help.

I squatted down to look into her face. She was
pathetic, hardly in shape to help anyone, including
herself. Far back within tunnels of fat were tiny sparks
of life, dull gray against black. Hopeless eyes, almost
lifeless.

Her voice was a husky whisper. "Well?"

"I don't know where I am. I just got here, and I
have to know. Can you help me?"

"Help *you!* I died, and then *this* happened to me!"

"Died?"

"How else do you get into Hell?" Her voice rose
to demand attention despite my shocked surprise. The
full force of her breath washed over in waves. "What
did I do? I don't *deserve* this! I don't belong here *at
all*," she wailed. "I was beautiful. I could eat like a
horse and burn it off in an hour. Then I woke up
here, like *this!*" Her voice dropped to a low, confidential murmur. "We're in the hands of infinite power
and infinite sadism."

I shied back. Another one.

"Is there nothing you can do?" Benito asked her.

"Sure. I can chase banners to keep slim. What's

the point of that? They won't let you do anything meaningful."

I shuddered. It could have been me. "Why would anyone do this to you?"

"I . . . think it must have been because ten-million fat people were cursing me." Her voice turned venomous. "Fat, fat, fat people with no willpower and no self-respect."

"Why?"

"For doing my job! For trying to help people, trying to save them from themselves! For banning cyclamates, that's why! It was for their own good," she ranted. "You can't trust people to be moderate about anything. Some people get sick on cyclamates. They have to be helped. And this is what I get for helping them!"

"We're trying to escape. Want to come with us? Benito thinks we can get out by going down to the center of this crazy place."

A little spark of interest flared in her eyes, and I held my breath. My open mouth had sent me floating down the side of a building; when would I learn to keep it closed? If she came with us we'd never get away. What good was she?

She struggled to get up, then collapsed against her rock. "No, thank you."

"Right." I started to say something else in parting, but what? If anything went at all right, I'd never see her again. I just walked away, and she let her head slump back into the mounds of fat that bulged at her neck.

As we walked away, Benito asked, "What are cyclamates?"

I slapped at a gnat. The gnats were everywhere, stinging us both, but Benito didn't bother to slap at them. "Sugar substitute. For people who want to lose weight."

He frowned. "If there is too much to eat, surely it would be better to eat less and share with those who have none."

I looked at his big paunch and said nothing.

"I too am in Hell," he reminded me.

"Ah. And they can do what they did to her to you . . ." I shuddered. We were lucky.

"I take it you did not agree with her policy?"

"Idiots. If they'd fed as much sugar to the control rats as they gave cyclamates to the experimental group, they'd have killed the controls first. Instead, they doomed a lot of people to fat. There wasn't a good substitute for cyclamates. I know one guy who bought up cases and cases of a cyclamate diet drink just before the ban hit. He used to give cases of 'vintage Tab' as Christmas presents. They were appreciated, too."

Benito said nothing.

"I know a couple who used to drive up to Canada every so often just to buy cyclamates. It was a *stupid* policy." I looked back over my shoulder at the shapeless pink mound. "Still, it seems a little extreme, what they did to her."

"It is not just?"

"How can you call that *just?*" I didn't say anything else, but I remembered what she'd said. " 'We're in the hands of infinite power and infinite sadism.' "

And just who in Hell was Benito? A paying customer having sport? A damned soul like me? Or one of the paid crew of Infernoland? He talked like a religious fanatic; he seemed to take everything at face value.

Did I dare follow him? But what else could I do? One thing was certain: if he could think that woman had been treated justly, he was not much better than a devil himself.

Hey, Carpentier. Would an artificial Hell have artificial devils? I looked at Benito more closely. He was partly bald. There were no horns on his forehead.

We seemed to be covering a lot of ground, as if the effect of too much distance to the wall had been played in reverse. Suddenly we were part of a crowd, all streaming toward the river. Nobody was pushing them along, but they didn't seem friendly and they didn't talk among themselves. Each one was huddled in toward himself, not looking where he was going. Or she, there were a lot of women.

The ferryboat captain had a long white beard and eyes like burning coals. He screamed in rage when anyone was slow getting aboard. We were pressed together on deck, a mass of us so tightly packed that we couldn't move.

"You again!" He'd turned his burning eyes on Benito. "You've come here before! Well, you won't escape again!" He swung a long billyclub at Benito. It hit with a crack that I thought would break my guide's skull, but it only staggered him.

More people packed the decks until I couldn't even see. Finally I felt the boat begin to move. By then I'd have been glad to stay behind, but there was no way off the boat.

Two voices whispered intensely near my ear:

"Why didn't you stop when I screamed?"

"Because you *startled* me into taking my *foot* off the brake. At least I'll never have to listen to your backseat driving again—"

"But we're in Hell, darling. They'll probably put us in a car with no brakes. Maybe they'll give you a horn. You'll like that."

"Shut up! Shut up!"

She did, and quiet descended. No crowd is that quiet. It was as if nobody had anything to say to anyone.

We bumped solid ground. "All off," Charon shouted. "Damned souls! Damned forever! You cursed God, and now you'll pay for it!"

"Damn God and everyone else!" "Piss on you!" "Up the people!" "You're mucking bastards, all of you, get off my *foot!*" "But I don't *belong* here." "What'd I do? Just tell me—" "Damn the lot of you, I died a *man!*"

We pushed and shoved and danced to keep our feet in the swarm. At least we were on the other side. The crowd was hurrying downhill, along a road that ran between thick, high walls. I hung back, hoping Benito would go with the rest. No such luck. The road turned and twisted so we couldn't see what was ahead, but that was good because after a while we were alone.

I tried to climb the wall. It was a tough scramble, and I kept falling back. After the fourth time I sat there below the wall and whimpered.

"Would you like help?" Benito asked.

"Sure. I thought you said the only way out was downhill."

"It is, but we have time to explore. Try again, I will lift you."

He practically threw me over the wall. He didn't look that strong. I sat on top for a second and looked down at him. He seemed to be waiting for me to help him up.

And now what, Carpentier? Fair's fair, he helped you. Yeah, but why? Leave him behind, he's trouble.

But he knows things I don't. And he got me out of the bottle.

*Did he? He says he poured you out of a bottle
the size of a fifth of rum! Leave him.*

I didn't get the chance to decide. While I was thinking it over, Benito began climbing like an alpiner, using
tiny cracks and bumps I could hardly see. Pretty soon
he got one hand on top of the wall and pulled himself
up. He wasn't breathing hard, and he didn't say anything about my sitting there and watching instead of
helping.

I turned to look at the countryside. After all, this
Infernoland seemed to be modeled on Dante's. A quarter of a century ago the *Inferno* had been a required
book for a course in Comparative World Literature.
I'd paid as little attention to the book as I could get
away with. I remembered almost nothing, but certainly the place had not been pleasant. God's own
torture chamber, very medieval.

Vague images came back to me now: devils with
pitchforks, trees that talked and bled, giants and centaurs, fire, snakes . . . but were those from the authentic
Inferno, or were they hangovers from Oz books and
Disney cartoons? *Never mind, Carpentier. You're not
going any further.*

4

IT WAS LOVELY ON THE OTHER SIDE OF THE WALL. I jumped down onto firm ground, grassy and pleasant. The air was clean, as at the top of a mountain, with that fresh smell you get only after a hard backpack into remote country. The gnats were gone. We walked toward the villas, lovely things, square-built, the colors of stone by twilight.

There were crowds around us. Men and women and children—a lot of children, far too many, all watching us with big round eyes (or almond eyes, Hell was thoroughly integrated). Adults and children alike were curious, but none of them said anything.

They didn't want to be near us, either. They shrank away as we approached.

It was embarrassing. I thought we must be carrying the smells of the Vestibule area, the fetid stench of roses and decay. We'd have to find a place to wash.

"I think I'm going to like it here," I said.

Benito looked at me curiously, but he only said, "Pleasant, isn't it? Here there is no punishment."

The word grated. *Punishment* implies authority,

someone with more power and a moral position
superior to yours. I couldn't accept that. We were in
the hands of the Builders of Infernoland, and I'd
learned all about their moral position on the other
side of the black river.

But I didn't flare up at Benito. Lightly I asked,
"These, then, are the privileged customers of Hell?"

"Yes." Benito did not smile. "They never sinned.
They would have reached Heaven if they had known
the Church."

"And the children?"

"Unbaptized."

I'd heard that about Catholic beliefs. Even in
Infernoland it seemed a little rough on the kids. "I
thought they got Limbo."

"Call it Limbo if you wish. This is the First Circle
of Hell." He paused, uncertain. "There are legends
that say the children will be born again."

There were as many children here as there were
adults! As if the Builders had gotten a discount for
quantity. Hmmm. Could these creatures be androids?

It could have come down to a matter of economics.
Android infants would be cheaper than android adults:
smaller, fewer reflexes. Would it be cheaper to build
androids than to find and capture human beings? I
couldn't know, not without knowing the source: who
the Builders were or why *I* was here—placed here
without my consent or knowledge, by an unknown
hand. If me, then why not a thousand others? A
billion?

Benito wouldn't be much help. He didn't seem to
question anything he saw.

Robot or human, child or adult, they didn't seem
unhappy. Except those near us . . . "Benito, what's
the matter with them?"

"They sense that we do not belong here. I come

from deeper in Hell, and the smell of the depths is on my soul."

"But I don't."

His smile was grim. "They will not accept you either."

I wasn't so sure of that. If I found a way to clean up, and different clothing . . . hmm. Knock someone on the head, steal his toga; why not? Well, partly because they'd tear me apart if they caught me. And partly because there was no privacy here. The villas, maybe. Or—

I pointed upslope toward what might have been a domed planetarium, the nearest building in sight of us. "What's that?"

He looked. "I have never seen it before."

"Come on."

He came, but reluctantly. "We might not be permitted entry. This is a public building, but we are not of the appropriate public."

"We—" I stopped because a white-bearded patriarch swathed in purple-bordered white bedsheets had grasped me roughly by the arm. He asked a rude question in gibberish.

"Go peddle your papers," I informed him.

He frowned. "Recent English? I asked of you why you invade a place not meant for you."

"I'm taking a survey. Are you happy here? Do the arrangements satisfy you?"

He snorted. "No."

"Then," asked Benito, "why not leave? There is a way out."

The bearded man looked him over, while several passersby stopped to listen. He said, "In what direction does it lie?"

"Downslope. One must travel all the way to the center. To know evil is one path to knowing good."

It was lousy dialogue. The bearded man thought so too. "I do not question your knowledge of the depths of Hell," he said pointedly. "I think you lie."

"Why would I? We plan to leave Hell—" Benito was interrupted by raucous laughter. A crowd was gathering, and it wasn't friendly.

"You can all leave." Benito seemed deadly serious. "Come with me, deeper and deeper into Hell. Learn to hate evil—"

"Hatred for salvation?" one of the oldsters asked. "A curious route to salvation."

Benito seemed to know him. "Yet, Epictatus, that is what you must learn. Not to hate men, but to hate their sins. And *that* you cannot do moderately. You *know* the truth, now. You know that reason alone is not enough. You must ask for grace . . ."

I slipped out during the sermon. They were standing there politely waiting for him to finish. What might have been a mob scene had become a formal debate.

How long would that last? Benito was pushing them in a direction they wouldn't even consider, and they didn't like him at all. They'd looked at me the same way; candid contempt, and the high bitter flavor of mockery. They wanted out, and they didn't believe there was any way out, and they were damned well not going to listen long to a man they thought didn't belong with them.

Benito was preaching hatred, and they hated *him*. He should have had more sense. Like me.

The dome: it couldn't be a planetarium. There was no sky here. Conceivably it was a bathhouse where I could wash off the stench and possibly find an unguarded toga. I climbed toward it.

There were no guards. I walked between Doric pillars, up black marble steps to an expanse of black marble floor. Half a dozen people were talking in a circle. They seemed lost in distance, but as far away as I was, when they caught sight of me they turned their backs firmly and continued talking.

The language wasn't familiar at all.

The place was as empty as anything I'd seen since I left the area of the bottles. Six rude sons of bitches, and a thing in the center of the black marble floor. It might have been a sculpture, it might have been a machine. A thick silver ring twelve feet tall, standing on edge, and a control board at its base.

The console looked operational. There were labels, in English. A switch (marked ON, OFF), a joystick, and a notch with a knob in it. The notch ran the whole length of the console.

I tried the joystick. It went in all six directions: left, right, forward, back, push down, pull up. When I used the switch the space within the ring clouded, then became starry space.

It *was* a planetarium.

When I pushed on the joystick nothing happened.

I took a closer look at the markings along the notch. They were logarithmic, labeled in parsecs/second. The knob was all the way to the left.

I moved it hard right and tried the joystick again.

The universe came up and hit me in the face. Whoosh! Stars shot past and around me; a sun came at me and exploded into a fraction of a second of intolerable brightness and was gone. And I was flat on my back a couple of yards from the console.

That was some planetarium!

The half-a-dozen natives were watching me with some amusement. Screw 'em. I went back to the console, moved the knob down to one parsec/second, then to a tenth of that. Tried the joystick.

This time the motion was just obvious. I steered

toward a blue-white star; moved the knob to slow
as I approached it. Moved into it.

The brightness should have burned my eyes out. It
wasn't even painful. Odd . . .

I went through the center of the star (X-ray blue)
and came out the other side (tremendous prominences
leaping out ahead of me) and into space. What now?
Find a planet? A different star? Stars were easier to
find in this sparkling emptiness, but I'd *love* to dive
into an Earthlike world. To search out the layers of
it, to see the glowing nickel-iron heart. Let's see, that
not-too-brilliant white fleck could be a yellow dwarf.
I moved the knob—

A large hand fell heavily on my shoulder.

I twitched like a man electrocuted. I turned, and
there was the mob scene I thought I'd left behind me:
fifty-odd large, heavy men surrounding me and Benito
and the Anywhere Machine.

The white-bearded man who spoke English said,
"You are leaving."

I said, "Dammit! Why? Nobody else is using the
damn machine. I've waited all my life for something
like this!"

"We do not want you here," he said. "We waited
because we hoped a messenger of the gods would
come to remove you. We might have asked him questions . . . but we have tolerated you too long. As
for the machine—" One side of his mouth twitched
upward. "If you can carry it you may take it with
you."

I cursed him. I stopped when his wide-shouldered
friends converged. Several of them wore armor! They
moved away in a tight circle with Benito and me in
the center.

I whispered, "Benito, can't you stop them?"

He looked at me. "How?"

Yeah.

But if I'd known what waited below, I'd have fought them.

5

EVEN WHILE THEY MARCHED US TOWARD THE WALL, Benito never gave up.

"You may leave this place!" he shouted. "Hector! Aeneas! You are not cowards, to stay where it is pleasant when there is everything to gain elsewhere! Come with us!"

They ignored him.

They were compact and tough inside their armor: too tough to fight, even if they were men, which I doubted. *Hector, Aeneas:* I knew the names. I remembered the Abe Lincoln robot at Disneyland. Could the armor be part of them? With inspection plates—

"Where is Vergil?" Benito raved. "He is no longer here, is he? And the Emperor Trajan?"

"We had our chance," said the taller, broader one. "We didn't take it. There will be no other."

"Have none come here since?" Benito demanded.

The soldiers barked bitter laughter. "Many."

38

"Is it reasonable to suppose that they will never have the opportunity to leave?"

We had come to the wall. "We'll think about it," one said. "Now out with you. Go where you belong." The gate slammed shut behind us.

I went for the wall on the other side. I examined it without joy. The footholds Benito had used would better have fitted a spider.

Benito watched with a wry smile. "You never give up, do you?"

"No."

"Perseverance is commendable. You will need it, but you must develop other virtues, such as prudence. What will happen if you enter the First Circle again?"

"Maybe they won't catch us this time. I won't go near anyone until I've changed clothes and taken a bath."

"Do not tempt the angels," Benito said. He was quite serious. Yeah, and why not? I was expecting devils in Infernoland. Why not angels?

"That messenger they hoped to see. They *wanted* him to come."

"*They* did, yes. But we are fugitives, Allen."

There were no handholds. This time Benito wouldn't help. I was still trying to climb the wall when a flash flood of people spilled into the far end of the alley. As they foamed toward us in dreadful silence I made one last attempt to go up the wall. Then they swept us up and floated us away.

We were in a marble palace. It was enormous, without furniture. The walls were covered with frescoes of bulls and dolphins and pretty girls wearing flounced skirts and little jackets that opened in front to show bare breasts. The palace was lit with torches in bronze holders along the walls, and there wasn't any sign of modern technology at all.

Except for the palace itself. It wound on and on, chamber after chamber, huge staircases with great pillars inscribed in languages I couldn't read. It was too big; it must have been prestressed concrete or something better. I would have liked to stay and look around, but we were embedded in the flow of the crowd. Nobody spoke or paid us any attention. I was glad for Benito's company. Crowds of strangers bug me, and this one was worse than New York commuters, everyone wrapped up in himself.

We spilled into an enormous room open at the far end. I had a good view through the pillars. The ground sloped sharply away into the bleakest landscape I'd ever seen. The castle was perched on the side of an enormous bowl, a world-sized bowl. Far down into it were the glimmers of fires and the shadow of smoke. I couldn't see far into the smog that hung over everything.

There was a throne at the far end of the audience chamber. An alien occupied it. He was vaguely bovine, but I'd have taken him for an oversized man if it hadn't been for his tail.

Tail!

"What *is* that?" I demanded.

"Minos. Judge of the Dead," said Benito.

The Builders had mixed some Egyptian or Cretan mythology with their Christianity. That, or they'd had to warp their landscape to fit a genuine alien. I could believe a cropping beast becoming an intelligent biped, given time and impetus and perhaps an assist from biological engineers. I'd written stories about that kind of thing.

Could Minos be one of the Builders?

People went up to present themselves to the monster. I couldn't hear what the girl in the yellow dress was telling it, but it grinned and nodded. Abruptly its tail looped out and wrapped around and around the girl. It lifted her.

The tail stretched like the limbs of Plastic Man in the old comic books. The girl shot between two pillars and dwindled, dwindled, dwindled to a speck. Minos' tail must have been tens of miles long at that point. It came snaking back through the air, while the speck that was the girl sank like a single snowflake.

My willing suspension of disbelief went all to hell. I started to giggle hysterically.

Nobody noticed. Nobody but Benito, who watched curiously as I gathered the shreds of my self-control, took him by the arm, pointed at "Minos" and said, "He can't *do* that!"

He was doing it again! The tail stretched out between the pillars like an infinite length of snake, dropped a man in a postman's uniform into the murky air, and came coiling back.

But there wasn't room! Even ignoring the moment arm—that much weight at the end of that much length should have toppled him, and how could such a length of tail, *flexible* tail, be strong enough to stay almost straight? But ignore that, and tell me where there was room for tens of miles of tail to be coiled inside his body?

His feet weren't anchored; I watched until I saw them both move. The tail wasn't stored in the floor, then.

"Are you all right?" Benito asked.

My vision was graying out; my whole body had

a buzzing foot's-asleep feeling. I said, "I'm going
to faint."

"You can't faint here. Hold fast." His hand gripped
my shoulder.

A dark-haired woman, quite pretty, was encoiled in
the tail until she nearly vanished, lifted, and sent spin-
ning off down the bowl. A man in a cabbie's uniform
was next. Three loops of tail and out he went into
space. And another, and another—

There were thousands here. We'd starve before we
reached our turn.

But I didn't feel hungry, and hadn't felt hungry
since I left the bottle, and that was hours ago. Also,
something was wrong with time. "Minos" was in no
hurry. Quite the opposite. He took plenty of time to
deal with each case, and there were plenty of cases;
yet the crowd thinned out much faster than it should
have.

Where were they going? I never saw anyone leave
the room, but there had to be other audience cham-
bers, people slipping off into side passages. There
must have been hundreds, perhaps thousands, of
copies of "Minos."

*Ridiculous mummery. But the tail, Carpentier! Hid-
den in hyperspace, or snaking out of an alternate
time track? If the Builders have that kind of technology, how long were you dead? Ten thousand years?
A million?*

It was our turn. We approached together. Not many
had come up in pairs.

"Sodomites, huh?" Minos said. "Seventh Circle,
Third Level. Or have you got something worse to
confess?"

I said, "I refuse to answer on grounds that my—"

He looked a lot like an angry bull when he frowned, and nothing at all like a machine. He turned to Benito. "You've been here before. Why have you left your proper place?"

"Is that your affair? You see I roam freely through Hell."

"Yes. How?"

"It has been willed that I may do so. You have no right to interfere."

Minos waved at me. "And this one?"

"He has come from the Vestibule," Benito said. "You will note that he comes of his own accord. You may not judge him."

"Lawyers." Minos laughed. "I have problems with lawyers. There are so *many* places appropriate to that breed. Where are you two going, then?"

"Down."

"Back to the First Circle."

We'd spoken simultaneously. Minos laughed. "Back you will not go. Are you sure you don't want me to judge you, Allen Carpenter? My judgment is just and fair. You could choose worse for yourself than justice."

"Cease!" Benito commanded. I jumped. He was a changed man. Power seemed to gather around him as he struck a pose, massive chin jutting out in defiance, his face both calm and stern. Once upon a time he had been used to obedience.

"I am permitted to judge . . ." Suddenly Minos sounded petulant.

"You have already judged me. What other power have you? And this man is not under your jurisdiction. Leave us alone to go in peace."

"Not back up."

"No. Down."

Minos laughed. He waved toward the steps leading

down into the bowl from his throne. "Depart. Thou art sent!" He was still laughing as we started down those steps, the mocking laughter in our ears until we lost sight of the palace.

6

WE WERE ALL RIGHT AS LONG AS THE STEPS CON-
tinued. Unfortunately they soon trailed away into a
broken slope that still dropped at forty-five degrees
or so. At the same time a wind began to rise. Benito
and I turned to face the slope and backed down on
toes and knees and hands.

In fact, the hurricane in my head (Where does
the Minos-thing keep its tail? What is Benito, that he
gives orders to an inhuman that judges all others
who come before it? Is this Hell for a science-fiction
writer, where physical laws are whimsical and puzzles
have no answers?) was nothing compared to the hurricane we were backing into. We moved flat against the
slope, clutching at the rock and digging into the dirt
for footholds.

Benito yelled, "Minos called you Carpenter. Not
Carpentier."

I'd been wondering how the monster knew. "I was
born Carpenter," I shouted down at Benito. "I added

the 'i' to make the name more interesting, easier to
remember. I wrote under Carpentier." And when I
talked to myself (I didn't add) it was Carpentier I
talked to. I'd started that in an effort to memorize
the new pronunciation.

We'd backed onto a broad ledge. I stayed flat as
I looked around.

Someone was dancing to the music of the howling
wind.

He was bones and paunch and long flying hair just
graying unevenly at the temples. He jumped and
danced and flapped his arms like a bird, grim deter-
mination on his homely face.

I hollered into the wind. "Hey, friend—"

He didn't wait for the question. "If I could just
get off the ground!" he wailed. "The guy in the
helmet's got a *dozen!*"

Hey, yeah, I'd been right the first time! It was a
futuristic loony bin geared for psychodrama on the
grand scale! Let them work out their delusions here,
and maybe they'd be fit for whatever unimaginable
society they'd flunked out of . . . And I had answers
to all the questions, in that wonderful moment before
I followed his eyes upward.

The air was full of flying people.

They weren't exactly guiding their flight. The wind
had them. Here it churned them in a momentary
funnel, then flung them outward. There they came in
a straight blast; it hit a shoulder of the mountain and
churned the trapped beings into eddy currents. The
people flew like Kleenex in a hurricane, but they
looked like people, and they howled like Kansans
caught outside in a flash tornado.

Most of them were flying in man-and-woman pairs.
But, yeah, there was one guy surrounded by a good

dozen girls, all in a whirling clump at the top of a rising air column.

The bony guy on the ledge ran off flapping his arms. There were others along the base, men and women, all trying to fly. I had different ideas. I gripped the rock hard and stayed flat.

"The Carnal," Benito screamed into the wind. "Those who warped all that mattered in their lives for lust. I imagine those at the base of the cliff were unsuccessful lovers. We will be in less danger on the next ledge." He started crawling.

"Benito! That's it!" I cried. "We'll fly out of here!"

He turned in astonishment. It was a mistake. The wind slipped under his raised shoulders and lifted him and flung him at me.

I got him by the ankle. He nearly tore me loose, but I had a handhold in a split rock and I hung on. He doubled on his own length and pulled himself down my forearm until he was flat to the ground again.

"Thank you," he bellowed.

"S'okay. I wish you could have seen your expression." I was rather pleased with myself, as if I'd managed to catch a glass somebody's elbow had knocked off a table. *Good reflexes, Carpentier!*

"We'll fly out of here," I screamed happily into his ear. "We'll fly over the wall. We'll build a glider!"

"I was stubborn too, once. Perhaps I still am. Is this really your wish, Allen?"

"Damn right. We'll build a glider. Listen, if we're light enough to be blown away by the first wind, we probably won't need much more than a big kite! Hey, let's get out of this wind and talk it over."

We crawled.

* * *

The weather changed as we lost altitude. It didn't get any better. The wind died down; we didn't need to clutch at the rocks, and we could hear ourselves speak. But a freezing drizzle started.

Now that I was thinking *glider*, the loss in altitude bothered me. "We need a place to build it," I said. "Out of the wind. We need fabric, a lot of fabric, and we need wood. We probably need tools."

Benito nodded. "There is a place, a great swamp, the Styx. Trees grow there. As for the fabric and the tools, we can cross the Styx and get them from the wall."

"How many walls have you *got* here?"

Benito smiled grimly. "None like this one ahead. Red-hot iron."

I believed him. Nothing subtle about Infernoland. "How far down is it? We're losing altitude with every step."

"A good distance yet." Benito laughed. "A glider. You may be the first ever to think of that. If we can launch from the hill above Styx, we can use the thermal updraft above the red-hot walls. Ecch," he said, about the time I stepped backward into freezing slush.

We'd reached another level region. I stood up and looked around. Freezing muck in all directions. Human beings lay full length in it, like half-immersed logs. The rain was turning to sleet. Cold garbage washed against my ankles.

"Behold the low-rent district," I said.

I got a chuckle from Benito. "Not yet," he said, and if I hadn't had the shivers before I got them then. He swept his arm about him and said, "The Gluttonous."

"I don't want to know. Come on, let's get through this."

We waded out into it.

In the darkness, and half-blinded by sleet, I managed not to step on any half-buried victims. Some raised their heads to watch us pass, showing us uniform looks of weary despair, then sank back after we were gone.

Men and women in about equal numbers, they ranged from pleasantly plump to chubby to gross. Three or four were as bad as the woman in the Vestibule. I wondered if they'd be pleased to know about her.

And once I wiped frozen slush from my eyes, cursing imaginatively under my breath, and when I dropped my hand he was staring at me: a long-haired blond man built like an Olympic athlete.

"Allen Carpentier," he said sadly. "So they got you too."

I looked close and recognized him. "Petri? Jan Petri! What are you doing here? You're no glutton!"

"I'm the least gluttonous man who ever lived," he said bitterly. "While all of these creeps were swilling down anything that came near their mouths, from pig meat to garden snails—and you too, for that matter, Allen—I was taking care of myself. Natural foods. Organic vegetables. No meat. No chemicals. I didn't drink. I didn't smoke. I didn't—" He caught himself up. "I didn't hire you as my lawyer. Why am I bending your ear? You're here too. You were one of the PIGS, weren't you?"

"Yeah." He meant the Prestigious International Gourmand Society, whose purpose in life was to go out and eat together. I'd joined because I liked the company. "But I'm not staying. This isn't my slot."

He wiped slush from his face to see me better. "So where are you going?"

"Out of this place. Come along?" He'd be unpleasant company till we got him a bath, but I knew he wouldn't slow us down. There never was a health nut to match Petri. He used to run ten miles a day. I figured he'd be a lot of help building the glider.

"How do you get out of Hell?"

So they'd convinced him too. "We go downhill for a while. Then we'll—"

He was shaking his head. "Don't go down. I've heard about some of the places downhill. Red-hot coffins and devils and you name it."

"We're not going very far. We're going to build a glider and go over the walls."

"Yeah? And then where?" He seemed to think it was funny. "You'll just get yourself in more trouble, and for what? You're better off if you just take what they give you, no matter how unfair it is."

"Unfair?" Benito asked.

Petri's head snapped around. "Hell yes, unfair! I'm no glutton!"

Benito shook his head, very sadly. "Gluttony is too much attention to things of the earth, especially in the matter of diet. It is the obsession that matters, not the quantity."

Petri stared a moment. Wearily he said, "Bug off," and sank back into the freezing muck. As we left him I could hear him muttering to himself. "At least I'm not *fat* like those animals. I take *care* of myself."

I was annoyed with Benito. "You didn't have to insult him. We could use his muscles. *Hey*—"

Benito heard the panic in my voice. "Yes?"

"I was at Petri's funeral! All that attention to his

health, and then he got caught in the Watts riots. But
they damn sure didn't freeze him! They cremated
him!"

"Freeze him?"

I didn't bother to explain. They'd cremated Petri,
burned him to ash and gasses. How could he have
been revived? How could the Builders of this Infernoland even have found specs for a robot analogue? Or
a cell for cloning? Or . . . anything? Cremated is as
dead as you can get!

Do the Builders have a time camera? Physical
principles unknown, but to re-create Petri they have
to be able to photograph the past. So we give them
that, and the space-warping fields, and the genetic
engineering that created Minos and freed Carpentier
from the need to eat or drink or sleep, and the
weather control, and the reduced mass of people in
the winds, and the engineering technology that built
Infernoland itself.

*Carpentier, if they're that powerful, do you really
want to fight them?*

Of course not. I only want out!

"You're very thoughtful," said Benito. "Watch your
step."

I stopped at the brink of a precipice. Then I
followed Benito down a wandering, dangerous trail.
It switchbacked along the face of the cliff, and in
many places it would have been easy to go over the
edge. That scared me a lot. After all, I'd done it
before . . .

At least we were going down on our feet, and the
sleet had stopped.

Things were definitely looking up. Still, there were
funny noises from the gloomy area below, sounds

my mind registered as construction work. *Crash*. A long pause, in which voices screamed orders too distant to make out.

   Crash.

THE TRAIL LED OUT ONTO A FLAT PLAIN OF HARD baked clay. As we reached the bottom Benito stopped me silently, with an arm held straight out across my chest. I was willing. I had heard the rumble and the shouting coming toward us.

It rolled past us at a good clip: a boulder four or five yards across, nearly spherical, bounding across the cracked adobe, surrounded by a shouting mob. They were urging it along, running alongside and butting the mass with their heads and shoulders, a mob of men and women dressed in the finest rags I'd ever seen. There were the remains of evening gowns and slashed velvet Restoration clothing, academic robes and Gernreich original creations, all torn and filthy.

The leader wore striped trousers and swallowtail coat and a ring that would have choked a hippopotamus. "This time!" he screamed at the top of his voice. "This time we'll . . . get them!"

"We can pass now," Benito said calmly.

"What was *that* all about?"

CRACK!

I looked to my left. Two nearly identical masses of pale-blue translucent stone stood rocking back and forth. Eighty or ninety humans in decaying opulence lay about the rocks as if they'd been flung in handfuls.

A few started to get up. The leader shook his fist and screamed, "Hoarders! Misers! Next time— Come on, men, we need a bigger lead time!" More got up, shaking their heads dazedly, and two groups attacked the two huge stones and began painfully rolling them in opposite directions. The other outfit, the one furthest away, was dressed differently: also in rags, but these had never been much to start with.

"Hoarders and Wasters," said Benito. "Natural enemies. They will try to crush each other with those rocks for all eternity."

"Benito, I'd swear those rocks . . ."

"Yes?"

"Skip it. I'm getting so I'll believe anything." We started across the plain. A couple of hundred yards ahead of us was a hedgerow of some kind, and sounds filtered through it. The misers were rolling their rock back that way, getting good distance for another run. We followed until they reached the hedges and stopped. Then they turned to, pushing it the other way. A prim-looking bearded man in the remains of a dark suit from the 1890's shouted toward the other mob. "You threw away the good in your lives! Now pay!"

I couldn't stand it any longer. I grabbed a wild-eyed matron by the shoulder. She struggled to get away. "Let me go! We have to crush those wasteful—"

"Ever manage to do it?"

"No."

"Think you will this time?"

"We might!"

"Yeah, sure," I said. "What would happen if you stopped rolling the rock and took a break?"

She studied my face for signs of idiocy. "They'd cream us."

"Suppose you both stopped?"

She pulled away from me and ran to put her shoulder to the boulder. The mob heaved it over a bump. She shouted back to me. "We couldn't trust *them*. Even if we could . . . we can't stop. Minos might . . ."

"Might take it away," I guessed. "I *thought* I knew that color."

Several of them glanced at me suspiciously. A couple of the men left the rock to advance on me.

"Hey! Hold on! I couldn't steal it by myself. I don't *want* to."

They relaxed. One, a man wearing the remains of a peasant smock, said, "Many of us hae been here for unco time. Yon Queen Artemesia says when first she came, there were still facets upon't. It must hae been a bonny sight." He sighed wistfully.

It must hae been, yeah. *Hey, Carpentier, how long would it take to wear all the corners off a twelve-foot diamond?* I turned back toward Benito. He was talking to someone on the ground.

It was a man with both legs crushed. The rock must have rolled over him. He was still in shock, because he wasn't screaming in pain, but he would be. Blood seeped from the jellied mess that had been his legs.

"For pity's sake," he said, "pull me out of the way. Maybe they won't get me a few times, and then I'll be able to keep away from them—"

He'd had it. Mind gone with his body. It was just

as well. We ought to be taking him to a hospital, but why bother? He'd had it.

"We are leaving Hell," Benito said. "First we go down—"

"Oh no! I know what they do to you down there! Just move me, just a little, please?"

I wondered where to put him. The ledge was hard and flat, baked adobe, with no cover between the cliff and the hedgerow. But we couldn't leave him out here. I took him under the arms and dragged him over against the cliff to die in peace.

"I thank you," he whispered. "What's your name?"

"Allen Carpentier."

He seemed to brighten. "I had all your books."

"Hey! Did you?" Suddenly I liked this man.

"Too bad I don't have my collection. I could get your autograph on them. I had . . . all of everyone's books. Did you ever hear of my collection? Allister Toomey?"

"Sure." I'd known many book collectors, and they'd all heard of Allister Toomey, to their rage and sorrow. Toomey had spent a considerable inheritance on books, all kinds of books, from double four-edges to first editions to pulps and comic books that were just getting to be worth owning. Much of what he had owned had been unique, irreplaceable. He'd kept them all in a huge barn he'd managed to hang onto somehow.

He'd spent everything else on books: there was no money left to take care of them. They moldered in that barn. Rats and insects got into them, rain dripped through the roof. If he'd sold a few of them he'd have been able to take care of the rest. I'd known a lot of collectors, and they all had a tendency to brood over Allister Toomey.

"I guess I don't have to ask why you're here."

"No. I was both a . . . hoarder and a waster. I lay between both groups . . . I suppose it's fair enough. I wish I'd taken . . . one or another of those offers. But what could I sell?"

I nodded and turned away. He continued talking, to himself now. "Not the complete Analog collection. Not the Alice in Wonderland. It was autographed. Autographed!"

Good-bye, Allister Toomey, who'd died twice now. I waited with Benito until the mob swarmed past with their bouncing boulder, then we ran across.

CRACK!

We found a hole in the hedgerow and scrambled through.

There was only a narrow ledge beyond the hedgerow, then a cliff. Thick mists hid the bottom, but it was a long way down. There didn't look to be any way over it.

We walked along for miles. There were other groups behind the hedgerow (CRACK!) all shouting and screaming (CRACK!) in various languages.

Then the sounds changed. Machinery, rivet guns, hammers ringing, the sounds of workmen and their tools.

Tools! We'd need tools for the glider. I began to run ahead.

A tremendous chunk of the ledge had collapsed, and the chasm ran right across, from the cliff on the downhill side to the base of the cliff towering above. A stream ran through it, and it had cut the gorge even deeper. Far below we could see people working frantically on a dam.

Another group was just as frantically tearing it down.

At our own level there was a similar contest. One

group was trying to build a bridge across the gorge,
and another worked to disassemble it. Fifty yards in
either direction were more bridge builders and de-
stroyers. It seemed like a lot of wasted effort.

I looked to Benito, but he only shrugged. "I have
never been to this part before. I do not think Dante
came here either."

The group just in front of us were steelworkers,
slapping together I beams, girders, plates, anything
they could manage, fastening it with hot rivets and
hammers. A small forge blazed away to heat rivets.
I looked at all the work without comprehension—
until I saw Barbara Hannover.

Suddenly it came to me. I'd known Barbara a long
time. She wasn't cruel, and she didn't hate people,
but she loved wildlife more. Whatever anyone proposed, a new bridge, a new freeway, housing development, mine, power plant, oil well, or wheatfield,
she had a million reasons why you couldn't do it. I
honestly think she'd have let all the Kansas wheatfields
go back to prairie and buffalo if she could have
thought of a way to manage it.

Add to her fanatic streak a Harvard Law School
degree and one of the sharpest brains in the country,
and it was easy to see why lovers of progress shuddered
when she took an interest in what they were doing.

And naturally she was tearing the bridge down. I
had an idea and looked closer at the construction
workers. If Barbara was in this part of Infernoland,
Pete couldn't be far away . . .

And there he was, bucking rivets. Pete and Barbara had been married for a while. A short while.
Just as she couldn't see a housing tract without wanting eviction writs and bulldozers, he couldn't see a
nice place on the trail without wanting to improve
it with a log cabin. I'd gone hiking with him once.

The whole fifty miles was one long development plan, with ideas for improving the trail, building hostels, constructing artificial beaver dams, putting in hand-rails where the climb was steep . . . I almost killed him before we got back to the car.

"It makes sense," I told Benito. "Artistically. The way anything else down here makes sense. Pete and Barbara were both fanatics."

Neither of them had noticed me. I couldn't see how steelworking tools would help anyway. But upstream was a wooden trestle bridge, with a group just finishing it while another tried to get at it with saws.

I looked at the saws and lusted. With a saw and nothing else we could build a glider. Other things would be useful, but they were easier to make than a saw would be. I had to have one.

The funny thing was that they used each other's tools. One guy would be hammering away to put a beam in place, and another would be sawing it in half—and while they screamed insults at each other, they did nothing else. The rules in Infernoland were more complicated than I'd have thought.

Or the robots were programmed funny.

But that sure looked like Pete and Barbara.

I waited until a progressive type laid down his saw, then started for it. Too late. A thin-faced woman grabbed it and had at the trestle-piece he'd been trimming to fit.

The next time I was quicker. When she set the saw aside for an ax, I grabbed it. There was a drill bit on the ground next to it, just a twisted chunk of steel more valuable than its equivalent in diamonds, and I got that too.

You'd have thought they *were* diamonds. Madam Hawkface started for me with the ax, and her builder companion was right behind. He didn't need an ax. He could have made three of me.

"Run!" I shouted.

Benito heard. We dashed for the trail leading down into the gorge. It was narrow and twisted, but it looked safer than what we were leaving.

I'd done one thing. I'd got those two crews to cooperate for the first time since Infernoland was opened to the public.

Unfortunately, what they wanted to cooperate on was tearing me to pieces. The trail turned a corner, then swooped down the cliff. We followed it.

8

THERE WAS A LEDGE TEN FEET BELOW THE LIP OF the cliff, and we stopped for a moment to catch our breaths. I thought I felt the cliff tremble and asked Benito about it.

"It is not any place to stay," he warned. "Allen, you will find that there is no safe place in Hell. Wherever you stop—well, you won't like it."

"I can believe that." The thing to do was get out of here, and the more I thought about it, the better the glider looked. Now I had a saw that I could use to cut frames and ribs and stringers, if I could find anything to cut.

I still wondered what we'd use for fabric, but somewhere there had to be a storehouse for the costumes. The gowns Benito and I wore would do. It was a close-woven fabric, very tough, and it shed most of the dirt and muck we'd crawled through. I lifted the hem and tested the weave by blowing through it. It didn't let much through. It would do fine.

The ledge heaved again. I wondered if this were something for our benefit, then laughed at myself.

Earthquakes on call? The Builders were powerful, but *that* powerful?

We scrambled along the ledge until we were stopped by a waterfall pouring out in front of us. The water was black and dirty, and it stank like a sewer outfall, but the water rushed downward, and it had carved a bed in the cliffside. There were handholds in the sides of the notch the stream had carved.

How long would it take a stream to carve that? It would depend on what the rock was made of. And of course the Builders could have carved the notch themselves, though it looked natural enough.

After a while we reached the bottom of the cliff. The ground fell away at a steep angle. We found a path down it, along the stinking stream, twisting and turning along lower and lower, with steep cliff edges in places.

It would be an ideal place to launch a glider if we could get one up the slope. Drag it up here and over to one of the drop-offs, and push. Yeah. It looked better all the time, but first we had to build the glider, and what was I going to build it out of? I wanted to see those trees. I clutched the saw closer to me.

Benito was staring at me. I stared back.

"Forgive me," he said. "You hold that tool in a way I have seen before."

"Yeah?"

"By monks riddled with self-doubt, and clutching a crucifix to reassure themselves their religion is true."

"We'll *need* this. We'll need other things too. Wood, and rope for the glider—"

"Will that do?" He pointed downward.

We were almost at the bottom now. We faced a stinking swamp. Thick fog hid most of it, with only temporary glimpses through. Things thrashed around in the filthy water, but there were also bushes and

trees hung with vines. Wood! Vines! Certainly I could
build a glider out of those! "Now all we need is fabric.
There must be a supply dump in this place. Or a
laundry. Something."

Benito sighed. "There is."

"Great! Can we get a lot of those gowns?"

"It will not be easy."

"Easy?" I laughed. "Who cares, as long as we get
out of here!"

Benito's determined look was very like a bulldog's.
"Very well. I will help you get what you need. I will
help you build your glider. I will help you fly it, in
whatever direction you choose. In return, you will
promise me that if this mad scheme fails, you will come
with me to the real exit."

"Yeah, sure, sure." I wasn't really listening. I was
too interested in the swamp below us.

The things bubbling around in there were people.
Some of them just lay there half submerged, bubbling
out filth and talking nonsense. Others fought each
other, for what I couldn't make out. They roiled the
stinking waters, washing up slimy things. Thick fog
hung all around, and I had only glimpses of anything
more than a few feet away.

"This way." Benito waded out into the slop. He
seemed to know what he was doing, because it wasn't
very deep, just to our ankles. The goop squished inside my sandals, slimy and thoroughly unpleasant.
Every now and again there was solid ground a few
inches above the muck.

We picked our way through low-hanging trees and
bushes. I fingered the wood and tried my saw on one
of the trees to cut off a branch. It seemed strong
enough and quite springy. I hacked off a chunk of
vine, and it was too tough to break.

We could! We really could build a glider!

As we got deeper into the swamp there were fewer people, but I could hear curses in every language I'd ever imagined, people screaming at each other, and the sounds of blows. Sometimes a filthy shape would try to climb up onto the ground where we walked, but others would grab it and pull it back into the mire. I shuddered. Why did they do that?

"The wrathful," Benito said. "And the sullen. The worst offenders in upper Hell." He was about to say something else, but he ran into something lying on the trail and almost fell.

It was a man, filthy with the muck, lying in fetal position. His eyes were open and staring at us. He glared, not at us, but at the universe in general.

"Hello," I said.

"Come with us," Benito added. "There is a way." He didn't sound hopeful, and of course there wasn't any response. "Remember there is a way. Downward, accepting everything—"

"Come on, he's catatonic." It bothered me, Benito preaching to a rubber-doll catatonic. Was my loony-bin theory right after all? Psychodrama on the grand scale?

Then why was I here? And Jan Petri, and Pete and Barbara? It was as if the Builders had revived everyone who had ever lived! Then set out to cure the crazy ones. Did they think I was one of those?

There was another one on the trail, and he wasn't catatonic at all. He stood there glaring at us, while others thrashed in the muck at either side of him. To get past we'd have to wade out into that, and from the ripples we would not only be over our heads but among the fighters. They'd never let us out.

"Excuse us," Benito said pleasantly. "The trail is wide enough for us to pass if you will step forward two paces."

"Bugger off."

"Surely you will not stand in our way?" Benito was still very pleasant, but there was an edge to his voice.

"Took me a hundred years to get up here," the figure said. *"You* never *have* been in the muck. If it's good enough for me, it's good enough for you."

He was a big man with powerful arms, and he seemed to mean it.

"Stand aside," Benito said. He was giving orders now. "You may come with us if you will—and if you can, which I doubt. But you will not prevent us from going." Benito's voice still had the ring of authority that had cowed Minos, and it shook the guy momentarily.

"Don't I know you?" he said. He stared at Benito. "I'm sure I know you. Well, whoever the hell you are, get past me the same way I got up here."

"Friend, you leave us no choice," Benito said.

"Aha! I *do* know you! You're Ben— Hey! Let go! Hey!"

Benito grasped him by the shoulders and lifted him as easily as I would a child. I gaped as Benito flung him out into the marsh. He wasn't even breathing hard. "Come, Allen."

"Yeah. Sure." I followed numbly, wondering who Benito really was. A professional wrestler? Circus strong man? What he'd done wasn't impossible. I'd seen it done before, but not often, and Benito didn't look that strong.

9

EVENTUALLY WE GOT THROUGH THE TREES AND BRUSH to open water. There was a big black tower at the edge. I couldn't see anyone in the tower, but suddenly there was a light in the top window. It flashed, ruby-red, out across the marsh.

Red? Ruby? A laser! Not magic, just a laser signal from an old stone tower. Far out in the murk over the water there was a flash of light, blinking, the same color as the signal.

"Phlegyas will come for us now," Benito said. "You must be careful. Say nothing you don't have to say, and as little of that as possible. Let me handle him."

"Sure. Why?"

"Because we are fugitives and we are approaching the, ah, administrative centers of Hell. There are demons here. Guards. They can do terrible things to us."

"Can't they just." I'd seen enough atrocities already. Were the Builders the crazy ones? They seemed to like pain.

From somewhere behind us there were screams of

rage and agony, and splashing noises. I thought I saw ripples in the open water ahead of us too.

Then something took shape in the gloom ahead, something moving toward us.

It was a boat. A big man, bearded, with a low gold crown on his head, stood in the stern with an oar in a sternlock. He sculled slowly, but that boat *moved*. I almost laughed. He certainly wasn't putting out enough effort to get that kind of speed. The boat must have a hidden water jet or something.

"I have you again!" the man crackled. "Ah, Benito, caught again. Good work!" He looked at me closely, and his grin faded. "Who are you?"

I didn't answer.

"Were you sentenced to lower Hell?"

"Phlegyas, mind your own business," Benito said. "Bring the boat to the shore. I do not care to wade in your filthy swamp."

"Don't like cold, eh?" Phlegyas seemed to find that funny. "Well, you won't have cold feet long, where you're going! Get in, Benito, get in. The other one has to stay here, of course. I have orders concerning you, but not him." He looked at me again. "You don't have a pass from Minos? No papers? You can't come."

"He will come," Benito said. "This has been willed where what is willed must be. Now bring the boat to shore."

Phlegyas shrugged. "All right, all right, you have the formula." His voice was a nasty whine of complaint. "It's sure been hell here since Dante published that book. You'd be surprised how many try that on me. Nothing I can do about it, either."

We scrambled onto the boat and sat gingerly. I noticed that the boat didn't sink deeper by an inch. Didn't we weigh anything? In that case we could walk on the swamp! But that was silly, because the swamp

rippled and bubbled with people—and we'd sunk to
the ankles in the muck. I could smell the stink on my
feet.

Every now and then a nose would appear above the
water as someone caught a breath, then vanished again.
How many were there in that swamp? I could hear
screams of rage and agony and pain, and cursing in
all languages, but I couldn't see any details in the half-
light and the fog.

Phlegyas sculled rapidly, and the boat shot away
from the bank. The fog enclosed us in a circle of dark
water rippled with shouting faces and with the chicken
guts and other filth that poured down from the land
of the Hoarders and the Wasters.

Sometimes a filthy claw would reach from the water
to clutch at the gunwhales, and then Phlegyas would
smash it with a six-foot pole he kept in a socket ready
to hand. He sculled easily with one hand.

"You know, that formula doesn't work with the real
supervisors," he said. He reached to straighten his
crown and gave us a sour look. "They took the power
of decision away from me. I made a couple of mistakes, just a couple of lousy mistakes, and now they
think they can do better than me. Over two thousand
years of service here, and upstarts have more power
than me. It isn't fair, you know. Bastards. Stupid bastards. But they won't let you in without a pass, you
watch and see."

"Old man, be silent," Benito said.

"Humph." Phlegyas sculled more rapidly. The boat
shot through the water. Now I could make out dim
glowing red. The fog began to lift, and we could feel
the heat.

There were walls ahead of us. They had towers, and
some of them were cherry red. The radiated heat was
already uncomfortable. A low, wide mudbank stretched

out from the walls to the swamp, and I could see a landing dead ahead, at the end of a narrow bay.

We headed toward it. A man came out through a doorway in the wall. He was old and bent, and he hobbled. He carried a box about a yard square and an inch deep.

He shuffled to the water's edge and used a shovel to fill his box with mud. Then he turned and ran, his robe flying out behind him as he darted back into the door he'd come so slowly out of. It didn't make sense.

I turned to Benito, but he only shrugged. He didn't know either.

We passed the entrance to the bay. "You may let us out at this landing," Benito said.

"Nope." Phlegyas continued to scull.

"It would be more convenient."

"Yep."

"Then why don't you do it?" I demanded.

"Because I don't have to," Phlegyas answered. He continued to scull until we reached another landing. "Regulations say ferry terminal to ferry terminal, and that's where I go. Nothing about stops in Himurali-bima's Bay."

Benito frowned, but we didn't say anything. The boat reached the dock area. There was no one to meet us, and I wasn't sorry.

"Off, off," Phlegyas shouted. "There's more coming. No rest for an old man, none at all. Off, off." He reached for his cudgel, and we scrambled ashore before he could smash us with it. As soon as we were off he was sculling away, headed for the other shore like a motorboat.

The city was maybe a quarter-mile away across hard stinking mud. The walls were hot, although not as hot here as further away. A mile to our left was a tower that glowed cherry red.

Thermals! There'd be thermals here, if a glider could get across the swamp. It would take luck, and we'd have to drag it pretty high up that cliff to make it, but it could be done.

"Be very careful," Benito said. "I will have to deceive the officials. Do not undeceive them."

"You mean you're gonna lie? Oh, Benito, that's sinful. You could go to Hell for telling lies."

He took it seriously. "I know. It is one reason I am here."

"Um, but this *is* in a good cause . . ."

"I thought my deceits were in a good cause." He shrugged. "The Commandment is against false witness, and by extension against malicious deceit, and fraud, and perversions of honesty and honor. We shall not do that, and as you say, it is in a good cause. Or so I hope. We tread dangerous ground, Allen."

"Come on," I said. I started off toward the door I could see ahead of us. Fat chance I'd ever make that joke with *him* again.

It was getting warmer all the time. Off to our left, near the blazing-hot tower, were the remains of a *big* gate, torn off its hinges. Things walked guard duty in front of it. They were just far enough away, and there was just enough fog and steam, that I couldn't see them clearly. But the shapes seemed odd, twisted out of true. I didn't want to ask about them.

We came to a Dutch-type door open at the top and with a counter on the lower half. Heat poured out through the opening. A bored-looking man in a high stiff collar, something out of a Dickens novel, was inside in a little office. His face was narrow and pinched, and the heat couldn't have improved his disposition. He had a desk like a woodcut from the Scrooge story, a tall thing he stood at. There wasn't a chair or a stool in the room. We waited at the counter.

And waited, and waited, getting warmer and warmer, while the clerk fussed with papers on his desk. He seemed to be reading every line on an enormous form a dozen pages thick. Every now and then he used a red pencil to mark something. When he continued to turn the pages and scrawl notes without even looking at us, I pounded on the counter.

"Are we invisible?" I demanded.

"A moment, sir. Just a moment, please. We're very shorthanded here, sir. You'll have to wait, sir." He made each "sir" a curse.

"You would be well advised to attend us." Benito's voice had that edge to it, a note of warning. The clerk looked around uneasily. He obviously didn't recognize either of us. Hardly surprising.

"Your papers, please."

"We have none," Benito answered.

"Oh my, oh my, one of those days," the clerk muttered. "Well, if you haven't any papers, you can't come in. The rules are very strict. You'll have to go back for papers." He turned back to his desk and started looking over the files on it.

"We have an errand inside," Benito said. "You do not help your record by delaying us."

The clerk looked back nervously. He examined us closely again, noting the slime on our gowns and the stench of our sandals. That seemed to cheer him. "What is your station inside?" he asked.

"No fixed post," Benito answered.

"I can't help you, sir. I'm only record-keeper for the Sixth Circle. Next window, please." He turned back to his desk. We waited. Benito whistled something monotonous. Finally the clerk turned back. "You still here, sir? I *told* you, next window, please."

"It is to the Sixth Circle that we must go now."

"Why didn't you *tell* me," the clerk complained.

"Very well." He reached into a cabinet and produced what looked like manuscript books and short stubs of pencil. "If you don't have the proper papers, you'll have to fill out these forms."

They were twenty pages long, covered with small blanks, and there were nine copies. Not only wasn't there any carbon paper, but the blanks were arranged differently on each copy, although they all asked for the same information.

"I think we will not bother," Benito said.

I flared up. "What the hell do you want all this for? Great-grandmother's blood type! Why should I fill this out?"

"You *have* to." The clerk was getting more and more irritated. "You can see they're all blank. You can see they have to be filled out. Right at the top, see, it says, 'Replacement for lost papers, application for, D-345t-839y-4583, to be submitted in nine copies.' I can't do anything for you without that information."

"Aren't there exceptions?"

"Of *course* there are exceptions, *sir*. One was made over two thousand years ago. Before my time, but they still talk about it." He shuddered. "But you are obviously not Him. Is either of you a living man? Can either of you summon angels? Those are in the book too." He glanced at a shelf of loose-leaf folios above his desk. "Volume sixty-one, page eight ninety-four, paragraph seventy-seven point eighty-two—I'm *glad* we changed to the decimal system, but most of us didn't like it—it says very plainly, anyone who can summon angels may pass. But if you're applying under that ruling you'll have to go to the main gate. *Don't* prove you can do it. Just go to the main gate, and they'll take care of you."

"But you will not let us pass," Benito said. "Not

even if I tell you that if you do not you will be in grave trouble?"

"I know my duty. You will not come through."

"Very good. You have done well," Benito said. "If you had let us in, we would have reported it. Now you have a favorable report coming. Who is your supervisor?"

The clerk stared at Benito. "Mrs. Playfair. Formerly a postmistress. But—"

"Oh, my," said Benito. "I won't be able to help you after all. It would do no good to give the report to *her*."

The clerk was unsettled. "Why not, sir?" The "sir" wasn't a curse any longer.

"I am not permitted to say."

"Ah. You mean—" He gulped. Whatever he imagined was going to happen to Mrs. Playfair worried him excessively. "But what will happen to her people? What will become of *me*?"

Benito looked crestfallen. "You know the rules—"

"But I've done everything *properly!* My files are in perfect order—oh dear, oh dear, I *told* her she shouldn't have let that man in the records room, I *told* her he wasn't properly credentialed, I *told* her! It was all her fault, I *told* her . . . my files are in perfect order. And they won't even look at them, they'll just—" He was actually wringing his hands as he looked around his office at his desk and files.

Benito frowned. "It would be a waste to have you in the boiling pitch—"

"IN THE PITCH!" the clerk screamed.

"Are you certain your files are in perfect order?" Benito demanded.

"Of *course* they are! Here, you can see for yourself." He did something that opened the gate.

Benito and I crowded in. Benito took down a volume of the rule book and leafed through it. "Keep this up to date, do you? All revisions in place as they come in? Where are your unfiled revision sheets?"

"There are none," the clerk said primly.

"Hmm." Benito lifted the forms on the clerk's desk. "*This* is not in order!" He leafed through quickly.

"But I hadn't checked the seventh copy yet!" the clerk moaned. "I was doing that when you interrupted me! You can't report me for that, I was trying to give you service, and——"

Benito handed the forms back. The clerk looked through and extracted a bulky set. There was pencil all over the first six pages, then the writing medium changed to something darker. Benito looked at it curiously. "This is hardly legible."

"He used up his pencil," the clerk said. "Volume four, page ninety-eight, paragraph six, states that no applicant can have more than one pencil. So I made him fill it out with something else. He used blood."

"His own?" I asked.

"Where else would he get blood?" The clerk turned to Benito. "Who *is* this man?"

"In my custody. Witness. Not your case, don't worry about it." He handed back the forms. "This seems to be in order."

"Thank you." There was relief all over the clerk's face.

"One item was very difficult to read. You should be more careful next time."

"Yes, sir. Certainly, sir. Are you finished with it?"

Benito nodded. The clerk took the form—copy seven of nine copies—and tossed it into a wastebasket in the corner. It burst into flames. I stared. A man had used his own *blood* to fill that out? I glanced at the forms the clerk had handed us.

Sure enough, at the top of copy seven, it said "DE-

STROY." Copy eight went to "APPLICANT" and copy
nine was "TO BE ROUTED TO THE STATISTICAL SEC-
TION."

"What will be the charges against Mrs. Playfair?"
the clerk asked, his voice low and confidential.

Benito frowned. "I understand there are shortages
in uniforms and supply—"

"But we don't have anything to do with that."

"Precisely," Benito said knowingly. Comprehension
dawned on the clerk's face. He nodded.

"We're going to check that now," Benito said. "Keep
up the good work, uh—"

"MacMurdo. Vincent MacMurdo. You'll remember?"

"Certainly." Benito opened the inner door and held
it for me. I went through, trying not to hurry.

10

Benito followed and closed the door behind him. I slumped against the wall, convulsed by silent laughter.

I jumped away fast. The wall was burning hot. I smelled scorched cloth. Another second and I'd have had a bad burn.

We were in a corridor that stretched to infinity in both directions. It was about ten feet high and wide, and there were doors at intervals along it. People hurried in both directions, paying us no attention.

And there were all *kinds* of people! Men and women in flowing robes, in US Post Office uniforms, in colonial costumes, in the high collars the Dickensian clerk had worn, military uniforms, Chinese mandarin robes, modern business suits, coveralls with insignia of planets and stars and sunbursts, a whirl of scurrying humanity shoving past us as if we weren't there.

Nobody was going to notice us for our funny clothing.

The old man we'd seen outside rushed past us, almost running. He carried a box of fresh mud and poked at it with a stick as he ran. We watched as he turned through a door and out of sight.

Someone had stopped beside us and was laughing. He wore a Roman toga.

"Do you speak English?" I asked.

"Certainly." He was still laughing.

"Who *was* that?" I asked.

The laughter stopped, and the man glared. He was carrying some kind of wood plank with wax on it. There were letters cut in the wax. "You are new here?" he demanded.

"From another division," Benito said quickly. He lowered his voice. "Special assignment."

The Roman drew away from us. "Surely you have no interest in Himuralibima? He is our most honored civil servant."

Benito gave a knowing look. I still had a blank stare.

"Hammurabi's secretary, you know. Invented record-keeping."

"Ah," I said. *Hammurabi? Oh, all right, he's Hammurabi's secretary. And I am Napoleon Bonaparte.* "You'd think after all these years they'd let him slow down a little."

"But he *can't*," the Roman protested. "They've offered him retirement, but he has to fill out the proper forms, and in his case, of course they're in cuneiform. And you have noticed how hot it is in here?"

I couldn't stand it. I tipped my head back and roared with laughter. It rolled out, gales of laughter, choking me, as I thought of that first bureaucrat trying to complete his retirement papers before the mud dried from the heat . . .

. . . Himuralibima's *Bay?*

Benito merely nodded. "Fitting. I am certain you have work, Signor—?"

"Uh, of course," the Roman said. "Your pardon." He pushed past us and walked briskly down the corridor. Our clerk came out of his office. The Roman stopped, and they talked in whispers.

"Allen, must you ask unnecessary questions?" Benito demanded.

"I'm a writer. Of *course* I ask questions."

"Please do not. Not in here. For the moment we are safe. They think—" He motioned with his eyes.

I turned my eyes only. The Roman had stopped someone else and was whispering to him. The man he'd stopped, a young man in 1930's US Army uniform, nodded. Pretty soon he stopped someone and both looked clandestinely at us. They stopped others . . .

"They're telling stories about us," I said.

"Yes. Let us hope they are telling the proper ones. Now we must find the supply center."

Wherever we went we were preceded and followed by whispers. People got out of our way, too. If we wanted to go through a door, if we even looked like we wanted to go through a door, there was a scramble to hold it open for us.

"They sure are scared of you," I said. "They know who you are." Which was more than I did.

"I think few of them have seen or heard of me," Benito answered.

Oh, really? "You know your way around here."

"No. I know my way around bureaucracies. This one is no different from any other."

"You were a bureaucrat once?"

He hesitated. "I suppose you might say so."

"Exactly what—"

An anguished voice drowned me out. We were passing an open door, and a woman's voice screamed in rage and pain: "But that form is twenty-seven pages long! All that for one tool?"

I looked in, caught a familiar hawklike profile, turned back and kept walking. "Don't look now," I said out of the corner of my mouth.

The other voice followed us. "You should keep better track of your handsaw. The rules are very clear . . ."

At the next door there was a long line of naked people, fat men, pretty girls, ugly women, studs, every form and variety of mankind: the reception desk at a streakers' convention. They were trying to get to a counter where some fat guy handed them clothing while two beanpole women took information down on more forms.

What was this? The supply center for Infernoland? Were these employees, or spectators, or—

—or what?

We got in line, the only ones with clothing who did. A thin guy in a medieval bachelor gown came in, went behind the counter, and whispered to the supply clerk. The clerk summoned his two old biddies, and they whispered together.

Finally one of the women came out from behind the counter. She wore a coverall of a kind I didn't recognize, dark blue with strange insignia. "What may we do for you?" she asked. She was trying to be pleasant, and it was obvious that she'd never learned how.

"This man was given the wrong clothing," Benito said. "He is wearing the same thing I am. In our section we do not give a junior courier the uniform of a supervisor."

She frowned. Benito didn't look like he was dressed as a supervisor. He looked like an escapee from the violent ward. So did I. But he only stared back, and after a while her eyes dropped. "What should he wear?" she said.

"Loincloth. And there are nine senior men in my section who have loincloths and no gowns. It is intolerable."

"Oh." She didn't know what to make of that. She went back and whispered to the other biddy.

Meanwhile the line moved up. The clerk looked at papers and then at the fat man at the head of the line. He went into the shelving stacks behind the counter and came back with bright gaudy clothes, slashed velvet sleeves and tight trousers. They were obviously too small.

"Ungood. Double plus ungood. Too small. Wrong period," the fat man protested.

"Tough shit, buddy. We all got our troubles. Next!"

The biddies came over to him and whispered. He looked at us. "Uh, you sirs—can I help you?"

Three helped carry the gowns, and a fourth brought up the rear with stacks of papers flowing with seals and ribbons. Benito paid no attention to me; he just walked ahead as if he assumed we'd all follow, which we did.

We turned a corner, and he stopped. "This will do," he said. "Give those things to Allen. You have your work to do, and this is his task."

"Certainly, sir. Is there nothing else we can do for you?" This one wore a policewoman's uniform, vaguely American, though the shield was shaped strangely. She talked without using articles. When she spoke to her subordinates she used a language I didn't know. I was afraid to ask her death date.

"I said this will do," Benito said. "We will be met by others. You may go."

"Thank you, sir." The sow turned and stalked away, followed by the others.

When she was out of sight Benito seemed to wilt. His straight posture was gone, the high angle of the chin vanished, and he slumped.

Then he laughed. "So. Nothing changes. Now we must get out of here before someone tells this story to an internal security agent."

"They think—what do they think? That we're important officials?"

"No. Of course not. They know we are only pretending that."

"Then what—"

"But they cannot be sure. We *might* be important officials. But most of them think we are secret police."

"But how do you know there *are* secret police?"

Benito looked very sad. "Allen, there have to be. You cannot run a bureaucratic state without them. Come."

We found a door to the outside, and Benito surrendered one of the documents he'd collected. We passed through and were out on the mud flats again. A stinking breeze wrapped itself around me, deliciously cool, and I said, "Ahh . . ."

Far to our right the old man had just filled his box of mud again. He ran for the gate, writing frantically.

11

I WAS SMILING AS I TURNED. THE ROBES I HELD
stacked on my head, an ungainly load. "Now what?"

Benito was staring across the swamp. "I don't
know."

"Ah?"

"We cannot possibly persuade Phlegyas to take us
back. I fear we must swim." He set his own stack of
robes down, shook out the top robe and used it to tie
the rest together.

Swim? Through *that?* It wasn't the garbage that
turned me off. It was the bubbling of angry people in
and under the water. If we met anyone like the guy
Benito had thrown back into the water . . . if we met
half a dozen of them while loaded down with heavy
wet stacks of robes! "Wait a minute, Benito. Let's try
something else."

"Lead on, then, Allen."

I stopped to tie my bundle as Benito had tied his.

Then I turned right along Himuralibima's Bay. The choice was deliberate: here there were windows and doors along the wall.

I was wading thigh-deep and not liking it, but it was the only way to learn what I wanted to know. At worst I was postponing our swim. At best—"We've got plenty of time. You keep saying so."

"So we do. I wonder what you expect to find."

My foot brushed something soft.

She was clearly visible beneath two feet of water: a long-boned black woman with her hair floating like seaweed around a slack face. I asked a stupid question. "Is she dead?"

"Of course," said Benito.

She was curled in fetal position. She stayed rigid as I rolled her to bring her head above water. There was no sign of decay, and no sign of life. But I felt for a pulse in her neck and found it.

"Catatonic." And I started to get mad. "Another catatonic. Of all the dirty things. *We* don't persecute crazy people for crimes. What right do the Builders have to put crazy people in Hell?"

"The Builders?"

"Never mind. Of all the dirty things. Benito, can you handle two bundles for a minute?"

He took my robes on his other shoulder. He waited while I reached into the water to adjust the woman's position.

Catatonia. It's a rare enough disorder, but almost incurable. You can find one or two catatonics in almost any mental hospital. They afford opportunity for endless jokes, all identical, for a catatonic will take any position you put him into and hold the pose indefinitely.

Every intern thinks he is the first to see the possibilities. He will lead the resident catatonic to the hospital cafeteria, place him just outside the door, and leave him there with his thumb to his nose or his middle finger rigidly extended. Hilarious!

Sometimes he gets a surprise . . .

I had to stand on her knees to straighten her legs, but finally I got them stretched out in front of her. She was still leaning too far back, her eyes staring at infinity through a half-inch of scummy water. Still standing on her knees for leverage, I reached beneath the water, took her shoulders and pulled her up to sitting position.

Now she'd be able to breathe.

. . . sometimes he gets a surprise, your antic intern. He will have just finished adjusting the patient's hand with thumb properly to nose, when the hand becomes a fist and the fist becomes a missile warhead. Catatonics are hideously strong. They have to be, to hold one position forever.

And she was sitting down. She lashed straight out and tried to punch a hole through my groin. She damned near made it. I whooped and doubled over, sucking air. Sucking, as it turned out, filthy water as I rolled helplessly over into the swamp.

I tried to uncurl. My lungs still wanted to suck water. Inch by inch, I fought my mouth to the surface, drew a lungful of sweet stinking air, and screamed.

Benito was sloshing toward me. I gestured him back. If he dropped the robes to help me, they'd quadruple in weight!

He stopped. I waited for the pain to ease a little, then tried to stand up. When I put weight on my legs it felt like she'd hit me again. I moved toward shore, doubled over.

The woman's lower lip was just at the surface of the water. She held her arm straight out, fist clenched. "Don't make waves," I told her sourly as I passed. She didn't respond, and she still looked dead. Water streamed from her nose.

I didn't stop for any more catatonics. Gradually I was able to straighten up. Benito followed patiently, carrying both bundles, both of us wading thigh-deep in water. I ignored the floating garbage. It wasn't getting me any dirtier than I already was.

The texture of the bottom had changed. Beneath a film of frictionless mud there were tilted slabs that had sharp corners and tended to slide . . . I stopped. Benito stopped behind me.

I said, "Feel that?"

Benito didn't get it. "What should I feel?"

"Himuralibima's Ford, that's what! No telling how far it goes, but it should get us a good distance across the swamp. Here, give me that." I took one of the bundles and started into the swamp. The footing was chancy, the slabs tended to slide, but it was better than swimming.

And I, feeling that I had earned the right to brag, bragged. "All along I wondered where the dried mud was going. It'd shrink a little when the water evaporated, but even so, that bay is *huge*. Where do they dump the slabs after Himuralibima gives up? Maybe I'd find a mountain of them. Or maybe they don't want a pile of ruined clay slabs in their working area. Maybe they're afraid of getting ticked off for sloppiness.

"So, I was right. Someone's been dumping the slabs in the bay. Every hundred years he has to walk a little further. Otherwise they'd show above the surface."

"Very clever, Allen."

"Thank kew." No telling how far it would go, but we were a good distance into the swamp, and the water was only up to our calves. *Hold your breath and make a wish, Carpentier. Or just hold your breath, the water could be over your head any second.*

We were nearly across before it ended. The slabs dipped, and I followed the dip, walking on eggs, with the stack of robes balanced on my head. I was chin deep where the mud turned squishy soft.

So far, so good. I found an underwater ridge and followed that, going waist deep, then higher. I was wading ashore, with Benito behind me, when our luck ran out.

The broad-shouldered man who blocked our path was the same who had blocked our path before. He shied back when he recognized us, and then he saw our situation and grinned.

I turned back to Benito. "Mind if I try this?"

"If you think it will help."

"I wrote science fiction, remember? I ought to be able to explain a complicated idea to a moron."

I hadn't lowered my voice. The broad-shouldered man advanced on us, saying, "Who's a moron?"

"Don't worry about it," I told him. "You've got worse problems than that. Remember the flying lesson?"

His grin was back. "I'd like to see old Benito try that with his arms full of bedsheets!"

"He won't be able to," I said, keeping my speech slow and distinct. "He'll have to put them down. In the swamp." Pause. "They'll get all dirty." Pause. "Imagine what that will do to his temper."

I watched his eyes. It was getting through to him.

I said, "Why don't you step aside while you think it over?"

"Some guys would rather talk than fight," he said contemptuously. He turned and stalked back to his point of high ground.

PART II

"THINGS ARE DEFINITELY LOOKING UP FOR ALLEN Carpentier."

"I beg your pardon?" Benito was looking out at the marsh, at decaying trees embedded in fog.

"We've got a quiet place to work, I've made some flint tools, and there's everything we need for the glider. What more could we want?"

Benito sighed, and I got back to work. The first job was to find a place to loft the glider. We were on a little area of high ground, no more than thirty yards square and nestled up against the base of the cliff. The bad-tempered character was between us and everyone else. He wouldn't let anyone else past, and he wasn't about to bother us. I could just see his back through the mist.

First things first. I used a log to flatten out an area larger than the glider would be, then cut a long springy sapling for a ruler. After a while I had a whole collection of saplings of various lengths and thicknesses.

You draw the rough outlines, then spring the batten

—in this case one of the saplings—across the important points. That makes a smooth fair curve. It was the way the Wright Brothers designed airplanes, and it was the way the Douglas Gooney Bird was designed. It wasn't until World War II, long after the age of flight was underway, that airplanes were designed on drafting tables. Before that they were done on the loft floors, the same way that boats were designed for centuries.

I don't know how long it took me to get it right. I wasn't in any hurry, and Benito never tried to rush me. After a while he even developed some enthusiasm.

Did you ever try to set up ribs and make them keep their shape by tying them with vines? When the ribs are whatever you can cut off swamp willows? As a lesson in patience the job has few equals . . .

Eventually it looked liked a glider. The wings weren't precisely symmetrical, and the control surfaces pivoted on wooden bearings with dowels shaped by flint knives and thrust into holes enlarged by flint drill bits; the fabric was sewn with vine tendrils shoved through holes poked with a thorn; but it *looked* like a glider.

I remembered the Cargo Cults of the South Seas.

The islanders had been sorry to see the airplanes go after World War II ended. Native magicians had made mockups of airplanes and landing fields. It was sympathetic magic intended to bring back the real airplanes and the great days of cargo and trade. I told Benito about the Cargo Cults, amusing him greatly, and only later realized what had brought them to mind.

What I was building would never look like more than a crude imitation of an airplane. But it would fly!

I spent as much time making tools as I did working on the sailplane. A bow drill: take one bow, as for shooting arrows; get a good curve in it, and instead of an arrow, take a piece of sapling. Wrap the bow-string around the piece of sapling. Attach the drill bit to one end. You need a hard block in which the top of the sapling chunk will rotate freely because you've worn a depression in it. Hold that block in one hand, put the drill point where you want it, and draw the bow back and forth with the other hand. The sapling turns. The point turns. In about a week you can drill a hole.

I'd heard that boatbuilders in Asia preferred their bow drills to American electrics. They must have been crazy.

I worked. There were no distractions. The Builders must have altered my body radically. I didn't get hungry, thirsty, horny, or sleepy, and I never had to go to the bathroom. I wondered what I had become. What was my power source now? A power source with no food intake and no waste outlet? If it was beamed power, Benito and I would be turning our-selves off when we dropped the glider beyond the wall.

Beyond the wall . . . I hadn't thought much about that. What would we find outside? Dante had de-scribed a dark wood, a wilderness. Why not? A low-gravity world, native vegetation allowed to run wild . . .

No guarantees, Carpentier. There might be nothing but Infernoland itself, a tremendous cone built in air-less space, with a point mass, a quantum black hole for instance, mounted at the tip to provide gravity. In that case we were dead.

I kept working.

And eventually, there it was. The Fudgesickle, by Carpentier and Company. "This is a demo, madam. The finished model will have many other desirable features, such as landing gear and seats for the crew, and metal fastenings . . ."

"Will that hold together?" Benito didn't seem particularly worried. His tone was more one of abstract curiosity.

"I think so. We shouldn't put much strain on it, but I've noticed we don't weigh what we should. Infernoland seems to be built on a lower gravity planet than Earth."

"Yours is the most curious delusion I have yet encountered here. Well, if it will fly, we may as well try it. The sooner you are done with this idiocy, the sooner we can reach the center and escape."

I could have killed him. So the Fudgesickle wasn't a thing of beauty. It would fly! And it was a lot better way out than his.

I didn't try to kill him for three reasons. First, he'd break my neck. Second, he *had* been useful as a guide; he'd gotten me the fabric. Third, I needed his help getting the Fudgesickle high enough on that cliff above us for a launching.

We pulled the glider up the slope and carried it until the land fell away as a steep cliff. The swamp bubbled like sludge, with sickly lights glowing among the odd-shaped bushes and trees.

"If we crash down there, we'll never get out," I said. "Can you fly this thing?"

"I have flown them." Benito laughed, with real humor.

"What?"

"I have done this before. We launched the glider from a much higher cliff. An Austrian soldier came to get me out of a sticky situation." He settled himself at the controls.

Something familiar about that story . . . but Benito was looking out at the swamp, and I didn't ask him. He looked awfully big and heavy to be a glider pilot, and I had to remember that we didn't weigh what we should. I strained against the fuselage and shoved outward.

It wouldn't have worked if we hadn't been mass-less or nearly so. Even then I kept wondering about that. It chewed at my soul the way a ragged tooth attracts the tongue. How could we have weight and no mass? The wrong weight, and . . .

Infernoland. Disneyland of the Damnable. How long had they kept me in that bottle? Clarke's Law kept running through my head, an old axiom of science fiction: "Any sufficiently advanced technology is indistinguishable from magic."

In my time it would take magic, the supernatural, to make that many people, not weightless, but *mass-less*. It wasn't even possible in theory to extract the inertia and leave the weight. But *they* could do it, the Builders, the God Corporation. Why? It must have cost a lot. Just how big a paying audience did they have?

Who was watching us now?

I heaved against the plane, and then there was no room for thought. The plane dropped like a rock, with me hanging onto the tail, crawling forward to get into the rear seat. Benito knew how to fly, all right. He let us dive, just missing the cliff, until we had built up speed; then he leveled out, taking us above the swamp and toward the red-hot city.

Dis. Dante had described it, glowing with red-hot mosques, with demons on the walls to guard it. I didn't see any demons. I'd take them on faith. If the Builders could build Minos, they could make demons.

We were about a hundred feet above the swamp, and keeping steady altitude. There must have been warm air rising from the hellish brew below us. Then we were over the wall, and Benito banked sharply left to catch the updraft. The plane rose steadily, gliding along the gentle curve of the wall.

Benito shouted, "This won't do any good, you know."

"We're getting higher, aren't we?" I pointed down. The swamp had shrunk until I could see the gentle curve of the cliff beyond it. Cliff and red-hot wall were concentric arcs of circles.

The view to the right went down forever. Beyond what seemed the biggest maze ever built, steam rose in a thick curtain. Through wind-torn rents in the steam I could glimpse factories belching out ugly black dirt, a line of electric pylon towers, a yellow glow of desert . . . on and on, down and down.

What had it all *cost?* Thousands of times as much as Disneyland. What kind of people would build Infernoland and people it with unwilling damned souls?

If this worked out, I would never know.

We were higher than the cliffs to our left. It seemed that we had climbed fast, faster than we had any right to. But we were nearly weightless and completely massless. The plane had only its own structural weight to lift. We continued to rise until we were in the hideous gray fog that served Infernoland for a sky.

It stank: excrement, oil, smog, sickness, slaughterhouses, everything hideous. There wasn't even the honest smell of sweat and locker rooms.

"We'll have to turn now," Benito said. "We can't stay in the updraft if we can't find it."

"That's right. Go!"

We banked left, then straightened out. The fog began to thin. We were doing it! Passing over the rings we'd struggled through. A wind full of weightless people bounced us about, then let us go. We passed over Minos' palace. It was even bigger than

I'd thought. There was the wall ahead. We were going to make it.

Have at you, Builders! You can't keep a science-fiction writer in Hell!

Even so, no hero worth writing about would have left Infernoland with so many questions unanswered. He would have led a revolution against the Builders, and never mind the odds. The plane would have been for reconnaissance, not escape.

Heinlein, van Vogt, "Doc" Smith, Robert Howard, all the men who wrote of mighty heroes: what would they think of me now? *Who cares? Go, Carpentier! Go, go!*

The villas of the First Circle slid below us.

And suddenly we were losing altitude again. The plane dipped sharply just over the cold river. I should have known it would.

"We're not high enough!" I shouted.

"Obviously. What now?"

"Take us back to the thermals! Get up higher, we can try it again."

"As you wish." He didn't say it wouldn't work. He just banked left again and headed us back down into the bowl. Toward the winds.

Even below the gray fog, Infernoland's lighting was not good. Gloom and night, all the way down. Infernoland was a vast funnel, leading down, down . . . down where Benito said we had to go. And we were flying there.

Suddenly we were in the winds. People flew about us like flurries of autumn leaves, some together, some alone. Aerial whirlpool ahead, which Benito avoided. And off to the left a straight updraft, flailing human shapes rising helplessly toward Infernoland's invisible roof. Just before they vanished into the gray stinking fog, the air column topped out and they streamed away to both sides.

"There," I said. I pointed.

Benito shrugged expressively.

"I'm getting pretty damned tired of your defeatist attitude!"

He banked toward the updraft. Suddenly we were rising as in an elevator. I caught startled faces, and some of the whirling victims tried to swim toward us through the air, but they were rising faster than we were. They couldn't catch us. I was glad. Massless they might be, but if I could feel wind roaring past my ears and tugging at my hair, then people clinging to the wings would foul the airstream. We'd all crash.

We left the updraft and were carried along with the others. Sure enough we were just at the edge of the fog, so that we could hardly see below. This was it! We were as high as we'd been above Dis, and much closer to the wall. "Now!" I shouted.

Benito even grinned at me as he turned toward the wall. This time we'd make it!

As he banked, something bulky hit him in the face and knocked him back into the seat, then slipped past and wrapped itself around me. I struggled to rip it off, and it fought back. We'd picked up a passenger.

"Let me at the controls! I used to be a glider pilot!" The hitchhiker pulled himself off me and scrambled into the other seat.

Benito didn't resist. "Let him fly," he said.

The plane turned sickeningly. We had lost altitude. I could see over the stranger's shoulder: cliffside, swampland, a glowing red line—

A tailspin, and we were beyond the place of the winds, headed back into the inner circles of Inferno-land.

He pulled us out of the spin. Nothing subtle about

it. He just stopped the spin with the ailerons, then pulled back on the tailflaps and hung on. Presently we were flying level again, headed toward the swamp. The stranger looked back at us, showing a lean, cheerful face beneath short, wind-tossed hair. "Where to?"

"Up and out. Over the wall."

"Good thinking, but there's a problem." He waved toward the cliff. We were well below the level of the winds.

I said, "There are red-hot walls down there. Good thermals. We'll spiral around them until we're high enough, then get back into the winds——"

"Not me."

"We have to! There are updrafts in the winds. Before you interfered we were high enough to get out of this place."

"Down is correct," Benito said.

"Not the way you mean!"

He shrugged. "It is the only way we can go now."

"No question about that." We headed out over the swamp again, feeling the rising air that was just strong enough to keep us level. If we didn't find an updraft we'd crash in the swamp.

The trouble was, we were looking for something invisible. You can't see a wind, you can only see what it does. I was looking for heat turbulence, or formations that might break a horizontal airstream and send it upwards; *anything*. There'd been no problem spotting updrafts when the wind was full of actors or draftees or whatever they were.

Ahead through the murk we could see the cherry-red glow of the walls of Dis. It looked a bit like the first sight of a town in the middle of the Nevada desert, and for a moment I thought of food and coffee and one-armed bandits, and girls . . .

We were over a hot-spot in the swamp. A shape

rose from the murk and shook a fist at us. He had a big bushy Afro hairdo. He lost interest when another man in a voluminous white gown and high pointed cap rose up to scream at *him*. They were locked in battle when we left them.

"Take it easy," I told our pilot. "I think I saw the left wing bend way up when you pulled us out of the spin."

"Yeah, I saw it too. What did you build this thing out of?"

I told him. He looked uneasy. I asked, "What kind of gliders are you used to?"

"Hypersonic."

"Eh?" said Benito.

"Huh?" I said.

The stranger chortled. "Jerome Leigh Corbett, at your service. I was a space-shuttle pilot. I had a dozen flights on my record, and then . . . You ever have one of those days?"

"Damned right," I said. Benito laughed and nodded.

We seemed to have enough altitude to reach the hot walls. They were close enough that we could make out details through the murk and the red glow. Corbett seemed to know what he was doing.

There were ripples in the dark mud below. A hand thrust itself upward, middle finger extended. There was no movement in the cobwebs and slimy moss hanging from the bushes, no wind, nothing; only the ripples in the mud.

"One of those days," Corbett said. "First, a twenty-six-hour hold while we replaced one of the solid boosters. That was only irritating. We lost one of the three main motors going up. Then after we made orbit one of the fuel tank clamps jammed. Either of you know what a space shuttle looks like?"

I said I did. Benito said he didn't.

"Well, the tank is big and bulky and cheap. We carry the main motors down aboard the dart, the winged section, but we leave the tank to burn up in the atmosphere. If we couldn't get the tank loose there wouldn't have been any point in going down."

"Did you?"

"Sure. We fired the orbital motors in bursts until the clamp sprang open and let us loose. Then we had to use more fuel to get back to our orbit. We were supposed to dump cargo and change orbit, but there wasn't enough fuel. We had to go down."

Benito was looking totally confused. It must have been gibberish to him. I asked, "What happened?"

"I don't know. I spacewalked out and looked at the fuel tank clamp. I swear there was nothing wrong. But maybe the metal fatigued, or maybe the hatch over the clamp lock got twisted—anyway, we were halfway down and going like a meteor when we got a burnthrough under the nose. I heard the maintenance techs—they were the cargo I couldn't jettison —screaming in the instrument room, then the whole nose peeled back in front of me. I woke up by that ferryboat. The crowd pushed me along to Minos, and he threw me into the whirlwind."

"And why were you there?" Benito asked.

Corbett grinned. "Being a shuttle pilot carries a lot of prestige. The girls liked me."

We were over the walls of Dis now, and banked to catch the rising air. My seat surged comfortingly against me . . . and the left wing bent in the middle. The Fudgesickle turned on its side and dropped.

Corbett dropped the nose. The wing, relieved of pressure, straightened out. But when he tried to pull up it bent again. We'd have been better off if the loose section had ripped away, but it hung on, dragging us back.

Corbett did his best. He tried to fly with the broken wing, the flap raised high on the right wing to compensate. We got some lift that way, but there wasn't any doubt: we were going to crash.

Inside the walls of Dis there were tombs. Dozens, hundreds, thousands of tombs, some glowing red hot, others dark. The whole landscape was littered with them.

On the walls themselves were—beings. They didn't look much like the cute little devils in Disney cartoons. They raged at us, and Corbett, seeing them, dove for speed to get out of their sight.

The wing folded entirely. Corbett played the controls like a virtuoso at an organ, heading out over the tombs and toward a steamy clear area beyond and below them, but we were too low and falling lower, into the tombs—

We dropped into their midst. The plane kissed the top of one tomb, bounced, and smashed nose on against a wall of red-hot iron.

13

FLAME ROARED UP AROUND ME, AS IF A FUEL TANK had caught. I pulled myself loose and rolled out, clawing frantically with my hands as the flames washed over me. When I tried to get to my hands and knees my right leg wouldn't work. I pulled myself along the ground, dragging the useless leg behind me, whimpering with fear while the fire raged behind and the air I breathed grew unbearably hot.

I didn't stop until I was forty feet away. My fingernails were torn, and my hands cut on the flinty ground. I rolled over onto my back to look behind me, afraid to look at my leg, knowing I'd have to. What had I done to myself?

Someone was screaming.

I ignored the deep throbbing incoherent pain in my leg to look back at the crashed glider. Benito had been thrown clear in the crash. Now he was running back toward the glider.

Corbett was trapped in the wreckage, rammed up against the red-hot iron tomb, screaming like a damned soul. I didn't even consider trying to get him out. He'd be dead in seconds. His skin would already have charred away, and he was breathing superheated air and smoke. How could he scream like that with seared lungs? He was a dead man.

Benito hadn't thought of that. He ran straight back into the flames. I watched in disbelief as he pulled at Corbett's arm, getting nowhere, while fire roared about him. Benito took flaming wreckage in his hands and heaved it away, clawing to get Corbett out.

Idiot! He'd leave me stranded here, my leg ruined, with no guide and no one to help me! I sat up and tried to go to his aid, but agony flashed in my leg. I had to look down.

I stared at two splintered ends of red-and-white bone protruding through my thigh. Bright blood spurted through the torn skin. Arterial bright, impossibly red. I couldn't take my eyes away.

Once before I'd broken a bone. I'd caught a football wrong in high school, and a knuckle cracked. It had made me sick, not just the pain, but the thought of that broken thing inside me. I could hardly walk to the clinic. Now I stared at two ends of a broken thighbone while my life's blood jetted out with each pulse. I expected to faint. But nothing happened, and presently I thought of making a tourniquet before all my blood was gone.

There was only my robe. I gripped the hem in my teeth and pulled with both hands. It wouldn't tear, and wouldn't tear, and bright blood jetted in the air.

Benito! I was lying with a broken bone and a terrible wound, but I could be saved! Why was Benito wasting his time on a hopeless case, a man he'd barely met, a *hitchhiker*? It wasn't fair.

Corbett was still screaming as Benito tore at the wreckage. Where did the pilot find the strength? He should be finished, lungs burned out, heart stopped, but he went on screaming mechanically as if the sounds of pain were being ripped out of him.

The pilot came lose suddenly, and they both went sprawling backward. Benito got up and dragged the pilot over to me. Benito was parboiled and hairless, his hands blistered and burned. Corbett was a charred corpse, black from end to end, with blood-rare steak showing through cracks in the char. There were no eyes left in the sockets. And still sounds came through the swollen blackened lips. I wanted to stop my ears.

"Stupid!" I said. "Stupid, stupid, stupid! In a minute he'll be dead anyway!"

"He will heal," said Benito. "He is dead already."

"*Heal?*"

"Certainly."

Agony surged in my leg. I looked down . . . and couldn't look away. I watched in helpless fascination.

The blood had stopped pumping. The bone ends gradually vanished as skin crawled out to cover them. It crawled on, closing the wound, leaving my leg in an odd tented shape. Without my willing it the leg straightened slowly.

An old scar I'd once got fishing slowly reappeared where before there had been bloody jagged bone end. The pain turned to a ferocious itch. That went away too.

I was healed.

Corbett had stopped screaming. Now he only moaned softly. I looked, afraid to look, afraid not to. The char was flaking off him in thick patches. The skin beneath was bright sunburn red, not at all like raw meat. His tattoo, like my scar, came up from underneath his skin like a self-developing photograph. He groaned again and opened his eyes.

There were eyes in the sockets. Corbett looked at me

and smiled weakly. "Can't die again, I guess. Wished I could for a time there."

"It is a pointless and evil wish," said Benito. "The dead cannot die."

"No." Corbett began an inspection of his body.

I stood up uncertainly. Benito watched, saying nothing. I was able to stand. I could walk. I did. I went off a way, toward the glowing tomb, until the heat was nearly unbearable, and I stared at it.

We'll have to change our theory, won't we, Carpentier? Corbett's no robot. The Builders would have had to put new, sunburned skin under the skin to be charred. They would have had to plan all this ahead of time. They would have to be omniscient.

And what about your leg, Carpentier? *What about your leg?*

Biological engineering. Rapid regeneration. That, to add to their other powers. They can warp space and possibly time. They can take the mass from a human body and leave the weight. They can put Minos' tail into—where? Hyperspace? They've got fine-tuned weather control and infinitely adaptable robots.

And they can engineer your body, Carpentier, *your* body, in such a way that it heals in minutes, and do it without your knowing they gave you that ability.

Getting a little thin, isn't it, Carpentier? A neat set of rationalizations, but it won't work. How are these Builders different from God Himself? What can God do that they can't?

And back at the edge of my mind I couldn't help remembering the last thing I'd screamed in the bottle.

Corbett had got up and was peeling saucer-sized flakes of charred skin from his chest and shoulders. "Hot here," he said.

I nodded and abandoned my reverie. It was hot. Even the tombs that weren't glowing were just below red heat. Here and there flames shot up from open pits. It must have been painful for Corbett with his new skin.

I remembered where we were. Inside the walls of Dis. How were we to get out again? We were surrounded by hot glowing tombs, flames, fire, heat everywhere, except in one direction where darkness showed through the red glow.

"We have to get out of here," I said to Benito. "We'll roast to— We'll roast." To death? We couldn't die. Can't die twice, Carpentier.

"Of course we must leave," Benito said. "Recall your promise. I helped you with the glider, and it did not work. Now you have no choice. We go downward."

"Which way?" For that moment I didn't care.

"I am not sure. We may as well go where it is more comfortable." He led us off toward the dark. It drew us onward, promising relief from the heat and the choking air. We threaded our way between heated tombs and great vatlike pits with fire dancing from them. Huge lids that would just cover them lay beside each one.

The edge of the hot region was the beginning of a white marble maze. The heat stopped as if we'd gone through an insulated doorway, but there was no door. I wasn't even surprised. It would take more than invisible heat barriers to surprise me now.

Corbett staggered into a corridor and sank down with a happy sigh, his back against cool marble. He wriggled to get his head clear of the brass fixtures.

We were in an endlessly sprawling building. The corridors were about fifteen feet wide and nearly that high. Every wall was covered with square-cut marble slabs and rows of brass plates and slender brass . . . what? Vases? I read some of the plates. *Name, birth-*

date, date of death. Sometimes an insipid poem. These were burial vaults, and those brass things were vases, and of course there were no flowers in them. The corridor stretched on endlessly, and there seemed to be branches at frequent intervals. Millions of tombs . . .

"More unbelievers," I said.

"Yes," Benito answered.

"But I was an unbeliever. An agnostic."

"Of course."

"Why of course?"

"I found you in the Vestibule," said Benito. "But now you know the truth."

A two-syllable response stuck in my throat. The truth was an elusive thing, here in Infernoland. I could talk about advanced technologies until Hell froze over, and Benito would still call them miracles.

I'd watched a miracle. A compound fracture had healed before my eyes. And I was no robot!

But this place had to be artificial. It was a construct, a design. I *knew* that.

All right, Carpentier. An artifact implies an artificer. There has to be a designer. Pick a Chief Engineer for the Builders, and call him . . . what? Good fannish names, like Ghod, Ghu, Roscoe, the Ceiling? No. Call him Big Juju.

Question, Carpentier. In what way do Big Juju's abilities differ from God Almighty's?

Size? This place is the size of a small planet. Carpentier, you've no way of knowing Big Juju can't build even bigger. Worlds, stars, whole universes.

Natural laws? He suspends them at will. A world-sized funnel, as stable as a sphere would be in normal space. And—and he can raise the dead. Me! Corbett, who couldn't *possibly* have been frozen. Jan Petri the health-food addict, *cremated,* Carpentier, burned

to a pile of greasy ashes and a few chunks of bone,
and now risen so that he can be tortured.

Big Juju can create. He can destroy. He can raise
the dead and heal the sick. Was more ever claimed
for Christ?

I looked back at the red-hot tombs. They still
glowed with heat, but none of that reached us in
these cool marble halls. "There are people in those
tombs?"

Benito nodded. "Heretics."

The word was frightening. Heretics. They believed
in the wrong gods, or worshiped the right god in the
wrong way. For that they were raised from the dead
so they could be tortured in hotboxes.

Iago says it. *"Credo in un Dio crudel."* I believe
in a cruel God. And that you must believe, Carpentier.
The ability to make a universe does not presuppose
moral superiority. We have seen no strong evidence
that Big Juju's moral judgments are better than our
own. Would God torture people?

I half-remembered Sunday school lessons. No. But
also, yes. It was one reason I was an agnostic. How
could I worship a God who kept a private dungeon
called Hell? That might be all right for Dante
Alighieri, a Renaissance Italian! But Carpentier has
higher standards than that!

A voice floated from within my mind, a tired voice
whispering out of a mound of fat. *We're in the hands
of infinite power and infinite sadism.*

We were in the private museum park of Big Juju.
"We've got to get out of here."

"Too right," said Corbett. He paused. "Music?"

I listened. There was music playing from somewhere within these marble corridors. Something
chintzy-sweet, a minor work by a major composer,
played for every melodramatic sweet note in it. Arti-

ficial good cheer in Hell. "It fits," I said. "Granted we're damned, how do we get out? Which way?"

Benito looked around him. "I have never been in this part before."

"Not back out there," Corbett insisted. "Not unless we have to."

"Right. We've got time," I said. And I started laughing.

It was an awful sound. It bounced around in the maze and came back at me from all directions, transmuted to racking sobs. I tried to stop. Corbett and Benito were staring. I tried to tell them:

"I was right. Just once, I was right. All that time in the bottle, all that guessing, and I was right just once. Immortality! When they woke me up they had immortality." Dammit, I *was* crying.

Corbett took my arm. "Come on, Allen."

We went inward.

14

THE CORRIDORS BRANCHED AWAY, ENDLESS CROSS-corridors in an endless corridor, and every one of them the same, wall after wall of marble-sealed caskets, each with its empty bronze vases for flowers. Our footsteps echoed hollowly. Our sandals hadn't been touched by the flames. The sprightly music continued, never getting louder, and the light never changed, neither gloomy nor bright. On and on, corridor after corridor. Finally we halted.

"We haven't turned," I said.

Corbett nodded. "Do a one-eighty and we can get out of here. Let's."

Half-facetiously I rapped on a bronze nameplate and read off the name and dates. A translucent human shape formed before me. I stared in horror, then shrugged. What was a ghost among ghosts?

"Pardon me," I said. "Can you direct us toward the wall of Dis?"

The ghost's voice was faint and reedy. "Wall? Dis?" Faint laughter. "They must have added more extensions to the Mausoleum. I don't remember anything like that in Forest Lawn."

"Very funny. This isn't Forest Lawn."

The ghost seemed vexed. "I was supposed to be buried in Forest Lawn. I paid for it before I died. It was in my will. Where am I?"

"Would you believe Hell?"

More faint laughter, as if from a great distance. "Certainly not. I don't even believe in ghosts." And then there was nothing but the wall.

I jumped when Corbett spoke behind me. "It's a risk, but are you game to try a cross-corridor? I think if we turn left and keep going straight we'll be headed up again."

The scenery changed. Now there were niches with urns in them, much closer together. We came to a T intersection and turned and returned to the right direction when we could. Then another T and a Y and a big round empty space with corridors off in all directions and a big monument in the very center . . .

. . . and we were in the good section of town. The sarcophagi were no longer buried in the walls. At the ends of short alcoves were huge marble oblongs, ornately carved, guarded by traditional statuary. Knights and vague sexless winged beings that were supposed to be angels and might have been faggots; reproductions of famous religious statuary; original creations, all done with enormous competence, all in monstrous bad taste. Sculpted Bibles open to John 3:16. Replicas of European cathedrals, done in perfect scale, bronze toys.

One alcove was blocked off by a brass gate and enormous lock. All the nameplates were of the same family, all ornately carved with relief pictures and bronze replicas of their life's signatures. We looked in, grinned at each other, and went on.

Pride. Unbelievably ornate monuments purchased at unbelievable price: expensive tombs turned prisons. I wondered if they matched monuments left behind on Earth. Sure, I decided. Big Juju has a sense of fitness.

Fitness?

In this one case, yes, fitness.

The corridors twisted again and again. The dead were high walls on all sides of us. Our footsteps were dull intrusions on music for the proud dead. The dead walked among the dead. Dead. Dead. *Dead. Dead!* Word and reality echoed with each step. Word and reality hammered at my soul. Dead. Dead. Dead. Presently I sat down against cool marble.

"Allen? What is the trouble?" Benito's anxious voice was far away.

"Come on, let's get moving. This place gives me the creeps." Corbett shoved at me with his toe. "C'mon."

I tried to speak. It wasn't worth the effort, but finally I heard my own voice saying, "We're dead. Dead. It's all over. We tried to make lives for ourselves, and we didn't make it, and we're dead. Oh, Corbett, I wish I'd died like you."

The gay sweet music mocked me. Dead. Dead. Dead.

Green light blinked on and off in the corner of my eye. It was annoying, a disturbance, an irritant in the thick cotton closing about me. I could see the source without turning my head, but it was an effort to move my eyes. Why bother? But the light winked on and off, and eventually I looked at the source, a neon sign blinking far down at the dead end of a corridor of the dead. It echoed my thought:

SO IT GOES
SO IT GOES
SO IT GOES

—off and on, endlessly, in green neon.

Unreachably far away, on another world, in another time, Allen Carpentier had been buried like a potato in a closed coffin ceremony. The fans had come to the funeral, some of them, and a few writers had come, and afterward they'd gone off to have a drink and talk about new writers. Carpentier was dead, and that was all there was to it. I could speculate forever about Big Juju's moral superiority, I could wander forever through Hell, and so what?

SO IT GOES
SO IT GOES

Corbett's voice came dimly. "We may have to leave him. I saw this happen to a guy, once, in the war. He's going autistic."

"I have seen it also. Many times. Would you leave him here?"

I thought Benito was shaking my shoulder.

SO IT GOES
SO IT GOES
SO IT GOES

—what was the blinking neon sign doing in this place?

A horrible suspicion filtered through the blankets around my brain. I pushed Benito away and surged to my feet. I walked, wobbling, toward the blinking light. So it goes?

At the end of the corridor was a tremendous square-cut edifice in black marble. The epitaph beneath the neon sign was long and wordy, couched in words of one syllable and short, simple sentences. A man's life history, a list of books and awards—

Corbett and Benito stared when I came back. Corbett said, "You look like you're ready to kill somebody."

I jerked my thumb behind me. At first I couldn't speak, I was that angry. *"Him.* Why him? A science-fiction writer who lied about being a science-fiction writer because he got more money that way. He wrote whole novels in baby talk, with sixth-grade drawings in them, and third-grade science, and he *knew* better. How does he rate a monument that size?"

Benito's smile was lopsided. "You envy him that tomb?"

"If you must know, I was writing better than he ever did before I left high school!"

"Being dead hasn't hurt your ego," said Corbett. "Good. We thought we'd lost you."

"He's got *vases* bigger than the bottle they put me in!"

"You were an agnostic. Selfish, but not viciously so," Benito said. "If I judge rightly from the size of his tomb, he must have founded his own religion. And possibly worshiped himself."

"No, they were jokes, sort of. But he did found at least two, not that there ever were any followers, or that he even intended there to be. One of them had everyone telling comforting lies to everyone else. The other was the Church of God the Fairly Competent. Maybe I should have gone in for something like that."

"Why didn't you?" Corbett asked.

"Because what's the point of mocking people who've found something to believe in." I turned toward the big, gaudy edifice. *"That's* the point."

Benito shook his head wonderingly. "I question your sanity. He is in there. You are out here, free to escape."

I didn't answer, but he was right. We turned away. For a time I could see the green reflection blinking ahead of us.

SO IT GOES

We were lost in endless corridors of the dead. Benito walked in stolid patience, but Corbett's face had acquired a grim, set look, desperation barely held in check. I kept my own thoughts to myself.

But I remembered Big Juju's ability to distort space and time.

We'd come a long way. Perhaps there *was* no way out.

And what if we did get out of the maze?

Benito said we had all eternity. Eternity in Infernoland. Or in Hell. Big Juju or God, it didn't matter; the problem was to escape.

I'd built a glider once, and it had flown. Get me through the wall, get me fabric for the wings, and I'd do it again.

But I'd have to do it without Benito.

You promised you'd go with him, Carpentier. Down to the center, out his way. You can keep your word or you can break it; but if you break it, it'll be without his help.

Suppose he's crazy? Or an agent for Big Juju?

Then you're on your own.

Nuts. Benito might be able to trick the damned bureaucrats into giving us whatever we wanted. I couldn't kid myself I'd be able to. Fabric I could get—at worst, by peeling it off catatonics—but how to get through the wall? I'd seen demons on the rim. More demons guarded the gate.

I glanced sideways at Benito. Stolid patience, and iron faith in God and the maps of Dante Alighieri. And Carpentier's given word. If we ever got out of this maze, he'd go down. We could follow or not.

I felt heat ahead. We turned a corner and found a wall of red-hot urns. The floor seemed to slant uphill.

Corbett whooped. "This way! To the wall!" His voice sounded out of place in the mausoleum. I waited for Benito to protest, but he said nothing, and I wondered if he knew something we didn't.

"We could make quite a safari," Corbett shouted. He was over-joyful at finding a way out. "Just open these urns and pour out the ashes."

"I went further than that, once," Benito told us. "I attempted to establish a local government."

"Didn't work?"

"No."

"Why?"

There was no answer. It became apparent that there wouldn't be one. Something else to think about.

We hit a T corridor and were back in cool marble. We followed it a short way, anxious lest we find ourselves back in the endless tombs. It turned left again. I rounded the turn ahead of the others and found myself facing red heat. I shaded my eyes—

"Your papers, please?"

I squinted through my fingers.

I faced a towering wall of red-hot iron, with a divided door in it. There was a counter on the lower closed half of the door, and someone behind it, half-hidden in the dark interior framed by bright red light. He held a stack of papers. The bored face showed no sign of recognition. It might have been the same clerk or a different one.

"Papers? Come on, I haven't got all eternity." He pushed the stack of papers toward me. "You'll have to make these out before you can go uphill. It's in the rules."

I backed around the corner. To the questioning looks of the others I said, "Don't ask. Just turn around."

We went back the way we'd come, looking for a right turn. Presently we found it, and—

"Your papers, please?"

I walked toward the booth, but I was studying the gate behind the clerk. Iron glowing red, but it was only waist high. We could jump it.

The counter turned white hot as I approached.

"Papers? You'll have to fill out the forms. No exceptions."

I looked to Benito. He shrugged and turned away. After a moment I followed, hating him. He wasn't going to help.

And he'd known it all along. We had to go downhill.

15

THE MUSIC WENT WITH US WHEREVER WE WENT: nature themes, melodramatic sweetness, singing violins, but never funeral dirges or somber tones. The cheerful music was more depressing than any funeral march.

Gradually I realized we could hear something else as well. I don't know if it had been with us the whole time, waiting for us to become aware of it, or if it began as we threaded our way deeper into Hell.

The sounds came from the tombs. Groaning. Whimpers. Croaks of rage. Mumbled curses. Once even gay whistling, a tune that jarred against the canned music.

Gradually the clammy air warmed. It was our first sign that we were moving out of the maze.

We followed currents of warming air. Where the air turned steamy hot we found a doorway.

Unnerving sounds reached us through the doorway: screams of agony torn from throats that could contain them no longer, blended with animal war cries and the most vicious curses I'd ever imagined.

Corbett plunged ahead, but Benito caught him. "Carefully," he warned us.

We looked out and down. The ground fell straight away from the doorsill, first vertically, then angling down to a forty-five-degree slope. The dirt was baked adobe with jagged edges of protruding flint.

The bottom of the cliff was obscured by steam, much like the marsh outside Dis, but this was hot. The steam roiled about, leaving occasional clear patches. Gradually the picture formed.

We were looking at an enormous discolored lake. The shore curved away to either side until steam hid the endpoints. Men and women stood waist deep in steamy red water, and they howled. They were packed like a public pool on a Kansas summer Saturday, and they wanted out.

Some tried it, but they didn't make it. Armed men patrolled the shore between us and the scarlet water. The guards were dressed for a costume ball, in the military garb of all places and all times, but they walked like sentries whose officers are watching. Their eyes were uniformly on the lake, and they held weapons ready.

Weapons: there was every hand weapon known to history. Pistols, bows, scythes, crossbows, throwing-sticks, slings, pikes and lances, AR-15 rifles, all held at the ready. When someone attempted to leave the lake, the sentries fired.

I saw a woman in black military uniform cut nearly in half by a burst from an automatic rifle. She shrieked in agony and waded deeper into the lake, where she stood, healing.

Healing. The implications of our inability to die began to get through to me then.

One man in a long beard wore a golden crown on his head and clustered crossbow bolts through his chest. He was stubborn. He'd move toward the shore. The crossbowmen would fire, and he'd stagger back,

the scream hissing through clenched teeth. He'd pluck
the bolts from his chest and throw them contemptuously into the water—and wade toward shore again.

And again. And again. He was a fool, but a brave
one.

"I take it the guards won't be on our side," I
whispered.

Benito shuddered. "No. On the contrary, if they
catch us, we—" He didn't finish, but he didn't have to.

The guards looked silly in those costumes. I knew
some of them. Nazi swastikas and American GI's.
Coldstream Guards and Cameron Highlanders. Blue
and gray of the Civil War. World War I helmets. Red-
coats and the blue-and-buff of Washington's Continen-
tals. Fuzzy-wuzzies and Chinese Gordon's Tommies,
and more: Roman legion, Greek hoplite, vaguely
Asiatic uniforms, long gowns and wicker shields,
spears with golden apples on the hilts; and more still,
yellow men in animal fur, red and black men in little
besides war paint, blue men stark naked. Blue?
Britons in their woad, marching beside legionnaires,
followed by men and women in coveralls carrying tiny
machine guns of a variety I'd never seen.

And they watched the lake, constantly, vigilantly.
"They won't see us up here," I said. "Now what?"

"We must cross the lake," said Benito. "There is a
place, far around, where it is only ankle deep. Elsewhere it rises to above our heads in the deepest parts.
The damned stand at a depth appropriate to the violence they did on Earth."

"That water looks hot. It steams."

"It is boiling blood." Benito laughed without humor.
"What would you expect for the violent?"

A frozen moment stretched endlessly. Then Corbett
shouted, "We can't walk into that! No!"

"Jerry—"

"I've been burned before, remember? We'll never make it! When our ankles are cooked we'll go to our knees. When the legs are cooked we'll be lying in it!"

"Yet you see that every man and woman in the lake is standing."

The calm voice halted Corbett's panicky monologue. He looked. I'd already seen that Benito was right. If they could stand, their cooked legs must still be operating. They also wouldn't stop hurting . . .

"The guards will not allow us to wander freely in Hell," Benito cautioned us. "Without instructions regarding our sentence, they may well force us to the deepest spot and keep us there. You have noted that their weapons do not kill, but they can disable."

Let's stay here, Carpentier. I'm starting to like the music.

"They must not notice us. We must do as little screaming as possible." Benito spoke seriously, without a trace of humor. Benito had been in Hell so long that suffering was not remarkable to him, or even unusual.

"There may be a better way," Corbett said slowly. He pointed. "Allen, what do you see?"

"An island." Half-obscured by steam, it stood very low in the lake a good mile to our right. It was more crowded than the water around it, the water that Benito said was boiling blood.

Poetic justice. Infinitely exaggerated, as everything was here. No doubt the people boiling down there were murderers in life, or torturers, or kidnappers, arsonists perhaps. The violent. Well, at least we knew how to get across. "Benito, can we cross on the island?"

He stared pop-eyed, his big square jaw thrust forward. "I had no idea there was an island in Acheron. Dante did not describe it."

"I suppose he mentioned boiling blood?"

"Of course. He also described the ford I used before. The ford is heavily guarded, and perhaps the island would be better." He considered. "Dante did not mention the ship in Acheron either."

"Ship?"

"Yes, Allen, a wooden sailing ship sunken on the other side of Acheron. The decks are just awash with blood. I have been aboard it. There are grills in the deck and souls beneath the grills."

"Slave traders," Corbett speculated.

"Probably," said Benito.

But how had Benito been aboard? Was that where he had escaped from? Or from deeper down? I didn't dare ask, yet how could we trust him until we knew his crime?

How could we not?

"Slave traders aren't our problem," Corbett said. "I suppose the best plan would be to circle up here until we're just opposite the island, then make a run for it."

We looked at each other and nodded agreement.

We turned back inside to parallel the shore, passing walls of shelves packed with crematory urns. I savored the cool, damp air. I was going to miss it. The cliff edge was just beyond that wall.

Why bother, Carpentier? Why not stay here?

No. We've got to get out of here. Minos would track us down eventually, and then what? We have to escape.

Hey, Carpentier, what makes you think there's a way out?

I don't want to think about that. There has to be a way out. Benito says there is. Dante described it—

A way out for him, yes! A living man whose guide called on angels!

There is a way out of Hell and we're going to find it, because we can't die trying, because there's nothing else to do but sit for eternity. Eternity.

I'm scared, Carpentier.

Me too. Let's talk to the others. They're scared like you. Talking helps.

"The guards," I said. "They bother me two ways."

Corbett said, "It's *boiling* that bothers me."

"I don't think I'll like being shot full of arrows and bullets," I said. "But worse than that, what the blazes are they *doing* here?"

Corbett just laughed. They were guarding, his look said.

"They did violence they believed justified," said Benito. "They fought for what they thought was a higher cause."

"And there aren't any soldiers in Heaven?"

"I'm sure there are. But these enjoyed their work." His voice took on a note of sadness. "They enjoy it still. They do not seek to escape."

"It's weird. They're serving the Builders, or Big Juju, or God, whatever we call the master of this place. If they're serving God they ought to be in Heaven!"

Benito shrugged. "Or Purgatory. Perhaps. Theology is not my specialty. The next doorway is just ahead, be careful."

He wouldn't say more, but I remembered the uniformed servitors in Disneyland and wondered if the guards worked in shifts. Did they have homes to go to when they got off work? Did they go home and tell their wives about their day?

We waited, peeking around the doorjamb to watch the shore. The island was just opposite, no more than fifty yards offshore, obscured by clouds of steam and no easier to see than it had been from a mile away.

A band marched past, robed and unarmed. "Inquisition priests," Benito murmured. "They would call the temporal authorities. The soldiers."

They receded. A handful of barbarian women passed, arms and shoulders the color of their bronze armor. They carried bows and shortswords. Behind them was another group, also women, wearing olive-drab fatigues and carrying submachine guns. They passed out of sight, and the shore was clear.

"Run," Benito ordered.

We ran. There was a ten-foot drop to the steep slope. I landed on my feet and kept running in a half-controlled fall. Jagged flint edges tore at my feet. When I hit the beach I kept running, because I knew I'd never be able to *walk* into the boiling lake. The wandering clouds of steam wrapped me round, hid me from the guardians, and I ran toward the chorus of screams. The smell was overpowering, fresh blood and clotted blood, copper bright and polluted foul.

Corbett was ahead of me. He splashed into bubbling red fluid and screamed. He stood, covered to his knees, screaming in pain. Benito plunged in, waded through the stuff like a damned robot and gripped Corbett's arm to keep him from turning back. Then I was in it myself. I fell into a trench and was instantly waist deep.

The pain hit me weirdly, as if I'd stuck my finger in a light socket. Stunning. Unreal. All my senses were scrambled. I knew the smell of pain, its sight and sound, and there was nothing to see or hear but pain. I couldn't control my limbs. They thrashed and twitched, almost spilling me full length into the stuff.

Still jerking like a marionette, I turned toward shore. Nothing could be worth this much pain.

Half a squad of Green Berets stood there studying us. They had friends: small men in black pajamas.

I turned back. We were committed now. Through a gap in the steamy mist I had seen their eyes; dull, expressionless, intent on their task: and their task was to let no one leave the blood.

"The island," I screamed. "To the island!" But I didn't move and neither did the others. We stood where we were and screamed.

"The island!" Corbett laughed hysterically, laughter and pain and horror. "We can't use the island—"

I screamed, "What?"

"Stupid! Look!"

He was right. I cursed the rolling clouds that had hidden it from view. They were shoulder to shoulder over every square inch of the island. I never saw a more vicious mob. They were armed haphazardly, with clubs and crude daggers of what seemed to be splintered bone. Even as I watched, someone trying to climb out of the blood was repelled by half-a-dozen stab wounds. He staggered away, howling, leaving a foaming red wake.

Benito came up to me, still pulling Corbett by the arm. "We must wade around the island."

I couldn't move. Suddenly he took my shoulder in his powerful grip and began to plunge through the boiling red, towing both of us like children. I remembered his strength. There was no point in struggling with him. I didn't want to. I wanted *out,* but my limbs would not obey. The pain was paralyzing.

You could read the agony on Benito's face. He hurt as we did. But he plunged on. He shouted, "Deeper down, there is a place where souls are not even allowed to cry! Here there is no law against screaming!"

"Yeah! Cheer me up!" I screamed.

We halted. There were guards on the shore. A man in a high peaked hat stared through binoculars. We didn't dare move.

There are two ways to treat constant excruciating agony. Both involve screaming. You may try to suppress the screams, and they will force their way through your teeth; or you can just let it out. Similarly, you can concentrate on the source of pain and try to minimize it: a current of not-quite-boiling blood here on the left, get into it! Stand on tiptoe, you gain an inch . . .

Or you can tell yourself it will heal and concentrate on something else.

There was turmoil on the island. People were shouting at one of their number. He stood with his feet planted wide and his hands raised high over his head. The hands held the haft of a spear: a length of wood that might have been a broken oar or a tree sapling, and a leaf-shaped blade poised a few inches above his feet. Poised to strike, but at what? Hands reached to shake his shoulders, and he snarled in an agony different somehow from all the moans around him.

I tried to hear. By now the wordless moaning of the thousands of waders, even my own, had become a background noise, had faded like the sickening smell of boiling blood. I caught disjointed phrases.

"Kill 'em! Kill 'em before—"

"Billy, if you won't do it, let us through!"

"Idiot, you hafta, they'll be all around us in a minute—"

The man with the spear bellowed, "No!"

And the ground seemed to erupt beneath his feet.

He kicked at whatever was gripping his ankles. He kicked himself free and ran for the island's shore. Others got out of his way, then surged to close the gap. Behind him, that portion of the island was heaving as in an earthquake, and clubs and knives were rising and falling with horrible rhythm.

"Billy" splashed knee deep into boiling blood and stopped at once. As he sucked air for his first shocked scream, three separate hands thrust forward against his back. He splashed face down. Two surging waves washed against the bathers around him.

He was up in a flash, his spear ready for war. I was sure he'd try to fight his way back onto the island. But he didn't. He turned and waded away, in our direction. A foot short of my nose he said, "Friend, it's not polite to stare."

"Sorry. What happened back there? Will they let you back?"

He glared back at his erstwhile neighbors. "Those bastards couldn't stop *me*." He sounded like he was holding his breath . . . as we all did, because each of us was trying to talk around a scream. It was almost funny, that sound. "I . . . never thought it would hurt so much," he said.

"Why didn't you stay?"

"Couldn't take the killing."

"What?"

Benito and Corbett had crowded close to listen. "Billy" studied me, his face contorted in agony. "Don't know about the island, do you?"

I shook my head. The Afrika Korps had gone, but cuirassiers with muskets had replaced them. We still dared not move.

"We on the island, we killed people, just like you in the swimming hole. But we all had some excuse, some reason we had to kill. Like me. There was a range war going on. We wasn't even the ones that started it."

I said, "Yeah?"

He took it wrong. "You think maybe we could have stopped it? Gone along with the amnesty?"

I didn't know what he was talking about and didn't much care. His blue eyes had turned killer in that moment. I said, "Don't mind me. I'm in Hell too."

That calmed him, and changed him. He was younger than me and shorter than me, and the short amateurish

haircut gave him a pleasant boyish look. Though the
hair was plastered down with blood . . . "Then there's
Harry Vogel," he continued, "he was robbing a liquor
store and the owner pulled his mask off. He'd seen his
face, so he had to die, see? And Rich and Bonny An-
derson, they kidnapped a kid, and it would have been
okay, but he got away. Got as far as a great big street
called a freeway, then some kind of machine hit him."
He looked down, then continued talking, hurriedly, as
if that would block the pain. "Bonny's here, Rich isn't.
Rich got religion. Hey, we got Aaron Burr on the island!
And that guy who ran the Andersonville prison
camp—"

"I get the idea. If they thought they had to do it,
they don't get hurt as bad."

"Yeah." Billy looked down a his waist. "It hurts. I
think this hurts as much as anything I ever did except
die. But I wouldn't go back. No." But he looked back
and wasn't sure. He said it again. "No! I won't ever kill
anyone again!"

"That's twice you've—"

"Well, that island ain't any common dirt, you know.
It's mostly judges and congressmen and lawyers and a
few jury members and crooked sheriffs—"

"Wait! Wait!" I remembered the island surging up
around him. "The island's people? Live people?"

I swear he was enjoying my reaction. "Yeah. We have
to keep 'em crippled. It's what Minos does to them for
letting known killers loose on the public that was paying them to protect them. Some was jury members that
took bribes, and lawyers that fiddled with the evidence,
and congressmen that passed laws against putting a man
in jail if the evidence wasn't got in a special kind of
way . . . I don't know. That kind of law is all new to
me. The island was a lot smaller when I came here."

"And they keep coming back to life!" I was this shocked: I had forgotten to hurt.

"Friend, they sure do. And we have to keep persuading them not to move, one way or another. Otherwise they'd just swim away, and where'd we be?"

"Waist deep in boiling blood?"

He tried to laugh. "Well, I guess I'd rather boil. If they could die it'd be okay, but they can't. Let 'em alone long enough and they try to get up. I can't take it anymore."

I felt Benito's hand on my shoulder. "Allen, the shore is clear of guards. I think we can move."

Corbett was already raising a wake. I started after him, tottering on stiffened legs. On impulse I turned back. "Why not come with us? It can't be any worse lower down."

His eyes sparked with hope. "Maybe you're right."

16

WE WADED THROUGH BOILING BLOOD, GOING UP TO OUR chins before the bottom sloped up again. After an eternity we reached the other shore and let ourselves fall, each wrapped silently and solipsistically in his own pain. We lay in full view on what seemed to be rough white concrete. Four targets. If the guardians wanted us they could have us.

A long time later, Corbett found the strength to roll over. "They're all along the far shore," he reported. "Watching us. Nazis, Indians—"

Benito said, "Never mind. They will not hurt us. They do not bother those who wish to go deeper into Hell."

"That's a relief," said Corbett.

I wasn't so sure, but I held my peace. I inspected my feet, legs, buttocks. The meat was loose on my bones. I should have been dead down there; it should have stopped hurting. *Fat chance, Carpentier.*

And Billy, who must have hurt just as much as I did, was smiling to himself. I snarled, "What are you so damned happy about?"

"First off, this is the first chance I've had to lie down

in a hundred years. Second, I don't have to kill anyone, even if they yell at me. Third, I didn't much like the company on that island. Maybe I'll like you better."

"Maybe. Who were you?"

"William Bonney. Just a cowhand that got done unto and did some back."

"Bonney?" Corbett sat up suddenly. He'd healed much faster than I had. "Billy the Kid?"

"Friend, there are a dozen men on the island that all claim they was Billy the Kid."

"And you?"

"I'm the real one."

I could see the wheels going round in Corbett's head. Were we supposed to spend eternity wondering if he were telling the truth? Corbett said, "Have it your way. I was a spaceship pilot."

"What? You mean like you been on the Moon?"

"Right."

Benito grunted and surged to his feet, then sat down hard with another grunt of pain. From the waist down he showed bright red skin, very tender looking. Like Corbett he'd healed fast, but he wasn't in condition to scout.

I asked, "Benito, what are we headed into? It's for sure we can't go back."

"The Wood of the Suicides lies ahead. A pleasant place, comparatively, if we can avoid the dogs."

"Dogs?"

"The Wood is punishment for the sin of suicide," Benito explained. "Each tree holds the soul of one who took his own life. They are not dangerous to us. But the Violent Wasters also suffer there, and the dogs are their punishment. There will not be many of the dog packs. It is almost an obsolete sin."

Corbett looked up. "Since when is a sin obsolete?"

"Customs change. In Dante's time there were men

who would hold a party at which they would burn part of their wealth, to show how wealthy they were."

"Potlach!" I cried.

"Gesundheit," said Corbett.

"No, dammit, listen. There was a West Coast Indian tribe that used to do just what Benito's talking about. Hold a party, burn a lot of valuables. They used to compete at it. I never knew the Italians did the same thing."

"They did," said Benito. "Their punishment is to run through these woods pursued by wild dogs. If the dogs catch them they tear them apart."

Billy was sitting up. "They heal after *that?*"

I was healing! My legs and buttocks still hurt, but the flesh was firm, and I could move the muscles. I watched, fascinated, as new skin grew before my eyes.

"The dogs and the souls they pursue should be rare," Benito said, "and the trees can do us no harm. We should find this stretch easy." He stood up. "Are we ready?"

My feet were still tender, and Billy was complaining about his. But it didn't sound like we'd have to run anywhere. Corbett and Benito were healed.

We set off, deeper into Hell. It had become an obsession with me. Anything was better than waiting—and if I spent too much time remembering the agony in the lake, we'd *never* get started.

We left concrete for dirt. When we topped a gentle rise, the ground was suddenly all erosion gullies, hard red and yellow clay studded with gravel and gashed by flash floods. We had to scramble in and out of them. Some had water at the bottom, water filthy with broken bottles and bottle caps, used condoms, floating grease, occasional bursts of brightly colored dyes, chemicals that burned our sandaled feet. Nothing grew here; there were dead stumps of trees and dried brown vines reaching upward like dead old women's fingers. Strange smells moved on the air: incongruous whiffs of automobile exhaust, acids, burning oil and rubber.

Billy grunted. "I don't see no trees, Benito. Where'd you put the damn trees?"

"We should have reached the Wood long since. I do not understand. But we must go on."

We scrambled out of the gully and looked downward. We had a vista of Hell.

It looked like Hell on Earth. Nothing grew. We had to shout above a continual racket. In the distance rectangular shadows showed through the gloomy half-light and thick smog. Buildings? Factories?

I said, "Progress has caught up with your woods, Benito."

A clattering sounded nearby, within a cloud of roiling smoke. A woman ran out of the smoke, terror on her face, hair streaming behind her. She wore a torn evening gown with diamond brooch and earrings, high-heeled shoes with jeweled ornaments. She ran holding the skirt high.

Billy shouted and tried to stop her. She dodged him and ran on. The clattering grew louder, and a bulldozer roared out of the smoke. A man ran just ahead of the blade. The 'dozer trailed smoke, and it was gaining on the fugitive. There was no driver.

Billy was in the bottom of the gully, curled up, his head wrapped in his arms. When the monster was past I went down to Billy. He was muttering to himself, and when I touched him he twitched galvanically. He leapt to his feet in fighting stance.

"I was never afraid of no man that ever lived," he said. "But I was scared of that. What was it?"

"Bulldozer. For moving dirt."

Billy stared into the smog, his face wondering. "You could tear down whole mountains with things like that."

"We did," Corbett said. "There's more than one way to be a violent waster."

Billy frowned. "How's that?"

"Pollution. This must be the place for people who ruin the environment." Corbett's face showed his disgust. "They did this to the Earth."

"But who gets chased by them things?"

"Real-estate developers, I guess. Housing-tract speculators. We shouldn't have too much trouble here." Corbett looked at us. "Or do we?"

I'd always been a conservationist myself. If Big Juju's poetic justice ran true to form, I'd be safe enough.

Or would I? Had I fallen by accident? I'd certainly put myself on that window ledge. If a bulldozer buried me here, would I become a tree?

"Let's go," said Billy. "This place gives me the willies."

We moved off by tacit consent.

"Where we going, anyway?" Billy asked.

"Past this round there is desert," Benito said. "A fiery desert, too hot for life, with flame falling from the sky. I know of only one way to cross it, and that is the way Dante used. A stream runs through the desert, the overflow from the lake of blood. It cools the desert as it moves through it."

"Miraculously," I said. I'd intended it to be contemptuous, but it hadn't come out that way. I'd seen too many miracles, all unpleasant.

Benito nodded. "Of course. We must find this stream, or we cannot cross. It runs through the Wood. Comrades, we must find the Wood." He turned left and walked on.

"Why this way?" Billy laughed. "You ain't got any idea where that Wood is."

"No, but we must reach it if we walk far enough. It is only a matter of time."

Yeah, we had plenty of that. And Hell was a series of concentric circles, God only knew how big around. It might take years, and so what?

"Why not go the other way?" Billy insisted.

Benito shrugged. "Dante always turned left on his way down. But we will turn right if you like."

"Naw. It ain't important."

17

THE NOISE, THE SMELLS, THE DESOLATION CONTINUED. The damned were here, placed by a macabre humor. Phantom heads rose from oil pools. Some were pecked incessantly by oil-smeared birds. A river ran past like an open sewer, and men and women lined the banks, mourning. The wails were constant in our ears, wails and roaring motors and clanking machines.

We looked into some of the huge buildings and pulled back out fast. Inside the noise was overwhelming. Here a sizzling hum of electricity, there a scream of metal grinding on metal, elsewhere a roar of flame. There were more of the damned in those buildings, and they were hard at work.

Our way led through one of the immense factories. Not a head lifted to see us pass. Incomprehensible widgets passed on an endless belt, and men and women screwed on nuts and tightened them and fitted the bottoms and the handles, endlessly. We followed the endless belt for miles until it went through a wall. On the other side more of the damned were taking the widgets apart. Machinery hummed, and conveyors took the parts back to the other side of the wall.

We left the building to find oil derricks raising and lowering their heads like giant prehistoric birds. We crossed a strip mine, and Benito pointed out that it was laid out very like Hell itself: a vast series of descending circular terraces. But there was nothing at the bottom except stagnant water.

A towering oil-fueled power plant of spidery framework and miles of pipes and valves poured power into a cable thick as my waist. Transmission towers took the cable downhill.

I peered along its length, but the murk defeated me. How did they use electricity in Hell? But outside the power plant was an athletic man chained to a wheelless bicycle set in concrete in front of the exhaust pipe of the generator. Black smoke poured around him, almost hiding him from view.

As we watched he began pedaling furiously. The hum of the gears rose to a high pitch—and the generator inside died. There was a moment of quiet. The man pedaled with sure strokes, faster and faster, his feet nearly invisible, his head tucked down as if against a wind. We gathered around, each wondering how long he could keep it up.

He began to tire. The blur of his feet slowed. The motors inside coughed, and black smoke poured out. He choked and turned his head away, and saw us.

"Don't answer if you'd rather not," I said, "but what whim of fate put you here?"

"I don't *know!*" he howled. "I was president of the largest and most effective environmental protection organization in the country! I *fought* this!" He braced himself and pedaled again. The hum rose, and the generator died.

Billy was completely lost. He looked to Benito, but our guide only shrugged. Benito accepted everything. I knew better. This couldn't be justice, not even Big Juju's exaggerated justice. This was monstrous.

Corbett had to be guessing when he suddenly asked, "You opposed thermonuclear power plants?"

The guy stopped dead, staring as if Corbett were a ghost. The dynamo lurched into action and surrounded him with thick blue smoke.

"That's it, isn't it?" Corbett said gently. "You stopped the nuclear generators. I was just a kid during the power blackouts. We had to go to school in the dark because the whole country went on daylight saving time to save power."

"But they weren't safe!" He coughed. "They weren't safe!"

"How did you know that?" Benito asked.

"We had scientists in our organization. They proved it."

We turned away. Now I knew. I could quit looking for justice in Hell. There was only macabre humor. Why should that man be in the inner circles of Hell? At worst he belonged far above, with the bridge-destroyers of the second ledge. Or in Heaven. *He* hadn't created this bleak landscape.

I couldn't stand it. I went back. Benito shrugged and motioned to the others.

Within the cloud of blue smoke his face was slack with exhaustion. "It wasn't just the problem of where to bury the waste products," he told me. "There was radioactive gas going into the air." He spoke as if continuing a conversation. I must have been his only audience in years, or decades.

"You got a rotten deal," I said. "I wish I could do something."

He smiled bravely. "What else is new?" And he started to pedal.

I glared at the nothing sky, hating Big Juju. *Carpentier declares war*. When I looked down, Benito was fumbling through saddlebags attached to the stationary bicycle.

The man cried, "What are you doing?"

Benito took out papers. The man snatched at them, but Benito backed away. He read, "Dear Jon, I could understand your opposition to us last year. There was some doubt about the process, and you expressed fears all of us felt. But now you know better. I have no witnesses, but you told me you understood Dr. Pittman's demonstration. In God's name, Jon, why do you continue? I ask you as your sister, as a fellow scientist, as a human being: why?"

He began pedaling again, ignoring us.

"You knew?" I demanded. He pedaled faster, his head bent. I leaned down and put my face close to his. "You knew?" I screamed.

"Fuck off."

Big Juju wins again. Too much, but appropriate. As we walked away, Jon screamed after us, "I'd have been *nothing* if I gave up the movement! Nothing! Don't you understand? I had to stay as president!"

We plunged on. Once we caught lungfuls of something unidentifiable. We were getting used to that by now. This time we wound up at the bottom of an erosion gully, kicking and twitching, unable to control our muscles.

"N-n-nerve g-g-gas," said Corbett.

We lay there for hours. Days perhaps. Eventually the wind shifted, and our legs could work again. Benito and Corbett scrambled up the side of the gully, then came back for Billy and me. As usual we were the last to heal. Big Juju's biological engineers hadn't done as good a job on us. We scrambled to the top.

Beyond the gully we saw trees.

That was all we could see through the sniffles and the tears and the dark, smoky air: a sharply bordered forest, some distance away.

We began to run. Trees. Real living things! or close to it; nothing was really alive in this terrible place. But trees! We ran, wearing fierce grins, noses lifted as if the air were already sweet . . .

Closer, they were not so inviting. Gnarled trunks, black leaves . . . Not Mother Nature herself could have called them pretty. Clumsy birds flapped above them. The forest ended abruptly at a border of flat ground. No, not ground. I stopped at the edge, confused.

The others ran heedlessly out onto the flat black borderland.

It was a road. Blacktop, and a white double line down the center. I called, "Hey, wait a . . ."

Things roared past and drowned my voice. Too fast to tell what they were, but I knew the sound: the whip of air, followed by a shriek of brakes. I screamed, "Run!"

Corbett was already running for his life. Benito and Billy stared at me; then Benito just took my word for it and ran toward me. Billy looked where I was looking . . . and for him it was already too late.

They looked like black Corvettes, 1970's models, but they were lower-slung and more rakish-looking. They'd stopped and turned and were coming back, accelerating hugely, leaving opaque black clouds of smoke. Billy made up his mind to run; he turned, and they were on him. Billy flew high, hit hard, and rolled like a beanbag: no bones.

I started swearing. The cars roared away . . . two
of them did. The third turned hard, right off the road.
It rolled over once and landed upright and came for
us, bouncing and rattling, but accelerating. Its headlights came on blindingly.

I stopped swearing and looked for cover.

"What are they?" Benito screamed.

"Cars. No drivers," Corbett told him. "I saw. Empty
race cars. They must guard the forest."

I looked for cover: something to hide behind, or
even a jumble of broken rock too rough for a car.
Nothing. The black demon bore down on us.

"There!" I pointed, and ran. It was an oil slick,
depth unknown, and it would bloody well have to do.

I ran straight into the pool. My foot landed on something that jerked away and sent me sprawling. When
I pulled my face out of the oil another black, dripping
face looked back at me. "Sorry," I said.

"That's okay. We all got our own problems here,"
said the stranger, and he sank beneath the oil.

Benito was waist deep and wading deeper. Corbett
hesitated at the edge, looked disgusted, looked behind
him . . . squealed and dived sideways. I ducked under.
The glare of headlights was branded on my closed eyes.

A wave of oil splashed over me. I lifted my head,
and there it was: a rakish black sports car, hubcap-
deep in the oil pool. Its motor was a demon-snarl; its
wheels spun frantically. It found some traction from
somewhere: it edged backward, found more traction
and surged out of the pool just as Corbett went over
the door in a flying dive.

The horn screamed in rage. The car backed, then
turned in a tight circle. I think it was trying to roll
over. It never made it. The motor died, the killer car
rolled to a gentle stop.

Corbett stood up in the driver's seat, grinning all over his face. The keys dangled from his hand.

Benito and I waded out, streaming oil.

Corbett had the hood of the murder car up and was inspecting the motor. "I used to race a little," he said. "I can probably drive this. What do you say, shall we cross the desert in comfort?"

"You look it over," I told him. Benito and I went to see about Billy.

He lay twisted as no living man could be. We straightened him out. His body was mushy and limp. So was one side of his head. The good eye opened and looked at us.

Benito bent over Billy and took one of his hands between his own. "I don't know if you can hear me," he said. "I want you to know that you will heal. It will hurt, but you will heal."

I beckoned Benito out of Billy's hearing. I asked, "Should we take him with us?"

"I think so. He will be of no help until he heals, but what of that? He should be safe enough in an automobile. He can ride in the passenger seat."

We rejoined Corbett at the car.

"I don't know the make," he told us. "It's got a big mill, but the tuning is lousy. You saw how much smoke it was pouring out. I've been checking the brakes, and they look good—"

"The question," said Benito, "is whether it will obey the steering wheel and other controls. We saw it driving itself."

"Yeah." Corbett frowned, studying the car as one would search the face of a prisoner of war. Would he give information? Would it be the truth? "The top's down. We can always jump clear," he said. "No point

in taking chances, though. Why don't you two get
under cover, and I'll take her for a spin."

There wasn't any cover. We stood at the far edge
of the oil pool, ready to jump, as Corbett turned the
ignition key. He drove the car around for a while, trying it on rough and smooth terrain. He brought it back
and prudently took the key before he got out.

"Seems okay. I'll stay in low gear the whole trip.
That way nothing can happen fast. If the gearshift
starts moving by itself I'll give a yell."

"There's one more problem," I said. "Four of us.
Two seats. Benito, shall we ride on the fenders?"

"I have no better suggestion."

The change was gradual. The air got hotter. Then
there were no more oil pools. The dead ground gave
way to hot dead sand, and Corbett worried aloud about
the tires. A minute later he'd forgotten the tires; he
was too busy slapping away fat flakes of burning matter.

18

IT SNOWED FIRE. GREAT BURNING FLAKES FELL slowly from the dead gray sky and settled on us. We slapped frantically. Billy was slumped like a corpse while fireflakes dropped to his skin and clung. I could reach his head by stretching backward along the fender, and I pulled a saucer-sized chunk from his face. His one good eye thanked me.

We rolled across a burning sandy waste. The fireflakes vanished when they touched ground, but not when they touched flesh. Another evil miracle. The car weaved drunkenly, then shifted into second and picked up speed.

I called back to Corbett. "Did you do that?"

"Yeah! You want to be out here forever?"

"Not really." The sand was flat enough for higher speed—provided we could control the car.

Billy grunted in soft protest. I could imagine his fear. He'd never seen a car before or gone faster than a horse could run.

Fire bored into my back where I'd exposed it

stretching to help Billy again. I slapped it off and wished for a Cadillac.

Cadillacs *belong* in Hell. There's something about the car that rots the driver's brain. Every time some damn fool has almost gotten me wrecked by running a red light or jumping lanes or parking where no car ought to be, said idiot has been driving a Cadillac. There *had* to be Cadillacs in Hell—and if we'd captured one of those, we'd be riding in air-conditioned comfort! Instead of riding a fender and slapping fireflakes!

Clusters of souls danced frenetically on the blazing sand. Some stopped, amazed, to watch us pass. A couple of times Corbett tooted the horn at them. He was cursed for his trouble, but he wasn't mocking them. There was nothing he could do.

I called across the low hood to Benito. "Who are they?"

Benito was busy tearing burning gunk out of his hair. "They sinned against Nature," he yelled back.

"What does that mean?"

"Unnatural love. Man for man, woman for woman—"

Man for sheep, woman for vibrator . . . poor bastards. I wondered about the gay couple who'd owned the house next door to mine. Quiet neighbors, friendly middle-aged people like any married couple without children. Were they here?

I turned my head and hunched up so that the fireflakes hit the side of my face instead of the front. I couldn't slap fast enough. The windshield gave Billy some protection now that we were moving.

The fire burned holes in my skin. *You'll heal, Carpentier. You'll heal, if we ever get out of here.*

But what about them? They danced, they slapped at themselves; they ran in circles; they screamed at us to stop and cursed us when we didn't, with an insane jealousy that I understood perfectly. They'd be here forever.

This, just for being queer? But it was no surprise to me that God's justice and mine didn't agree. I thought about my neighbors and shuddered. *Credo in un Dio crudel . . .*

The industrial section of Hell was only a yellow tinge to the sky behind us. Ahead was nothing but more desert. We must be about halfway across, I thought.

Suddenly the car surged forward with the bit in its teeth.

Corbett froze in panic. The motor screamed in inhuman fury as the car accelerated. In a second we'd be moving too fast to stop. I tucked my head in my arms and rolled off the fender.

Look, I wasn't running out on my buddies. The car was going to crash, and they'd have a better chance if one of us could move, right? It was what I was thinking, anyway.

The motor choked off while I was still in the air.

I hit rolling. I came up screaming and dancing. The other souls hadn't been dancing for joy either. The pain was as bad as the boiling blood.

The car rolled to a stop, and I ran for it, yelling and swearing at the fireflakes.

Suddenly a girl was running alongside me. She'd have been pretty once. Now her hair was raggedly scorched, and her body was covered with burns. "Can you take me out of here?" She screamed.

"We'll be lucky to get out ourselves. There's no room!" I kept running until I reached the car.

The girl stayed right with me. "Please, I'll do anything if you'll take me out of here. *Anything.*"

"That's nice," Corbett told her. To me he said,

"We're in big trouble. The gas pedal just damned well floored itself. I had to turn off the ignition."

"Couldn't you—"

"Couldn't I what? Pull the pedal up with my toes? Allen, this car is haunted. It hates us."

"What's wrong?" the girl asked. She got no answer.

It was hard to think with the fire settling on me. I danced around the car, shouting, "We'd better think of something. In a minute or two we'll be under a pyramid of people." The damned were running toward us from all directions.

"Raise the bonnet," Benito commanded. "Corbett, see to Billy."

I got the hood up. We looked inside, and Benito said, "Now, Corbett, move the accelerator."

Something wiggled behind the engine.

"Allen, you saw? That moves the petrol feed. You must control it with your fingers."

It was a hell of an awkward position, sprawled across the fender with my head and hands under the hood. The motor was as hot as the sand. I couldn't avoid touching it. But I pulled at the widget and cried, "Okay! I got it! Corbett, go! Go like a bat!" The crowd was very near, and they couldn't *all* hang on. Benito motioned to the girl, and she took the fender in front of me.

The car roared and surged into a converging circle. Most of them dodged for their lives. One went under the wheels. Another, a big athletic type with long black hair halfway down his back and a scraggly beard, got the edge of the right door and swung up on the trunk lid. A small-boned blond man had come with him. "Frank!" the companion called. "Frank! Don't leave me!"

"Sorry, Gene. Nothing I can do. No room for both of us."

"Frank!" The car gunned ahead as Corbett got it under control again. A thin voice followed us. "Frank! I went to Hell for you . . ."

Frank had managed to crawl up to get an arm around Corbett's neck. He squeezed. "All right, buddy, turn this thing around! We're going to Havana!"

"Fine. Whatever you say," said Corbett. Frank grinned and slacked off his grip on Corbett, but he didn't let go.

Now we had Frank on the trunk; Billy in the passenger seat, groaning a little, still unable to move; Benito on the left front fender; me in the motor compartment trying to stay clear of the hot engine, my legs dangling out to the right; and the girl forward on the right front fender, her feet on the bumper. Corbett had his problems driving. He had to lean way out to the left to see around the open hood.

Billy was able to scream now.

"For God's sake, brush the fire off him, Frank!" Corbett yelled.

"Screw that. Screw God too. Get moving."

We moved. Corbett yelled, and I slacked off on the gas to let him shift to second. That was fast enough. The car fought, the hot metal tugged against my fingers like something alive, but I could control the speed. At least we weren't hitting any bumps.

"Heeehaaah!" Frank screamed in joy. "Better'n the last chicken run! I'll make you guys honorary Hell's Angels! We're tough, you know? Toughest bunch in the world, you know? Hick sheriff was so scared of us he called the state fuzz. We run for it. I had the lead. Come around a curve and the whole road was full of fuzzmobiles. I got two fuzz smearing myself."

"Your friend back there—" I shouted.

"Gene? We did some swinging times, man. Had a whole stable of 'em. Boys, girls, but the only one

they let me keep here was Gene. Maybe I'll miss him."
He didn't look back.

"Could you get that fire off my leg?" I asked the
girl.

"Naw! Enough trouble holding on here."

"You said you'd do anything!" I clenched my teeth
in agony. There was fire on both legs now, and I
couldn't slap. I couldn't let go of the spring, and I had
to hold on with the other hand. The car was still fighting me. "Get that fire off or we'll throw you off!"

"Awright, awright, you don't have to get nasty."
She slapped a couple of times and got the worst away.

"Who are you?" Benito asked.

"Doreen Lancer," she yelled above the roaring
motor. "Go-go dancer. One night some bastard raped
me and strangled me. At least, he tried to rape me!"
She laughed bitterly. "He didn't seem to know how to
go about it!"

"So what the hell are you doing here?" Frank demanded.

"Don't know! I liked it every which way. Most of
the types I meet here are fags—"

"I'm no goddamn fag!" Frank yelled.

"Do not blaspheme," Benito told him, predictably,
I guess.

"Fuck off! Talk to me that way and I'll twist this
bastard's neck off!" The car lurched as he choked Corbett.

"No!" Doreen screamed. "We'll crash! This is our
only way out! Leave him alone—Look, don't hurt him,
and when we get out we can really swing, right?"

I laughed. I couldn't help it.

"What's so funny?" she demanded.

"It's not a romantic situation!" I bellowed. I wasn't
even sure there could be sex in Hell, and I hadn't
found any opportunity to try. Or inclination, either.

I bellowed again when she slapped my testicles. It hurt as much as it had when I was alive. I pulled the accelerator widget out, tugging with all my strength, letting the car slow.

"I'm sorry!" she yelled. "I was getting the fire off, I swear, that's all I was doing! I'm sorry . . . hey, you wanna be a threesome with Frank and me?"

I let the car speed up again. We had to get out of here. But I'd never had an offer I liked less.

"I can see something ahead!" Corbett shouted. "We're getting to the edge!"

"About time," Frank said. We rolled on. "Just remember, pretty boy, I'm in charge here," he added, and Corbett grunted in pain. Frank must have emphasized his words.

The horizon was sharp ahead. I could barely see over the motor. Corbett saw it too. "Kill the power!" he yelled. Brakes screeched, and he twisted the wheel hard.

I climbed out of the motor. The fireflakes were thicker here than in the middle of the desert. We ran, hopping—

Frank still had Corbett by the neck. "This the way out of here? What are you trying to pull?"

There was a sheer drop ahead of us. It was gloomy down there. I couldn't see the bottom. Several hundred feet, anyway. "Now what?" I asked Benito.

"The quick way would be to jump." He was dead serious. "Jump and wait to heal, then go on."

The girl backed away, staring at him. "You're crazy! Crazy! I should have known better than to trust guys like you! All the promises you make—" She didn't finish, but ran back into the desert, crying.

"That's done it!" Frank yelled. "You're sure as Hell going over that cliff, all right, because I'm going to throw you!" He had Corbett by the neck, and he dragged him toward the cliff edge. "First you, then your loudmouth friend, then the fat one, and then—"

He'd forgotten Billy. We all had. It was a mistake for Frank. Billy launched himself from the car without warning. He landed on Frank's back and seized the long hair with one hand, pulled the head back, and wrapped his arm around Frank's neck. His knee gouged into the Hell's Angel's back, bowing him into an arc. "Friend, I don't think I like you."

I yelled, "Billy! Are you all right?"

"Yeah."

"You weren't moving—"

"Been able to move awhile now. Didn't seem like a good idea to let this creep know it. Jerry coulda crashed this thing if we were fightin' while it was movin'."

I thought about the self-control it would take to sit still under a rain of sticky fire.

"What'll I do with the Gila monster, Benito?"

"Leggo! I was only kidding!" Frank yelled. "You guys got no business giving me false hopes! It was all your fault—" He stopped talking because Billy's arm had closed his throat.

"Do not harm him," Benito said quietly.

"Yeah?" Billy let him go. "Friend, you're not tough. You don't know what tough is. Now get away from us." The pale-blue eyes seemed infinitely deep, and cold even in this place of fire.

"You may come with us if you like," Benito told Frank, "although I do not think you are ready. With your attitude you might well find a worse place than you have now. Still, you are welcome to join us."

"Go to Hell!" Frank screamed. He thought that was funny. "Go to Hell! Go to Hell!" He ran away into the desert, laughing, screaming, trying to keep both feet off the hot sand at once.

Benito looked at us, waiting.

"I'll jump if you say so," Billy said. "Looks bad, though. I can tell you, being crushed flat ain't no fun."

I gulped. "I will too." I wondered if I meant it.

"There may be a better way," Benito said. "We must find the stream. Corbett, can you drive?"

"Sure."

We turned left. I had the whole fender to sprawl on now. The car seemed more docile, too, but I wasn't going to trust it. I didn't really have to—I was getting good at manipulating the gas widget.

We came to a horde of people dressed in the finery of all ages: velvet robes, flare pants, alligator shoes. Corbett shouted at me. "Stopping!" He turned off the key before I could do anything, and the car rolled to a halt.

Fireflakes fell on us. "Now what?"

Corbett was out of the car and looking at a beefy man in gaudy tunic, crimson sash, and black glove-leather boots. There was a big leather wallet hung on a golden chain around his neck, and he stared into it, not looking up. The fireflakes had burned holes in his tunic and scorched his hair.

Corbett stood in front of him. When the burly man didn't look up, Corbett stooped over so that his face was in line with the wallet. "Give me my money!" Corbett shouted.

"You son of a bitch, you owe *me!*"

"But I've had this problem, see, my girl is . . ." Corbett began.

"I don't want to hear any stories, I just want my money! Arrgh!" A big fireflake settled on the crown of his head. He tried to brush it off.

"Hang tough," Corbett said. He came back to the car chuckling. "Long Harry there loaned me some cash, once. Six for five—every week."

I nodded. There were lots of others there, crying into their purses. The rain of fire seemed heavier here. "Let's get going." I didn't like Corbett gloating over them—but if anybody deserved to be here, it was them. Loan shark is as low a form of life as there is.

We didn't drive so fast that we couldn't talk. "Funny thing about Harry," Corbett said. "He had to give up the loan shark business. Had a customer with a hit man for a friend. Took his buddy Lem to see Harry, but Harry wouldn't listen. Just kept saying 'Give me my money.' So Lem had a talk with Harry."

"Lem?" Billy asked. He sounded puzzled.

"Yeah. I don't know what he told Harry, but just after that all of Harry's customers were off the hook. Just had to pay what they'd got in the first place."

"Lem," Billy said. "Little guy? About my size? Big scar over his left eye?"

"Yeah," Corbett said. "You know him?"

"Kind of. They used to let him onto the island for a day. One day a year. The rest of the time he was out in the blood. I always did wonder why."

"We are coming to the stream," Benito said. "The fire does not fall there."

19

THE RIVER WAS NARROW BUT FAST. ITS ROAR WAS different somehow from that of water, and it was still bright scarlet. The air was thick with the smell of blood.

Nonetheless we walked down and bathed our half-broiled feet in it. Afterward we walked the cool mud of the bank with our sandals off until we reached the waterfall. There we watched endless tons of blood falling into the darkness.

I said, "Now what?"

Benito scowled in indecision. "It is a risk. The monster Geryon carried Dante and Vergil into lower Hell. But they were on a holy errand. We are not. I have known Geryon. He is not worthy of trust."

"The password," I remembered.

" 'This has been willed where what is willed must be.' Yes. Shall we try it?"

"Better'n jumping." Billy looked at Benito. "It is, ain't it? What can he do to us? Eat us?"

"Summon Minos."

"Let's try it," said Corbett. "We've gotten this far without anyone doing that."

"Are we agreed, then? Good. Now we must summon Geryon. We need a signal, something to get his attention. Dante flung a rope into the abyss."

"A signal," said Corbett. "Does it have to be subtle?"

"I should not think that subtlety would be necessary."

"We wouldn't want Geryon to think we're crude, would we? Some delicate change in the environment, just noticeable enough to attract his attention. Let me see." Corbett walked back to the car and switched on the ignition. He went around to the back and unscrewed the gas cap.

A fireflake fell past his nose. He blew on it, guiding it into the gas tank. The tank lit with a *whoosh*. Hurriedly Corbett reached into the car and shifted it into first gear. We stood well back and watched it roll over the edge.

"Subtlety is all," said Corbett.

The car fell like a battlefield flare. It passed and illuminated a compact body already rising through the murk.

"He knew we were here." Corbett was flat on his belly with his face over the cliff's edge. "We didn't need a signal."

"He will not come without a signal," said Benito.

The car was a towering flame at the base of the cliff. Lighted from below, Geryon was a compact shadow with a slender, twisting tail. He floated up to us, his features growing clear. He hovered at our height, smiled reassuringly at us with a startlingly human face, then slid forward onto the rock ledge, leaving his tail hanging free in space.

Geryon was as big as a rowboat, and wingless. His

hind feet were webbed, built for swimming. His almost human head was hairless, the mouth wide, the chin broad and strong, the nose very wide and flat, with large nostrils. The head sloped back to round shoulders, without benefit of neck.

His arms were human enough, the size of my own. On Geryon they were disproportionately small. Something was funny about the hand: the fingers were short and thick, designed for ripping.

I could see him as an air-breathing aquatic beast that had developed human intelligence. I wondered about his nose. It was big enough to feed him air fast, hooded to keep water out. Reasonable, but different from the cetacean design.

His pelt had the look of medieval tapestry: golden knots and figures on a blue-gray background. Lovely; a trifle flashy. And adequate camouflage if he was used to hovering just beneath sunlit water.

Altogether he was a believable alien, excluding his ability to fly. I didn't like that. Bad enough if Infernoland had been built by humans. What if it had been built by interstellar conquerors for their own amusement?

Geryon's voice was deep, with a queer buzzing quality. "Hello, Benito. Three of them? Isn't that a bit much?"

Benito was brusque. He didn't like Geryon. "This has been willed where what is willed must be. In any case, you must have noticed how the damned flow in like a river in flood—"

"Haven't I just. Swamping you, are they? I think the end of the world must be near. Hell is getting full," said the alien. "Well, we who serve God's will in Hell have precious little of free will, eh, Benito? Climb aboard, you. I hope you all can hang on."

He had spoken jovially, with no bitterness and only the merest trace of mockery.

My foot kicked something rigid as I tried to board Geryon's reasonably flat back. I looked down. It wasn't easy to see, but there was metal belted about Geryon's belly, machinery covered with material the same color as his gaudy pelt.

Antigravity?

I settled behind the monster's head. Billy's arms closed about my waist. Corbett was behind him, and Benito last, braving the twin stings in the forked tail. Geryon grinned at me over his shoulder and pushed back from the edge.

Billy's arms tightened convulsively. I saw that his eyes were closed tight, his teeth clenched.

My view of Hell was darkness and firelit smokes, the fires tracing concentric arcs. Geryon tilted to one side and dropped in a slow spiral. The scarlet waterfall dashed itself to foam and spray on the rocks. Billy was squeezing the breath from me, but I didn't complain. I heard whimpering noises being squeezed from him.

We touched down.

I said, "Your first flight, Billy?"

"Yeah."

"We're down. You can let go."

"Yeah." He unlocked his arms in stages and climbed down on shaky legs. I followed.

Geryon floated up a few feet and hovered. "Hey, Benito," he called. His voice was full of artificial camaraderie, more menacing than threats. "Why is it, Benito, that the people you travel with don't ever come back?" The monster lifted toward the sky, chortling.

Carefully casual, Corbett asked Benito, "You've been here before?"

"I have rescued others," Benito answered.

"How many?"

"Six. One at a time. No matter how many come with me at first, no more than one at a time ever seems to reach the exit point. Perhaps this time we will be more fortunate."

"What happens to the others?" I asked.

"Why did you come back?" Corbett demanded.

We'd both spoken at once, and Benito chose to answer neither of us.

"Have you seen the exit?" Corbett asked.

Benito's voice was colorlessly grim. "Yes."

"And gone beyond it?"

"No. But it follows Dante's route, which leads to Purgatory. I came back to find others in need of guidance. Do *you* object, Allen Carpentier? Should I have left you in the bottle?"

"Hey, hey, hey!" Billy was dancing with impatience. "If we're going, let's *go!* What's all the jawing about?"

Benito nodded and led us off downslope. We felt exposed on level ground, and Geryon couldn't be the only flying thing. He hadn't reported us (had he?), but that was no guarantee that something else wouldn't. We moved swiftly across what seemed to be solid rock, always downhill, further into murk and gloom, until we came to a cliff edge.

There was a ditch in front of us, seventy or eighty feet deep and perhaps twice that wide. It was divided in the middle by a low wall of rock. Just off to our left was a passageway in the dividing rock wall. The divider was low enough that we could see over it, lower than the height of a normal man—

—and the ditch was full. Masses of humanity moved in a standard traffic pattern, all hurrying along, not quite running, leftbound on the far side, rightward on the near side. They moved *fast*.

They moved fast because there were beings with

whips urging them along. It took a moment for that to register.

Okay, Carpentier, you're in Hell and there are demons in Hell. There were things on the red-hot wall that might have been demons if you could have seen them clearly through the fog. There's Geryon, certainly a monster. *Of course* Big Juju can make demons.

But I hadn't wanted to believe it.

Now I was looking at them. They were blackskinned rather than the red I'd expected, and they were at least ten feet tall. They had horns and tails and were uglier than I could have imagined. They used whips twice as long as themselves. They screamed at the laggards:

"Along with you, Big Morris, there's no ass to sell here!"

"Git along, little dogie, git along, git along . . ."

Wails and groans rose from the pit, and screams of pain and rage. Snap! Crack! Chunks of flesh flew from the backs of those who slowed down.

"Who . . ." whispered Corbett. He ran out of voice and had to try again. "Who are they?" He was frightened, and why not? I was scared out of my mind. The demons were looking up at us—

—but they went back to their tasks, gleefully lashing the crowd. I recognized one of the runners. He was a famous movie director-producer, idolized by millions when I was younger. He was on the near side, but as he reached the passageway in the dividing wall the demon stationed there lashed him until he went through and joined those scurrying in the other direction.

I'd never met him, but I knew who he was. And I knew who these people must be.

Benito confirmed my suspicions. "Panderers on this side, seducers on the other. Come, we must find a bridge." He turned left, and we followed uncertainly.

"I . . . was a seducer," Corbett said uncertainly.

I remembered the convention atmosphere and what happened the night before I died. "Me too."

Benito snorted. "Did you ever have a woman against her will?"

"No—"

"Or make her drunk, or drug her?"

"Well—" Did pot count? "Nobody who didn't know what to expect."

"Never had to," Corbett said matter-of-factly.

"Or use threats of force?"

"Don't be silly." Corbett resented the implication. "I told you, it wasn't necessary."

"The Italian does not properly translate as your English seducer, which is hardly more than casual fornication," Benito said seriously. "I think perhaps the better word is 'rape.' "

Now we could see the bridge ahead of us: a stone arch. It looked very old.

"Jerry!" A voice called from the pit. "Jerry! Come on down, Jerry. You *belong* here!"

It stopped Corbett cold. He looked down into the pit. "Julia?"

"Come on down, Jerry. Share *everything* with me. You taught me how, Jerry—"

"How can a girl be a rapist?" I demanded. She was, or had been, quite pretty, but now her face was distorted by pain and exhaustion. The demons were watching her stand there as she panted and shouted up to Corbett, and they didn't interfere.

"Deceit. Fraud," said Benito. "Those who induce others to what they know is wrong, as well as those who force their will on others."

I turned to Corbett and *Shut up, Carpentier! None of your business* closed my mouth.

"You taught me everything, Jerry," she was calling.

"I could still love you. Come down with me. Where else can you go now?"

"Out! Down to the center and out!" Corbett screamed to her.

The demons howled maniac laughter. The girl laughed with them. "Oh, Jerry, do you *believe* that? Don't you know that the deeper you go, the worse it is, and you can't *ever* go back, and you can't get out? It's worse down there, Jerry. Wait till you see who's below us! Here you have *me*, Jerry. Stay where you belong. There's no escape down there. Don't you know what's carved on the gates of Hell, Jerry? All hope abandon!"

"I'm not afraid of what's below!" Corbett was getting hysterical. "I never did any of the things they punish you down there for—"

She laughed again. "The only perfect man who ever lived! Are you *sure*, Jerry? Then why do they let you *go* there? And what makes you think you'll get justice anyway? Come down with me before its too late to—HYEEEE!"

The demons had called time on her. Crack! Snap! The whips sounded like popcorn popping. Julia sprinted, screaming with the rest. The flesh of my back rippled. I wanted to shut my ears.

"Come." Benito took Corbett's arm. "Come. Do not let her seduce you again."

"Uh?" Corbett looked at Benito as if he'd only just met him. "It did happen that way, now you mention it. Or did it? Maybe I do belong in that pit."

"If you do, you will be there. For the moment you are not. Ergo—come along."

We walked in silence, each wrapped in its own thoughts. What if the girl was right? Were we plunging deeper and deeper, never to return? What was below us? Had I committed any of the appropriate crimes? "Benito, what's ahead?"

His dry lecture voice couldn't mask the screaming as we walked the rim. "No more!" "Not again!" "Wait, I'm in the wrong place!" "It was just *one* book, just one. *I needed the money!*" "You big ugly sonofabitch, you—" *Crack!*

"Of the ten *bolgias*—canyons—of this circle of Hell, this is the only divided one. Each canyon is crossed by a bridge, except that all the bridges are down across the sixth canyon. We must descend into it. It will be no problem."

"Benito, how in God's name can you ignore those screams?" Corbett demanded.

"They have no more than they deserve," Benito said simply. Either he hadn't the empathy of a turtle, or . . . or what? "Now, we will have trouble at the fifth *bolgia*. It is the pit of grafters, and the demons are on the rim, not down in the canyon."

"Ugh." I'd forgotten most of the Inferno, but I could never have forgotten that image: a troop, an army of devils, ill-mannered and sadistic, a military organization of ugly hate. They'd almost got Dante despite his safe-conduct. "What's after this circle?"

We had reached an arching bridge of rough stone. It had no handrails and was about ten feet wide, a slender arch above that pit of screaming runners. It sloped up so steeply that I dropped to all fours to climb.

"Jerry! Come down, Jerry!" It was the girl again. Corbett stiffened.

"What's next?" I prompted Benito. "After the ten canyons what will we find?"

"Very little," Benito answered. "The great ice plain, where traitors are punished. Those who betrayed their blood kin or their benefactors."

"Not me," Corbett said. He seemed to feel better. "And then?"

"We cross to the very center. There is a hole. We crawl through it, past the center of the world, and find ourselves climbing up again."

"And I can believe as much of that as I like?"

"Certainly. Why should you not believe it?" Benito was genuinely puzzled.

"It's nonsense," said Corbett. "We'd be in free-fall by the time we got there."

"Jerry!"

Corbett shuddered. The voice floated upward again. "Don't be a fool, Jerry. It's bad down there at the center. And they *never* let you out."

"Did I really put her there?" Corbett wondered. "Maybe I have betrayed a benefactor. She was kind to me and—"

"Come on, no woman's worth what they're gettin'," Billy said. "We stick together. I never let a buddy down in my life, and I'm goin' down to the center. Now come on."

Corbett lost some of his tension. "If you're really Billy the Kid, that's right. At least, that's what the movies showed." He began moving again, over the arch of the bridge and downward. "Benito, your description is still nonsense. Not only would there be free-fall at the center of the Earth, but this isn't Earth to begin with. A cavity this size, under the Earth? Can you imagine the *pressures?* And we'd get seismograph readings on it with every earthquake. No, we have to be somewhere else."

"Sure," I said. "Infernoland. Somebody built it, following Dante. But the geography's been the same as the Inferno all the way so far, so what do we care if it's an artifact?"

"It is an artifact," Benito said, "in the sense that God designed and built it."

"Okay," said Corbett. "I was never a good atheist. Not a churchman either. Still, Benito, I've seen designs for bigger structures than this. Bigger than Earth, for that matter. Our real problem is, did Dante really see this place himself? And can we trust his reports?"

That was a good question, but I had a better one. How far could we trust Benito? He had never mentioned earlier trips.

Just how did Benito get back uphill after those trips? How did he earn this privilege of running free through Hell? Geryon had said "we" when speaking of both himself and Benito. "We who serve God's will in Hell."

Benito was an unlikely angel . . . and Geryon an untrustworthy witness, I reminded myself. But this was the Devil's realm, and Benito wandered at whim.

All right, Carpentier: just what *is* the punishment for a soul who defies God's final command? God or Big Juju, I had plenty of evidence that He was vindictive. He put me in the Vestibule, and I violated my sentence. Minos warned me. Is this the final retribution against Carpentier? To go even deeper into Hell, with no way back, to find my own level and have it worse than He condemned me to?

Or. Suppose this really is Infernoland, a bigger and more powerful Builder's playground. Why would the Geryon-type engineers have built anything *but* the Inferno? They clearly enjoyed seeing humans suffer. Would they get a similar kick from human pleasure? All the professors told me the *Inferno* was by far the most interesting of the three books of *The Divine Comedy*.

Benito was talking again. "I have always assumed that Dante made his trek in a vision. When he woke he had forgotten many of the details. He filled them in with research in theology and dogma and philosophy and natural history and with his own whims and prejudices and special hatreds. But the basic vision was sound and true. Be careful here."

The bridge dropped steeply at the end. The inner rim of the trench was twenty feet lower than the outer. We went down backward. The lip of another pit was a hundred yards away. A cacophony of sound rose from it. We stopped for a moment.

"For instance," Benito said, "Dante's work gives the impression that he met large numbers of Italians—"

"Sounds perfectly reasonable to me," said Corbett. We tried to laugh, but this wasn't a place for laughing.

Benito merely continued as if he hadn't heard. "Improbable numbers of Italians. Large numbers of famous ancients. He met writers, poets, politicians, but no Hottentots, Eskimos, Askaris, or American Indians. This seems unlikely."

"Then you don't trust Dante after all?"

"Jerry, that was not my point."

I said, "Benito, we've met an embarrassing sufficiency of Americans."

Billy laughed. "Plenty on the island, too."

Benito was startled. "It's true. And Hilda Kroft and I met Germans. And—"

"Man tends to notice his own folks," said Billy. "Let's get moving."

We angled toward a bridge spanning the next ditch. Benito still looked disturbed. Why? *That* disturbed *me.*

The smell stopped us joltingly at the second pit. It was like being dropped into a sewer. We didn't even try to look over the edge.

"Who's down there?" Billy asked.

"Flatterers," Benito said shortly, and turned toward the bridge.

We followed. "I don't get it," Corbett said.

"In every place of power, throughout all time, the rulers have been surrounded by flatterers. In many places flattery has been the path to power and wealth. In others it is only a good living. Yet everywhere the flatterers tend to push aside the men of real wisdom. Flattery is so much safer than telling unpleasant truths."

"Not in America," said Corbett.

"This I doubt," said Benito. "But you should know best."

"Never buttered up the boss? I sure have," said Billy.

I felt uncomfortable. What was I doing at the moment I died but flattering the fans? I glanced over at Corbett, and he looked no better. Flattery? We'd all tried it. What did they do to flatterers?

We clustered at the bridge approach and stood looking at it. The smell was thick as putty. I could feel it clinging to me, and I squirmed. Corbett said, "How are we going to cross that?"

"Fast," I said. "Don't breathe." I didn't move. I hadn't worked up the nerve.

"Come on, pals!" Billy hit the bridge at a dead run. As he went over the arch and disappeared from view, we heard him yell. The other side of the bridge would be steep. I hoped he'd rolled to the end and not over the edge. I wasn't ready to dive in after him, and I didn't hear anyone else volunteer.

"Billy?" I shouted. There was no answer.

"He's all right," Corbett said. His voice was hollowly reassuring. "Sure he is."

We looked at each other. We took deep breaths.

We scrambled up the arch, and when we could stand, we ran.

Was Billy down there? I made the mistake of looking from the top of the arch.

Down into a river of shit, chest-deep. A respectable crowd waded through it.

Disgust can freeze you as solid as fear. At my side, Corbett stopped to look where I was looking. He made a retching sound, took my arm and tried to pull me on. I couldn't move. I'd recognized someone I knew.

I called down. "George!"

Heads turned up. They were disguised by what was smeared across their faces, but that was George, all right. I tried to remember his last name and couldn't.

But he knew me. He shrank away with his sticky arms hiding his sticky head.

Benito had come back up the bridge. "Billy is safe." He spoke with the pinched voice of a man holding his breath. "Who was that?"

"An old friend. An advertising man, wrote fiction in his spare time. Not very good stories, but he wasn't a bad guy. How did he get here?"

"Immoderate flattery. There is no other way to reach this pit. Allen, Jerome, there is no profit in standing here. You cannot enjoy the view."

Immoderate flattery? It fit, in a way. Big Juju's way. Most advertising is immoderate praise of a product or its users. But like every other torture I'd seen in Hell, it was just too damned much! I wanted to tell George . . . what? That he'd been wronged? That I'd get justice for him no matter what it took? That I couldn't save him and I couldn't save myself and everything was useless because we were in the hands either of a cruel God or heartless aliens? I don't know. But I'd remembered one of his own ads, and I shouted it down to him. It was not to mock him! Only to get his attention!

"You *deserve* to belong to the Xanadu Country Club!"

The response was an explosion of voices. Smeared stinking heads rose, mocking voices called. "The wethead is dead!" "Aren't you glad you use Dial? Don't you wish everybody did?" "I'm Glenda! Fly me!" "Hazel, it turned *blue!*" "Always have . . . *always* will!"

And we three who peered into the moat, we saw where the shit came from.

Another macabre joke. Every one of them had been fitted with a second anus. It became apparent only when they tried to speak.

Corbett bent double, heaving, a ghost trying to expel emptiness from the ghost of his belly. I tried to help him, but he backed away fast. He didn't want to be touched. The convulsions went on and on.

I tried to turn away from the edge, but it was too late. George screamed up at me, in agony. "Allen! Why?"

"I'm sorry!" I should have left him alone.

Benito spoke in an actor's voice, calm but carrying. "There is a way out of Hell."

He got insults and laughter, but a few listened.

"You must climb the pit. Cooperate if you must. It will be hard, but you can do it if you try long enough. Then you must move inward. The route to Heaven is at the center of Hell."

Smeared faces turned away. George stayed to answer. His laugh had tears in it. "Me, in Heaven? With shit dribbling down my chin? I'd rather stay here."

Another called. "Listen, when you get there, tell Him. Tell God we will praise Him day and night! I have written a new hymn to His name! Tell Him!"

Benito turned sadly away.

I looked for Corbett—and found him at the outer end of the bridge. He was crying and hiccoughing and trying to run. I shouted, "Corbett! Wrong way!"

He turned. "No chance! I don't belong here! I'm supposed to be in the winds!"

"You'll never get up the cliff."

"I will! Somehow, I will! I belong up there, not down here with—" He flapped his arms helplessly. Corbett had no word for these thoroughly damned souls with whom Corbett would not associate. He went away from us.

Billy was waiting at the inner end of the bridge. He watched us come down, then, "Where's Jerry?"

Benito shook his head. "Pride. He was too proud to stay."

PART III

※-|※-|※-|※-|※-|※-|※-|※-|※

20

THE THIRD GULLY WAS NARROWER AND CLEANER. From the edge it looked empty, so that I wondered if there were a sin nobody would commit, or one nobody thought of. But lights danced dimly down there . . .

From the arch it was clearer. I made out long rows of holes cut into the stone. The holes had raised stone rims. Most of them were occupied, each by a pair of human feet sticking straight up into the air. The feet danced. Flames burned on their soles.

"Another obsolete sin," said Benito. "Selling holy offices. Simony."

Billy said, "Huh?"

I translated for him. "Those guys would take money to make you a priest."

There were signs by some of the holes. "Wharton School of Theology. Earn your Th.D. in just ten weeks! Write Registrar for application."

And another: "Meditation. The new way to inner peace and serenity. Meet the greatest guru of all time. Registration fee, $350."

Billy was aghast. "God does *that* to them? Just for *that?*"

"They stole what belongs to God," Benito said. "There are popes in those baptismal fonts. And many others. The denomination does not seem important. What matters is the sale of the gifts of God."

Why would aliens care about that? Well, Carpentier?

"Benito, I don't like it here," Billy said.

I patted his shoulder. "Me neither. Let's get out." I felt the urge to run. At least I was safe from this pit. We all were. We'd never had heavenly gifts to sell.

The bridge over the fourth gully was just ahead, and I glanced into it from the top, intending to run on past. The strange sight held me. The damned flowed beneath us, and their heads had been turned back to front. Most of them were women.

"Fortune tellers," Benito said before I could ask. "They tried to see the future by magic."

And now they were not even allowed to watch where they were going. I shivered, thinking that a science-fiction writer might well end up here. But no, I'd never used magic. Only logic, and it hadn't kept me out of Hell. "Why aren't all the scientists and economic prognosticators here?" I asked. *"They* try to foresee the future."

"Most of these appealed to Satan for aid. He gave it to them . . . or not. It is the appeal that weighs against them." He turned to move on.

Then I recognized one of the damned.

A little elderly lady, very prim and proper. She'd been a teacher in my nephew's school. Now she walked with her head turned backward, and tears ran down her spine and between her buttocks. I screamed. The damned looked up at me.

"Mrs. Herrnstein! Why?" I shouted.

She looked away. Then she stopped and looked up. Face and back turned toward us. She'd always been thin, and I'd never thought of her as particularly feminine. Certainly she wasn't feminine now. "I belong here, Mr. Carpentier," she called. "Please leave. I don't want to be watched."

"You *belong* here?" I could *not* see Mrs. Herrnstein with a crystal ball.

"Yes. Whenever I had a pupil who had difficulty learning to read, I used—I was a bad teacher, Mr. Carpentier."

"You were a *good* teacher! You taught Hal more in a year than he learned in five!"

"I was a good teacher with good pupils. But I could not be bothered with the ones who weren't so bright. If they had trouble learning to read, I said they had dyslexia."

"Are you here because of bad diagnoses?" This was monstrous!

"Dyslexia is not a diagnosis, Mr. Carpentier. It is a prediction. It is a prediction that says that this child can never learn to read. And with that prediction on his record—why, strangely enough, none of them ever do. Unless they happen on a teacher who doesn't believe in educationese witchcraft."

"But—"

"It was witchcraft, Mr. Carpentier. Please go now." She walked on, crying uncontrollably, her face toward us as she walked away. I watched until she was out of sight.

"She does not belong here," I insisted.

"Then perhaps she will not be here long," Benito answered dispassionately. "Yet—you will note that she did not agree with your judgment."

"Then she's wrong too!"

"Why do you feel so competent to judge every-one, Allen?"

"Get it through your thick head that it's *Big Juju* I'm judging—"

"It is God you are judging," he thundered.

"All *right*, it's God I'm judging. If He can judge me, I claim the right to judge Him!"

Billy seemed horrified by what I was saying. I was sorry for that. But Benito laughed and said, "How will you implement your judgment against God Himself?"

The only possible answer to that was a feeble one, maybe, but I used it. "By withholding my worship. Benito, do you realize that the God you worship keeps a private torture chamber?"

"Hardly private."

"Private or public, the God Allen Carpentier worships will have to meet higher standards than *that!*"

Benito didn't speak for a moment. Then he said, "We must hope our shouting was not heard. Look ahead."

From our position at the top of the arch we had a good view of the rims of the next gully. On both sides of the gap, horned black demons moved. They were larger than men, a little smaller than the demons in the first ditch, but like them they had horns and tails, and their skin was black ebony, very different from a black man's skin. They carried—

"Pitchforks?"

"Certainly," said Benito.

I couldn't help grinning a little. Pitchforks! I'd forgotten that detail. Had Walt Disney's cartoonists ever realized why their devils carried pitchforks?

"They must not see us," Benito said. "None of us

are safe from them. They guard the pit of the grafters, of those who stole from positions of trust."

Billy shuddered. "Reckon they'd like me," he said. "Guess I took a few things from my bosses in my day. Not much, but some."

"Not me. Free-lance writers don't have bosses," I said. Then I remembered the advance from Omniverse Publishing, nine years before I died. Somehow the novel had never jelled, and *let's play it safe here, Carpentier. Demons wouldn't understand the publishing business.*

There was cover at the bottom of the bridge. It was all a jumble of boulders. We waited our chance, then sprinted down the bridge while none of the demons were nearby. We were hidden before another group came past. We huddled together between the rocks.

"Too bad the bridges are staggered," I whispered. "We could have gone right across." The next bridge was thirty or forty yards to the left, with a troop of twenty-odd demons between.

"For us this is the second most dangerous place in Hell," whispered Benito. "We must reach the next bridge without being seen. Cross at a dead run, and do not stop at the next pit. Run straight into it. There are no bridges in any case, and we could not reach one if any existed. The demons are on both sides of the pit."

Billy shifted restlessly. "Don't like running from nothing."

"We must," Benito said simply. He pointed. A demon strode past.

A roughly human form nine feet tall, equipped with horns and hooves and a twitching tail. A capriform humanoid.

How glib, Carpentier. Capriform humanoid? Demon! Why play games with yourself?

The demon was carrying a human being, carrying him like a bowling ball, his claws inserted deep into the man's back. The man writhed and struggled. The demon didn't seem to notice. He called to three of the others. "How many New Yorkers this week?"

They joined him in front of our rock. One twitched his tail up to his mouth. Teeth like butcher knives gnawed at the end. "Twelve."

"Make it thirteen. And it's still Thursday on Earth. If Hideous wins the pool again I'll rip his face off."

"You could forget to report this one."

"Why not?" The first demon lifted his human burden to study it. "He hardly counts anyway. He stole a few hundred bucks from a friend who needed an eye operation." He addressed the man: "*You* won't tell on us, will you?"

"No. I swear," said the man. His voice was choked with agony.

"And you won't show your head above the pitch? Because if we see any sign of you—" The demon hefted his pitchfork suggestively. "We'll pull you out and tear you in little pieces and scatter you widely. It hurts a *lot*."

"I won't tell," said the man.

"Good," said the demon holding him, and he flung him. The man dropped below the rim with a mournful howl that ended in a sound half splash, half thud.

"What's down there?" Billy whispered.

I answered, "Boiling pitch."

"What'd he do?"

"Graft."

"I kept wanting to try to save him."

Benito said, "I would not save him if I could."

The demons passed on. Like the warriors around the lake of blood, they looked always into the pit, always away from us. If we were careful we could move, one at a time, flitting from rock to rock to—

"Gotcha!" a demon shouted, and I had a heart attack, right out there between two inadequate boulders. All they had to do was come and collect me, but they weren't looking. They were clumped at the rim, jabbing down.

A human form came up dripping gobbets of black pitch and trying to wriggle free of the tines of two pitchforks. I heard, "Boss Tweed, ain't it? We been checking with some of those dead men that're supposed to have voted your ticket— Hold him, Crazyred!" The man lurched free of one pitchfork, but the other held him fast. They beached him. They began to play with him.

I touched Billy's shoulder. "Don't look. We can get a good way while they're busy."

We crawled like snakes. By the time the shade of Tweed had stopped screaming, we were opposite the bridge. I looked back once and had to close my eyes. The demons had opened him up and spread him out like a frog in biology class; but unlike the frog, he was still trying to get away.

Benito crouched like a sprinter. "Ready?"

"Yeah."

"Right."

We ran.

I heard a great bass roar of rage. I didn't look back. But as I went over the arch, last in line, I saw that the demons on the far side of the gully were running to meet us.

One was going to make it.

I stopped. Only for an instant; then I plunged down the arch behind Benito.

But Billy had doubled his speed.

The demon reached the end of the bridge off

balance and skidding. "Come to Poppa!" he roared, and swung his pitchfork around.

He was a nanosecond late. Billy shot past the tines and ran up the demon and swarmed over the huge head.

The demon bellowed and tried to reverse eighteen feet of iron pitchfork. Benito slammed shoulder-first into his knee. The demon half-turned, and I hit the other knee sideways. Both huge legs went out from under the demon, left him blind and falling.

Half a ton of demon slammed into the rock.

Billy rolled away. The demon moaned and tried to gather his knees to his chest.

"Now run!" cried Benito. *"Billy!"*

A troop of demons was almost on us. I raced for the next pit, stopped at the edge. Where was Billy?

Billy had retrieved the demon's pitchfork and was raising it for the kill.

I yelled, "Never mind that!" and then it was just too late. Billy yelled triumph and brought the pitchfork down hard. He raised it for another thrust, and they had him. I jumped into space alongside Benito. Three-inch fingernails clicked shut behind my neck.

21

THE SIDE OF THE GULLY WAS ROUGH ROCK FALLING almost sheer. I glimpsed it in free-fall, and when I saw that there were no handholds I simply gave up. A couple of seconds later I lay broken at the bottom, staring up at the non-sky.

In the sea of pain I couldn't tell what was broken and what was only bruised. But I remembered that you're not supposed to move an accident victim. I didn't try to move.

Rustling near me.

"Benito?"

"Over here."

"Are you hurt?"

"Yes."

"Me too."

"We are out of their path, I think. We need only wait to heal."

Whose path? I was afraid to turn my head, but I turned my eyes. I found myself looking up along the fluted robe of a life-sized golden statue. No information there.

I said, "What about Billy?"

"Poor Billy. His urge to violence betrayed him."

"Don't be so damned philosophical. We've got to get him out of their hands!"

"How?"

"Well . . . first we wait to heal, I guess. Where would they put him? In the pitch with the Tammany types?"

"Look up along the edge of the gully."

Something like an endless length of rope was falling in loops across the sky. It dropped very slowly, as if almost weightless. As it came near I saw that it was thicker than rope, and there was a tuft on the end . . . Where had I seen something like that recently?

Above our heads it hesitated, then descended like a blind worm. For seconds it was hidden behind the rock slope. Then it began to rise . . . and the end was coiled around something that moved. Billy.

"Minos," I said. "It's his tail."

"Yes."

Before we could move, Billy would be back on the island in the river of blood—or in the river itself; he'd left the island of his own free will. He was beyond our reach. I sighed and turned my eyes from the tiny struggling figure and the infinite sprawl of Minos' tail.

And the statue had moved.

It had gone past me about one yard. I turned my head, regardless of consequences. My neck wasn't broken. And there were two bare human feet beneath the hem of the golden robe. One moved a good six inches as I watched.

"Benito. There are men in those things."

"And women too," said Benito. "Religious hypocrites."

He stood up carefully, testing to see if anything had healed. Apparently it had. He tried to help me up, but pain yelped in my ribs. I sat down against the slope to wait some more.

Golden robes moved past like snails. There were men and women in those golden idols, but I saw only bare feet and shadowed faces within enormous hoods. One stopped, and turned with the same excruciating slowness that characterized his walk, and said, "Are you lost?"

Benito said we weren't. I asked, "Are you?"

"Why, no. I think this is my proper place." His accent was thick and hard to identify. "I have been here long enough to be convinced that God thinks so too."

"How long is that?"

"Over a thousand years have passed on Earth, I'm told."

"That's a little hard to swallow," I said. "The English language isn't that old."

"I know," said the priest. "We teach each other. I learned this language from one who came here recently, an Amie Semple MacPherson. There is little else to do as we wander this endless channel, and you may imagine that it is easier to teach each other than to search for some companion who speaks our own language."

"Why," I asked, "don't you stop and sit down?"

The tired gray eyes studied me from within the golden cowl. "I could fall on you. But it may be that you do not know what you say. If I stop this robe grows hot. It is too hot now. It grows hot slowly, and it grows cool slowly. Now, good-bye." He began to turn away.

Benito said, "We could walk along with you."

"That would please me." He finished his turn and took one lurching footstep.

I got up. The ruined ribs only twinged. "How heavy is that robe?" I asked.

"I never weighed it. They tell me it is gilded lead. Perhaps a ton?"

"What did you do?"

"Does it matter? I was young, I had not been a priest for many years. But the end of the thousand years since Christ was born were drawing to a close. People began to fear the end of the world. I urged them to give away their property. To the Church. We became very wealthy."

"You could have given it back, afterwards."

"We did not."

"Did all of you end up here? The whole order?"

"No. Some truly thought the world would end. Some believed a wealthy Church could serve souls better. But I never believed the Second Coming could be predicted, and I enjoyed the wealth. I—do you need to know more? It was a good thing to be in the Church in those days."

Benito tapped my shoulder and pointed. "There is our way out. The rubble from the bridge."

It had been a bridge, high and arching like those we'd crossed before. Now it was a sloping pile of shattered rock. I looked at it curiously, but it didn't seem different from any other rock I'd seen, and I could see that normal laws of material strength didn't hold down here. It wasn't a surprise.

"What happened to it?" I wondered. "Earthquake?"

"I am told that all Hell shook at the moment of Christ's death," said the ex-priest.

"So says Dante," Benito added. "Afterwards, He came to Hell and threw down the great gate in the wall of Dis."

"He must have been mad about something. I suppose being crucified could do that to you."

"I would be less flippant, Allen. Look around you." Before I could answer, Benito had started climbing the ruined bridge.

It was still a ridiculous picture. Christ was supposed to be gentle. Using a whip on the temple money-changers was one thing; behaving like a comic-book hero was something else. I tried to imagine the bleeding, wounded, near-naked figure ripping those tremendous iron gates from their hinges, while the halo flamed angrily about His Head—

Then gave it up and climbed up after Benito. I tested each foothold, but some of the slabs slid down anyway. Near the top the rockslide ended, and we climbed by fingerholds and toeholds. There it was that I had to repress a sudden, violent urge to giggle.

Benito wouldn't have appreciated it. But—no wonder Christ was so upset. Some clerk must have tried to hand Him Form D-345t839y-4583.

The seventh pit was enormous. I stood at the end of the bridge and marveled at the thin fairy-span arching across. Carbon steel wouldn't have taken the stress; yet it was made of stone without mortar, like the fallen bridge behind us. Another miracle, and so what?

We started across.

It was dark down there. What I could see had a vaguely reptilian flavor to it: constant slow slitherings, and sudden flurries of violent motion.

Benito pulled at my arm. "Why do you dawdle, Allen?"

"What's down there?"

"Thieves. Theft is the most profitable of sins, and

very popular. Tell me, Allen, do you expect to see anything that pleases you?"

He had me there. I didn't. But— "I'm a writer. I've got ten men's curiosity. What's the hurry? Are we in danger here?"

"I remind you that we are fugitives."

I stared in astonishment. "Geryon could have stopped us. Minos could have stopped us. They didn't."

"The demons behind us would have. Oh, very well, Allen. The real danger is at the next pit. We must cross that quickly."

"Okay." And I looked down again.

Reptilian, yeah. There were men and women down there . . . and lizards ranging in size from Chihuahua to Great Dane, and snakes whose range was even greater. I watched a tiny scarlet lizard leap from a crack in a rock to bite a man on the neck. The man burned like flash paper, dazzling me. When I looked again he was congealing from a cloud of smoke.

Benito was watching me, not them. Let him wait.

The land was strewn with rocks of all sizes. A stout gray-haired woman came toward us, running a tortuous path, her eyes fixed on her path. It didn't help. Somehow she stepped between two rocks and fell sprawling, yelling in despair. The python that had been following her caught up as she tried to run on the ruined foot. It climbed her leg and bit her on the navel.

Woman and snake, they lay immobile. They began to change.

"Allen—"

I made a shushing gesture. They were changing, the snake sprouting arms and legs and head hair, the woman melting into a smooth limbless shape. Presently there was nothing left of the woman.

The slender man who had been a snake stood up smiling. "Thanks, Gladys," he said, and walked away.

"He stole her shape," I said. "I'll be buggered. He stole her shape!"

"She will grow it back. In life she was probably a buyer of stolen goods, what do you call it? A fence."

"Yeah. Wow."

"Are you ready?"

"Yeah." I turned and followed him. Wow. He stole her shape. How does a science-fiction writer explain that? A computer-drawn hologram. Could be. It was pretty dark down there. But I didn't believe it.

The bridge dipped. We climbed down. Benito turned left on the ledge between the seventh and eighth pits. Benito was clearly uneasy. Interesting things were happening in the darkness on my left, but I looked into the darkness on my right for the danger Benito expected.

It looked like a swarm of fireflies, or like a freeway seen from an airplane, or—

> This aye night, this aye night,
> Every night and all,
> Fire and sleet and candlelight,
> And Christ receive thy soul.

Sleet I'd found in the Circle of Gluttons, and fire on the desert. Here at last was the candlelight: huge candle flames moving in darkness.

From the next bridge it was no clearer. Benito kept trying to hurry me along. "You will not see anything here. Are you so fond of Hell that you would linger?"

Slender flames moved down there in the yellow-and-black murk . . . and stopped, and clustered beneath us. I said, "Who are they?"

"Dante calls this the Bolgia of the Evil Counselors."

"That doesn't tell me a lot. And I still don't know what you're afraid of."

A voice answered from below . . . a voice with little of the human in it. It thrummed like a harp. It was coming from the tip of one of the huge flames. "He is afraid of his own homecoming."

I looked at Benito. He nodded, not looking at me.

"Come down!" one of the flames called to Benito. It was eerily compelling, that thrumming voice. The tip of the flame wavered, turned to me. "Throw him down, you, if you're an American! That's Mussolini! Benito Mussolini!"

Jolted, I turned to Benito. He shrugged.

Mussolini?

Another voice thrummed from the pit. "You *are* American. I know your accent. Do you understand? That's Mussolini! Throw the bastard down here where he belongs!"

"Who are you?"

"Does it matter? I approved the firebombing of Dresden."

A British voice spoke from the flames. "And I led the mission. We may belong here, Yank, but so does that Eytie swine."

Benito was backing away. When I went toward him, he turned and ran. I caught him at the edge of the next pit and tripped him. He fell heavily to the ground, and I sat on him. He was no match for me. "Mussolini!" I shouted.

"I pulled you out of a jinn bottle!" he protested.

"And led me here, deeper into Hell! I knew it all along!" Mussolini. What better choice for the Devil's agent, to wander through Hell corrupting souls already half corrupted? Hitler was probably loose too. If we'd run across him I'd have guessed earlier. I remembered all my suspicions, and all the unexplained things that had happened on the trip down. No wonder he could give orders!

Well, I knew who he was now, and I knew where he belonged. We were at the edge of the ninth pit, but I took him by the heels and dragged him back to the eighth. He thrashed like a fish. He clutched at rocks and pulled a couple out of the ground, for all the good that did him.

The pit flamed beneath us with the crowd gathered to welcome Benito home.

I rolled him over the edge. He gave a low cry as he dropped. Before he struck bottom he burst into flame. His was very bright, brighter than most around him.

I turned and went on.

22

I WALKED UNTIL I HAD TO STOP, UNTIL THE GROUND dropped away at my feet. There I stood like a machine whose program has run out. After all, where would I go?

Now I was utterly alone, with nobody to tell me about the geography of Hell, or warn me of the dangers—

—or make me go deeper into horror after horror when all I wanted to do was stop. Mussolini. Benito Mussolini, Il Duce of Italy. He hadn't even tried to deny it.

What an idiot I'd been. Why hadn't I recognized him, with that massive square jaw and high forehead? I remembered reading about him in history books. Benito Mussolini had escaped from his castle-prison in a glider flown by Hitler's Commando, Skorzeny, one of the most romantic figures of that war. No wonder Benito could fly a glider!

Mussolini the fascist. He invented fascism! Killer and leader of killers, thug, ally of Adolf Hitler . . . back to the anonymous flame, Mussolini, evil genius behind the Italian king. Down you go, Benito, who poured me from a bottle.

I stood there a long time before I realized what I was seeing.

In the ninth pit the damned staggered and lurched, slipping in bloody mud, leaving more blood to make the path more slippery for those behind. They seemed dazed survivors of some lost battle.

One showed no obvious wounds, except for his erect posture and painfully stiff walk. I stared at his face, where a macabre joke had been played. It was pale and lean, and calm; no one would have guessed that he was in pain; but the eyes burned with hate. The mustache was in an unfamiliar style, straight, but twice the width of his mouth. And the sharp white canine teeth protruding over his lower lip would have had anyone over the age of six shouting, "Vampire!"

Well ahead of him was a sturdy fat man with a striking bearded face and blood running from a cut throat. The face was familiar. I studied him, trying to remember where I'd seen that face.

He stared back. Then he roared in fury wrapped in a Shakespearean accent. "Varlet! Who might you be, that stare so arrogantly at England?"

"Huh?" I shook myself. "Carp— Carpenter."

"Come down, woodworker, and I will have your eyes nailed shut!"

I realized I had been staring, rudely, at people who had trouble enough without that. More of Big Juju's victims. "Sorry. Does it help if I tell you the wounds will heal?"

I could see the shock rippling down the line, and suddenly they were all screaming curses and waving their fists. One man threatened with his severed arm held like a club.

"Dolt! Ass who mocks us!"

"What did I say?"

"You cannot be such a fool!" "England" cried. "We are nearly healed now! We reach the point in the circle where—" He stopped, looking ahead, forgetting me entirely. "I see him now," he said in a voice without life or hope.

I looked. The bridge was ahead of them, and under it was a king-sized version of all the other demons we'd passed, twenty feet tall, carrying a slender sword. He grinned, showing teeth nearly a foot long.

I had to cross the bridge anyway. I walked toward the demon.

He was killing them. They marched toward him, hanging back when they could until others pushed ahead, and he killed them. He picked a man up and sliced him from the crotch to the throat, set him down and let him walk on. Empathic pain lashed through me, and a line from a joke ran crazily through my head. About a cowboy who'd been thrown onto a barbed wire fence. He'd shown Texas courage; he'd remounted the horse and gone on. *Of course he had to let the stirrups out a little . . .*

The fat man looked sick and scared. His face clicked suddenly into place: a painting, very famous. Henry the Eighth.

I kept walking.

I was crossing the bridge when Henry reached the demon. The sword was not a sword, I saw now. It was an overdeveloped fingernail on an overdeveloped middle finger as thick as a strong man's thigh. It flicked like a rapier and severed Henry's head, and the demon handed Henry his head, and Henry walked on. The sharp horn tip of the sword flicked suddenly up before my face.

I stopped.

"Who may you be, O privileged one, who run so free through Hell?"

I got my throat working. "Allen Carpenter."

"Where away, Carpenter?"

"I don't know. Inward." With all the feelings that had been burnt out of me, one was left. Curiosity. Whatever Benito had planned for me, it lay downward, inward.

The dead had stopped to wait, with understandable patience, for the demon to finish his conversation. I waved downward. "Who are they?"

The demon seemed in no hurry. "Sowers of discord. People who advocated hatred, started wars, refused to end wars—you know, the opposite of the peacemakers. This is a special collection. Religious schizmatics. Generally founded their own churches for their own purposes. You want political types, or lawyers who talked people into divorces they didn't want and lawsuits they didn't need, you've got to go to another part of the pit."

"Oh."

The demon looked fondly at "England's" receding back. "Henry there wanted a divorce. The Church wouldn't give him one. So he made himself a Church that would. Clever?"

"On the evidence, not very."

The demon stooped to pick up the man with the Fu Manchu mustache and the vampire teeth. "Dracula here didn't found any churches. He—"

"*Dracula!* I thought he was— Dammit, he *was* just a legend."

"There *are* legends about him. In his homeland, Transylvania, mothers still frighten their children with his name. Dracula was just a title. Means dragon. His real name was Vlad; they called him Vlad Tepes, Vlad the Impaler. He spent his whole life torturing and killing Turks in the name of Christ. Otherwise he'd be uphill, eyelash deep in boiling blood. About half the people he killed were his own subjects, by the way."

Small wonder Vlad the Impaler walked funny. A wooden stake was sticking two feet out of his anus. The demon didn't need his sword. He just pushed the stake up until it didn't show, set the man down, and let him walk on. Walking funny.

The demon picked up another. "Johann here was the only man God would reveal the exact time of Doomsday to. He could save a small party of the Chosen, chosen by him, that is. All you had to do was turn all your property over to him." The demon grinned enormously. "And you, Carpenter? Did you ever create a church of your very own?"

"I—" Oh, boy.

The sword's bloody tip swung away and back, rapier-quick. I ducked and ran. I fell flat on the bridge as the sword flashed again. The demon couldn't quite get at me at that angle. But the arch of the bridge dipped low, there at the end.

I rose to sprint position, poised, took off. At the base of the arch the sword flicked toward me at knee height. I jumped it and kept running, right across and into the space above the next pit.

The side was steep. I hit once, and bounced, and hit the bottom very hard.

There was no unconsciousness in Hell. There was only pain and the awful strain of trying to draw a breath. Deep down behind the pain a tiny voice was saying, *You don't need to breathe, Carpentier. You're dead.* But I wanted to breathe, I needed to breathe, and not a sip of air could I draw.

Eventually the air did come, in sips, then gulps. I

tried to straighten out. It felt as if I were breaking my own back. Maybe my back *was* broken. But the sword would have been worse.

Could I feel my feet? Yes.

Okay. Your spine's intact. Just lie here awhile. It will heal. Sure, we always healed.

Hey, Carpentier. Why was it Benito always healed before you did?

Why shouldn't he? He was one of the paid staff.

Then why did he get hurt at all?

A woman's voice said, "What've you got?"

"Uh?" I still couldn't get more coherent than that.

"What've you got?" she repeated patiently. I moved my head around, slowly. It was dark and gloomy. I became aware of hideous screeching sounds, moans, screams of pain and rage, snarling dogs, the cacaphony of Hell.

She was sitting against the sloping side of the trench, naked, her body marked with pustules and the scars of older eruptions of the skin. She didn't seem more able to move than I was.

But the pain in my back was easing. I said, "Broken back, probably. What've *you* got?"

"Everything. Syphilis. Gonorrhea. Yaws. Trench mouth. Everything you can think of."

"Uh huh. I know what *you've* been doing."

She wailed, "But I *didn't!* That's why it's so unfair!"

My eyes were getting accustomed to the gloom that hung thick down here in the pit. There were others lying about the floor and the sides of the gully. Most of them looked deathly ill.

Across from me was a man scrabbling among thousands of pills. There must have been every variety of medication ever invented or imagined: tablets, capsules of many hues, bottles of liquids, tiny pills and pills that would choke a horse. He groaned in pain as he held up a pill and squinted at it. Finally he decided: he flung the pill back into the bathtub of them next to him.

He sat for a moment. Then he moaned, pressing his hands hard against his belly. "It's eating me alive!" he screamed. He scrabbled for another pill. This time he gulped it without looking at it. It didn't seem to help, because he screamed even louder and went back to his inspection routine.

I looked a question at the girl. She shrugged. "He sold cancer cures. They only worked if you didn't go to a doctor. Somewhere in that pile there may be a pill that cures him."

"What about the rest?"

"Some don't do anything. Some make it worse."

I shuddered, then froze as something came howling past on all fours, foam dripping from its jaws. I'd thought it was an animal, but it wasn't. It was a man.

"Counterfeiters. Counterfeiters always get rabies," said the woman. "If they bite you it takes a long time to heal."

And I couldn't move! There was nothing to do but watch.

Men and women with peeling scabs and an itch that drove them to tear at themselves. A man with no ears, unable to move and screaming for water.

"Listen!" he shouted. "Tell Satan! Anyone! Tell Satan there is a plot to overthrow him. For water I will reveal the names of the plotters! Tell him!"

They were all deathly ill, and they were all in pain—

—except one, and he was startling by contrast. He sat against the slope of the gully, a few feet from the girl and across from me. A middle-aged cherub, comfortably overweight, his blue eyes twinkling above a mad and happy smile.

Certainly he was mad. Was it a sickness of the mind, or had some vile bacterium reached his brain?

I had to get out of here. The most ferocious contagious diseases ever to wrack mankind were all around me. I tried to move, and stopped at once. My legs wouldn't obey, and it felt as if my spine were being twisted in a vise. Had I caught something already? Spinal meningitis, maybe?

The madman's wandering blue eyes found me. He said, "I was a psychiatrist."

"I didn't ask." In fact, I'd already learned more of Hell than I really wanted to know. I only wanted out. *Don't tell me any more!* I closed my eyes.

"They trusted me," the mad voice said happily. "They thought we knew what we were doing. For fifty bucks an hour I listened to their life stories. Wouldn't you?"

He subsided. The woman said, "He's crazy."

"Thanks. I really wondered about that," I told her without opening my eyes.

"Listen, you fell in over the edge. Have you been upslope? Have you seen a lot of what's up there?"

"A lot."

"What do they do to, shall we say, ladies of the evening?"

I opened my eyes. She was tense, waiting for my words.

"I didn't notice anything special for whores. Why?"

"I, I . . . Listen, some girls don't actually sleep with the customers. They take a gentleman to a motel, they get their money in advance, then they disappear. Sometimes you can do better than that. You're just getting down to business when your boyfriend walks in the door. You see?"

"Sure." I'd been robbed that way a couple of times in England.

"Well," she said, "you'd think that wouldn't be as bad as being an actual . . . prostitute." And she looked at me.

Somehow the memory was very dim now, of a time on Earth when a London girl had propositioned me, taken my money, and vanished from a bathroom with an unsuspected second door, leaving me in rage and frustrated lust. If I'd caught her I'd have killed her. But that was long ago, and nothing looked bad next to where I was now.

So I lied. "They'd be downslope from here. I haven't been there yet."

Satisfied, she sank back and forgot me in the examination of her ruined body.

The mad psychiatrist noticed me again. "We were just playing," he said dreamily. "Tinkering with something we didn't understand. I knew. Oh, I knew. Let me tell you—"

"Don't tell me." They kept hurting at me, all of them!

"He was a catatonic. He was like a rubber doll. You could put him in any position, and he'd stay there for hours. We tried all sorts of things in those days. Shock therapy, insulin shock, lobotomy. Punish the patient for not noticing the outside world."

"Or for not noticing you."

I meant it to hurt, but he nodded happily. "So we put him in a hotbox and started raising the temperature. We watched him through a window. First he just sweated. Then he started to move around. At a hundred and thirty he said his first words in sixteen years. *'Get me the fuck out of here!'*"

The mad eyes found me, and his face seemed to cave in. The cherubic smile vanished. Urgently he said, "Get me the fuck out of here!"

"I can't. I'll be lucky to get out myself." I tried

moving again. There was pain, but not enough to keep me in that place. I stood gingerly and started up the slope.

The girl cried, "You can't do that! Come back here! Come back!"

I kept going. There were rocks to pull myself up, cracks to use as footholds. I'd climbed just far enough when another hydrophobia case raged past, biting and chewing on everyone he passed. A rock rolled from beneath my foot, and pain grated in my spine as I caught myself.

The rabid man screamed at the psychiatrist, but the cherubic look had returned and he was smiling dreamily at the opposite wall. When I reached the top I remembered who had been in the last pit of the Eighth Circle. Frauds. Falsifiers. False witnesses.

23

THAT WAS THE LAST OF THE BOLGIAS. NOW THE WAY led across an empty, rocky land. I turned and looked at the ten canyons rising upward behind me, light flickering from some, others marked by rising smoke or roiling heated air. It had not been a pleasant journey.

Far ahead, through a twilit gloom that would just have had drivers turning on their headlights, I saw what seemed a cluster of great towers. There was nothing else to see, nothing at all.

Benito's evil counsel had brought me this far. Now it was too late. I could get back a little way, probably to the fifth pit, possibly as far as the cliff. But I'd never talk Geryon into taking me up that cliff . . . and there were just too many places where Allen Carpentier might belong.

Could I talk the monster into summoning Minos? That could get me all the way back to the Vestibule. Yeah, and into the bottle again. If I were lucky. I hadn't forgotten that burrowing this far into Hell might be a crime in itself. Minos had told me that I could choose far worse for myself than "justice." Maybe I'd already made the choice.

Or . . . I could just sit down. In this empty borderland I could spend a good piece of eternity before some angel noticed me.

I sat down.

It was very peaceful.

It was, in fact, the only completely empty spot I'd seen in Hell. Why? Maybe it was reserved for some brand new sin, something that hadn't been invented yet . . . say, a development of brain research or genetics. At some time in the indefinite future I might have to vacate fast.

Meanwhile, it was better than the bottle. I could see my navel.

Time passed without leaving footprints. Days, I think. The stinks of Hell were still in my nostrils. The ever-present background noise might have been soothing if I hadn't known what it was: millions of moans and cries blended by distance. But nobody was hurting me or hurting at me. I didn't have to watch people getting sliced up, or burned, or riddled by diseases, or smashed by demon cars, or distorted into obscene shapes.

I sat and dreamed of the past. I wondered idly about the looming towers I could see in the dark distance. I wondered at Benito's ultimate purpose in luring me here. But none of it seemed to matter. I thought that even curiosity had been burned out of me.

That would have been nice. I would have liked to turn my mind off for a long time. But it wouldn't turn off. Whatever quiet I'd found here, there was still Hell around me, and I hurt with the need to know why.

God had created human souls; could He not uncreate the failures? God had created sleep; could He not put the failures to sleep, forever? There were no good excuses for Hell. I thought of some unsettling bad ones:

The universe would fly off its axis if Hell's agony did not balance Heaven's bliss.

Or: Part of Heaven's bliss was the knowledge that lots of nasty people were suffering terribly.

Or the old standby: We were in the hands of infinite power and infinite sadism.

I got restless. The towers kept catching at my eye: blurred gray shadows on the horizon. Skyscrapers? A city in Hell? Quarters to house the maintenance crew for Infernoland? Or were they the true entrance, the tourist entrance?

But I was only playing with plots. I didn't believe in Infernoland anymore. This was Hell, and I knew it. I finally realized what was really bothering me.

To all intents and purposes I was back in the bottle.

I got up. I walked toward the towers. No harm in looking.

They weren't towers.

They were giants, enormous humanoids, buried in the earth from the navel down. I stopped well out of their reach to study them. Their enormous eyes found me and pinned me to the landscape like a butterfly on a board, then shifted away. I was not worth their attention.

I was glad. Unreasonably I felt that those tremendous deep eyes could see everything there was to know about me.

One was mad. He looked down at me hopefully and said, "Ildurb fistenant imb?" His face fell when I did not respond. Alien language, alien being. What were these aliens doing in human Hell?

Not serving Big Juju. Not hardly. Miles of chain bound their arms to their sides.

There were giants in the Bible and Titans in mythology. But no archaeologist had ever found human bones this size. And how could they survive Earth's gravity? The square-cube law should have flattened them into mountains of hamburger.

Maybe they weren't from this universe at all. An attacking army from another universe made by another creator? The science-fiction writer in me, the late Allen Carpentier, wanted very much to see their legs and feet. They must be disproportionately large and sturdy to support their weight . . . unless they had developed in a lighter gravity field . . .

While Carpentier the trapped damned soul was examining the chains that wrapped another of the giants.

For the giants were buried just outside a chin-high wall: their chins, not mine. The wall looked too smooth to climb. I walked up to the chained giant, ready to jump, but it wasn't necessary. The chain looked like anchor cable. Whoever had wrapped it round him had a fine eye for detail. He'd have been lucky to shrug his eyebrows.

Now, what would Benito have done here? Climbed the giant, of course.

The thought of climbing such a monster gave me pause. Yet I was sure I could do it. Up the chain, stepping in the links, as far as his shoulder; beware of snapping teeth. Then onto the wall and down.

If Benito had told the truth . . . if what I remembered of Dante was true . . . I would then be in the last Circle of Hell, the Circle of Traitors. Traitors to nation, to overlord, to benefactor, to parents and siblings. A great ice plain, and the traitors embedded in it. There would be nothing but the cold to stop me from crossing it, and I knew I couldn't freeze to death.

It looked so easy. What had Benito left out?

I remembered the great ice plain well enough. The college boy had been jolted at finding part of Hell already frozen over. Benito hadn't said anything that jarred with my own memories of Dante.

But there had to be a joker in the deck somewhere. Benito had been a power in Hell. He'd given orders to others of Hell's minions. He'd demonstrated demonic strength against a tank of a man in the great swamp.

Carpentier, why didn't he do that to you?

Maybe it was guilt that stopped him. He'd writhed and torn at the ground, but he hadn't actually hit me, not once. He'd uprooted jagged rocks while trying to use them as anchors, but he hadn't tried to hit me with them. And for all his presumed safe-conduct, he was back where Minos had sentenced him, with the Evil Counselors.

Maybe Satan or God or Big Juju had rendered some kind of judgment against Benito. With me as the agent.

But *why hadn't Benito fought?*

The giant tried to shake himself. The chains barely rustled.

No danger there.

You writhe and you struggle, but there's no way around it. Me too, giant. From every possible direction it looked the same. It was going to be unreasonably easy for Allen Carpentier to enter the Circle of Traitors . . . the place of punishment for those who had betrayed their benefactors.

I thought it over for a long time. Then I turned and started back.

24

GOING BACK WAS HARDER. THE DIP AT THE LOWER END of the tenth bridge was steeper, and now I was climbing it. I crossed the pit without looking down and climbed backward down the high end of the bridge.

I saw the next bridge close by, and made for it.

A sword's point flicked up before my eyes. I stopped. Surely he'd been under a different bridge? I'd skewed my path deliberately. But a half-human, half-bestial head beyond the sword's point shook itself negatively.

"You can't go back, Carpenter."

"I have to."

The blade hung before me, rock-steady. I could have chinned myself on it. I half-stepped forward and the blade moved too fast to follow. Now it pricked the tip of my nose.

I shrugged and turned back.

I took no chances. I crossed the inner pit again and circled through the wasteland beyond. Two bridges away, I crossed again—on my belly. I slid down the high end of the bridge and kept crawling along the ridge above the ninth pit. He couldn't be under *all* the bridges.

Couldn't he just. Like the damned clerk. He was waiting when I tried to stand up. At this, the low side of the pit, he had the angle on me. "You can't go up-hill," he said. "I really don't know how to make it plainer."

"I'm from the Vestibule," I said. "I don't belong here."

"You never created your own Church, Carpenter?"

Oh, dammit! "Listen, those weren't in competition with God or anybody! All I did was make up some religions for aliens. If that was enough you'd have every science-fiction writer who ever lived!"

"We've got *him*," said the demon, and he pointed with the sword.

I forgot the sword entirely. I leaned far out over the edge of the pit to see. "What in Hell—to coin a phrase—is that?"

It was, in a sense, the last word in centaurs. At one end was most of what I took for a trilobite. The head of the trilobite was a gristly primitive fish. Its head was the torso of a bony fish . . . and so on up the line, lungfish, proto–rat, bigger rat, a large smooth-skinned beast I didn't recognize, a thing like a gorilla, a thing like a man, finally a true man. None of the beasts had full hindquarters except the trilobite; none had a head except the man. The whole thing crawled along on flopping fish-torsos and forelegs and hands, a tremendous unmatched centipede. The human face seemed quite mad.

"He founded a religion that masks as a form of lay psychiatry. Members try to recall previous lives in their presumed animal ancestry. They also recall their own past lives . . . and that adds an interesting blackmail angle, because those who hear confession are often more dedicated than honorable. Excuse me."

For the line of victims had bunched up while we talked. The demon turned and sliced at them rapidly, to a tune of screams and curses. The centaur creature he sliced into its separate components, and it went past him in a parade, on arms and forelegs and wriggling fishy fins. The sword flicked up again just as I'd decided to make a break for it.

A bead of blood formed at the tip of my nose. "I'm not like him," I said quickly. "He played the game for real. With me it was just a game." I backed away until the tenth *bolgia* was an emptiness beneath my heels. He couldn't reach me now. "Take the Silpies. They were humanoid but telepaths. They believed they had one collective soul, and they could prove it! And the Sloots were slugs with tool-using tentacles developed from their tongues. To them, God was a Sloot with no tongue. He didn't need a tongue; He didn't eat, and He could create at will, by the power of His mind." I saw him nodding and was encouraged. "None of this was more than playing with ideas."

The demon was still nodding. "Games played with the concept of religion. Enough such games and all religions might look equally silly."

"You can't do this!" I shouted. "Listen, there's a friend of mine in the Eighth Bolgia, and it's my fault he's there, and I've got to get him out!"

"Did anyone promise you it would be easy? Or even possible?"

"Whatever it takes," I said, and thought I meant it.

"Step closer."

I walked to the edge. Carpentier shows his good faith.

The sword flashed twice. I heard and felt the tip grate along my ribs. It left two vertical slashes along my chest and belly. I reeled back with my arms wrapped around myself to hold my guts in.

The demon was watching me steadily. What could he be waiting for?

I knew. I stepped forward and dropped my arms. Carpentier shows his inability to learn.

The sword flashed twice more, leaving two deep horizontal slashes, perhaps mortally deep. A living man would have fainted from shock. I couldn't.

"Games," said the big evil humanoid. "Your move."

I studied the slashes and the flowing blood. Shock did seem to be slowing down my thought processes, but presently I saw what he meant. I said, "What do I use for a pencil?"

"You'll think of something."

I studied my fingernails. I thought of something.

I gouged a ragged X in the top left square of the diagram. The sword flashed to place an O in an adjacent corner.

I climbed the first slope of the bridge on fingers and toes. When I could walk I held my arms wrapped around myself, holding me in. The pride of my victory seemed excessive for a stupid game of ticktacktoe.

As I left the bridge I heard him call, "Carpenter?"

I turned my head.

"Best two out of three?"

My imagination was dead of shock. The only dirty word I could think of was one I'd never use again, not after seeing the place of the flatterers. I just kept walking along the rim.

The eighth pit was a canyon filled with firelight. "Benito!" My voice echoed hollowly between the canyon walls. "Benito!"

Some of the flames wavered. Thrumming voices,

retarded by the transfer from voice to flame tip, floated upward.

"Leave the damned to suffer alone."

"Benito who?"

"Bug off, you!"

The canyon stretched endlessly away in both directions in a gentle curve. If it was a full circle, it could hold millions. How was I to find Benito?

"Benito!" There was panic in my voice. The strain hurt my slashed chest. "Benito!"

"Benito Mussolini? He just passed me going *that* way—"

"No, it was the other direction."

"You're both wrong. Mussolini's in the boiling lake."

A fat lot of help I'd get here. And if I found him, what then? How was I going to get him out?

How did he get out in the first place? Maybe he'd already left again. A frustrating thought, because I couldn't do a thing about it, and it would mean I'd played my game with the demon for nothing. I hoped Benito was already out, but I had to assume he was still in there.

The canyon wasn't all that deep. What I needed was a climber's rope. Yeah, an asbestos one, stupid! Benito was on fire! For that matter, I hadn't seen any ropes anywhere.

I thought for a second about the chain on the giant. It would mean passing the demon twice—

No. Even if I got the chain loose, it was too heavy to move, and the freed giant would probably crush me for my trouble. I was glad I didn't have to decide to face the demon's sword again. I don't know what I would have done.

Well? *Think, Carpentier! There are tools in Hell. Sure, boats carry rope. Now we're getting somewhere. A heavy rope, kept wet while Benito climbs— Wait a minute. How do we climb the cliff when there's no rope yet? There haven't been any boats since the gaudy alien Geryon took us down. Tackle Geryon again?*

And if it doesn't work, back in the bottle while Benito burns?

Benito was smarter than I was. Maybe he'd think of something. "Benito!"

Mocking, thrumming voices answered.

I thought of fourteen feet of sword blade attached to a twenty-foot demon. Disable the demon (with what?), cut the blade loose (how?), send it down to Benito. But could he climb something that sharp? Or would he lose his fingers immediately? Did fingernail burn?

Waitaminute! There were smaller demons, higher up, carrying iron pitchforks!

I made for the bridge. In a few steps I was running. If I slowed down I'd want to stop, because I was terrified of what I planned.

I was in too much of a hurry. I was trotting toward the base of the tremendous bridge over the chasm of thieves when something flashed scarlet from behind a rock. I turned, frowning . . .

. . . and there was agony, flashing out from my neck to engulf me and drown me. I felt my bones soften and bend.

The pain drew back like a broken wave receding, but it left a blackened mind. I was confused; I couldn't think. A homely bearded man bent over me, saying urgent words that made no sense.

"Which way is out?" He was huge, I realized. A giant. I stepped toward him—and I was tiny and four-legged; my belly scraped the ground. A lizard. I was a lizard.

The bearded man repeated himself, enunciating each word. "Which way is out? How can I leave Hell?"

Vengeance. I advanced on him. Bite the son of a bitch! He backed away, still talking, but I couldn't understand him.

He stopped and seemed to brace himself.

I leapt. I sank my teeth into his belly. He howled, and I dropped to the ground, writhing in new agony.

When my mind cleared I was a man. I rolled away fast from the red lizard and didn't stop until there was a rock between us. The lizard stayed where he was, watching me.

I was making for the next bridge when his words came back to me. My dumb reptile brain had registered them only as sounds.

"You can't speak!" he'd wailed. Then, "Tell me! I'll let you bite me, but tell me the way out!"

He was a scarlet splash on a gray rock. Still watching me.

I pointed downslope, toward the lake of ice. "There! All the way to the center, if I haven't been lied to myself!"

I glanced back once after I'd crossed the next bridge. The lizard was poised on the rim, staring down. As I watched, he made his decision. He leapt into the pit.

Now what was that all about? *Never mind, Carpentier, you've got other concerns . . .*

25

FAR BELOW ME, THE GOLDEN MONKS STOOD LIKE SO many statues. Every couple of seconds one or another would rock forward as if its base were unstable. The broken bridge dropped in a cascade of rock.

I stopped to catch my breath (Habit, Carpentier! You could give that up), then went down the broken slope with some care. It would have been easy to break an ankle.

I had reached the floor of the canyon before I noticed that one of the monks had turned completely around to stare at me. His slate-gray eyes were the oldest, the weariest I had ever seen, and I recognized them.

He said, "Didn't you pass here a week ago?"

"A few days, I think. And you've only come this far?"

"We hurry as fast as we can." The gray eyes studied me. They were so tired; they made me want to sag down and rest. "May I ask, what game are you playing? Are you a courier or something equally unlikely?"

"No. I—" Why not tell the truth? He wasn't about

to run tell someone. "I've got to steal a pitchfork from one of the ten-foot demons in the next pit over."

"Don a cloak like mine," he said. "See what it does to your sense of humor."

I sank down against the bank. Those tired eyes . . . "I'll wear the cloak," I said. "You get Benito out of the Pit of the Evil Counselors. Okay?"

"I beg your pardon?"

"I pushed a good friend into the Pit of the Evil Counselors. If I can't—"

"But why would you do a thing like that?"

I howled. It startled me more than him. I'd been about to say something else entirely. But no words came, and I threw back my head and howled. The tears streamed down my face.

The monk said something in a foreign language. He tottered toward me and stopped. He didn't know what to do. "There, there," he said. "It will be all right. Don't cry." With a touch of bitterness he added, "Everyone will notice."

There was a howl as big as the world inside me. It wanted out, and it was stronger than I was. I howled.

The priest muttered to himself. Aloud he said, "Please. Please don't do that. If you will only stop crying, I will help you get your pitchfork."

I shook my head. I got out a whimpered, "How?"

He sighed. "I cannot even take off my robe. I do not see how I can help. Perhaps I could act as bait somehow?" He lifted his head, his teeth grinding with the effort, to look up along the cascade of broken rock.

I stood up. I patted him on his leaden back: *Clunk, clunk, clunk.* "You've got your own problems." I girded up my mental loins and started up the slope.

Loose rocks rolled under my feet. This was the high side of the gully. It took a long time to get to the top. I had just one advantage: part of the bridge still projected out from the cliff. I climbed in its shadow and stopped underneath. I waited.

After all, what could a demon do to me? Rip me to pieces? I'd heal.

Drop me into the pitch forever?

Throw me into the Pit of the Thieves?

One of the horned black demons strolled past, his head turned to study the pitch on the other side of the ridge. He held six yards of iron pitchfork balanced in one hand. All I had to do was leap out and grab it.

I let him go. When he was past I began to shake. The beast had three-inch claws, ten. And eight-inch tusks, two. And Carpentier was a coward.

I heard clanking and puffing below me. I turned and saw an amazing sight. The priest was coming up behind me.

I watched him. I didn't believe it, but it was true: he was actually in motion. He sounded as if he were dying again, but every so often his hand or his foot would move and he'd be two inches higher. When I finally made myself believe what was happening, I scrambled down the cliff, got under him and pushed up on the rigid hem of his robe. I doubt it helped. I might as well have been trying to lift the world.

We reached a flattish fragment of rock just under what was left of the bridge. There we rested. The death rattle was in his throat. His eyes were closed. His face glistened.

"Thousand years," he got out. "Been walking . . . thousand years . . . in this lead coffin. Legs like trees." Then, "Was a priest. A priest. Supposed to . . . keep people *out* of Hell."

"I still don't know how we're going to do it." The *we* was courtesy, and he deserved it. But what could he do?

"Get me up," he said.

I got my arms under his robe. It was warm. Together we got him upright, somehow. Then I looked
up . . . at a demon's hooves.

The demon looked down at us, grinning. "You
know," he said pleasantly, "you're the first one ever
got this far out of the tar."

I said, "You're making a mistake. I'm not—" Then
I leapt for it. The pitchfork struck sparks from the
rock where I'd been, but I was in midair, falling.

I landed hard on a ragged-edged boulder. I rolled
immediately, ready to dodge again.

The priest was gripping the business end of the
pitchfork!

The demon bellowed and pulled. For an instant he
had lifted the priest off the rock, robe and all. Then
the priest sagged back, still gripping the tines.

I tried to climb up to help.

The priest took two steps back and off the edge of
the rock.

The demon bellowed for help. He was trying to lift
half a ton of leaden robe, and it wasn't working out.
I had almost reached them when the demon cried out
and let go. The priest dropped through space.

I crawled down to him.

The robe was bent like tinsel and cracked down
the front. The edges glowed yellow. He'd been told
wrong; the robe was solid gold. When I touched it it
burned my fingers.

The priest was mangled inside. He looked violently
dead, except for his eyes, which followed me. If I
didn't get him out of the robe he'd fry. But you don't
move an accident victim—

He'll heal, Carpentier. We all heal, to be hurt again.
I pulled him out by his feet. The robe wasn't con-
toured to let him pass, but it didn't matter. He came

out like a jellyfish. He must have broken every bone in his body.

I spoke, not to the soft-looking head but to the gray eyes alone. "You'll heal. When you heal, there's a way out of Hell. Benito says so. Go downhill. Downhill."

The eyes blinked.

"I've got to rescue Benito," I said. I pulled him over to the side so nobody would step on him. I picked up the pitchfork and left.

"Benito!"

I walked the ridge between the pits, calling like a lost soul. The answering voices all sounded the same, anonymous, thrumming, inhuman. "Here I am, fellah!" "Benito who?" "Who dares disturb the silence of Hell?"

"Benito!"

"Allen?"

That had to be him! But a dozen voices took it up. "Allen!" "Here I am, Allen! What kept you?"

"Benito! I've come to get you out!"

I listened for the Italian accent . . . and heard it. "Never mind. I belong here. I should not have tried to leave."

All the flames looked alike, but I thought I had him placed now. I reached down with the pitchfork. "Bugger that! Grab the end!"

The other flames were wandering off. Benito said, "It is not long enough in any case."

It wasn't. I looked along the rim. There was a rough place where I might climb down partway.

Benito tried to stop me. "You are being stupid. If you fall, you will burn like the rest of us!"

"Can you reach the end?"

"Go away, Allen. This is my proper place."

I was ten feet below the rim and almost out of foot-

holds. The pitchfork was heavy and awkward. I tried
to go further, setting my feet very carefully.

"All right," Benito said suddenly. The huge flame
moved to engulf the tines. I felt a feather touch on the
haft, and the flame began to rise from the pit.

He called, "Can you hold me?"

I laughed wih relief. "You don't weigh as much as
an ounce! I could lift a thousand of you!" After all
I'd been through, suddenly it was going to be easy.

The flame rose higher along the haft . . . and I felt
the first warming of the metal.

I waited until I was sure I could filter the panic
from my voice. Some of it may have got through anyway. "Benito? Hurry."

"Is something wrong?"

"No, never mind. Just hurry." I was afraid he'd let
go.

The metal was uncomfortably warm.

It grew hot.

Down there where a huge flame was rising in dreamy
sloth, the metal began to glow dull red. He wouldn't
notice; his own bright flame would blind him to it. Up
here it was too hot to hold, but I held on, my teeth
clenched against the scream.

The scream grew bulky in my throat. I stopped
breathing to hold it in. If Benito gave up now to save
me pain, I'd never, never find the courage to do this
twice.

The metal was cherry red around the flame. My
hands began to sizzle. I wasn't breathing, but the smell
of cooked meat worked its way into my nose. I
couldn't imagine how my hands still held. I was clenching them with everything I had, but the muscles and
nerves must be cooked through. Charred through. I
knew that smell too: dinner ruined. My head was

thrown back, my eyes clenched tight. There was no sensation but the fire.

"You can let go," said Benito. He was beside me, clinging to the cliff, his body no longer hidden by the flame.

I tried to let go.

My hands were charred fast to the haft. I tried to knock the pitchfork loose. It came loose, all right, and slid bumping into the eighth *bolgia* with my charred hands still attached.

Benito had to virtually lift me up the cliff.

26

WE WENT INWARD. I FOLLOWED BENITO, NURSING MY charred wrists. He had to haul me up the last bridges by the slack of my robe. The pain never stopped. The nerves gave no sign of having been cauterized by the red-hot iron. The charred bone broke away; the black flesh split to expose red flesh.

It'll heal, Carpentier.

Oh, *shut up*. And call me Carpenter. Carpentier the Famous Author is dead.

In the empty borderland between the tenth pit and the giants, we sat down. Presently Benito spoke. "Thank you."

"Yeah. I'm sorry I pushed you in."

He didn't say anything. I said, "I thought I had to do it. I thought it was *right*."

Still nothing. "Look," I said, "I was raised to believe that Benito Mussolini and Adolf Hitler were identical monsters."

Benito sighed. "Sometimes, toward the end, perhaps we were. I didn't start that way. I meant well." He laughed bitterly. "I had good intentions. We know what is said to be paved with those."

"Tell me about it."

He spoke musingly, without looking at me. "After the war I saw my country humiliated. No one believed in anything. Corruption everywhere, laboring people working against wealthy people, middle class working against the government, everyone fighting each other and everyone ruining each other. If they'd only work together—we were Romans, once. We ruled the world. We could be great again, instead of a joke for Clemenceau and Lloyd George to swat aside."

"So you made people work together?"

"I gave Italy hope. For years I even stopped Hitler from taking Austria. Allen, if I'd chosen the side of the Allies in the second war, would I have as great a place in history as Stalin?"

I couldn't say anything to that.

"Yet he killed ten-million peasants. Adolf never equaled that record. As for me, in the early days we used castor oil, not clubs." He sighed. "But you can never stop, once you begin seeing what is better for people than they know themselves. The opposition will make a thorough mess of everything you've done, and you know they will destroy the country. What do you do? Destroy the opposition. Now they really have grievances. Bigger opposition, more police needed to suppress them. But I meant well. I loved my people to the day they killed me."

" 'The purpose of power is power.' "

"*What?*" Benito was badly shocked.

"Never mind. Quote from a novel, *Nineteen Eightyfour.* So then you tried to set up a government here?"

"For my sins, I did." Benito's sudden laugh was like my own howling in the sixth *bolgia:* there was an agonized laugh in him, and it clawed its way through his throat. "Oh, Allen! And you think you've seen Hell! A government among the Evil Counselors— When I tried to get out they stopped me; they needed me as figurehead. Never mind, I got out anyway. I *had* to."

"But you never did anything but good for me. Or anyone else you met, down here."

"How are your hands?"

We looked. Two tiny infant's fists were forming at the lumpy bones of my wrists. "We must wait until they heal. You will never climb with those!" He laughed.

We sat and talked. Hours went by.

"I think the worst was when they shot my cabinet people. Italians shooting men whose only crime was to love Italy and trust me—" He shuddered. "Those are strange scars on your chest."

"I had to play games with the demon in the tenth *bolgia*. Funny, we didn't see him coming back."

"Games?"

Reluctantly I told him. It could have been embarrassing, but it wasn't. He didn't thank me again. Instead he smiled and said, "Do you still believe that Hell is a place of entertainment?"

"No. I didn't even then. I think Geryon convinced me."

"Geryon?"

"Yeah. You may not have noticed, but Geryon is the only nonhuman in Hell who really looks like an ET, an extraterrestrial, something from another world. He's consistent. Not like those patchwork demons, animal traits grafted on a human frame. And when I climbed aboard him I kicked machinery around his waist."

"So?"

I had to laugh. "Oh, *really*, Benito! An antigravity belt? When they've already proved they can take the mass and weight out of anything they like? Geryon was lying. Lying without saying a word."

"And it was Geryon that convinced you? You have seen no proper miracles?"

"I saw one."

I told him where the pitchfork had come from. "That priest climbed the broken bridge in half a ton of gold. He hung from the demon's pitchfork until the demon had to let go, and he *knew* what would happen then."

Benito smiled. "Yes, that was a miracle."

"Too right. I know a miracle when I see one."

"Then you are more fortunate than most of us." He looked thoughtful. "Geryon has looked a little different each time I have seen him."

"That worried me too. Just how often have you made this trip?"

"Six times. Each has been easier for me, although not for the one who accompanied me to the exit. As I told you, it does not matter how many start. Only one leaves."

"And there really is a way out . . . There was a time when I thought you were just leading me into something more horrible. I'm still scared, but not of that."

"Now there remains only the lake of ice. You have nothing to fear."

"I'm afraid to relax. Too often I've thought I was through the worst part."

His look probed my soul. "When the iron began to grow warm in your hands—"

"Tell me all about it."

"I think not. But now there is only the ice. It will be colder than anything you can imagine, but we can endure it. Nothing can bar us now! Soon we reach the center, and then—" He stopped.

"And then?"

"You will see." He looked me in the face. "I think you have enough courage."

"Even now I feel it leaking away. Spit it out, Benito."

"We will meet Lucifer and pass him. Ignore anything he says. When we have passed that, go uphill to Purgatory." He paused. "Without me."

"But you've traveled this route? You know where it leads?"

"No, and yes. I have not traveled it, but I know where it leads."

"How?"

"By faith, and by Dante's description."

"Dante's been wrong a couple of times. Admit it, Benito: you don't know what happened to those six you rescued."

"I know. But I have not seen."

"Do you want to leave Hell? Or are you afraid of what's there?"

"How are your hands?"

They were a child's hands now, still too small to support my weight.

"You didn't answer my question."

"I would leave Hell if I could. I belong here, so long as there are lost souls to be rescued."

"You sent six men and women into the unknown, but you were afraid to go yourself."

He didn't answer, only looked at me.

I stood up. "Come on. My hands'll heal before we need them."

They healed.

We climbed the torso of a chained giant. It was easier than mountain climbing, and harder: mountains don't shake, mountains don't snap at you with teeth the size of medieval shields. We stepped across space from the giant's shoulder to the flat top of a wall. From the wall I watched Benito slide down on the seat of his pants, if he'd been wearing pants. A pity he hadn't found a better way down in six previous trips.

I slid after him.

Imagine one of the Great Lakes frozen over, seen on a moonless night. Maybe it looked like that. I'd never seen any of the Great Lakes. To me it was an ice-skating rink for a society of teleports: big enough to hold, say, one percent of a population of five billion. The wall behind me seemed arrow-straight; the dark ice, infinite.

A breath of a breeze whispered around us and leeched all the warmth from our massless souls. I stiffened with the shock, then crouched down and tried to shelter in my own arms.

Benito was standing. "That will not help. Nothing helps," he said patiently. "You must bear the cold."

If he could do it . . . I stood up and closed my eyes tight against the soft, unreasonably cold breeze. Surely it was below freezing, *way* below freezing. How cold was it? If it could kill a man in minutes, or seconds, I'd never know it. I couldn't die.

"Benito? Burst into flame again for your good friend."

"I would if I could. My apologies, Allen." Benito took my arm. We walked.

It had certainly been worth asking.

Was it water ice we walked on? For all of me, it could have been dry ice, or frozen nitrogen, or something even colder.

I kicked something that cursed me without emotion. I tried to open my eyes. The wind's tears had frozen them shut. I pulled them open, painfully, with my fingers.

"Leave them open," Benito said without pity, "and they will freeze open."

When the urge came to blink I fought it. Then there was no need, for my eyes would not close. I looked back at what I'd kicked. I said, "Sorry."

The face was handsome, photogenic, dignified in middle age, undignified in the way it grimaced and bent to the ice for shelter. Had I seen that face sometime, on television? Maybe. The man was buried to his chin in the ice. At the sound of my voice he cried, "Wait! Are you American?"

"Aren't we all? I can't seem to find anything but."

The head called to another head sitting like a cabbage on the ice. "George! Maybe we can settle this now." It turned back to me. "Late American? Do you know anything about the ABM controversy?"

"Sure. Antiballistic missiles to knock down incoming missiles. The controversy was over whether to build the ABM system."

"Wonderful! All right, sir. George was a Democrat, and I was a Republican. The Democrats were against building the system. The Republicans were in favor of it. But which of us was right?"

"I haven't the faintest idea," I said. "Do you really have nothing better to talk about than that?"

"No!" the man I'd kicked said sharply. "We do not! One of us had to be right! So why are we both here?"

The cold wasn't just getting to me; it had gotten me. I wanted *out*, not conversation. I said, "Other crimes, maybe."

"One of us was wrong," George said. "Senator Gates here thought the system was a waste of money, but he went along with his party. He—"

"It was more than a waste of money! It used up efforts we could have spent on a laser system! Sir,

I've seen how accurate a laser defense system could be against incoming missiles. But politics dictated that I must support the ABM system. I went along."

"I don't know anything about the darned lasers," George said, "except they were highly experimental. Experimental weapons did a lot for the Nazis, didn't they?" He snorted contempt, then sneezed on the freezing air. "I was convinced that the ABM system was needed to defend the country against an atomic attack. But our party platform was in favor of military cutbacks. Officially, so was I."

"Now, sir," Senator Gates said to me, "we can't both have been wrong."

"I think I'm getting the picture. You both *thought* you were wrong."

". . . yes."

"And a mistake could wipe out the United States of America."

Neither answered.

"For what it's worth," I said, "we're still getting Americans in Hell. Corbett died much later than you."

"Thank you," said ex-Senator Gates, and they both turned their faces to the ice again.

"But you were both traitors in your minds."

"Thank you for your help," said ex-Senator George. It was a dismissal.

We walked with care, to avoid kicking heads. There were certainly enough of them. But now it was worse; here the dead had been buried supine, and we would have been stepping on faces.

Once I missed my step and came down hard on a human face. The ice across its eyes crackled under my feet, and I leapt back fast. "Sorry!"

"Thanks," I heard.

"Mistake."

"Thanks, oh, thanks," it said, weeping. "I haven't cried in years. The damned ice froze across my eyes, and I couldn't cry. Thanks."

I felt awful. This was an awful place. "That's okay," I said. I bent and picked the remaining shards of ice from her eyes. "What'd you do?"

"I don't want to say."

"Okay."

I tore the ice visors from a couple of dozen pairs of eyes. Always they froze over again almost immediately. Only one ever said "Thanks." Finally I gave it up. There were just too many.

And the next head I passed screamed, "The ice! Stupid! Tear off the ice! You did it for the others!"

I stopped. "Who're you?"

"None of your business!"

I turned away.

"The ice! Wait! Al Capone, I'm Al Capone! You want names? That's Vito Genovese, trying to turn his face! Wait, I'll show you Lepke! Wait!" He was shouting against a chorus of voices trying to drown him out. I kept walking.

When the noise was behind us Benito said, "I knew Vito Genovese."

"Was he worth talking to?"

"No. Were you thinking of going back? It's cold, Allen."

Sound whispered all around us. Partly it was the breeze, which had stiffened. Partly it was the chattering of teeth. I'd suppressed that reflex in myself; it wasn't warming me at all.

But in all that expanse of ice, there was only one point of motion. I caught it in the corner of my eye, way off to one side. Doubted my senses. Kept looking. Saw it again.

"Benito?" I pointed.

He found it. "I had no idea. I thought I was the only one."

"You may be. It seems to be one man. And a dog."

They had noticed us, and they angled to meet us. As they came closer I saw my mistake. The dog was a lizard, its scarlet color leeched from it by the cold. And the man was the black-bearded thief who had stolen my shape at the seventh pit.

We studied each other. No greeting seemed appropriate. Finally I gestured and said, "Benito Mussolini. I'm Allen Carpenter."

"Jesse James. This lizard is Bob Ford."

"What was that all about, that business there at the bridge?"

"A bunch of us got together," said Jesse. "We thought maybe we could cooperate in getting one of us out. It turned out a man couldn't throw a lizard far enough. But we could stand a human pyramid against one of the walls, and the top man could throw a lizard at the bridge. I was the lizard."

"Funny nobody thought of it before."

He sighed. "It's getting those animals to work together, that's the problem. All the time we were trying to make the pyramid, some of us in the lizard form kept biting the ones in human form. We didn't get anything done till we had a dozen big lizards to guard us while we made the pyramid."

"Figures. Why'd you jump back?"

"I had to tell them which way was out."

"You might not have got out again. They might not even have let you take human form again."

He nodded.

I remembered something. A line from a song. "It was little Robert Ford, that dirty little coward, I wonder how does he feel, for he ate of Jesse's bread, and he slept in Jesse's bed, and he laid Jesse James in his grave . . ." "Bob Ford. Didn't he kill you? Shot you while you were taking a bath?"

"Hanging a picture. Yeah, he shot me, all right. I was following your advice—for which I thank you, stranger." He laughed. "And there was Bob Ford's head sitting on the ice. I thought it over for a while. I wandered around and around him, wondering what I could do to him, and wondering if I still hated him." The lizard was rubbing affectionately against his leg. "I finally bit him on the nose."

It hit me like a stiff shot of good whiskey. "You can get out of the ice!"

"Sure, friend. I just reached into that man-shaped bubble and picked up a lizard. Well, which way now?"

"Inward," Benito said. "Let us go. It is cold here."

That had to be the most unnecessary statement of all time. We moved inward, and the wind came up. It was blowing right in our faces. Pretty soon it was a real howler, as bad as the circle of the winds. I wondered if Corbett had ever got back there . . .

The wind whistled past us and lifted Jesse off the ice. The lizard squealed and leaped after him, and the wind caught it too. Man and lizard were bowled end over end across the ice, then lifted and flung high and outward. I watched them dwindle.

"So close," I said. "They were so close!"

"They were not ready," Benito said. "Perhaps they must see what is done to others. Theft and treachery may not have been all they did. It is even possible that they will be blown all the way back to the Vestibule and must make their way back. Come."

"But—"

"They know the way, Allen. Come!"

"All right." We bowed our heads against the wind and staggered on. The wind had been entirely too

selective for coincidence. It had thrown Jesse and
Ford an unguessable distance without knocking me or
Benito off our feet. I thought it was a good omen
. . . for us.

27

SUDDENLY THERE WERE NO MORE HEADS. THERE WAS only the ice, and the wind that had blown the others away. We leaned into it and kept moving.

I said, "Hell has run out of sins?"

"Look down."

Hell had not run out of sinners. They were buried beneath the ice in weird positions. Once I looked down, and then no more.

We walked crouched, wrapped in our own arms, to no purpose. The wind had early sucked every erg of heat out of us.

I saw motion ahead, high up.

As we drew near a shadowy mass loomed around the suggestion of motion. Pterodactyls on a mountain? Restless, rhythmic motion, like the wings of enormous birds. And gradually it all came clear.

There was a humanoid form, a hairy torso more than a mile tall. We stood at the bottom, at waist level, and looked up at three vast faces whose features were almost lost in distance. Bat wings flapped on either side of each face, and the wind was now beating down at our heads.

This was a very different picture from the dapper gentleman who offers to buy your soul. Or from Milton's epic hero, proud and unrepentant. One could not imagine playing riddles or chess games with this hideous, miserable, helpless mountain. I studied it almost without fear.

All three pairs of jaws were moving in the same rhythm as the wings. Something fluttered around the lips . . .

"Benito, what's he chewing on?"

"Are you sure you want to know?"

"Skip it. Which way is out? *Hey*—" I reached to stop him, not fast enough. Benito was striding straight toward Lucifer.

He stopped at the edge of the ice.

The ice ended short of Lucifer himself. There was three feet of empty space all around the enormous waist.

And no navel. I couldn't have missed it. It would have been big enough to hide a battleship.

"You must climb down," said Benito.

I looked into the gap. "After you."

He shook his head. "I cannot leave. There are others to rescue."

"I don't go without you."

"You have not shown such fear before."

"It's not all fear. You've rescued seven of us, now rescue yourself. You've earned it. If this doesn't lead to where you think it does, we can help each other get back."

"What if I turn back now, leaving you here?"

I'd wondered about that myself. "I don't know, and that's the truth. But there's a moral problem. You're a better man than I am—"

He smiled sardonically. "I? The murderous dictator you pushed into the eighth pit?"

"You've changed since you reached Hell. You've given *me* no evil counsel. I guess that's the point. If you haven't changed in Hell, if you haven't earned the right to leave, then I haven't and won't. If you can't go, I can't."

"I, I think I can go. I choose not to."

"If you can leave Hell, you'll have to prove it."

He studied my face . . . and then he smiled a joyful, luminous smile. He turned and stepped across the gap and had two fistfuls of coarse hair. And a sound beat down at our heads, a wind with an almost subsonic voice in it.

"Carpentier."

I looked straight up. Lucifer's middle face was looking down the curve of Lucifer's chest. Two fluttering human legs protruded like a ghastly cigarette from the corner of the mouth. It spoke, and the deep bass voice blew down to me.

"What will you tell God when you see Him?"

I didn't answer.

"Will you tell Him that He could learn morality from Vlad the Impaler?"

Benito was far below, clinging like a tick in the billowing hair, waiting for me. I stepped across and worked my way down. As I did, my weight seemed to increase, against all the laws of physics. It scared me. I was back in Infernoland, climbing down into the quantum black hole Big Juju had used for artificial gravity . . .

Benito looked up at me curiously. "What did he say to you?"

I shook my head.

We descended, getting heavier. There was a point

where I must have weighed tons, and all of it pushing inward toward my navel. No quantum black hole
crushed and swallowed me. I hadn't really expected
one. Benito worked his way around until his feet
pointed at me, and kept climbing. I followed his example.

Now we climbed up. Once I found breath to laugh
at the picture we would have made: two men climbing
at least half a mile of hairy leg, like ticks in the Devil's
hair. I half-expected to pass a dong the size of the
Empire State Building, testicles like twin Astrodomes.
There was nothing but hair.

The climb seemed endless, but it ended, not in
ice but in an echoing grotto of gray rock, dimly lit.
The Devil's hooves still loomed over us, big enough
to stamp a city flat.

We lay on our backs on the smooth rock, panting.
Somewhere a running stream made a bright, happy
gurgling sound. The dim light came from a single
bright pinpoint source overhead. The rock curved inward over our heads, but it never closed. It stretched
away like the neck of an inverted funnel, straight up
for an unguessable distance.

Presently I got up and found the stream and drank
from it. The water was clear and sweet. There is the
peace of deep sleep, and once I had thought there
would be peace in death. I drank again, then lay
with my fingers trailing in the water. Peace in death:
I'd found it.

But Benito was on his feet. "Onward!" he cried,
and began to climb. The handholds were not difficult,
and he moved like a spider monkey, or like a fat
man who no longer weighs anything at all.

He looked down from the inward-tilting gray slope
of grotto roof. "A four-thousand-mile climb, if Dante

was half right!" he bellowed cheerfully. "Are you coming?"

"I'm afraid not."

"What did you say?"

"No!"

I sighed in exasperation when I saw him climbing back down, but I'd half-expected it. He dropped the last few feet, and it did seem he fell like a settling balloon, too slowly. "What was it Satan said to you?"

"He asked me what I would say to God."

"Well?"

"I have to know something before I can speak to God at all."

Benito waited.

"I have to know the purpose of Hell."

"Come and ask Him!"

"You don't get it. Every torture in Hell was too much too late. Punishment? But it's *infinite* punishment for things that are *little* in comparison. Dracula caused a lot of people a lot of pain and death, but it *ended*. George only lied to people to make them buy things! And what about the fat lady in the Vestibule area?

"What's the *point*? To teach us a lesson? But we're *dead*. Revenge, punishment? Completely out of proportion. Balance? Does the universe need as much pain in it as pleasure? I couldn't *take* Heaven if that was the case."

"There is a reason, and the reason is good. I *know*."

"Yeah? I don't. There's only one *possible* excuse for Hell, and I almost missed it in the ravings of a crazy psychiatrist. It has to be the final training ground. If nothing can get a soul into Heaven in its *life*, there's still Hell, God's last attempt to get his attention. Like a catatonic in a hotbox, like me in that bottle, if Hell won't make a man yell for help, then it was still worth a try."

Benito was nodding. "You may be right. You may have found the purpose of Hell."

"Yeah. Yeah, but do you see where it leaves me? *Everyone* in Hell has to be able to leave once he's learned enough about himself. *Everyone,* even the trees in the Wood of the Suicides, even the poor devils in the boiling pitch and the sullen types anchored under the lake. Even the ones who think they're satisfied, the ones in the First Circle. And I can't leave Hell until I'm sure they can do it."

Benito nodded. "We go back."

"No, no, you idiot!" I was furious. "How can I tell anyone he can leave unless I know you did it? You're going up! And I'm going to watch you do it!"

He thundered, "Carpenter, you must still learn humility!"

"Granted. And you?"

"But they need me. They . . . ah. They have you."

"They have me." I put out my hand. "Good-bye, Benito. Good luck. I hope you find—"

He stepped past my hand and wrapped his arms around me and squeezed all the air out of me. I said something like, "Huff!", and hugged him back. We held the embrace for a long moment. Then Benito released me and turned away fast—I couldn't see his face—and started climbing.

I lay flat on the rock and looked up. At the end of the vertical tube, the pinpoint light source had all but vanished, leaving Benito nearly invisible. Many hours later the light brightened again, and I knew I was seeing the sun. Benito was a dark fleck that moved if I watched it long enough.

He had made good progress before the light dimmed and went out.

The water sounds burbled back from the rock walls. I lay with my arms folded behind my head, taking joy in laziness. The peace of this place was almost tangible. Worrying seemed inappropriate here: a breach of good manners.

What did they do to Billy? Did the priest get out all right? How could any thinking being do such a thing to Mrs. Herrnstein? I've got to get back—

But I felt no sense of urgency. The damned had all the time there was, and so did I. Hell was the violent ward of a hospital for the theologically insane. Some could be cured.

I would have to return to Hell. I was afraid of that; not afraid of the pains, or that the demons would catch me, because the pains would heal, and pain in the right cause is a badge of honor. As to the demons, there'd be no chance they could hold me. Not now. I knew.

No. My fear was of the doubts that would return. They would come, and I'd just have to live with them, and fight them with my memory of these few moments of peace. There were no doubts here. None at all.

The light was back, and there was a tiny mote in it that moved even as I watched. My eyes were better than human now; else I'd never have seen him at all.

The light was dimming with sunset when the mote moved out of it and left it clear.

"ONE OF THE GREATEST LIVING SUSPENSE WRITERS"

—CBS Radio

"His name on the jacket is a guarantee of pleasure."
—*Washington Star-News*

"One of the most highly acclaimed suspense novelists of the decade"
—*The Bookshelf*

"Francis is right up there at the top among the best mystery writers in the world."
—Stanley Ellin

"Dick Francis continues to be the hottest author going to the post. He improves with every offering."
—*Columbus Enquirer*

Published by POCKET BOOKS

Dick Francis

FOR KICKS

PUBLISHED BY POCKET BOOKS NEW YORK

POCKET BOOKS, a Simon & Schuster division of
GULF & WESTERN CORPORATION
1230 Avenue of the Americas, New York, N.Y. 10020

ISBN: 0-671-83499-1

First Pocket Books printing October, 1975

10 9 8 7 6 5 4 3

POCKET and colophon are trademarks of Simon & Schuster.

Printed in the U.S.A.

1

The Earl of October drove into my life in a pale-blue Holden which had seen better days.

I noticed the car turn in through the gateposts as I walked across the little paddock toward the house, and I watched its progress up our short private road with a jaundiced eye. Salesmen, I thought, I can do without. The blue car rolled to a gentle halt between me and my own front door.

The man who climbed out looked about forty-five and was of medium height and solid build, with a large, well-shaped head and smoothly brushed brown hair. He wore gray trousers, a fine wool shirt, and a dark, discreet tie, and he carried the inevitable briefcase. I sighed, bent through the paddock rails, and went over to send him packing.

"Where can I find Mr. Daniel Roke?" he asked. An English voice, which even to my untuned ear evoked expensive public schools; and he had a subtle air of authority inconsistent with the opening patter of representatives. I looked at him more attentively, and decided after all not to say I was out. He might even, in spite of the car, be a prospective customer.

"I," I said, without too much joy in the announcement, "am Daniel Roke."

His eyelids flickered in surprise.

"Oh," he said blankly.

I was used to this reaction. I was no one's idea of the owner of a prosperous stud farm. I looked, for a start, too young, though I didn't feel it; and my sister Belinda says you don't often meet a businessman you can mistake for an Italian peasant. Sweet girl, my sister. It is only that my skin is sallow and tans easily, and

5

I have black hair and brown eyes. Also I was that day wearing the oldest, most tattered pair of jeans I possessed, with unpolished jodhpur boots, and nothing else.

I had been helping a mare who always had difficulty in foaling: a messy job, and I had dressed for it. The result of my—and the mare's—labors was a weedy filly with a contracted tendon in the near fore and a suspicion of one in the off fore, too, which meant an operation, and more expense than she was likely to be worth.

My visitor stood for a while looking about him at the neat white-railed paddocks, the L-shaped stable yard away ahead, and the row of cedar-shingled foaling boxes off to the right, where my poor little newcomer lay in the straw. The whole spread looked substantial and well maintained, which it was; I worked very hard to keep it that way, so that I could reasonably ask good prices for my horses.

The visitor turned to gaze at the big blue-green lagoon to the left, with the snow-capped mountains rising steeply in rocky beauty along the far side of it. Puffs of cloud like plumes crowned the peaks. Grand and glorious scenery it was, to his fresh eyes.

But to me, walls.

"Breathtaking," he said appreciatively. Then turning to me briskly, but with some hesitation in his speech, he said, "I . . . er . . . I heard in Perlooma that you have . . . er . . . an English stable hand who . . . er . . . wants to go back home. . . ." He broke off, and started again. "I suppose it may sound surprising, but in certain circumstances, and if he is suitable, I am willing to pay his fare and give him a job at the other end. . . ." He trailed off again.

There couldn't, I thought, be such an acute shortage of stableboys in England that they needed to be recruited from Australia.

"Will you come into the house?" I said. "And explain?"

I led the way into the living room, and heard his exclamation as he stepped behind me. All our visitors were impressed by that room. Across the far end a great expanse of window framed the most spectacular part of the lagoon and mountains, making them seem even closer and, to me, more overwhelming than ever. I sat down in an old bentwood rocker with my back to them, and gestured him into a comfortable armchair facing the view.

"Now, Mr. . . . er . . . ?" I began.

"October," he said easily. "Not Mr.—Earl."

"October . . . as the month?" It was October at the time.

"As the month," he assented.

I looked at him curiously. He was not my idea of an earl. He looked like a hardheaded company chairman on holiday. Then it occurred to me that there was no bar to an earl's being a company chairman as well, and that quite probably some of them needed to be.

"I have acted on impulse, coming here," he said more coherently. "And I am not sure that it is ever a good thing to do." He paused, took out a machine-turned gold cigarette case, and gained time for thought while he flicked his lighter. I waited.

He smiled briefly. "Perhaps I had better start by saying that I am in Australia on business—I have interests in Sydney—but that I came down here to the Snowies as the last part of a private tour I have been making of your main racing and breeding centers. I am a member of the body which governs National Hunt racing—that is to say, steeplechasing, jump racing—in England, and naturally your horses interest me enormously. . . . Well, I was lunching in Perlooma," he went on, referring to our nearest township, fifteen miles away, "and I got talking to a man who remarked on my English accent and said the only other pommy he knew was a stable hand here who was fool enough to want to go back home."

"Yes," I agreed. "Simmons."

"Arthur Simmons," he said, nodding. "What sort of man is he?"

"Very good with horses," I said. "But he only wants to go back to England when he's drunk. And he only gets drunk in Perlooma. Never here."

7

"Oh," he said. "Then wouldn't he go, if he were given the chance?"

"I don't know. It depends what you want him for."

He drew on his cigarette, and tapped the ash off, and looked out of the window.

"A year or two ago we had a great deal of trouble with the doping of racehorses," he said abruptly. "A very great deal of trouble. There were trials and prison sentences, and stringent all-around tightening of stable security, and a stepping up of regular saliva and urine tests. We began to test the first four horses in many races, to stop doping-to-win, and we tested every suspiciously beaten favorite for doping-to-lose. Nearly all the results since the new regulations came into force have been negative."

"How satisfactory," I said, not desperately interested.

"No. It isn't. Someone has discovered a drug which our analysts cannot identify."

"That doesn't sound possible," I said politely. The afternoon was slipping away unprofitably, I felt, and I still had a lot to do.

He sensed my lack of enthusiasm. "There have been eleven cases, all winners. Ten that we are sure of. The horses apparently look conspicuously stimulated—I haven't myself actually seen one—but nothing shows up in the tests." He paused. "Doping is nearly always an inside job," he said, transferring his gaze back to me. "That is to say, stable lads are nearly always involved somehow, even if it is only to point out to someone else which horse is in which box." I nodded. Australia had had her troubles, too.

"We—that is to say, the other two Stewards of the National Hunt Committee and myself—have once or twice discussed trying to find out about the doping from the inside, so to speak—"

"By getting a stable lad to spy for you?" I said.

He winced slightly. "You Australians are so direct," he murmured. "But that was the general idea, yes. We didn't do anything more than talk about it, though, because there are many difficulties to such a plan and

8

frankly we didn't see how we could positively guarantee that any lad we approached was not already working for . . . er . . . the other side."

I grinned. "And Arthur Simmons has that guarantee?"

"Yes. And as he's English, he would fade indistinguishably into the racing scene. It occurred to me as I was paying my bill after lunch. So I asked the way here and drove straight up, to see what he was like."

"You can talk to him, certainly," I said, standing up. "But I don't think it will be any good."

"He would be paid far in excess of the normal rate," he said, misunderstanding me.

"I didn't mean that he couldn't be tempted to go," I said, "but he just hasn't the brain for anything like that."

He followed me back out into the spring sunshine. The air at that altitude was still chilly and I saw him shiver as he left the warmth of the house. He glanced appraisingly at my still bare chest.

"If you'll wait a moment, I'll fetch him," I said, and walking round the corner of the house, whistled shrilly, with my fingers in my teeth, toward the small bunkhouse across the yard. A head poked inquiringly out of a window and I shouted, "I want Arthur."

The head nodded, withdrew, and presently Arthur Simmons, elderly, small, bowlegged, and of an endearing simplicity of mind, made his crablike way toward me. I left him and Lord October together, and went over to see if the new filly had taken a firm hold on life. She had, though her efforts to stand on her poor misshapen foreleg were pathetic to see.

I left her with her mother, and went back toward Lord October, watching him from a distance as he took a note from his wallet and offered it to Arthur. Arthur wouldn't accept it, even though he was English. He's been here so long, I thought, that he's as Australian as anyone. He'd hate to go back to Britain, whatever he says when he's drunk.

"You were right," October said. "He's a splendid

9

chap, but no good for what I want. I didn't even suggest it."

"Isn't it expecting a great deal of any stable lad, however bright, to uncover something which has got men like you up a gum tree?"

He grimaced. "Yes. That is one of the difficulties I mentioned. We're scraping the bottom of the barrel, though. Any idea is worth trying. Any. You can't realize how serious the situation is."

We walked over to his car, and he opened the door.

"Well, thank you for your patience, Mr. Roke. As I said, it was an impulse, coming here. I hope I haven't wasted too much of your afternoon?" He smiled, still looking slightly hesitant and disconcerted.

I shook my head and smiled back and he started the car, turned it, and drove off down the road. He was out of my thoughts before he was through the gateposts.

He came back again the next day at sundown. I found him sitting patiently smoking in the small blue car, having no doubt discovered that there was no one in the house. I walked back toward him from the stable block, where I had been doing my share of the evening's chores, and reflected idly that he had again caught me at my dirtiest.

He got out of the car when he saw me coming, and stamped out his cigarette.

"M. Roke." He held out his hand, and I shook it.

This time he made no attempt to rush into speech. This time he had not come on impulse. There was absolutely no hesitation in his manner; instead, his natural air of authority was much more pronounced, and it struck me that it was with this power that he set out to persuade a board room full of hard directors to agree to an unpopular proposal.

I knew instantly, then, why he had come back.

I looked at him warily for a moment, then gestured toward the house and led him again into the living room.

"A drink?" I asked. "Whiskey?"

"Thank you." He took the glass.

"If you don't mind," I said, "I will go and change." And think, I added privately.

10

I showered and put on some decent trousers, socks, and house shoes, and a white poplin shirt with a navy-blue silk tie. I brushed back my damp hair carefully in front of the mirror, and made sure my nails were clean. There was no point in entering an argument at a social disadvantage. Particularly with an earl as determined as this.

He stood up when I went back, and took in my changed appearance with one smooth glance.

I smiled fleetingly, and poured myself a drink, and another for him.

"I think," he said, "that you may have guessed why I am here."

"Perhaps."

"To persuade you to take the job I had in mind for Simmons," he said without preamble, and without haste.

"Yes," I said. I sipped my drink. "And I can't do it."

We stood there eyeing each other. I knew that what he was seeing was a good deal different from the Daniel Roke he had met before. More substantial. More the sort of person he would have expected to find, perhaps. Clothes maketh man, I thought wryly.

The day was fading, and I switched on the lights. The mountains outside the window retreated into darkness; just as well, as I judged I would need all my resolution, and they were both literally and figuratively ranged behind October. The trouble was, of course, that with more than half my mind I wanted to take a crack at his fantastic job. And I knew it was madness. I couldn't afford it, for one thing.

"I've learned a good deal about you now," he said slowly. "On my way from here yesterday it crossed my mind that it was a pity you were not Arthur Simmons; you would have been perfect. You did, if you will forgive me saying so, look the part." He sounded apologetic.

"But not now?"

"You know you don't. You changed so that you wouldn't, I imagine. But you could again. Oh, I've no doubt that if I'd met you yesterday inside this house looking as civilized as you do at this moment, the thought

11

would never have occurred to me. But when I saw you first, walking across the paddock very tattered and half bare and looking like a gypsy, I did in fact take you for the hired help. . . . I'm sorry."

I grinned faintly. "It happens often, and I don't mind."

"And there's your voice," he said. "That Australian accent of yours . . . I know it's not as strong as many I've heard, but it's as near to cockney as dammit, and I expect you could broaden it a bit. You see," he went on firmly, as he saw I was about to interrupt, "if you put an educated Englishman into a stable as a lad, the chances are the others would know at once by his voice that he wasn't genuine. But they couldn't tell, with you. You look right, and you sound right. You seem to me the perfect answer to all our problems. A better answer than I could have dreamed of finding."

"Physically," I commented dryly.

He drank, and looked at me thoughtfully.

"In every way. You forget, I told you I know a good deal about you now. By the time I reached Perlooma yesterday afternoon I had decided to . . . er . . . investigate you, one might say, to find out what sort of man you really were . . . to see if there was the slightest chance of your being attracted by such a . . . a job." He drank again, and paused, waiting.

"I can't take on anything like that," I said. "I have enough to do here." The understatement of the month, I thought.

"Could you take on twenty thousand pounds?" He said it casually, conversationally.

The short answer to that was "Yes"; but instead, after a moment's stillness, I said, "Australian, or English?"

His mouth curled down at the corners and his eyes narrowed. He was amused.

"English. Of course," he said ironically.

I said nothing. I simply looked at him. As if reading my thoughts, he sat down in an armchair, crossed his legs comfortably, and said, "I'll tell you what you would do with it, if you like. You would pay the fees of the

12

medical school your sister Belinda has set her heart on. You would send your younger sister, Helen, to art school, as she wants. You would put enough aside for your thirteen-year-old brother Philip, to become a lawyer, if he is still of the same mind when he grows up. You could employ more labor here, instead of working yourself into an early grave feeding, clothing, and paying school fees for your family."

I suppose I should have been prepared for him to be thorough, but I felt a surge of anger that he should have pried so very intimately into my affairs. However, since the time when an angry retort had cost me the sale of a yearling who broke his leg the following week, I had learned to keep my tongue still whatever the provocation.

"I also have had two girls and a boy to educate," he said. "I know what it is costing you. My elder daughter is at university, and the twin boy and girl have recently left school."

When I again said nothing, he continued. "You were born in England, and were brought to Australia when you were a child. Your father, Howard Roke, was a barrister, a good one. He and your mother were drowned together in a sailing accident when you were eighteen. Since then you have supported yourself and your sisters and brother by horse dealing and breeding. I understand that you had intended to follow your father into the law, but instead used the money he had left to set up business here, in what had been your holiday house. You have done well at it. The horses you sell have a reputation for being well broken in and beautifully mannered. You are thorough, and you are respected."

He looked up at me, smiling. I stood stiffly. I could see there was still more to come.

He said, "Your headmaster at Geelong says you had a brain and are wasting it. Your bank manager says you spend little on yourself. Your doctor says you haven't had a holiday since you settled here nine years ago except for a month you spent in hospital once with a broken leg. Your pastor says you never go to church, and he takes a poor view of it." He drank slowly.

Many doors, it seemed, were open to determined earls.

"And finally," he added, with a lopsided smile, "the barkeeper of the Golden Platypus in Perlooma says he'd trust you with his sister, in spite of your good looks."

"And what were your conclusions, after all that?" I asked, my resentment a little better under control.

"That you are a dull, laborious prig," he said pleasantly.

I relaxed at that, and laughed, and sat down.

"Quite right," I agreed.

"On the other hand, everyone says you do keep on with something once you start it, and you are used to hard physical work. You know so much about horses that you could do a stable lad's job with your eyes shut standing on your head."

"The whole idea is screwy," I said, sighing. "It wouldn't work, not with me, or Arthur Simmons, or anybody. It just isn't feasible. There are hundreds of training stables in Britain, aren't there? You could live in them for months and hear nothing, while the dopers got strenuously to work all around you."

He shook his head. "I don't think so. There are surprisingly few dishonest lads, far fewer than you or most people would imagine. A lad known to be corruptible would attract all sorts of crooks like an unguarded gold mine. All our man would have to do would be to make sure that the word was well spread that he was open to offers. He'd get them, no doubt of it."

"But would he get the ones you want? I very much doubt it."

"To me it seems a good enough chance to be worth taking. Frankly, any chance is worth taking, the way things are. We have tried everything else. And we have failed. We have failed in spite of exhaustive questioning of everyone connected with the affected horses. The police say they cannot help us. As we cannot analyze the drug being used, we can give them nothing to work on. We employed a firm of private investigators. They got nowhere at all. Direct action has achieved absolutely

14

nothing. Indirect action cannot achieve less. I am willing to gamble twenty thousand pounds that with you it can achieve more. Will you do it?"

"I don't know," I said, and cursed my weakness. I should have said, "No, certainly not."

He pounced on it, leaning forward and talking more rapidly, every word full of passionate conviction. "Can I make you understand how concerned my colleagues and I are over these undetectable cases of doping? I own several racehorses—mostly steeplechasers—and my family for generations have been lovers and supporters of racing. The health of the sport means more to me, and people like me, than I can possibly say . . . and for the second time in three years it is being seriously threatened. During the last big wave of doping there were satirical jokes in the papers and on television, and we simply cannot afford to have it happen again. So far we have been able to stifle comment because the cases are still fairly widely spaced—it is well over a year since the first—and if anyone inquires we merely report that the tests were negative. But we *must* identify this new dope before there is a widespread increase in its use. Otherwise it will become a worse menace to racing than anything which has happened before. If dozens of undetectably doped winners start turning up, public faith will be destroyed altogether, and steeplechasing will suffer damage which it will take years to recover from, if it ever does. There is much more at stake than a pleasant pastime. Racing is an industry employing thousands of people . . . and not the least of them are stud owners like you. The collapse of public support would mean a great deal of hardship.

"You may think that I have offered you an extraordinarily large sum of money to come over and see if you can help us, but I am a rich man, and, believe me, the continuance of racing is worth a great deal more than that to me. My horses won nearly that amount in prize money last season, and if it can buy a chance of wiping out this threat, I will spend it gladly."

"You are much more vehement today," I said slowly, "than you were yesterday."

15

He sat back. "Yesterday I didn't need to convince you. But I felt just the same."

"There must be someone in England who can dig out the information you want," I protested. "People who know the ins and outs of your racing. I know nothing at all. I left your country when I was nine. I'd be useless. It's impossible."

That's better, I approved myself. That's much firmer.

He looked down at his glass, and spoke as if with reluctance. "Well . . . we did approach someone in England . . . a racing journalist, actually. Very good nose for news; very discreet, too; we thought he was just the chap. Unfortunately he dug away without success for some weeks. And then he was killed in a car crash, poor fellow."

"Why not try someone else?" I persisted.

"It was only in June that he died, during steeplechasing's summer recess. The new season started in August, and it was not until after that that we thought of the stable lad idea, with all its difficulties."

"Try a farmer's son," I suggested. "Country accent, knowledge of horses . . . the lot."

He shook his head. "England is too small. Send a farmer's son to walk a horse around the parade ring at the races, and what he was doing would soon be no secret. Too many people would recognize him, and ask questions."

"A farmworker's son, then, with a high IQ."

"Do we hold an exam?" he said sourly.

There was a pause, and he looked up from his glass. His face was solemn, almost severe.

"Well?" he said.

I meant to say "No," firmly. What I actually said was again, "I don't know."

"What can I say to persuade you?"

"Nothing," I said. "I'll think about it. I'll let you know tomorrow."

"Very well." He stood up, declined my offer of a meal, and went away as he had come, the strength of his personality flowing out of him like heat. The house felt empty when I went back from seeing him off.

The full moon blazed in the black sky, and through a gap in the hills behind me Mount Kosciusko distantly stretched its blunt snow-capped summit into the light. I sat on a rock up on the mountain, looking down on my home.

There lay the lagoon, the big pasture paddocks stretching away to the bush, the tidy white-railed small paddocks near the house, the silvery roof of the foaling boxes, the solid bulk of the stable block, the bunkhouse, the long, low graceful shape of the dwelling house with a glitter of moonlight on the big window at the end.

There lay my prison.

It hadn't been bad at first. There were no relations to take care of us, and I had found it satisfying to disappoint the people who said I couldn't earn enough to keep three small children, Belinda and Helen and Philip, with me. I liked horses, I always had, and from the beginning the business went fairly well. We all ate, anyway, and I even convinced myself that the law was not really my vocation after all.

My parents had planned to send Belinda and Helen to Frensham, and when the time came, they went. I daresay I could have found a cheaper school, but I had to try to give them what I had had . . . and that was why Philip was away at Geelong. The business had grown progressively, but so had the school fees and the men's wages and the maintenance costs. I was caught in a sort of upward spiral, and too much depended on my being able to keep on going. The leg I had broken in a steeplechase when I was twenty-two had caused the worst financial crisis of the whole nine years: and I had had no choice but to give up doing anything so risky.

I didn't grudge the unending labor. I was very fond of my sisters and brother. I had no regrets at all that I had done what I had. But the feeling that I had built a prosperous trap for myself had slowly eaten away the earlier contentment I had found in providing for them.

In another eight or ten years they would all be grown, educated, and married, and my job would be done.

In another ten years I would be thirty-seven. Perhaps I, too, would be married by then, and have some children of my own, and send them to Frensham and Geelong. . . . For more than four years I had done my best to stifle a longing to escape. It was easier when they were at home in the holidays, with the house ringing with their noise and Philip's carpentry all over the place and the girls' frillies hanging to dry in the bathroom. In the summer we swam or rowed on the lagoon (the lake, as my English parents had called it) and in the winter we skied on the mountians. They were very good company and never took anything they had for granted. Nor, now that they were growing up, did they seem to be suffering from any form of teen-age rebellions. They were, in fact, thoroughly rewarding.

It usually hit me about a week after they had gone back to school, this fierce aching desperation to be free. Free for a good long while: to go farther than the round of horse sales, farther than the occasional quick trip to Sydney or Melbourne or Cooma.

To have something else to remember but the procession of profitable days, something else to see besides the beauty with which I was surrounded. I had been so busy stuffing worms down my fellow nestlings' throats that I had never stretched my wings.

Telling myself that these thoughts were useless, that they were self-pity, that my unhappiness was unreasonable, did no good at all. I continued at night to sink into head-holding miseries of depression, and kept these moods out of my days—and my balance sheets—only by working to my limit.

When Lord October came, the children had been back at school for eleven days, and I was sleeping badly. That may be why I was sitting on a mountainside at four o'clock in the morning trying to decide whether or not to take a peculiar job as a stable lad on the other side of the world. The door of the cage had been opened for me, all right. But the tidbit that had been dangled to tempt me out seemed suspiciously large.

Twenty thousand English pounds . . . a great deal of money. But then he couldn't know of my restless state of mind, and he might think that a smaller sum would make no impression. (What, I wondered, had he been prepared to pay Arthur?)

On the other hand, there was the racing journalist who had died in a car crash. . . . If October or his colleagues had the slightest doubt it was an accident, that too would explain the size of his offer, as conscience money. Throughout my youth, owing to my father's profession, I had learned a good deal about crime and criminals, and I knew too much to dismiss the idea of an organized accident as fantastic nonsense.

I had inherited my father's bent for orderliness and truth and had grown up appreciating the logic of his mind, though I had often thought him too ruthless with innocent witnesses in court. My own view had always been that justice should be done and that my father did the world no good by getting the guilty acquitted. I would never make a barrister, he said, if I thought like that. I'd better be a policeman instead.

England, I thought. Twenty thousand pounds. Detection. To be honest, the urgency with which October viewed the situation had not infected me. English racing was on the other side of the world. I knew no one engaged in it. I cared frankly little whether it had a good or a bad reputation. If I went, it would be no altruistic crusade: I would be going only because the adventure appealed to me, because it looked amusing and a challenge, because it beckoned me like a siren to fling responsibility to the wind and cut the self-imposed shackles off my wilting spirit.

Common sense said that the whole idea was crazy, that the Earl of October was an irresponsible nut, that I hadn't any right to leave my family to fend for themselves while I went gallivanting around the world, and that the only possible course open to me was to stay where I was, and learn to be content.

Common sense lost.

2

Nine days later I flew to England in a Boeing 707.

I slept soundly for most of the thirty-six hours from Sydney to Darwin, from Darwin to Singapore, Rangoon and Calcutta, from Calcutta to Karachi and Damascus, and from Damascus to Frankfurt and London Airport.

Behind me I left a crowded week into which I had packed months of paper work and a host of practical arrangements. Part of the difficulty was that I didn't know how long I would be away, but I reckoned that if I hadn't done the job in six months I wouldn't be able to do it at all, and made that a basis for my plans.

The head stud groom was to have full charge of the training and sale of the horses already on the place, but not to buy or breed any more. A firm of contractors agreed to see to the general maintenance of the land and buildings. The woman currently cooking for the lads who lived in the bunkhouse assured me that she would look after the family when they came back for the long Christmas summer holiday from December to February.

I arranged with the bank manager that I should send postdated checks for the next term's school fees and for the fodder and tack for the horses, and I wrote a pile for the head groom to cash one at a time for the men's food and wages. October assured me that my "fee" would be transferred to my account without delay.

"If I don't succeed, you shall have your money back, less what it has cost me to be away," I told him.

He shook his head, but I insisted; and in the end we compromised. I was to have ten thousand outright, and the other half if my mission was successful.

20

I took October to my solicitors and had the rather unusual appointment shaped into a dryly worded legal contract, to which, with a wry smile, he put his signature alongside mine.

His amusement, however, disappeared abruptly when, as we left, I asked him to insure my life.

"I don't think I can," he said, frowning.

"Because I would be . . . uninsurable?" I asked.

He didn't answer.

"I have signed a contract," I pointed out. "Do you think I did it with my eyes shut?"

"It was your idea." He looked troubled. "I won't hold you to it."

"What really happened to the journalist?" I asked.

He shook his head and didn't meet my eyes. "I don't know. It looked like an accident. It almost certainly *was* an accident. He went off the road at night on a bend on the Yorkshire moors. The car caught fire as it rolled down into the valley. He hadn't a hope. He was a nice chap. . . ."

"It won't deter me if you have any reason for thinking it was not an accident," I said seriously, "but you must be frank. If it was not an accident, he must have made a lot of progress . . . he must have found out something pretty vital. It would be important to me to know where he had gone and what he had been doing during the days before he died."

"Did you think about all this before you agreed to accept my proposition?"

"Yes, of course."

He smiled as if a load had been lifted from him. "By God. Mr. Roke, the more I see of you, the more thankful I am I stopped for lunch in Perlooma and went to look for Arthur Simmons. Well . . . Tommy Stapleton—the journalist—was a good driver, but I suppose accidents can happen to anyone. It was a Sunday early in June. Monday, really. He died about two o'clock at night. A local man said the road was normal in appearance at one-thirty, and at two-thirty a couple going home from a party saw the broken railings on the bend and stopped to look. The car was still smoldering; they

21

could see the red glow of it in the valley, and they drove on into the nearest town to report it.

"The police think Stapleton went to sleep at the wheel. Easy enough to do. But they couldn't find out where he had been between leaving the house of some friends at five o'clock, and arriving on the Yorkshire moors. The journey would have taken him only about an hour, which left eight hours unaccounted for. No one ever came forward to say he'd spent the evening with them, though the story was in most of the papers. I believe it was suggested he could have been with another man's wife . . . someone who had a good reason for keeping quiet. Anyway, tht whole thing was treated as a straightforward accident.

"As to where he had been during the days before . . . we did find out, discreetly. He'd done nothing and been nowhere that he didn't normally do in the course of his job. He'd come up from the London offices of his newspaper on the Thursday, gone to Bogside races on the Friday and Saturday, stayed with friends near Hexhám, Northumberland, over the weekend, and, as I said, left them at five on Sunday, to drive back to London. They said he had been his normal charming self the whole time.

"We—that is, the other two Stewards and I—asked the Yorkshire police to let us see anything they salvaged from the car, but there was nothing of any interest to us. His leather briefcase was found undamaged halfway down the hillside, near one of the rear doors which had been wrenched off during the somersaulting, but there was nothing in it besides the usual form books and racing papers. We looked carefully. He lived with his mother and sister—he was unmarried—and they let us search their house for anything he might have written down for us. There was nothing. We also contacted the sports editor of his paper and asked to see any possessions he had left in his office. There were only a few personal oddments and an envelope containing some press cuttings about doping. We kept that. You can see them when you get to England. But I'm afraid they will be no use to you. They were very fragmentary."

22

"I see," I said. We walked along the street to where our two cars were parked, his hired blue Holden, and my white utility. Standing beside the two dusty vehicles, I remarked, "You want to believe it was an accident ... I think you want to believe it very much."

He nodded soberly. "It is appallingly disturbing to think anything else. If it weren't for those eight missing hours, one would have no doubt at all."

I shrugged. "He could have spent them in dozens of harmless ways. In a bar. Having dinner. In a cinema. Picking up a girl."

"Yes, he could," he said. But the doubt remained, both in his mind and mine.

He was to drive the hired Holden back to Sydney the following day and fly to England. He shook hands with me in the street and gave me his address in London, where I was to meet him again. With the door open and with one foot in the car, he said, "I suppose it would be part of your ... er ... procedure to appear as a slightly—shall we say—unreliable type of stable lad, so that the crooked element would take to you?"

"Definitely." I grinned.

"Then, if I might suggest it, it would be a good idea for you to grow a couple of sideburns. It's surprising what a lot of distrust can be caused by an inch of extra hair in front of the ears!"

I laughed. "A good idea."

"And don't bring many clothes," he added. "I'll fix you up with British stuff suitable for your new character."

"All right."

He slid down behind the wheel.

"Au revoir, then, Mr. Roke."

"Au revoir, Lord October," I said.

After he had gone, and without his persuasive force at my elbow, what I was planning to do seemed less sensible than ever. But then I was tired to death of being sensible. I went on working from dawn to midnight to clear the decks, and found myself waking each morning with impatience to be on my way.

Two days before I was due to leave, I flew down to Geelong to say good-bye to Philip and explain to his headmaster that I was going to Europe for a while; I didn't know exactly how long. I came back via Frensham to see my sisters, both of whom exclaimed at once over the dark patches of stubble which were already giving my face the required "unreliable" appearance.

"For heaven's sake shave them off," said Belinda. "They're far too sexy. Most of the seniors are crazy about you already and if they see you like that you'll be mobbed."

"That sounds delicious," I said, grinning at them affectionately.

Helen, nearly sixteen, was fair and gentle and as graceful as the flowers she liked to draw. She was the most dependent of the three, and had suffered worst from not having a mother.

"Do you mean," she said anxiously, "that you will be away the whole summer?" She looked as if Mount Kosciusko had crumbled.

"You'll be all right. You're nearly grown up now," I teased her.

"But the holidays will be so dull."

"Ask some friends to stay, then."

"Oh!" Her face cleared. "Can we? Yes. That would be fun."

She kissed me more happily good-bye, and went back to her lessons.

Belinda and I understood each other very well, and to her alone, knowing I owed it to her, I told the real purpose of my "holiday." She was upset, which I had not expected.

"Dearest Dan," she said, twining her arm in mine and sniffing to stop herself from crying. "I know that bringing us up has been a grind for you, and if for once you want to do something for your own sake, we ought to be glad. Only please do be careful. We do . . . we do want you back."

"I'll come back," I promised helplessly, lending her my handkerchief. "I'll come back."

The taxi from the air terminal brought me through a tree-filled square to the Earl of October's London house in a gray drizzle which in no way matched my spirits. Lighthearted, that was me. Springs in my heels.

In answer to my ring, the elegant black door was opened by a friendly-faced manservant, who took my grip from my hand and said that as his lordship was expecting me, he would take me up at once. "Up" turned out to be a crimson-walled drawing room on the first floor where round an electric heater in an Adam fireplace three men stood with glasses in their hands. Three men standing easily, their heads turned toward the opening door. Three men radiating as one the authority I had been aware of in October. They were the ruling triumvirate of National Hunt racing. Big guns. Established and entrenched behind a hundred years of traditional power. They weren't taking the affair as effervescently as I was.

"Mr. Roke, my lord," said the manservant, showing me in.

October came across the room to me and shook hands.

"Good trip?"

"Yes, thank you."

He turned toward the other men. "My two co-Stewards arranged to be here to welcome you."

"My name is Macclesfield," said the taller of them, an elderly, stooping man with riotous white hair. He leaned forward and held out a sinewy hand. "I am most interested to meet you, Mr. Roke." He had a hawk-eyed, piercing stare.

"And this is Colonel Beckett." October gestured to the third man, a slender, ill-looking person, who shook hands also, but with a weak, limp grasp. All three of them paused and looked at me as if I had come from outer space.

"I am at your disposal," I said politely.

"Yes . . . well, we may as well get straight down to business," said October, directing me to a hide-covered armchair. "But a drink first?"

"Thank you."

He gave me a glass of the smoothest whiskey I'd ever tasted, and they all sat down.

"My horses," October began, speaking easily, conversationally, "are trained in the stable block adjoining my house in Yorkshire. I do not train them myself, because I am away too often on business. A man named Inskip holds the license—a public license—and apart from my own horses, he trains several for my friends. At present there are about thirty-five horses in the yard, of which eleven are my own. We think it would be best if you started work as a lad in my stable, and then you can move on somewhere else when you think it is necessary. Clear so far?"

I nodded.

He went on, "Inskip is an honest man, but unfortunately he's also a bit of a talker, and we consider it essential for your success that he should not have any reason to chatter about the way you joined the stable. The hiring of the lads is always left to him, so it will have to be he, not I, who hires you.

"In order to make certain that we are shorthanded—so that your application for work will be immediately accepted—Colonel Beckett and Sir Stuart Macclesfield are each sending three young horses to the stables two days from now. The horses are no good, I may say, but they're the best we could do in the time."

They all smiled. And well they might. I began to admire their staff work.

"In four days, when everyone is beginning to feel overworked, you will arrive in the yard and offer your services. All right?"

"Yes."

"Here is a reference." He handed me an envelope. "It is from a woman cousin of mine in Cornwall who keeps a couple of hunters. I have arranged that if Inskip checks with her she will give you a clean bill. You can't appear too doubtful in character to begin with, you see, or Inskip will not employ you."

"I understand," I said.

"Inskip will ask you for your insurance card and an income tax form, which you would normally have brought on from your last job. Here they are." He gave them to me. "The insurance card is stamped up to date and is no problem, as it will not be queried in any way until next May, by which time we hope there will be no more need for it. The income tax situation is more difficult, but we have constructed the form so that the address on the part which Inskip has to send off to the Inland Revenue people when he engages you is illegible. Any amount of natural-looking confusion should arise from that; and the fact that you were not working in Cornwall should be safely concealed."

"I see," I said. And I was impressed, as well.

Sir Stuart Macclesfield cleared his throat and Colonel Beckett pinched the bridge of his nose between thumb and forefinger.

"About this dope," I said. "You told me your analysts couldn't identify it, but you didn't give me any details. What is it that makes you positive that it is being used?"

October glanced at Macclesfield, who said in his slow, rasping, elderly voice, "When a horse comes in from a race frothing at the mouth with his eyes popping out and his body drenched in sweat, one naturally suspects that he has been given a stimulant of some kind. Dopers usually run into trouble with stimulants, since it is difficult to judge the dosage needed to get a horse to win without arousing suspicion. If you had seen any of these particular horses we have tested, you would have sworn that they had been given a big overdose. But the test results were always negative."

"What do your pharmacists say?" I asked.

Beckett said sardonically, "Word for word? It's blasphemous."

I grinned. "The gist."

Beckett said, "They simply say there isn't a dope they can't identify."

"How about adrenalin?" I asked.

The Stewards exchanged glances, and Beckett said, "Most of the horses concerned did have a fairly high adrenalin count, but you can't tell from one analysis whether that is normal for that particular horse or not. Horses vary tremendously in the amount of adrenalin

27

they produce naturally, and you would have to test them before and after several races to establish their normal output, and also at various stages of their training. Only when you know their normal levels could you say whether any extra had been pumped into them. From the practical point of view, adrenalin can't be given by mouth, as I expect you know. It has to be injected, and it works instantaneously. These horses were all calm and cool when they went to the starting gate. Horses which have been stimulated with adrenalin are pepped up at that point. In addition to that, a horse often shows at once that he has had a subcutaneous adrenalin injection because the hairs for some way round the site of the puncture stand up on end and give the game away. Only an injection straight into the jugular vein is really fool-proof; but it is a very tricky process, and we are quite certain that it was not done in these cases."

"The lab chaps," said October, "told us to look for something mechanical. All sorts of things have been tried in the past, you see. Electric shocks, for instance. Jockeys used to have saddles or whips made with batteries concealed in them so that they could run bursts of current into the horses they were riding and galvanize them into winning. The horses' own sweat acted as a splendid conductor. We went into all that sort of thing very thoroughly indeed, and we are firmly of the opinion that none of the jockeys involved carried anything out of the ordinary in any of their equipment."

"We have collected all our notes, all the lab notes, dozens of press cuttings, and anything else we thought could be of the slightest help," said Macclesfield, pointing to three boxes of files which lay in a pile on a table by my elbow.

"And you have four days to read them and think about them," added October, smiling faintly. "There is a room ready for you here, and my man will look after you. I am sorry I cannot be with you, but I have to return to Yorkshire tonight."

Beckett looked at his watch and rose slowly. "I must be going, Edward." To me, with a glance as alive and shrewd as his physique was failing, he said, "You'll do. And make it fairly snappy, will you? Time's against us."

I thought October looked relieved. I was sure of it when Macclesfield shook my hand again and rasped, "Now that you're actually here, the whole scheme suddenly seems more possible. . . . Mr. Roke, I sincerely wish you every success."

October went down to the street door with them, and came back and looked at me across the crimson room. "They are sold on you, Mr. Roke, I am glad to say."

Upstairs in the luxurious deep-green-carpeted, brass-bedsteaded guest room where I slept for the next four nights, I found the manservant had unpacked the few clothes I had brought with me and put them tidily on the shelves of a heavy Edwardian wardrobe. On the floor beside my own canvas-and-leather grip stood a cheap fiber suitcase with rust-marked locks. Amused, I explored its contents. On top there was a thick sealed envelope with my name on it. I slit it open and found it was packed with five-pound notes, forty of them, and an accompanying slip which read "Bread for throwing on waters." I laughed aloud.

"Under the envelope October had provided everything from underclothes to washing things, jodhpur boots to raincoat, jeans to pajamas.

Another note from him was tucked into the neck of a black leather jacket.

This jacket completes what sideburns begin. Wearing both, you won't have any character to speak of. They are regulation dress for delinquents! Good luck.

I eyed the jodhpur boots. They were second-hand and needed polishing, but to my surprise, when I slid my feet into them, they were a good fit. I took them off and tried on a violently pointed pair of black walking shoes. Horrible, but they fitted comfortably also, and I kept them on to get my feet (and eyes) used to them.

The three box files, which I had carried up with me

29

after October had left for Yorkshire, were stacked on a low table next to a small armchair, and with a feeling that there was no more time to waste, I sat down, opened the first of them, and began to read.

Because I went painstakingly slowly through every word, it took me two days to finish all the papers in those boxes. And at the end of it I found myself staring at the carpet without a helpful idea in my head. There were accounts, some in typescript, some in longhand, of interviews the Stewards had held with the trainers, jockeys, head traveling lads, stable lads, blacksmiths, and veterinary surgeons connected with the eleven horses suspected of being doped. There was a lengthy report from a firm of private investigators who had interviewed dozens of stable lads in "places of refreshment," and got nowhere. A memo ten pages long from a bookmaker went into copious details of the market which had been made on the horses concerned: but the last sentence summed it up: "We can trace no one person or syndicate which has won consistently on these horses, and therefore conclude that if any one person or syndicate is involved, their betting was done on the Tote." Further down the box I found a letter from Tote Investors Ltd., saying that not one of their credit clients had backed all the horses concerned, but that of course they had no check on cash betting at racecourses.

The second box contained eleven laboratory reports of analyses made on urine and saliva samples. The first report referred to a horse called Charcoal and was dated eighteen months earlier. The last gave details of tests made on a horse called Rudyard as recently as September, when October was in Australia.

The word "negative" had been written in a neat hand at the end of each report.

The press had had a lot of trouble dodging the laws of libel. The clippings from daily papers in the third box contained such sentences as "Charcoal displayed a totally uncharacteristic turn of foot" and "In the unsaddling enclosure Rudyard appeared to be considerably excited by his success."

There were fewer references to Charcoal and the

following three horses, but at that point someone had employed a news-gathering agency: the last seven cases were documented by clippings from several daily, evening, local, and sporting papers.

At the bottom of the clippings I came across a medium-size manila envelope. On it was written: "Received from Sports Editor, *Daily Scope*, June 10." This, I realized, was the packet of cuttings collected by Stapleton, the unfortunate journalist, and I opened the envelope with much curiosity. But to my great disappointment, because I badly needed some help, all the clippings except three were duplicates of those I had already read.

Of these three, one was a personality piece on the woman owner of Charcoal, one was an account of a horse (not one of the eleven) going berserk and killing a woman on June 3 in the paddock at Cartmel, Lancashire, and the third was a long article from a racing weekly discussing famous cases of doping, how they had been discovered, and how dealt with. I read this attentively, with minimum results.

After all this unfruitful concentration, I spent the whole of the next day wandering round London, breathing in the city's fumes with a heady feeling of liberation, asking the way frequently and listening carefully to the voices which replied.

In the matter of my accent I thought October had been too hopeful, because two people, before midday, commented on my being Australian. My parents had retained their Englishness until their death, but at nine I had found it prudent not to be "different" at school, and had adopted the speech of my new country from that age. I could no longer shed it, even if I wanted to, but if it was to sound like cockney English, it would clearly have to be modified.

I drifted eastward, walking, asking, listening. Gradually I came to the conclusion that if I knocked off the aitches and didn't clip the ends of my words, I might get by. I practiced all that afternoon, and finally managed to alter a few vowel sounds as well. No one asked me where I came from, which I took as a sign

31

of success, and when I asked the last man, a barrow boy, where I could catch a bus back to the West, I could no longer detect much difference between my question and his answer.

On my way back I stopped at the Bank of Australia and made an arrangement about mail. I wanted to be able to write to my family sometimes and to receive letters from them, but I was afraid that the regular arrival of airmail from Australia would arouse comment. The Bank thought it decidedly odd, but agreed in the end to forward letters on to me in fresh (English) envelopes, adorned with English stamps.

I made one purchase, a zipper-pocketed money belt made of strong canvas webbing. It buckled flat around my waist under my shirt, and into it I packed the two hundred pounds: wherever I was going I thought I might be glad to have that money readily available.

In the evening, refreshed, I tried to approach the doping problem from another angle, by seeing if the horses had had anything in common.

Apparently they hadn't. All were trained by different trainers. All were owned by different owners; and all had been ridden by different jockeys. The only thing they had in common was that they had nothing in common.

I sighed, and went to bed.

Terence, the manservant, with whom I had reached a reserved but definite friendship, woke me on the fourth morning by coming into my room with a laden breakfast tray.

"The condemned man ate hearty," he observed, lifting a silver cover and allowing me a glimpse and a sniff of a plateful of eggs and bacon.

"What do you mean?" I said, yawning contentedly.

"I don't know what you and his lordship are up to, sir, but wherever you are going, it is different from what you are used to. That suit of yours, for instance, didn't come from the same sort of place as this little lot."

He picked up the fiber suitcase, put it on a stool, and opened the locks. Carefully, as if they had been

32

silk, he laid out on a chair some cotton underpants and a checked cotton shirt, followed by a tan ribbed pullover, some drainpipe charcoal trousers, and black socks. With a look of disgust, he picked up the black leather jacket and draped it over the chair back, and neatly arranged the pointed shoes.

"His lordship said I was to make certain that you left behind everything you came with, and took only these things with you," he said regretfully.

"Did you buy them?" I asked, amused, "or was it Lord October?"

"His lordship bought them." He smiled suddenly as he went over to the door. "I'd love to have seen him pushing around in that chain store among all those bustling women."

I finished my breakfast, bathed, shaved, and dressed from head to foot in the new clothes, putting the black jacket on top and zippering up the front. Then I brushed the hair on top of my head forward instead of back, so that the short black ends curved onto my forehead.

Terence came back for the empty tray and found me standing looking at myself in a full-length mirror. Instead of grinning at him as usual, I turned slowly around on my heel and treated him to a hard, narrow-eyed stare.

"Holy hell!" he said explosively.

"Good," I said cheerfully. "You wouldn't trust me, then?"

"Not as far as I could throw that wardrobe."

"What other impressions do I make on you? Would you give me a job?"

"You wouldn't get through the front door here, for a start. Basement entrance, if any. I'd check your references carefully before I took you on; and I don't think I'd have you at all if I wasn't desperate. You look shifty . . . and a bit . . . well . . . almost dangerous."

I unzipped the leather jacket and let it flap open, showing the checked shirt collar and tan pullover underneath. The effect was altogether sloppier.

"How about now?" I asked.

He put his head on one side, considering. "Yes, I

33

might give you a job now. You look much more ordinary. Not much more honest, but less hard to handle."

"Thank you, Terence. That's exactly the note, I think. Ordinary but dishonest." I smiled with pleasure. "I'd better be on my way."

"You haven't got anything of your own with you?"

"Only my watch," I assured him.

"Fine," he said.

I noticed with interest that for the first time in four days he had failed to punctuate any sentence with an easy, automatic "sir," and when I picked up the cheap suitcase, he made no move to take it from me and carry it himself, as he had done with my grip when I arrived.

We went downstairs to the street door, where I shook hands with him and thanked him for looking after me so well, and gave him a five-pound note. One of October's. He took it with a smile and stood with it in his hand, looking at me in my new character.

I grinned at him widely.

"Good-bye, Terence."

"Good-bye, and thank you . . . sir," he said, and I walked off leaving him laughing.

The next intimation I had that my change of clothes meant a violent drop in status came from the taxi driver I hailed at the bottom of the square. He refused to take me to King's Cross Station until I had shown him that I had enough money to pay his fare. I caught the noon train to Harrogate and intercepted several disapproving glances from a prim middle-aged man with frayed cuffs sitting opposite me. This was all satisfactory, I thought, looking out at the damp autumn countryside flying past; this assures me that I do immediately make a dubious impression. It was rather a lopsided thing to be pleased about.

From Harrogate I caught a country bus to the small village of Slaw, and having asked the way, walked the last two miles to October's place, arriving just before six o'clock, the best time of day for seeking work in a stable.

Sure enough, they were rushed off their feet: I asked

for the head lad, and he took me with him to Inskip, who was doing his evening round of inspection.

Inskip looked me over and pursed his lips. He was a stringy, youngish man with spectacles, sparse sandy hair, and a sloppy-looking mouth.

"References?" In contrast, his voice was sharp and authoritative.

I took the letter from October's Cornish cousin out of my pocket and gave it to him. He opened the letter, read it, and put it away in his own pocket.

"You haven't been with racehorses before, then?"

"No."

"When could you start?"

"Now." I indicated my suitcase.

He hesitated, but not for long. "As it happens, we are short-handed. We'll give you a try. Wally, arrange a bed for him with Mrs. Alnutt, and he can start in the morning. Usual wages," he added to me. "Eleven pounds a week, and three pounds of that goes to Mrs. Alnutt for your keep. You can give me your cards tomorrow. Right?"

"Yes," I said, and I was in.

3

I edged gently into the life of the yard like a heretic into heaven, trying not to be discovered and flung out before I became part of the scenery. On my first evening I spoke almost entirely in monosyllables, because I didn't trust my new accent, but I slowly found out that the lads talked with such a variety of regional accents themselves that my cockney-Australian passed without comment.

Wally, the head lad, a wiry, short man with ill-fitting dentures, said I was to sleep in the cottage where about a dozen unmarried lads lived, beside the gate into the

35

yard. I was shown into a small, crowded upstairs room containing six beds, a wardrobe, two chests of drawers, and four bedside chairs; which left roughly two square yards of clear space in the center. Thin flowered curtains hung at the windows, and there was polished linoleum on the floor.

My bed proved to have developed a deep sag in the center over the years, but it was comfortable enough, and was made up freshly with white sheets and gray blankets. Mrs. Alnutt, who took me in without a second glance, was a round, cheerful little person with hair fastened in a twist on top of her head. She kept the cottage spotless and stood over the lads to make sure they washed. She cooked well, and the food was plain but plentiful. All in all, it was a good billet.

I walked a bit warily to start with, but it was easier to be accepted and to fade into the background than I had imagined.

Once or twice during the first few days I stopped myself just in time from absentmindedly telling another lad what to do; nine years' habit died hard. And I was surprised, and a bit dismayed, by the subservient attitude everyone had to Inskip, at least to his face; my own men treated me at home with far more familiarity. The fact that I paid and they earned gave me no rights over them as men, and this we all clearly understood. But at Inskip's, and throughout all England, I gradually realized, there was far less of the almost aggressive egalitarianism of Australia. The lads, on the whole, seemed to accept that in the eyes of the world they were of secondary importance as human beings to Inskip and October. I thought this extraordinary, undignified, and shameful. And I kept my thoughts to myself.

Wally, scandalized by the casual way I had spoken on my arrival, told me to call Inskip "Sir"—and October "My Lord"—and said that if I was a ruddy communist I could clear off at once; so I quickly exhibited what he called a proper respect for my betters.

On the other hand, it was precisely because the relationship between me and my own men was so free and easy that I found no difficulty in becoming a lad among

36

lads. I felt no constraint on their part and, once the matter of accents had been settled, no self-consciousness on mine. But I did come to realize that what October had implied was undoubtedly true: had I stayed in England and gone to Eton (instead of its equivalent, Geelong), I could not have fitted so readily into his stable.

Inskip allotted me to three newly arrived horses, which was not very good from my point of view as it meant that I could not expect to be sent to a race meeting with them. They were neither fit nor entered for races, and it would be weeks before they were ready to run, even if they proved to be good enough. I pondered the problem while I carried their hay and water and cleaned their boxes and rode them out at morning exercise with the string.

On my second evening October came around at six with a party of house guests. Inskip, knowing in advance, had had everyone running to be finished in good time and walked around himself first, to make sure that all was in order.

Each lad stood with whichever of his horses was nearest the end from which the inspection was started. October and his friends, accompanied by Inskip and Wally, moved along from box to box, chatting, laughing, discussing each horse as they went.

When they came to me, October flicked me a glance and said, "You're new, aren't you?"

"Yes, my lord."

He took no further notice of me then, but when I had bolted the first horse in for the night and waited farther down the yard with the second one, he came over to pat my charge and feel his legs; and as he straightened up he gave me a mischievous wink. With difficulty, since I was facing the other men, I kept a deadpan face. He blew his nose to stop himself from laughing. We were neither of us very professional at this cloak-and-dagger stuff.

When they had gone, and after I had eaten the evening meal with the other lads, I walked down to the Slaw pub with two of them. Halfway through the first drinks, I left them and went and telephoned October.

"Who is speaking?" a man's voice inquired.

I was stumped for a second; then I said, "Perlooma," knowing that that would fetch him.

He came on the line. "Anything wrong?"

"No," I said. "Does anyone at the local exchange listen to your calls?"

"I wouldn't bet on it." He hesitated. "Where are you?"

"Slaw, in the phone booth at your end of the village."

"I have guests for dinner; will tomorrow do?"

"Yes."

He paused for thought. "Can you tell me what you want?"

"Yes," I said. "The form books for the last seven or eight seasons, and every scrap of information you can possibly dig up about the eleven . . . subjects."

"What are you looking for?"

"I don't know yet," I said.

"Do you want anything else?"

"Yes, but it needs discussion."

He thought. "Behind the stable yard there is a stream which comes down from the moors. Walk up beside it tomorrow, after lunch."

"Right."

I hung up, and went back to my interrupted drink in the pub.

"You've been a long time," said Paddy, one of the lads I had come with. "We're one ahead of you. What have you been doing—reading the walls in the Gents?"

"There's some remarks on them walls," mused the other lad, a gawky boy of eighteen, "that I haven't fathomed yet."

"Nor you don't want to," said Paddy approvingly. At forty he acted as unofficial father to many of the younger lads.

They slept one each side of me, Paddy and Grits, in the little dormitory. Paddy, as sharp as Grits was slow, was a tough little Irishman with eyes that never missed a trick. From the first minute I hoisted my suitcase

38

onto the bed and unpacked my night things under his inquisitive gaze, I had been glad that October had been so insistent about a complete change of clothes.

"How about another drink?"

"One more, then," assented Paddy. "I can just about run to it, I reckon."

I took the glasses to the bar and bought refills; there was a pause while Paddy and Grits dug into their pockets and repaid me eleven pence each. The beer, which to me tasted strong and bitter, was not, I thought, worth four miles' walk, but many of the lads, it appeared, had bicycles or rickety cars and made the trek on several evenings each week.

"Nothing much doing tonight," observed Grits gloomily. He brightened. "Payday tomorrow."

"It'll be full here tomorrow, and that's a fact," agreed Paddy. "With Soupy and that lot from Granger's and all."

"Granger's?" I asked.

"Sure, don't you know nothing?" said Grits with mild contempt. "Granger's stable, over t'other side of the hill."

"Where have you been all your life?" said Paddy.

"He's new to racing, mind you," said Grits, being fair.

"Yes, but all the same!" Paddy drank past the halfway mark, and wiped his mouth on the back of his hand.

Grits finished his beer and sighed. "That's it, then. Better be getting back, I suppose."

We walked back to the stables, talking as always about horses.

The following afternoon I wandered casually out of the stables and started up the stream, picking up stones as I went and throwing them in, as if to enjoy the splash. Some of the lads were punting a football about in the paddock behind the yard, but none of them paid any attention to me. A good long way up the hill, where the stream ran through a steep, grass-sided gully, I came across October sitting on a boulder smoking a cigarette. He was accompanied by a black retriever, and a gun and a full game bag lay on the ground beside him.

"Doctor Livingstone, I presume," he said, smiling.

"Quite right, Mr. Stanley. How did you guess?" I perched on a boulder near him.

He kicked the game bag. "The form books are in here, and a notebook with all that Beckett and I could rake up at such short notice about those eleven horses. But surely the reports in the files you read would be of more use than the odd snippets we can supply?"

"Anything may be useful . . . you never know. There was one clipping in that packet of Stapleton's which was interesting. It was about historic dope cases. It said that certain horses apparently turned harmless food into something that showed a positive dope reaction, just through chemical changes in their body. I suppose it isn't possible that the reverse could occur? I mean, could some horses break down any sort of dope into harmless substances, so that no positive reaction showed in the test?"

"I'll find out."

"There's only one other thing," I said. "I have been assigned to three of those useless brutes you filled the yard up with, and that means no trips to racecourses. I was wondering if perhaps you could sell one of them again, and then I'd have a chance of mixing with lads from several stables at the sales. Three other men are doing three horses each here, so I shouldn't find myself redundant, and I might well be given a raceable horse to look after."

"I will sell one," he said, "but if it goes for auction it will take time. The application forms have to go to the auctioneer nearly a month before the sale date."

I nodded. "It's utterly frustrating. I wish I could think of a way of getting myself transferred to a horse which is due to race shortly. Preferably one going to a far distant course, because an overnight stop would be ideal."

"Lads don't change their horses in midstream," he said, rubbing his chin.

"So I've been told. It's the luck of the draw. You get them when they come and you're stuck with them until they leave. If they turn out useless, it's just too bad."

We stood up. The retriever, who had lain quiet all this time with his muzzle resting on his paws, got to his feet also and stretched himself, and wagging his tail slowly from side to side, looked up trustingly at his master. October bent down, gave the dog an affectionate slap, and picked up the gun. I picked up the game bag and swung it over my shoulder.

We shook hands, and October said, smiling, "You may like to know that Inskip thinks you ride extraordinarily well for a stable lad. His exact words were that he didn't really trust men with your sort of looks, but that you'd the hands of an angel. You'd better watch that."

"Hell," I said, "I hadn't given it a thought."

He grinned and went off up the hill, and I turned downward along the stream, gradually becoming ruefully aware that however much of a lark I might find it to put on wolf's clothing, it was going to hurt my pride if I had to hash up my riding as well.

The pub in Slaw was crowded that evening and the pay envelopes took a hiding. About half the strength from October's stable was there—one of them had given me a lift down in his car—and also a group of Granger's lads, including three lasses, who took a good deal of double-meaning teasing and thoroughly enjoyed it. Most of the talk was friendly bragging that each lad's horses were better than those of anyone else.

"My bugger'll beat yours with his eyes shut on Wednesday."

"You've got a ruddy hope . . ."

". . . Yours couldn't run a snail to a close finish."

". . . The jockey made a right muck of the start and never got in touch . . ."

". . . fat as a pig and bloody obstinate as well."

The easy chat ebbed and flowed while the room grew thick with cigarette smoke and the warmth of too many lungs breathing the same box of air. A game of darts between some inaccurate players was in progress in one corner, and the balls of bar billiards clicked in another.

I lolled on a hard chair with my arm hooked over the back and watched Paddy and one of Granger's lads engage in a needle match of dominoes. Horses, cars, football, boxing, films, the last local dance, and back to horses, always back to horses: I listened to it all and learned nothing except that these lads were mostly content with their lives, mostly good natured, mostly observant, and mostly harmless.

"You're new, aren't you?" said a challenging voice in my ear.

I turned my head and looked up at him. "Yeah," I said languidly.

These were the only eyes I had seen in Yorkshire which held anything of the sort of guile I was looking for. I gave him back his stare until his lips curled in recognition that I was one of his kind.

"What's your name?"

"Dan," I said. "And yours?"

"Thomas Nathaniel Tarleton." He waited for some reaction, but I didn't know what it ought to be.

"T.N.T.," said Paddy obligingly, looking up from his dominoes. "Soupy." His quick gaze flickered over both of us.

"The high-explosive kid himself," I murmured.

Soupy Tarleton smiled a small, carefully dangerous smile—to impress me, I gathered. He was about my own age and build, but much fairer, with the reddish skin which I had noticed so many Englishmen had. His light-hazel eyes protruded slightly in their sockets, and he had grown a narrow mustache on the upper lip of his full, moist-looking mouth. On the little finger of his right hand he wore a heavy gold ring, and on his left wrist, an expensive wristwatch. His clothes were of good material, though distinctly sharp in cut, and the enviable fleece-lined quilted jacket he carried over his arm would have cost him three weeks' pay.

He showed no signs of wanting to be friendly. After looking me over as thoroughly as I had him, he merely nodded, said, "See you," and detached himself to go over and watch the bar billiards.

Grits brought a fresh half pint from the bar and settled himself on the bench next to Paddy.

"You don't want to trust Soupy," he told me confidentially, his raw-boned, unintelligent face full of kindness.

Paddy put down a double three, and looking round at us, gave me a long, unsmiling scrutiny.

"There's no need to worry about Dan, Grits," he said. "He and Soupy, they're alike. They'd go well in double harness. Birds of a feather, that's what they are."

"But you said I wasn't to trust Soupy," objected Grits, looking from one to the other of us with troubled eyes.

"That's right," said Paddy flatly. He put down a three-four and concentrated on his game.

Grits shifted six inches toward Paddy and gave me one puzzled, embarrassed glance. Then he found the inside of his beer mug suddenly intensely interesting and didn't raise his eyes to mine again.

I think it was at that exact moment that the charade began to lose its lightheartedness. I liked Paddy and Grits, and for three days they had accepted me with casual good humor. I was not prepared for Paddy's instant recognition that it was with Soupy that my real interest lay, nor for his immediate rejection of me on that account. It was a shock which I ought to have foreseen, and hadn't; and it should have warned me what to expect in the future, but it didn't.

Colonel Beckett's staff work continued to be of the highest possible kind. Having committed himself to the offensive, he was prepared to back the attack with massive and immediate reinforcements: which is to say that as soon as he had heard from October that I was immobilized in the stable with three useless horses, he set about liberating me.

On Tuesday afternoon, when I had been with the stable for a week, Wally, the head lad, stopped me as I carried two buckets full of water across the yard.

"That horse of yours in number seventeen is going tomorrow," he said. "You'll have to look sharp in the morning with your work, because you are to be ready to go with it at twelve-thirty. The horse box will take

43

you to another racing stable, down near Nottingham. You are to leave this horse there and bring a new one back. Right?"

"Right," I said. Wally's manner was cool with me; but over the weekend I had made myself be reconciled to the knowledge that I had to go on inspiring a faint mistrust all around, even if I no longer much liked it when I succeeded.

Most of Sunday I had spent reading the form books, which the others in the cottage regarded as a perfectly natural activity; and in the evening, when they all went down to the pub, I did some pretty concentrated work with a pencil, making analyses of the eleven horses and their assisted wins. It was true, as I had discovered from the newspaper cuttings in London, that they all had different owners, trainers, and jockeys; but it was not true that they had absolutely nothing in common. By the time I had sealed my notes into an envelope and put it with October's notebook into the game bag under some form books, away from the inquiring gaze of the beer-happy returning lads, I was in possession of four unhelpful points of similarity.

First, the horses had all won selling chases—races where the winner was subsequently put up for auction. In the auctions three horses had been bought back by their owners, and the rest had been sold for modest sums.

Second, in all their racing lives, all the horses had proved themselves to be capable of making a show in a race, but had either no strength or no guts when it came to a finish.

Third, none of them had won any races except the ones for which they were doped, though they had occasionally been placed on other occasions.

Fourth, none of them had won at odds of less than ten to one.

I learned both from October's notes and from the form books that several of the horses had changed trainers more than once, but they were such moderate, unrewarding animals that this was only to be expected. I was also in possession of the useless information that

44

the horses were all by different sires out of different dams, that they varied in age from five to eleven, and that they were not all of the same color. Neither had they all won on the same course, though in this case they had not all won on different courses, either; and geographically I had a vague idea that the courses concerned were all in the northern half of the country— Kelso, Haydock, Sedgefield, Stafford, and Ludlow. I decided to check them on a map, to see if this was right, but there wasn't one to be found chez Mrs. Alnutt.

I went to bed in the crowded little dormitory with the other lads' beery breath gradually overwhelming the usual mixed clean smells of boot polish and hair oil, and lost an argument about having the small sash window open more than four inches at the top. The lads all seemed to take their cue from Paddy, who was undoubtedly the most aware of them, and if Paddy declined to treat me as a friend, so would they. I realized that if I had insisted on having the window tight shut they would probably have opened it wide and given me all the air I wanted. Grinning ruefully in the dark, I listened to the squeaking bedsprings and their sleepy, gossiping giggles as they thumbed over the evening's talk; and as I shifted to find a comfortable spot on the lumpy mattress, I began to wonder what life was really like from the inside for the hands who lived in my own bunkhouse, back home.

Wednesday morning gave me my first taste of the biting Yorkshire wind, and one of the lads, as we scurried around the yard with shaking hands and running noses, cheerfully assured me that it could blow for six months solid, if it tried. I did my three horses at the double, but by the time the horse box took me and one of them out of the yard at twelve-thirty, I had decided that if the gaps in my wardrobe were anything to go by, October's big square house up the drive must have very efficient central heating.

About four miles up the road, I pressed the bell which in most horse boxes connects the back compartment to the cab. The driver stopped obediently, and looked

45

inquiringly at me when I walked along and climbed up into the cab beside him.

"The horse is quiet," I said, "and it's warmer here."

He grinned and started off again, shouting over the noise of the engine. "I didn't have you figured for the conscientious type, and I was damn right. That horse is going to be sold and has got to arrive in good condition. The boss would have a fit if he knew you were up in front."

I had a pretty good idea the boss, meaning Inskip, wouldn't be at all surprised; bosses, judging by myself, weren't as naïve as all that.

"The boss can stuff himself," I said unpleasantly.

I got a sidelong glance for that, and reflected that it was dead easy to give oneself a bad character if one put one's mind to it. Horse-box drivers went to race meetings in droves, and had no duties when they got there. They had time to gossip in the canteen, time all afternoon to wander about and wag their tongues. There was no telling what ears might hear that there was a possible chink in the honesty of the Inskip lads.

We stopped once on the way to eat in a transport café, and again a little farther on for me to buy myself a couple of woolen shirts, a black sweater, some thick socks, woolen gloves, and a knitted yachting cap like those the other lads had worn that bitter morning. The box driver, coming into the shop with me to buy some socks for himself, eyed my purchases and remarked that I seemed to have plenty of money. I grinned knowingly, and said it was easy to come by if you knew how; and I could see his doubts of me growing.

In midafternoon we rolled in to a racing stable in Leicestershire, and it was here that the scope of Beckett's staff work became apparent. The horse I was to take back and subsequently care for was a useful hurdler just about to start his career as a novice 'chaser, and he had been sold to Colonel Beckett complete with all engagements. This meant, I learned from his former lad, who handed him over to me with considerable bitterness, that he could run in all the races for which his ex-owner had already entered him.

46

"Where is he entered?" I asked.

"Oh, dozens of places, I think—Newbury, Cheltenham, Sandown, and so on—and he was going to start next week at Bristol." The lad's face twisted with regret as he passed the halter rope into my hand. "I can't think what on earth persuaded the Old Man to part with him. He's a real daisy, and if I ever see him at the races not looking as good and well cared for as he does now, I'll find you and beat the living daylights out of you, I will straight."

I had already discovered how deeply attached racing lads became to the horses they looked after, and I understood that he meant what he said.

"What's his name?" I asked.

"Sparking Plug . . . God-awful name, he's no plug. . . . Hey, Sparks, old boy . . . hey, boy . . . hey, old fellow . . ." He fondled the horse's muzzle affectionately.

We loaded him into the horse box and this time I did stay where I ought to be, in the back, looking after him. If Beckett was prepared to give a fortune for the cause, as I guessed he must have done to get hold of such an ideal horse in so few days, I was going to take good care of it.

Before we started back, I took a look at the road map in the cab, and found to my satisfaction that all the racecourses in the country had been marked in on it in india ink. I borrowed it at once, and spent the journey studying it. The courses where Sparking Plug's lad had said he was entered were nearly all in the south. Overnight stops, as requested. I grinned.

The five racecourses where the eleven horses had won were not, I found, all as far north as I had imagined. Ludlow and Stafford, in fact, could almost be considered southern, especially as I found I instinctively based my view of the whole country from Harrogate. The five courses seemed to bear no relation to each other on the map: far from presenting a tidy circle from which a center might be deduced, they were all more or less in a curve from northeast to southwest, and I could find no significance in their location.

I spent the rest of the journey back as I spent most of my working hours, letting my mind drift over what I knew of the eleven horses, waiting for an idea to swim to the surface like a fish in a pool, waiting for the disconnected facts to sort themselves into a pattern. But I didn't really expect this to happen yet, as I knew I had barely started, and even electronic computers won't produce answers if they are not fed enough information.

On Friday night I went down to the pub in Slaw and beat Soupy at darts. He grunted, gestured to the bar billiards, and took an easy revenge. We then drank a half pint together, eyeing each other. Conversation between us was almost nonexistent, nor was it necessary; and shortly I wandered back to watch the dart players. They were no better than the week before.

"You beat Soupy, didn't you, Dan?" one of them said.

I nodded, and immediately found a bunch of darts thrust into my hand.

"If you can beat Soupy you must be in the team."

"What team?" I asked.

"The stable darts team. We play other stables, and have sort of a Yorkshire League. Sometimes we go to Middleham or Wetherby or Richmond or sometimes they come here. Soupy's the best player in Granger's team. Could you beat him again, do you think, or was it a fluke?"

I threw three darts at the board. They all landed in the twenty. For some unknown reason I had always been able to throw straight.

"Cor," said the lads. "Go on."

I threw three more: the twenty section got rather crowded.

"You're in the team, mate, and no nonsense," they said.

"When's the next match?" I asked.

"We had one here a fortnight ago. Next one's next Sunday at Burndale, after the football. You can't play football as well as darts, I suppose?"

I shook my head. "Only darts."

48

I looked at the one dart still left in my hand. I could hit a scuttling rat with a stone; I had done it often when the men had found one around the corn bins and chased it out. I saw no reason why I couldn't hit a galloping horse with a dart: it was a much bigger target.

"Put that one in the bull," urged the lad beside me.

I put it in the bull. The lads yelled with glee.

"We'll win the league this season," they said, grinning. Grits grinned, too. But Paddy didn't.

4

October's son and daughters came home for the weekend, the elder girl in a scarlet TR-4, which I grew to know well by sight as she drove in and out past the stables, and the twins more sedately, with their father. As all three were in the habit of riding out when they were at home, Wally told me to saddle up two of my horses to go out with the first string on Saturday, Sparking Plug for me and the other for Lady Patricia Tarren.

Lady Patricia Tarren, as I discovered when I led out the horse in the half light of early dawn and held it for her to mount, was a raving beauty with a pale-pink mouth and thick curly eyelashes which she knew very well how to use. She had tied a green head scarf over her chestnut hair, and she wore a black-and-white harlequin skiing jacket to keep out the cold. She was carrying some bright-green woolen gloves.

"You're new," she observed, looking up at me through the eyelashes. "What's your name?"

"Dan . . . miss," I said. I realized I hadn't the faintest idea what form of address an earl's daughter was accustomed to. Wally's instructions hadn't stretched that far.

"Well . . . give me a leg up, then."

49

I stood beside her obediently, but as I leaned forward to help her, she ran her bare hand over my head and around my neck, and took the lobe of my right ear between her fingers. She had sharp nails, and she dug them in. Her eyes were wide with challenge. I looked straight back. When I didn't move or say anything, she presently giggled and let go and calmly put on her gloves. I gave her a leg up into the saddle and she bent down to gather the reins, and fluttered the fluffy lashes close to my face.

"You're quite a dish, aren't you, Danny boy," she said, "with those googoo dark eyes."

I couldn't think of any answer to her which was at all consistent with my position. She laughed, nudged the horse's flanks, and walked off down the yard. Her sister, mounting a horse held by Grits, looked from twenty yards away in the dim light to be much fairer in coloring and very nearly as beautiful. Heaven help October, I thought, with two like that to keep an eye on.

I turned to go and fetch Sparking Plug and found October's eighteen-year-old son at my elbow. He was very like his father, but not yet as thick in body or as easily powerful in manner.

"I shouldn't pay too much attention to my twin sister," he said in a cool, bored voice, looking me up and down. "She is apt to tease." He nodded and strolled over to where his horse was waiting for him; and I gathered that what I had received was a warning off. If his sister behaved as provocatively with every male she met, he must have been used to delivering them.

Amused, I fetched Sparking Plug, mounted, and followed all the other horses out of the yard, up the lane, and on to the edge of the moor. As usual on a fine morning, the air and the view were exhilarating. The sun was no more than a promise on the far distant horizon and there was a beginning-of-the-world quality in the light. I watched the shadowy shapes of the horses ahead of me curving around the hill with white plumes streaming from their nostrils in the frosty air. As the glittering rim of the sun expanded into full light, the colors sprang out bright and clear, the browns of the jogging horses topped with the bright stripes of the lads' ear-warming knitted caps and the jolly garments of October's daughters.

October himself, accompanied by his retriever, came up onto the moor in a Land Rover to see the horses work. Saturday morning, I had found, was the busiest training day of the week as far as gallops were concerned, and as he was usually in Yorkshire at the weekend, he made a point of coming out to watch.

Inskip had us circling around at the top of the hill while he paired off the horses and told their riders what to do.

To me he said, "Dan . . . three-quarter-speed gallop. Your horse is running on Wednesday. Don't overdo him but we want to see how he goes." He directed one of the stable's most distinguished animals to accompany me.

When he had finished giving his orders, he cantered off along the broad sweep of green turf which stretched through the moorland scrub, and October drove slowly in his wake. We continued circling until the two men reached the other end of the gallops, about a mile and a half away up the gently curved, gently rising track.

"OK," said Wally to the first pair. "Off you go."

The two horses set off together, fairly steadily at first and then at an increasing pace until they had passed Inskip and October, when they slowed and pulled up.

"Next two," Wally called.

We were ready, and set off without more ado. I had bred, broken, and rebroken uncountable race horses in Australia, but Sparking Plug was the only good one I had so far ridden in England, and I was interested to see how he compared. Of course he was a hurdler, while I was more used to flat racers, but this made no difference, I found; and he had a bad mouth which I itched to do something about, but there was nothing wrong with his action. Balanced and collected, he sped smoothly up the gallop, keeping pace effortlessly with the star performer beside him, and though, as ordered, we went only three-quarters speed at our fastest, it was quite clear that Sparking Plug was fit and ready for his approaching race.

I was so interested in what I was doing that it was not until I had reined in—not too easy with that mouth—and began to walk back that I realized I had forgotten all about messing up the way I rode. I groaned inwardly, exasperated with myself; I would never do what I had come to England for if I could so little keep my mind on the job.

I stopped with the horse who had accompanied Sparking Plug in front of October and Inskip, for them to have a look at the horses and see how much they were blowing. Sparking Plug's ribs moved easily: he was scarcely out of breath. The two men nodded, and I and the other lad slid off the horses and began walking them around while they cooled down.

Up from the far end of the gallop came the other horses, pair by pair. One of the lads in the third pair lifted his whip and gave his horse two resounding lashes on the flanks. The animal burst forward and flashed past the Land Rover at sprinting pace, pulling up with a jolt as the lad jabbed him in the mouth twenty yards farther on.

October yelled at him to come back and gave him the completest dressing down I had ever heard. His voice carried clearly in the frosty air. His body shook with anger as he gesticulated with his arms to ram home his disapproval. The lads leading their horses around with me grinned slyly at each other and winked.

One, coming alongside for a moment, said reflectively, "Always like that, his lordship is, if you touch one of his horses unnecessary like. You wouldn't think it, would you? I shouldn't give any of his horses a clout, if I was you."

"I won't," I said.

"Got a temper like a volcano, he has, if you hurt one of his horses."

"I'll remember that," I said. "Thanks for telling me."

He nodded and walked on. October finished his tirade and the dejected lad began to walk alone back to the stable, leading his horse. The show was over. The paired gallops went on as before, finishing with a bunch who weren't ready for anything faster than a canter.

When everyone had worked, most of the lads remounted and we all began to walk back down the gallop toward the track to the stable. Leading my horse on foot, I set off last in the string, with October's elder daughter riding immediately in front of me and effectively cutting me off from the chat of the lads ahead. She was looking about her at the rolling vistas of moor, and not bothering to keep her animal close on the heels of the one in front, so that by the time we entered the track, there was a ten-yard gap ahead of her.

As she passed a scrubby gorse bush, a bird flew out of it with a squawk and flapping wings, and the girl's horse whipped around and up in alarm. She stayed on with a remarkable effort of balance, pulling herself back up into the saddle from somewhere below the horse's right ear, but under her thrust the stirrup leather broke apart at the bottom, and the stirrup iron itself clanged to the ground.

I stopped and picked up the iron, but it was impossible to put it back on the broken leather.

"Thank you," she said. "What a nuisance."

She slid off her horse. "I might as well walk the rest of the way."

I took her rein and began to lead both of the horses, but she stopped me, and took her own back again.

"It's very kind of you," she said, "but I can quite well lead him myself." The track was wide at that point, and she began to walk down the hill beside me.

On closer inspection she was not a bit like her sister, Patricia. She had smooth silver-blond hair under a blue head scarf, fair eyelashes, direct gray eyes, a firm, friendly mouth, and a composure which gave her an air of graceful reserve. We walked in easy silence for some way.

"Isn't it a gorgeous morning," she said eventually.

"Gorgeous," I agreed, "but cold." The English always talk about the weather, I thought; and a fine day in November is so rare as to be remarked on. It would be hotting up for summer, at home. . . .

"Have you been with the stable long?" she asked, a little farther on.

"Only about ten days."

"And do you like it here?"

"Oh, yes. It's a well-run stable."

"Mr. Inskip would be delighted to hear you say so," she said in a dry voice.

I glanced at her, but she was looking ahead down the track, and smiling.

After another hundred yards she said, "What horse is that that you were riding? I don't think that I have seen him before, either."

"He only came on Wednesday. . . ." I told her the little I knew about Sparking Plug's history, capabilities, and prospects.

She nodded. "It will be nice for you if he can win some races. Rewarding, after your work for him here."

"Yes," I agreed, surprised that she should think like that.

We reached the last stretch to the stable.

"I am so sorry," she said pleasantly, "but I don't know your name."

"Daniel Roke," I said; and I wondered why to her alone of all the people who had asked me that question in the last ten days it had seemed proper to give a whole answer.

"Thank you." She paused; then, having thought, continued in a calm voice which I realized with wry pleasure was designed to put me at my ease. "Lord October is my father. I'm Elinor Tarren."

We had reached the stable gate. I stood back to let her go in first, which she acknowledged with a friendly but impersonal smile, and she led her horse away across the yard toward its own box. A thoroughly nice girl, I thought briefly, buckling down to the task of brushing the sweat off Sparking Plug, washing his feet, brushing out his mane and tail, sponging out his eyes and mouth, putting his straw bed straight, fetching his hay and water, and then repeating the whole process with the horse that Patricia had ridden. Patricia, I thought, grinning, was not a nice girl at all.

54

When I went in to breakfast in the cottage, Mrs. Alnutt gave me a letter which had just arrived for me. The envelope, postmarked in London the day before, contained a sheet of plain paper with a single sentence typed on it:

Mr. Stanley will be at Victoria Falls 3 P.M. Sunday.

I stuffed the letter into my pocket, laughing into my porridge.

There was a heavy drizzle falling when I walked up beside the stream the following afternoon. I reached the gully before October, and waited for him with the raindrops finding ways to trickle down my neck. He came down the hill with his dog as before, telling me that his car was parked above us on the little-used road.

"But we'd better talk here, if you can stand the wet," he finished, "in case anyone saw us together in the car, and wondered."

"I can stand the wet," I assured him, smiling.

"Good . . . Well, how have you been getting on?"

I told him how well I thought of Beckett's new horse and the opportunities it would give me.

He nodded. "Roddy Beckett was famous in the war for the speed and accuracy with which he got supplies moved about. No one ever got the wrong ammunition or all left boots when he was in charge."

I said, "I've sown a few seeds of doubts about my honesty, here and there, but I'll be able to do more of that this week at Bristol, and also next weekend, at Burndale. I'm going there on Sunday to play in a darts match."

"They've had several cases of doping in that village in the past," he said thoughtfully. "You might get a nibble there."

"It would be useful. . . ."

"Have you found the form books helpful?" he asked. "Have you given those eleven horses any more thought?"

"I've thought of little else," I said, "and it seems just possible . . . perhaps it's only a slight chance, but

55

it does seem possible that you might be able to make a dope test on the next horse in the sequence *before* he runs in a race. That is to say, always providing that there is going to be another horse in the sequence . . . and I don't see why not, as the people responsible have got away with it for so long."

He looped at me with some excitement, the rain dripping off the overturned brim of his hat.

"You've found something?"

"No, not really. It's only a statistical indication. But it's more than even money, I think, that the next horse will win a selling chase at Kelso, Sedgefield, Ludlow, Stafford, or Haydock." I explained my reasons for expecting this, and went on, "It should be possible to arrange for wholesale saliva samples to be taken before all the selling chases on those particular tracks—it can't be more than one race at each two-day meeting—and they can throw the samples away without going to the expense of testing them if no . . . er . . . joker turns up in the pack."

"It's a tall order," he said slowly, "but I don't see why it shouldn't be done, if it will prove anything."

"The analysts might find something useful in the results."

"Yes. And I suppose even if they didn't, it would be a great step forward for us to be able to be on the lookout for a joker, instead of just being mystified when one appeared. Why on earth"—he shook his head in exasperation—"didn't we think of this months ago? It seems such an obvious way to approach the problem, now that you have done it."

"I expect it is because I am the first person really to be given all the collected information all at once, and deliberately search for a connecting factor. All the other investigations seemed to have been done from the other end, so to speak, by trying to find out in each case separately who had access to the horse, who fed him, who saddled him, and so on."

He nodded gloomily.

"There's one other thing," I said. "The lab chaps told you that since they couldn't find dope you should look for something mechanical. . . . Do you know whether the horses' skins were investigated as closely as the jockeys and their kit? It occurred to me the other evening that I could throw a dart with an absolute certainty of hitting a horse's flank, and any good shot could plant a pellet in the same place. Things like that would sting like a hornet . . . enough to make any horse shift along faster."

"As far as I know, none of the horses showed any signs of that sort of thing, but I'll make sure. And by the way, I asked the analysts whether horses' bodies could break drugs down into harmless substances, and they said it was impossible."

"Well, that clears the decks a bit, if nothing else."

"Yes." He whistled to his dog, who was quartering the far side of the gully. "After next week, when you'll be away at Burndale, we had better meet here at this time every Sunday afternoon to discuss progress. You will know if I'm away, because I won't be here for the Saturday gallops. Incidentally, your horsemanship stuck out a mile on Sparking Plug yesterday. And I thought we agreed that you had better not make too good an impression. On top of which," he added, smiling faintly, "Inskip says you are a quick and conscientious worker."

"Heck . . . I'll be getting a good reference if I don't watch out."

"Too right you will," he agreed, copying my accent sardonically. "How do you like being a stable lad?"

"It has its moments. . . . Your daughters are very beautiful."

He grinned. "Yes; and thank you for helping Elinor. She told me you were most obliging."

"I did nothing."

"Patty is a bit of a handful," he said reflectively. "I wish she'd decide what sort of job she'd like to do. She knows I don't want her to go on as she has during her season, never-ending parties and staying out till dawn . . . Well, that's not your worry, Mr. Roke."

We shook hands as usual, and he trudged off up the hill. It was still drizzling mournfully as I went down.

57

Sparking Plug duly made the 250-mile journey south to Bristol, and I went with him. The racecourse was some way out of the city, and the horse-box driver told me, when we stopped for a meal on the way, that the whole of the stable block had been newly rebuilt there after fire had gutted it.

Certainly the loose boxes were clean and snug, but it was the new sleeping quarters that the lads were in ecstasies about. The hostel was a surprise to me, too. It consisted mainly of a recreation room and two long dormitories with about thirty beds in each, made up with clean sheets and fluffy blue blankets. There was a wall light over each bed, vinyl-tile flooring, under-floor heating, modern showers in the washroom, and a hot room for drying wet clothes. The whole place was warm and light, with color schemes which were clearly the work of a professional.

"Ye gods, we're in the ruddy Hilton," said one cheerful boy, coming to a halt beside me just through the dormitory door and slinging his canvas grip onto an unoccupied bed.

"You haven't seen the half of it," said a bony, long-wristed boy in a shrunken blue jersey. "Up that end of the passage there's a ruddy great canteen with decent chairs and a telly and a Ping-Pong table and all."

Other voices joined in.

"It's as good as Newbury."

"Easily."

"Better than Ascot, I'd say."

Heads nodded.

"They have bunk beds at Ascot, not singles, like this."

The hostels at Newbury and Ascot were, it appeared, the most comfortable in the country.

"Anyone would think the bosses had suddenly cottoned on to the fact that we're human," said a sharp-faced lad, in a belligerent, rabble-rousing voice.

"It's a far cry from the bug-ridden doss houses of the old days," nodded a desiccated, elderly little man with a face like a shrunken apple. "But a fellow told

58

me the lads have it good like this in America all the time."

"They know if they don't start treating us decent they soon won't get anyone to do the dirty work," said the rabble-rouser. "Things are changing."

"They treat us decent enough where I come from," I said, putting my things on an empty bed next to his and nerving myself to be natural, casual, unremarkable. I felt much more self-conscious than I had at Slaw, where at least I knew the job inside out and had been able to feel my way cautiously into a normal relationship with the other lads. But here I had only two nights, and if I was to do any good at all, I had to direct the talk toward what I wanted to hear.

The form books were by now as clear to me as a primer, and for a fortnight I had listened acutely and concentrated on soaking in as much racing jargon as I could, but I was still doubtful whether I would understand everything I heard at Bristol and also afraid that I would make some utterly incongruous, impossible mistake in what I said myself.

"And where do you come from?" asked the cheerful boy, giving me a cursory looking over.

"Lord October's," I said.

"Oh, yes . . . Inskip's, you mean? You're a long way from home."

"Inskip's may be all right," said the rabble-rouser, as if he regretted it. "But there are some places where they still treat us like mats to wipe their feet on, and don't reckon that we've got a right to a bit of sun, same as everyone else."

"Yeah," said the rawboned boy seriously. "I heard that at one place they practically starve the lads and knock them about if they don't work hard enough, and they all have to do about four or five horses each because they can't keep anyone in the yard for more than five minutes!"

I said idly, "Where's that? Just so I know where to avoid, if I ever move on from Inskip's."

"Up your part of the country," he said doubtfully, "I think."

59

"No, farther north, in Durham," another boy chimed in, a slender pretty boy with a soft down still growing on his cheeks.

"You know about it, too, then?"

He nodded. "Not that it matters; only a raving nit would take a job there. It's a blooming sweatshop, a hundred years out of date. All they get are riffraff that no one else will have."

"It wants exposing," said the rabble-rouser belligerently. "Who runs this place?"

"Bloke called Humber," said the pretty boy. "He couldn't train ivy up a wall . . . and he has about as many winners as tits on a billiard ball. You see his head traveling lad at the meetings sometimes, trying to press-gang people to go and work there, and getting the brush-off, right and proper."

"Someone ought to do something," said the rabble-rouser automatically; and I guessed that this was his usual refrain: "Someone ought to do something"; but not, when it came to the point, himself.

There was a general drift into the canteen, where the food proved to be good, unlimited, and free. A proposal to move on to a pub came to nothing when it was discovered both that the nearest was nearly two (busless) miles away and that the bright, warm canteen had some crates of beer under its counter.

It was easy enough to get the lads started on the subject of doping, and they seemed prepared to discuss it endlessly. None of the twenty-odd there had ever, as far as they would admit, given "anything" to a horse, but they all knew someone who knew someone who had. I drank my beer and listened and looked interested, which I was.

". . . nobbled him with a squirt of acid as he walked out of the bleeding paddock . . ."

". . . gave it such a whacking dollop of stopping powder that it died in its box in the morning . . ."

"Seven rubber bands came out in the droppings . . ."

". . . overdosed him so much that he never even tried to jump the first fence: blind, he was, stone blind . . ."

". . . gave him a bloody great bucketful of water

60

half an hour before the race, and didn't need any dope to stop him with all that sloshing about inside his gut."

". . . poured half a bottle of whiskey down his throat . . ."

". . . used to tube horses that couldn't breathe properly on the morning of the race until they found it wasn't the extra fresh air that was making the horses win but the cocaine they stuffed them full of for the operation . . ."

"They caught him with a hollow apple packed with sleeping pills . . ."

". . . dropped a syringe right in front of an effing steward."

"I wonder if there's anything which hasn't been tried yet," I said.

"Black magic. Not much else left," said the pretty boy.

They all laughed.

"Someone might find something so good," I pointed out casually, "that it couldn't be detected, so the people who thought of it could go on with it forever and never be found out."

"Blimy," exclaimed the cheerful lad, "you're a comfort, aren't you? God help racing, if that happened. You'd never know where you were. The bookies would all be climbing the walls." He grinned hugely.

The elderly little man was not so amused.

"It's been going on for years and years," he said, nodding solemnly. "Some trainers have got it to a fine art, you mark my words. Some trainers have been doping their horses regular, for years and years."

But the other lads didn't agree. The dope tests had done for the dope-minded trainers of the past; they had lost their licenses, and gone out of racing. The old rule had been a bit unfair on some, they allowed, when a trainer had been automatically disqualified if one of his horses had been doped. It wasn't always the trainer's fault, especially if the horse had been doped to lose. What trainer, they asked, would nobble a horse he'd spent months training to win? But they thought there was probably *more* doping since that rule was changed, not less.

Stands to reason, a doper knows now he isn't ruining the trainer for life, just one horse for one race. Makes it sort of easier on his conscience, see? More lads, maybe, would take fifty quid for popping the odd aspirin into the feed if they knew the stable wouldn't be shut down and their jobs gone for a burton very soon afterward."

They talked on, thoughtful and ribald; but it was clear that they didn't know anything about the eleven horses I was concerned with. None of them, I knew, came from any of the stables involved, and obviously they had not read the speculative reports in the papers, or if they had, had read them seperately over a period of eighteen months, and not in one solid, collected, intense bunch, as I had done.

The talk faltered and died into yawns, and we went chatting to bed, I sighing to myself with relief that I had gone through the evening without much notice having been taken of me.

By watching carefully what the other lads did, I survived the next day also without any curious stares. In the early afternoon I took Sparking Plug from the stables into the paddock, walked him around the parade ring, stood holding his head while he was saddled, led him around the parade ring again, held him while the jockey mounted, led him out onto the course, and went up into the little stand by the gate with the other lads to watch the race.

Sparking Plug won. I was delighted. I met him again at the gate and led him into the spacious winner's unsaddling enclosure.

Colonel Beckett was there, waiting, leaning on a stick. He patted the horse and congratulated the jockey, who unbuckled his saddle and departed into the weighing room. Beckett said to me sardonically, "That's a fraction of his purchase price back, anyway."

"He's a good horse, and absolutely perfect for his purpose."

"Good. Do you need anything else?"

"Yes. A lot more details about those eleven horses

. . . where they were bred, what they ate, whether they had had any illnesses, what cafés their box drivers used, who made their bridles, whether they had racing plates fitted at meetings, and by which blacksmiths . . . anything and everything."

"Are you serious?"

"Yes."

"But they had nothing in common except that they were doped."

"As I see it, the question really is what was it that they had in common that made it *possible* for them to be doped." I smoothed Sparking Plug's nose. He was restive and excited after his victory. Colonel Beckett looked at me with sober eyes.

"Mr. Roke, you shall have your information."

I grinned at him. "Thank you; and I'll take good care of Sparking Plug. . . . He'll win you all the purchase price, before he's finished."

"Horses away," called an official; and with a weak-looking gesture of farewell from Colonel Beckett's limp hand, I took Sparking Plug back to the racecourse stables and walked him around until he had cooled off.

There were far more lads in the hostel that evening, as it was the middle night of the two-day meeting, and this time, besides getting the talk around again to doping and listening attentively to everything that was said, I also tried to give the impression that I didn't think taking fifty quid to point out a certain horse's box in his home stable to anyone prepared to pay that much for the information was a proposition I could be relied on to turn down. I earned a good few disapproving looks for this, and also one sharply interested glance from a very short lad whose outsize nose sniffed monotonously.

In the washroom in the morning, he used the basin next to me, and said out of the side of his mouth, "Did you mean it, last night, that you'd take fifty quid to point out a box?"

I shrugged. "I don't see why not."

He looked around furtively. It made me want to laugh.

"I might be able to put you in touch with someone who'd be interested to hear that—for a fifty-percent cut."

"You've got another think coming," I said offensively. "Fifty percent . . . what the hell do you think I am?"

"Well . . . a fiver, then," he sniffed, climbing down.

"I dunno . . ."

"I can't say fairer than that," he muttered.

"It's a wicked thing, to point out a box," I said virtuously, drying my face on a towel.

He stared at me in astonishment.

"And I couldn't do it for less than sixty, if you are taking a fiver out of it."

He didn't know whether to laugh or spit. I left him to his indecision, and went off grinning to escort Sparking Plug back to Yorkshire.

5

Again on Friday evening I went down to the Slaw pub and exchanged bug-eyed looks with Soupy across the room.

On the Sunday, half the lads had the afternoon off to go to Burndale for the football and darts matches, and we won both, which made for a certain amount of back slapping and beer drinking. But beyond remarking that I was new, and a blight on their chances in the darts league, the Burndale lads paid me little attention. There was no one like Soupy among them in spite of what October had said about the cases of doping in the village, and no one, as far as I could see, who cared if I were as crooked as a corkscrew.

During the next week I did my three horses, and read the form books, and thought . . . and got nowhere. Paddy remained cool and so did Wally, to whom Paddy had obviously reported my affinity with Soupy. Wally showed his disapproval by giving me more than my share of the afternoon jobs, so that every day, instead of relaxing in the usual free time between lunch and evening stables at four o'clock, I found myself bidden to sweep the yard, clean the tack, crush the oats, cut the chaff, wash Inskip's car, or clean the windows of the loose boxes. I did it all without comment, reflecting that if I needed an excuse for a quick row and walked out later on, I could reasonably, at eleven hours a day, complain of overwork.

However, at Friday midday I set off again with Sparking Plug, this time to Cheltenham, and this time accompanied not only by the box driver but by Grits and his horse, and the head traveling lad as well.

Once in the racecourse stables, I learned that this was the night of the dinner given to the previous season's champion jockey, and all the lads who were staying there overnight proposed to celebrate by attending a dance in the town. Grits and I, therefore, having bedded down our horses, eaten our meal, and smartened ourselves up, caught a bus down the hill and paid our entrance money to the hop. It was a big hall and the band was loud and hot, but not many people were yet dancing. The girls were standing about in little groups eyeing larger groups of young men, and I bit back just in time a remark on how odd I found it; Grits would expect me to think it normal. I took him off into the bar, where there were already groups of lads from the racecourse mingled with the local inhabitants, and bought him a beer, regretting that he was with me to see what use I intended to make of the evening. Poor Grits: he was torn between loyalty to Paddy and an apparent liking for me, and I was about to disillusion him thoroughly. I wished I could explain. I was tempted to spend the evening harmlessly. But how could I justify passing over an unrepeatable opportunity just to keep temporarily the regard of one slow-witted stable lad, however much I might like him? I was committed to earning ten thousand pounds.

"Grits, go and find a girl to dance with."

He gave me a slow grin. "I don't know any."

65

"It doesn't matter. Any of them would be glad to dance with a nice chap like you. Go and ask one."

"No. I'd rather stay with you."

"All right, then. Have another drink."

"I haven't finished this."

I turned around to the bar, which we had been leaning against, and banged my barely touched half pint down on the counter. "I'm fed up with this pap," I said violently. "Hey, you, barman, give me a double whiskey."

"Dan!" Grits was upset by my tone, which was a measure of its success. The barman poured the whiskey and took my money.

"Don't go away," I said to him in a loud voice. "Give me another while you're at it."

I felt rather than saw the group of lads farther up the bar turn around and take a look, so I picked up the glass and swallowed all the whiskey in two gulps and wiped my mouth on the back of my hand. I pushed the empty glass across to the barman and paid for the second drink.

"Dan." Grits tugged my sleeve. "Do you think you should?"

"Yes," I said, scowling. "Go and find a girl to dance with."

But he didn't go. He watched me drink the second whiskey and order a third. His eyes were troubled.

The bunch of lads edged toward us along the bar.

"Hey, fella, you're knocking it back a bit," observed one, a tallish man of my own age in a flashy bright-blue suit.

"Mind your own ruddy business," I said rudely.

"Aren't you from Inskip's?" he asked.

"Yeah . . . Inskip's . . . bloody Inskip's . . . ." I picked up the third glass. I had a hard head for whiskey, which was going down on top of a deliberately heavy meal. I reckoned I could stay sober a long time after I would be expected to be drunk; but the act had to be put on early, while the audience were still sober enough themselves to remember it clearly afterward.

"Eleven sodding quid," I told them savagely. "That's all you get for sweating your guts out seven days a week."

66

It struck a note with some of them, but Blue Suit said, "Then why spend it on whiskey?"

"Why bloody not? It's great stuff—gives you a kick. And, by God, you need something in this job."

Blue Suit said to Grits, "Your mate's got an outsized gripe."

"Well . . ." said Grits, his face anxious, "I suppose he has had a lot of extra jobs this week, come to think—"

"You're looking after horses they pay thousands for and you know damn well that the way you ride and groom them and look after them makes a hell of a lot of difference to whether they win or not, and they grudge you a decent wage. . . ." I finished the third whiskey, hiccuped, and said, "It's bloody unfair."

The bar was filling up, and from the sight of them and from what I could catch of their greetings to each other, at least half the customers were in some way connected with racing. Bookmakers' clerks and touts as well as stable lads—the town was stuffed with them, and the dance had been put on to attract them. A large amount of liquor began disappearing down their collective throats, and I had to catch the barman on the wing to serve my fourth double whiskey in fifteen minutes.

I stood facing a widening circle with the glass in my hand, and rocked slightly on my feet.

"I want . . ." I began. What on earth did I want? I searched for the right phrases. "I want . . . a motor bike. I want to show a bird a good time. And go abroad for a holiday . . . and stay in a swank hotel and have them running about at my beck and call . . . and drink what I like . . . and maybe one day put a deposit on a house—and what chance do I have of any of these? I'll tell you. Not a snowball's hope in hell. You know what I got in my pay envelope this morning? Seven pounds and fourpence . . ."

I went on and on, grousing and complaining, and the evening wore slowly away. The audience drifted and changed, and I kept it up until I was fairly sure that all the racing people there knew there was a lad of Inskip's who yearned for more money, preferably in large amounts. But even Grits, who hovered about with an unhappy air throughout it all and remained cold sober himself, didn't seem to notice that I got progressively drunker in my actions while making each drink last longer than the one before.

Eventually, after I had achieved an artistic lurch and clutch at one of the pillars, Grits said loudly in my ear, "Dan, I'm going now and you'd better go, too, or you'll miss the last bus, and I shouldn't think you could walk back, like you are."

"Huh?" I squinted at him. Blue Suit had come back and was standing just behind him.

"Want any help getting him out?" he asked Grits.

Grits looked at me disgustedly, and I fell against him, putting my arm around his shoulders. I definitely did not want the sort of help Blue Suit looked as though he might give.

"Grits, me old pal, if you say go, we go."

We set off for the door, followed by Blue Suit, me staggering so heavily that I pushed Grits sideways. There were by this time, I noticed, a lot of others having difficulty in walking a straight line, and the queue of lads that waited at the bus stop undulated slightly like an ocean swell on a calm day. I grinned in the safe darkness and looked up at the sky, and thought that if the seeds I had sown in all directions bore no fruit, there was little doping going on in British racing.

I may not have been drunk, but I woke the next morning with a shattering headache, just the same: all in a good cause, I thought, trying to ignore the blacksmith behind my eyes.

Sparking Plug ran in his race and lost by half a length. I took the opportunity of saying aloud on the lads' stand that there was the rest of my week's pay gone down the bloody drain.

Colonel Beckett patted his horse's neck in the cramped unsaddling enclosure and said casually to me, "Better luck next time, eh? I've sent you what you wanted, in a parcel." He turned away and resumed talking to Inskip and his jockey about the race.

We went all the way back to Yorkshire that night,

with Grits and me sleeping most of the way on the benches in the back of the horse box.

He said reproachfully, as he lay down, "I didn't know you hated it at Inskip's . . . and I haven't seen you drunk before, either."

"It isn't the work, Grits, it's the pay." I had to keep it up.

"Still there are some who are married and have kids to keep on what you were bleating about." He sounded disapproving, and indeed my behavior must have affected him deeply, because he seldom spoke to me after that night.

There was nothing of interest to report to October the following afternoon, and our meeting in the gully was brief. He told me, however, that the information then in the mail from Beckett had been collected by eleven keen young officer cadets from Aldershot who had been given the task as an initiative exercise and told they were in competition with each other to see which of them could produce the most comprehensive report of the life of his allotted horse. A certain number of questions—those I had suggested—were outlined for them. The rest had been left to their own imagination and detective ability, and October said Beckett had told him they had used them to the full.

I returned down the hill more impressed than ever with the colonel's staff work, but not as staggered as when the parcel arrived the following day. Wally again found some wretched job for me to do in the afternoon, so that it was not until after the evening meal, when half the lads had gone down to Slaw, that I had an opportunity of taking the package up to the dormitory and opening it. It contained 237 numbered typewritten pages bound into a cardboard folder, like the manuscript of a book, and its production in the space of one week must have meant a prodigious effort not only from the young men themselves, but from the typists as well. The information was given in note form for the most part, and no space had anywhere been wasted in flowing prose: it was solid detail from cover to cover.

Mrs. Alnutt's voice floated up the stairs. "Dan, come down and fetch me a bucket of coal, will you, please?"

I thrust the typescript down inside my bed between the sheets, and went back to the warm communal kitchen-living room where we ate and spent most of our spare time. It was impossible to read anything private there, and my life was very much supervised from dawn to bedtime; and the only place I could think of where I could concentrate uninterruptedly on the typescript was the bathroom. Accordingly that night I waited until all the lads were asleep, and then went along the passage and locked myself in, ready to report an upset stomach if anyone should be curious.

It was slow going: after four hours I had read only half. I got up stiffly, stretched, yawned, and went back to bed. Nobody stirred. The following night, as I lay waiting for the others to go to sleep so that I could get back at my task, I listened to them discussing the evening that four of them had spent in Slaw.

"Who's that fellow who was with Soupy?" asked Grits. "I haven't seen him around before."

"He was there last night, too," said one of the others. "Queer sort of bloke."

"What was queer about him?" asked the boy who had stayed behind, watching television while I in an armchair caught up on some sleep.

"I dunno," said Grits. "His eyes didn't stay still, like."

"Sort of as if he was looking for someone," added another voice.

Paddy said firmly from the wall on my right, "You just all keep clear of that chap, and Soupy, too. I'm telling you. People like them are no good."

"But that chap, that one with that smashing gold tie, he bought us a round, you know he did. He can't be too bad if he bought us a round. . . ."

Paddy sighed with exasperation that anyone could be so simple. "If you'd have been Eve, you'd have eaten the apple as soon as look at it. You wouldn't have needed a serpent."

"Oh, well," yawned Grits. "I don't suppose he'll be

there tomorrow. I heard him say something to Soupy about time getting short."

They muttered and murmured and went to sleep, and I lay awake in the dark thinking that perhaps I had just heard something very interesting indeed. Certainly a trip down to the pub was indicated for the following evening.

With a wrench I stopped my eyes from shutting, got out of my warm bed, repaired again to the bathroom, and read for another four hours until I had finished the typescript. I sat on the bathroom floor with my back against the wall and stared sightlessly at the fixtures and fittings. There was nothing, not one single factor, that occurred in the life histories of all of the eleven microscopically investigated horses. No common denominator at all. There were quite a few things that were common to four or five—but not often the same four or five—like the make of saddle their jockeys used, the horse cube nuts they were fed with, or the auction rings they had been sold in; but the hopes I had had of finding a sizable clue in those packages had altogether evaporated. Cold, stiff, and depressed, I crept back to bed.

The next evening at eight I walked alone down to Slaw, all the other lads saying they were skint until payday and that in any case they wanted to watch Z *Cars* on television.

"I thought you lost all your cash on Sparks at Cheltenham," observed Grits.

"I've about two bob left," I said, producing some pennies. "Enough for a pint."

The pub, as often on Wednesdays, was empty. There was no sign of Soupy or his mysterious friend, and having bought some beer, I amused myself at the dart board, throwing one-to-twenty sequences, and trying to make a complete ring in the trebles. Eventually I pulled the darts out of the board, looked at my watch, and decided I had wasted the walk; and it was at that moment that a man appeared in the doorway, not from the street but from the saloon bar next door. He held a glass of gently fizzling amber liquid and a slim cigar in his left

71

hand and pushed open the door with his right. Looking me up and down, he said, "Are you a stable lad?"

"Yes."

"Granger's or Inskip's?"

"Inskip's."

"Hmm." He came farther into the room and let the door swing shut behind him. "There's ten bob for you if you can get one of your lads down here tomorrow night . . . and as much beer as you can both drink."

I looked interested. "Which lad?" I asked. "Any special one? Lots of them will be down here on Friday."

"Well, now, it had better be tomorrow, I think. Sooner the better, I always say. And as for which lad . . . er . . . you tell me their names and I'll pick one of them—how's that?"

I thought it was damn stupid, and also that he wished to avoid asking too directly, too memorably for . . . well . . . for me?

"O.K. Paddy, Grits, Wally, Steve, Ron . . ." I paused.

"Go on," he said.

"Reg, Norman, Dave, Jeff, Dan, Mike . . ."

His eyes brightened. "Dan," he said. "That's a sensible sort of name. Bring Dan."

"I am Dan," I said.

There was an instant in which his balding scalp contracted and his eyes narrowed in annoyance.

"Stop playing games," he said sharply.

"It was you," I pointed out gently, "who began it."

He sat down on one of the benches and carefully put his drink down on the table in front of him.

"Why did you come here tonight, alone?" he asked.

"I was thirsty."

There was a brief silence while he mentally drew up a plan of campaign. He was a short, stocky man in a dark suit a size too small, the jacket hanging open to reveal a monogrammed cream shirt and golden silk tie. His fingers were fat and short, and a roll of flesh overhung his coat collar at the back, but there was nothing soft in the way he looked at me.

At length he said, "I believe there is a horse in your stable called Sparking Plug?"

"Yes."

"And he runs at Leicester on Monday?"

"As far as I know."

"What do you think his chances are?" he asked.

"Look, do you want a tip, mister, is that what it is? Well, I do Sparking Plug myself and I'm telling you there isn't an animal in next Monday's race to touch him."

"So you expect him to win?"

"Yea, I told you."

"And you'll bet on him, I suppose."

"Of course."

"With half your pay? Four pounds, perhaps?"

"Maybe."

"But he'll be favorite. Sure to be. And at best you'll probably only get even money. Another four quid. That doesn't sound much, does it, when I could perhaps put you in the way of winning . . . a hundred?"

"You're barmy," I said, but with a sideways leer that told him that I wanted to hear more.

He leaned forward with confidence. "Now, you can say no if you want to. You can say no, and I'll go away, and no one will be any the wiser, but if you play your cards right, I could do you a good turn."

"What would I have to do for a hundred quid?" I asked flatly.

He looked around cautiously, and lowered his voice still further. "Just add a little something to Sparking Plug's feed on Sunday night. Nothing to it, you see? Dead easy."

"Dead easy," I repeated; and so it was.

"You're on, then?" He looked eager.

"I don't know your name," I said.

"Never you mind." He shook his head with finality.

"Are you a bookmaker?"

"No," he said. "I'm not. And that's enough with the questions. Are you on?"

"If you're not a bookmaker," I said slowly, thinking my way, "and you are willing to pay a hundred pounds to make sure a certain favorite doesn't win, I'd guess that you didn't want just to make money backing all

73

the other runners, but that you intend to tip off a few bookmakers that the race is fixed, and they'll be so grateful they'll pay you say, fifty quid each, at the very least. There are about eleven thousand bookmakers in Britain. A nice big market. But I expect you go to the same ones over and over again. Sure of your welcome, I should think."

His face was a study of consternation and disbelief, and I realized I had hit the target, bang on.

"Who told you . . ." he began weakly.

"I wasn't born yesterday," I said with a nasty grin. "Relax. No one told me." I paused. "I'll give Sparking Plug his extra nosh, but I want more for it. Two hundred."

"No. The deal's off." He mopped his forehead.

"All right." I shrugged.

"A hundred and fifty then," he said grudgingly.

"A hundred and fifty," I agreed. "Before I do it."

"Half before, half after," he said automatically. It was by no means the first time he had done this sort of deal.

I agreed to that. He said if I came down to the pub on Saturday evening I would be given a packet for Sparking Plug and seventy-five pounds for myself, and I nodded and went away, leaving him staring moodily into his glass.

On my way back up the hill I crossed Soupy off my list of potentially useful contacts. Certainly he had procured me for a doping job, but I had been asked to stop a favorite in a novice 'chase, not to accelerate a dim long-priced selling plater. It was extremely unlikely that both types of fraud were the work of one set of people.

Unwilling to abandon Colonel Beckett's typescript, I spent chunks of that night and the following two nights in the bathroom, carefully rereading it. The only noticeable result was that during the day I found the endless stable work irksome because for five nights in a row I had had only three hours' sleep. But I frankly dreaded having to tell October on Sunday that the eleven young men had made their mammoth investigation to

74

no avail, and I had an unreasonable feeling that if I hammered away long enough, I could still wring some useful message from those densely packed pages.

On Saturday morning, though it was bleak, bitter, and windy, October's daughters rode out with the first string. Elinor only came near enough to exchange polite good mornings, but Patty, who was again riding one of my horses, made my giving her a leg up a moment of eyelash-fluttering intimacy, deliberately and unnecessarily rubbing her body against mine.

"You weren't here last week, Danny boy," she said, putting her feet in the irons. "Where were you?"

"At Cheltenham . . . miss."

"Oh. And next Saturday?"

"I'll be here."

She said, with intentional insolence, "Then kindly remember next Saturday to shorten the leathers on the saddle before I mount. These are far too long."

She made no move to shorten them herself, but gestured for me to do it for her. She watched me steadily, enjoying herself. While I was fastening the second buckle, she rubbed her knee forward over my hands and kicked me none too gently in the ribs.

"I wonder you stand me teasing you, Danny boy," she said softly, bending down. "A dishy guy like you should answer back more. Why don't you?"

"I don't want the sack," I said, with a dead straight face.

"A coward, too," she said sardonically, and twitched her horse away.

And she'll get into bad trouble one day, if she keeps on like that, I thought. She was too provocative. Stunningly pretty, of course, but that was only the beginning; and her hurtful little tricks were merely annoying. It was the latent invitation which disturbed and aroused.

I shrugged her out of my mind, fetched Sparking Plug, sprang up onto his back, and moved out of the yard and up to the moor for the routine working gallops.

The weather that day got steadily worse until while we were out with the second string it began to rain heavily in fierce splashing gusts, and we struggled miserably

75

back against it with stinging faces and sodden clothes. Perhaps because it went on raining, or possibly because it was, after all, Saturday, Wally for once refrained from making me work all afternoon, and I spent the three hours sitting with about nine other lads in the kitchen of the cottage, listening to the wind shrieking around the corners outside and watching Chepstow races on television, while our damp jerseys, breeches, and socks steamed gently around the fire.

I put the previous season's form book on the kitchen table and sat over it with my head propped on the knuckles of my left hand, idly turning the pages with my right. Depressed by my utter lack of success with the eleven horses' dossiers, by the antipathy I had to arouse in the lads, and also, I think, by the absence of the hot sunshine I usually lived in at that time of the year, I began to feel that the whole masquerade had been from the start a ghastly mistake. And the trouble was that having taken October's money, I couldn't back out; not for months. This thought depressed me further still. I sat slumped in unrelieved gloom, wasting my much-needed free time.

I think now that it must have been the sense that I was failing in what I had set out to do, more than mere tiredness, which beset me that afternoon, because although later on I encountered worse things, it was only for that short while that I ever truly regretted having listened to October, and unreservedly wished myself back in my comfortable Australian cage.

The lads watching the television were making disparaging remarks about the jockeys and striking private bets against each other on the outcome of the races.

"The uphill finish will sort 'em out as usual," Paddy was saying. "It's a long way from the end . . . Aladin's the only one who's got the stamina for the job."

"No," contradicted Grits. "Lobster Cocktail's a flier . . ."

Morosely I riffled the pages of the form book, aimlessly looking through them for the hundredth time, and came by chance on the map of Chepstow racecourse in the general-information section at the beginning of the book. There were diagrammatic maps of all the main courses, showing the shape of the tracks and the positioning of fences, stands, starting gates, and winning posts, and I had looked before at those for Ludlow, Stafford, and Haydock, without results. There was no map of Kelso or Sedgefield. Next to the map section were a few pages of information about the courses, the lengths of their circuits, the names and addresses of the officials, the record times for the races, and so on.

For something to do, I turned to Chepstow's paragraph. Paddy's "long way from the end" was detailed there: 250 yards. I looked up Kelso, Sedgefield, Ludlow, Stafford, and Haydock. They had much longer run-ins than Chepstow. I looked up the run-ins of all the courses in the book. The Aintree Grand National run-in was the second longest. The longest of all was Sedgefield, and in third, fourth, fifth, and sixth positions came Ludlow, Haydock, Kelso, and Stafford. All had run-ins of over four hundred yards.

Geography had nothing to do with it: those five courses had almost certainly been chosen by the dopers because in each case it was about a quarter of a mile from the last fence to the winning post.

It was an advance, even if a small one, to have made at least some pattern out of the chaos. In a slightly less abysmal frame of mind, I shut the form book and at four o'clock followed the other lads out into the unwelcome rain-swept yard to spend an hour with each of my three charges, grooming them thoroughly to give their coats a clean, healthy shine, tossing and tidying their straw beds, fetching their water, holding their heads while Inskip walked around, rugging them up comfortably for the night, and finally fetching their evening feed. As usual it was seven before we had all finished, and eight before we had eaten and changed and were bumping down the hill to Slaw, seven of us sardined into a rickety old Austin.

Bar billiards, darts, dominoes, the endless friendly bragging, the ingredients as before. Patiently I sat and waited. It was nearly ten, the hour when the lads began to empty their glasses and think about having to get up the next morning, when Soupy strolled across the room toward the door and, seeing my eyes on him, jerked his head for me to follow him. I got up and went out after him, and found him in the lavatories.

"This is for you. The rest on Tuesday," he said economically; and treating me to a curled lip and stony stare to impress me with his toughness, he handed me a thick brown envelope. I put it in the inside pocket of my black leather jacket, and nodded to him. Still without speaking, without smiling, hard-eyed to match, I turned on my heel and went back into the bar; and after a while, casually, he followed.

So I crammed into the Austin and was driven up the hill, back to bed in the little dormitory, with seventy-five pounds and a packet of white powder sitting snugly over my heart.

6

October dipped his finger in the powder and tasted it.

"I don't know what it is either," he said, shaking his head. "I'll get it analyzed."

I bent down and patted his dog, and fondled its ears.

He said, "You do realize what a risk you'll be running if you take his money and don't give the dope to the horse?"

I grinned up at him.

"It's no laughing matter," he said seriously. "They can be pretty free with their boots, these people, and it would be no help to us if you get your ribs kicked in. . . ."

"Actually," I said, straightening up, "I do think it might be best if Sparking Plug didn't win. . . . I could hardly hope to attract custom from the dopers we are really after if they heard I had double-crossed anyone before."

"You're quite right." He sounded relieved. "Sparking Plug must lose; but Inskip . . . how on earth can I tell him that the jockey must put back?"

"You can't," I said. "You don't want them getting into trouble. But it won't matter much if I do. The horse won't win if I keep him thirsty tomorrow morning and give him a bucketful of water just before the race."

He looked at me with amusement. "I see you've learned a thing or two."

"It'd make your hair stand on end, what I've learned."

He smiled back. "All right then. I suppose it's the only thing to do. I wonder what the National Hunt Committee would think of a Steward conspiring with one of his own stable lads to stop a favorite?" He laughed. "I'll tell Roddy Beckett what to expect . . . though it won't be so funny for Inskip, nor for the lads here, if they back the horse, nor for the general public, who'll lose their money."

"No," I agreed.

He folded the packet of white powder and tucked it back into the envelope with the money. The seventy-five pounds had foolishly been paid in a bundle of new fivers with consecutive numbers; and we had agreed that October would take them and try to discover to whom they had been issued.

I told him about the long run-ins on all of the courses where the eleven horses had won.

"It almost sounds as if they might have been using vitamins after all," he said thoughtfully. "You can't detect them in dope tests because technically they are not dope at all, but food. The whole question of vitamins is very difficult."

"They increase stamina?" I asked.

"Yes, quite considerably. Horses that 'die' in the last half mile—and as you pointed out, all eleven are that type—would be ideal subjects. But vitamins were among the first things we considered, and we had to eliminate them. They can help horses to win, if they are injected in massive doses into the bloodstream, and they are undetectable in analysis because they are used up in the winning, but they are undetecable in other ways, too. They don't excite, they don't bring a horse back from a race looking as though Benzedrine were coming out of his ears." He sighed. "I don't know. . . ."

With regret I made my confession that I had learned nothing from Beckett's typescript.

"Neither Beckett nor I expected as much from it as you did," he said. "I've been talking to him a lot this week, and we think that although all those extensive inquiries were made at the time, you might find something that was overlooked if you moved to one of the stables where those eleven horses were trained when they were doped. Of course, eight of the horses were sold and have changed stables, which is a pity, but three are still with their original trainers, and it might be best if you could get a job with one of those."

"Yes," I said. "All right. I'll try all three trainers and see if one of them will take me on. But the trail is very cold by now . . . and joker number twelve will turn up in a different stable altogether. There was nothing, I suppose, at Haydock this week?"

"No. Saliva samples were taken from all the runners before the selling chase, but the favorite won quite normally, and we didn't have the samples analyzed. But now that you've spotted that those five courses must have been chosen deliberately for their long finishing straights, we will keep stricter watches there than ever. Especially if one of those eleven horses runs there again."

"You could check with the racing calendar to see if any have been entered," I agreed. "But so far none of them has been doped twice, and I can't see why the pattern should change."

A gust of bitter wind blew down the gully, and he shivered. The little stream, swollen with yesterday's rains, tumbled busily over its rocky bed. October whistled to his dog, who was sniffing along its banks.

"By the way," he said, shaking hands, "the vets are of the opinion that the horses were not helped on their way by pellets or darts, or anything shot or thrown.

But they can't be a hundred percent certain. They didn't at the time examine all the horses very closely. But if we get another one, I'll see they go over every inch looking for punctures."

"Fine." We smiled at each other and turned away. I liked him. He was imaginative and had a sense of humor to leaven the formidable big-business-executive power of his speech and manner. A tough man, I thought appreciatively; tough in mind, muscular in body, unswerving in purpose: a man of the kind to have earned an earldom, if he hadn't inherited it.

Sparking Plug had to do without his bucket of water that night and again the following morning. The box driver set off to Leicester with a pocketful of hard-earned money from the lads and their instructions to back the horse to win; and I felt a traitor.

Inskip's other horse, which had come in the box, too, was engaged in the third race, but the novice 'chase was not until the fifth race on the card, which left me free to watch the first two races as well as Sparks' own. I bought a race card and found a space on the parade-ring rails, and watched the horses for the first race being led around. Although from the form books I knew the names of a great many trainers, they were still unknown to me by sight; and accordingly, when they stood chatting with their jockeys in the ring, I tried, for interest, to identify some of them. There were only seven of them engaged in the first race: Owen, Cundell, Beeby, Cazalet, Humber. . . . Humber? What was it that I had heard about Humber? I couldn't remember. Nothing very important, I thought.

Humber's horse looked the least well of the lot, and the lad leading him around wore unpolished shoes, a dirty raincoat, and an air of not caring to improve matters. The jockey's jersey, when he took his coat off, could be seen to be still grubby with mud from a former outing, and the trainer who had failed to provide clean colors or to care about stable smartness was a large, bad-tempered-looking man leaning on a thick, knobbed walking stick.

81

As it happened, Humber's lad stood beside me on the stand to watch the race.

"Got much chance?" I asked idly.

"Waste of time running him," he said, his lip curling. "I'm fed to the back molars with the sod."

"Oh. Perhaps your other horse is better, though?" I murmured, watching the runners line up for the start.

"My other horse?" He laughed without mirth. "Three others, would you believe it? I'm fed up with the whole sodding setup. I'm packing it in at the end of the week, pay or no pay."

I suddenly remembered what I had heard about Humber. The worse stable in the country to work for, the boy in the Bristol hostel had said; they starved the lads and knocked them about and could only get riffraff to work there.

"How do you mean, pay or no pay?" I asked.

"Humber pays sixteen quid a week, instead of eleven," he said, "but it's not bloody worth it. I've had a bellyful of bloody Humber. I'm getting out."

The race started, and we watched Humber's horse finish last. The lad disappeared, muttering, to lead it away.

I smiled, followed him down the stairs, and forgot him, because waiting near the bottom step was a seedy, black-mustached man whom I instantly recognized as having been in the bar at the Cheltenham dance.

I walked slowly away to lean over the parade-ring rail, and he inconspicuously followed. He stopped beside me, and with his eyes on the one horse already in the ring, he said, "I hear that you are hard up."

"Not after today, I'm not," I said, looking him up and down.

He glanced at me briefly. "Oh. Are you so sure of Sparking Plug?"

"Yeah," I said with an unpleasant smirk. "Certain." Someone, I reflected, had been kind enough to tell him which horse I looked after; which meant he had been checking up on me. I trusted he had learned nothing to my advantage.

"Hmm."

A whole minute passed. Then he said casually, "Have you ever thought of changing your job . . . going to another stable?"

"I've thought of it," I admitted, shrugging. "Who hasn't?"

"There's always a market for good lads," he pointed out, "and I've heard you're a dab hand at the mucking out. With a reference from Inskip you could get in anywhere, if you told them you were prepared to wait for a vacancy."

"Where?" I asked; but he wasn't to be hurried. After another minute he said, still conversationally, "It can be very . . . er . . . lucrative . . . working for some stables."

"Oh?"

"That is"—he coughed discreetly—"if you are ready to do a bit more than the stable tells you to."

"Such as?"

"Oh . . . general duties," he said vaguely. "It varies. Anything helpful to . . . er . . . the person who is prepared to supplement your income."

"And who's that?"

He smiled thinly. "Look upon me as his agent. How about it? His terms are a regular fiver a week for information about the results of training gallops and things like that, and a good bonus for occasional special jobs of a more . . . er . . . risky nature."

"It don't sound bad," I said slowly, sucking in my lower lip. "Can't I do it at Inskip's?"

"Inskip's is not a betting stable," he said. "The horses always run to win. We do not need a permanent employee in that sort of place. There are, however, at present two betting stables without a man of ours in them, and you would be useful in either."

He named two leading trainers, neither of whom was one of the three people I had already planned to apply to. I would have to decide whether it would not be more useful to join what was clearly a well-organized spy system than to work with a once-doped horse who would almost certainly not be doped again.

83

"I'll think it over," I said. "Where can I get in touch with you?"

"Until you're on the payroll, you can't," he said simply. "Sparking Plug's in the fifth, I see. Well, you can give me your answer after that race. I'll be somewhere on your way back to the stables. Just nod if you agree, and shake your head if you don't. But I can't see you passing up a chance like this, not one of your sort." There was a sly contempt in the smile he gave me that made me unexpectedly wince inwardly.

He turned away and walked a few steps, and then came back.

"Should I have a big bet on Sparking Plug, then?" he asked.

"Oh . . . er . . . well . . . if I were you, I'd save your money."

He looked surprised, and then suspicious, and then knowing. "So that's how the land lies," he said. "Well, well, well." He laughed, looking at me as if I'd crawled out from under a stone. He was a man who despised his tools. "I can see you're going to be very useful to us. Very useful indeed."

I watched him go. It wasn't from kindheartedness that I had stopped him from backing Sparking Plug, but because it was the only way to retain and strengthen his confidence. When he was fifty yards away, I followed him. He made straight for the bookmakers in Tattersall's and strolled along the rows, looking at the odds displayed by each firm; but as far as I could see, he was in fact innocently planning to bet on the next race, and not reporting to anyone the outcome of his talk with me. Sighing, I put ten shillings on an outsider and went back to watch the horses go out for the race.

Sparking Plug thirstily drank two full buckets of water, stumbled over the second from the last fence, and cantered tiredly in behind the other seven runners to the accompaniment of boos from the cheaper enclosures. I watched him with regret. It was a thankless way to treat a greathearted horse.

The seedy, black-mustached man was waiting when

I led the horse away to the stables. I nodded to him, and he sneered knowingly back.

"You'll hear from us," he said.

There was gloom in the box going home and in the yard the next day over Sparking Plug's unexplainable defeat, and I went alone to Slaw on Tuesday evening, when Soupy duly handed over another seventy-five pounds. I checked it. Another fifteen new fivers, consecutive to the first fifteen.

"Ta," I said. "What do you get out of this yourself?"

Soupy's full mouth curled. "I do all right. You mugs take the risks, I get a cut for setting you up. Fair enough, eh?"

"Fair enough. How often do you do this sort of thing?" I tucked the envelope of money into my pocket.

He shrugged, looking pleased with himself. "I can spot blokes like you a mile off. Inskip must be slipping, though. First time I've known him to pick a bent penny, like. But those darts matches come in very handy. . . . I'm good, see. I'm always in the team. And there's a lot of stables in Yorkshire . . . with a lot of beaten favorites for people to scratch their heads over."

"You're very clever," I said.

He smirked. He agreed.

I walked up the hill planning to light a fuse under T.N.T., the high-explosive kid.

In view of the black-mustached man's offer, I decided to read through Beckett's typescript yet again, to see if the eleven dopings could have been the result of systematic spying. Looking at things from a fresh angle might produce results, I thought, and also might help me make up my mind whether or not to back out of the spying job and go to one of the doped horses' yards as arranged.

Locked in the bathroom, I began again at page one. On page sixty-seven, fairly early in the life history of the fifth of the horses, I read: "Bought at Ascot Sales, by D. L. Mentiff, Esq., of York for 420 guineas, passed on for 500 pounds to H. Humber of Posset, County Durham, remained three months, ran twice unplaced in maiden hurdles, subsequently sold again, at Doncaster, being bought for 600 guineas by N. W. Davies, Esq., of Leeds. Sent by him to L. Peterson's training stables at Mars Edge, Staffs, remained eighteen months, ran in four maiden hurdles, five novice chases, all without being placed. Races listed below." Three months at Humber's. I smiled. It appeared that horses didn't stay with him any longer than lads. I plowed on through the details, page after solid page.

On page ninety-four I came across the following: "Alamo was then offered for public auction at Kelso, and a Mr. John Arbuthnot, living in Berwickshire, paid 300 guineas for him. He sent him to be trained by H. Humber at Posset, County Durham, but he was not entered for any races, and Mr. Arbuthnot sold him to Humber for the same sum. A few weeks later he was sent for resale at Kelso. This time Almo was bought for 375 guineas by a Mr. Clement Smithson, living at Nantwich, Cheshire, who kept him at home for the summer and then sent him to a trainer called Samuel Martin at Malton, Yorkshire, where he ran unplaced in four maiden hurdles before Christmas (see list attached)."

I massaged my stiff neck. Humber again.

I read on.

On page 180, I read: "Ridgeway was then acquired as a yearling by a farmer, James Green, of Home Farm, Crayford, Surrey, in settlement of a bad debt. Mr. Green put him out to grass for two years, and had him broken in, hoping he would be a good hunter. However, a Mr. Taplow of Pusey, Wilts, said he would like to buy him and put him in training for racing. Ridgeway was trained for flat races by Ronald Streat of Pusey, but was unplaced in all his four races that summer. Mr. Taplow then sold Ridgeway privately to Albert George, farmer, of Bridge Lewes, Shropshire, who tried to train him himself but said he found he didn't have time to do it properly, so he sold him to a man a cousin of his knew near Durham, a trainer called Hedley Humber. Humber apparently thought the horse was no good, and Ridgeway went up for auction at Newmarket in November, fetching

290 guineas and being bought by Mr. P. J. Brewer, of the Manor, Witherby, Lancs . . ."

I plowed right on to the end of the typescript, threading my way through the welter of names, but Humber was not mentioned anywhere again.

Three of the eleven horses had been in Humber's yard for a brief spell at some distant time in their careers. That was all it amounted to.

I rubbed my eyes, which were gritty from lack of sleep, and an alarm clock rang suddenly, clamorously, in the silent cottage. I looked at my watch in surprise. It was already half-past six. Standing up and stretching, I made use of the bathroom facilities, thrust the typescript up under my pajama jacket and the jersey I wore on top, and shuffled back yawning to the dormitory, where the others were already up and struggling puffy-eyed into their clothes.

Down in the yard it was so cold that everything one touched seemed to suck the heat out of one's fingers, leaving them numb and fumbling, and the air was as intense an internal shaft to the chest as iced coffee sliding down the esophagus. Muck out the boxes, saddle up, ride up to the moor, canter, walk, ride down again, brush the sweat off, make the horse comfortable, give it food and water, and go in to breakfast. Repeat for the second horse, repeat for the third, and go into lunch.

While we were eating, Wally came in and told two others and me to go and clean the tack, and when we had finished our canned plums and custard, we went along to the tack room and started on the saddles and bridles. It was warm there from the stove, and I put my head back on a saddle and fell solidly asleep.

One of the others jogged my legs and said, "Wake up, Dan, there's a lot to do," and I drifted to the surface again. But before I opened my eyes the other lad said, "Oh, leave him, he does his share," and with blessings on his head, I sank back into blackness. Four o'clock came too soon, and with it the three hours of evening stables: then supper at seven and another day nearly done.

For most of the time I thought about Humber's name

cropping up three times in the typescript. I couldn't really see that it was of more significance than that four of the eleven horses had been fed on horse cubes at the time of their doping. What was disturbing was that I should have missed it entirely on my first two readings. I realized that I had had no reason to notice the name Humber before seeing him and his horse and talking to his lad at Leicester, but if I had missed one name occurring three times, I could have missed others as well. The thing to do would be to make lists of every single name mentioned in the typescript, and see if any other turned up in association with several of the horses. An electric computer could have done it in seconds. For me, it looked like another night in the bathroom.

There were more than a thousand names in the typescript. I listed half of them on Wednesday night, and slept a bit, and finished them on Thursday night, and slept some more.

On Friday the sun shone for a change, and the morning was beautiful on the moor. I trotted Sparking Plug along the track somewhere in the middle of the string and thought about the lists. No names except Humber's and one other occurred in connection with more than two of the horses. But the one other was a certain Paul J. Adams, and he had at one time or another owned six of them. Six out of eleven. It couldn't be a coincidence. The odds against it were phenomenal. I was certain I had made my first really useful discovery, yet I couldn't see why the fact that P. J. Adams, Esq., had owned a horse for a few months once should enable it to be doped a year or two later. I puzzled over it all morning without a vestige of understanding.

As it was a fine day, Wally said, it was a good time for me to scrub some rugs. This meant laying the rugs the horses wore to keep them warm in their boxes flat on the concrete in the yard, soaking them with the aid of a hose pipe, scrubbing them with a longhandled broom and detergent, hosing them off again, and hanging the wet rugs on the fence to drip before they were transferred to the warm tack room to finish drying thoroughly. It was an unpopular job, and Wally, who had treated me even more coldly since Sparking Plug's disgrace (though he had not gone so far as to accuse me of engineering it), could hardly conceal his dislike when he told me that it was my turn to do it.

However, I reflected, as I laid out five rugs after lunch and thoroughly soaked them with water, I had two hours to be alone and think. And as so often happens, I was wrong.

At three o'clock, when the horses were dozing and the lads were either copying them or had made quick trips to Harrogate with their new pay envelopes; when stable life was at its siesta and only I with my broom showed signs of reluctant activity, Patty Tarren walked in through the gate, across the tarmac, and slowed to a halt a few feet away.

She was wearing a straightish dress of soft-looking knobbly green tweed with a row of silver buttons from throat to hem. Her chestnut hair hung in a clean shining bob on her shoulders and was held back from her forehead by a wide green band, and with her fluffy eyelashes and pale-pink mouth, she looked about as enticing an interruption as a hard-worked stable hand could ask for.

"Hullo, Danny boy," she said.

"Good afternoon, miss."

"I saw you from my window," she said.

I turned in surprise, because I had thought October's house entirely hidden by trees, but sure enough, up the slope, one stone corner and a window could be seen through a gap in the leafless boughs. It was, however, a long way off. If Patty had recognized me from that distance, she had been using binoculars.

"You looked a bit lonely, so I came down to talk to you."

"Thank you, miss."

"As a matter of fact," she said, lowering the eyelashes, "the rest of the family don't get here until this evening, and I had nothing to do in that barn of a place all by myself, and I was bored. So I thought I'd come down and talk to you."

"I see," I leaned on the broom, looking at her lovely

face and thinking that there was an expression in her eyes too old for her years.

"It's rather cold out here, don't you think? I want to talk to you about something. . . . Don't you think we could stand in the shelter of that doorway?" Without waiting for an answer, she walked toward the doorway in question, which was that of the hay barn, and went inside. I followed her, resting the broom against the doorpost on the way.

"Yes, miss?" I said. The light was dim in the barn.

It appeared that talking was not her main object after all.

She put her hands around the back of my neck and offered her mouth for a kiss. I bent my head and kissed her. She was no virgin, October's daughter. She kissed with her tongue and with her teeth, and she moved her stomach rhythmically against mine. My muscles turned to knots. She smelled sweetly of fresh soap, more innocent than her behavior.

"Well . . . that's all right, then," she said with a giggle, disengaging herself and heading for the bulk of the bales of hay which half filled the barn.

"Come on," she said over her shoulder, and climbed up the bales to the flat level at the top. I followed her slowly. When I got to the top, I sat looking down at the hay-barn floor with the broom, the bucket, and the rug touched with sunshine through the doorway. On top of the hay had been Philip's favorite play place for years when he was little . . . and this is a fine time to think of my family, I thought.

Patty was lying on her back three feet away from me. Her eyes were wide and glistening, and her mouth curved open in an odd little smile. Slowly, holding my gaze, she undid all the silver buttons down the front of her dress to a point well below her waist. Then she gave a little shake so that the edges of the dress fell apart.

She had absolutely nothing on underneath.

I looked at her body, which was pearl pink and slender, and very desirable; and she gave a little rippling shiver of anticipation.

90

I looked back at her face. Her eyes were big and dark, and the odd way in which she was smiling suddenly struck me as being half furtive, half greedy; and wholly sinful. I had an abrupt vision of myself as she must see me, as I had seen myself in the long mirror in October's London house, a dark, flashy-looking stableboy with an air of deceitfulness and an acquaintance with dirt.

I understood her smile then.

I turned around where I sat until I had my back to her, and felt a flush of anger and shame spread all over my body.

"Do your dress up," I said.

"Why? Are you impotent after all, Danny boy?"

"Do your dress up," I repeated. "The party's over."

I slid down the hay, walked across the floor and out of the door without looking back. Twitching up the broom and cursing under my breath, I let out my fury against myself by scrubbing the rug until my arms ached.

After a while I saw her—her dress rebuttoned—come slowly out of the hay barn, look around her, and go across to a muddy puddle on the edge of the tarmac. She dirtied her shoes thoroughly in it, then childishly walked onto the rug I had just cleaned, and wiped all the mud off carefully in the center.

Her eyes were wide and her face expressionless as she looked at me.

"You'll be sorry, Danny boy," she said, and without haste strolled away down the yard, the chestnut hair swinging gently on the green tweed dress.

I scrubbed the rug again. Why had I kissed her? Why, after knowing about her from that kiss, had I followed her up into the hay? Why had I been such a stupid, easily roused, lusting fool? I was filled with useless dismay.

One didn't have to accept an invitation to dinner, even if the appetizer made one hungry. But having accepted, one should not so brutally reject what was offered. She had every right to be angry.

And I had every reason to be confused. I had been for nine years a father to two girls, one of whom was nearly Patty's age. I had taught them when they were little not to take lifts from strangers and when they were bigger how to avoid more subtle snares. And here I was, indisputably on the other side of the parental fence.

I felt an atrocious sense of guilt toward October, for I had had the intention, and there was no denying it, of doing what Patty wanted.

7

It was Elinor who rode out on my horse the following morning, and Patty, having obviously got her to change mounts, studiously refused to look at me at all.

Elinor, a dark scarf protecting most of the silver-blond hair, accepted a leg up with impersonal grace, gave me a warm smile of thanks, and rode away at the head of the string with her sister. When we got back after the gallops, however, she led the horse into its box and did half of the jobs for it while I was attending to Sparking Plug. I didn't know what she was doing until I walked down the yard, and was surprised to find her there, having grown used to Patty's habit of bolting the horse into the box still complete with saddle, bridle, and mud.

"You go and get the hay and water," she said. "I'll finish getting the dirt off, now I've started."

I carried away the saddle and bridle to the tack room, and took back the hay and water. Elinor gave the horse's mane a few final strokes with the brush, and I put on his rug and buckled the roller around his belly. She watched while I tossed the straw over the floor to make a comfortable bed, and waited until I had bolted the door.

"Thank you," I said. "Thank you very much."

She smiled faintly. "It's a pleasure. It really is. I like

horses. Especially racehorses. Lean and fast and exciting."

"Yes," I agreed. We walked down the yard together, she to go to the gate and I to the cottage which stood beside it.

"They are so different from what I do all the week," she said.

"What do you do all the week?"

"Oh . . . study. I'm at Durham University." There was a sudden, private, recollecting grin. Not for me. On level terms, I thought, one might find more in Elinor than good manners.

"It's really extraordinary how well you ride," she said suddenly. "I heard Mr. Inskip telling Father this morning that it would be worth getting a license for you. Have you ever thought of racing?"

"I wish I could," I said fervently, without thinking.

"Well, why not?"

"Oh . . . I might be leaving soon."

"What a pity." It was polite; nothing more.

We reached the cottage. She gave me a friendly smile and walked straight on, out of the yard, out of sight. I may not ever see her again, I thought; and was mildly sorry.

When the horse box came back from a day's racing (with a winner, a third, and an also-ran), I climbed up into the cab and borrowed the map again. I wanted to discover the location of the village where Mr. Paul Adams lived, and after some searching I found it. As its significance sank in, I began to smile with astonishment. There was, it seemed, yet another place where I could apply for a job.

I went back into the cottage, into Mrs. Alnutt's cosy kitchen, and ate Mrs. Alnutt's delicious egg and chips and bread and butter and fruitcake, and later slept dreamlessly on Mrs. Alnutt's lumpy mattress, and in the morning bathed luxuriously in Mrs. Alnutt's shining bathroom. And in the afternoon I went up beside the stream with at last something worthwhile to tell October.

He met me with a face of granite, and before I could say a word he hit me hard and squarely across the mouth. It was a backhanded expert blow which started from the waist, and I didn't see it coming until far too late.

"What the hell's that for?" I said, running my tongue around my teeth and being pleased to find that none of them were broken off.

He glared at me. "Patty told me . . ." He stopped as if it was too difficult to go on.

"Oh," I said blankly.

"Yes, oh," he mimicked savagely. He was breathing deeply and I thought he was going to hit me again. I thrust my hands into my pockets and his stayed where they were, down by his sides, clenching and unclenching.

"What did Patty tell you?"

"She told me everything." His anger was almost tangible. "She came to me this morning in tears . . . she told me how you made her go into the hay barn . . . and held her there until she was worn out with struggling to get away . . . She told the . . . the disgusting things you did to her with your hands . . . and then how you forced her . . . forced her to . . ." He couldn't say it.

I was appalled. "I didn't," I said vehemently. "I didn't do anything like that. I kissed her . . . and that's all. She's making it up."

"She couldn't possibly have made it up. It was too detailed. . . . She couldn't know such things unless they had happened to her."

I opened my mouth and shut it again. They had happened to her, right enough; somewhere, with someone else, more than once, and certainly also with her willing cooperation. And I could see that to some extent at least she was going to get away with her horrible revenge, because there are some things you can't say about a girl to her father, especially if you like him.

October said scathingly, "I have never been so mistaken in a man before. I thought you were responsible . . . or at least able to control yourself. Not a cheap lecherous jackanapes who would take my money—and

94

my regard—and amuse yourself behind my back, debauching my daughter."

There was enough truth in that to hurt, and the guilt I felt over my stupid behavior didn't help. But I had to put up some kind of defense, because I would never have harmed Patty in any way, and there was still the investigation into the doping to be carried on. Now that I had got so far, I did not want to be packed off home in disgrace.

I said slowly, "I did go with Patty into the hay barn. I did kiss her. Once. Only once. After that I didn't touch her. I literally didn't touch any part of her, not her hand, nor her dress . . . nothing."

He looked at me steadily for a long time while the fury slowly died out of him and a sort of weariness took its place.

At length he said, almost calmly, "One of you is lying. And I have to believe my daughter." There was an unexpected flicker of entreaty in his voice.

"Yes," I said. I looked away, up the gully. "Well . . . this solves one problem, anyway."

"What problem?"

"How to leave here with the ignominious sack and without a reference."

It was so far away from what he was thinking about that it was several moments before he showed any reaction at all, and then he gave me an attentive, narrow-eyed stare which I did not try to avoid.

"You intend to go on the investigation, then?"

"If you are willing."

"Yes," he said heavily, at length. "Especially as you are moving on and will have no more opportunities of seeing Patty. In spite of what I personally think of you, you do still represent our best hope of success, and I suppose I must put the good of racing first."

He fell silent. I contemplated the rather grim prospect of continuing to do that sort of work for a man who hated me. Yet the thought of giving up was worse. And that was odd.

Eventually he said, "Why do you want to leave without

95

a reference? You won't get a job in any of these three stables without a reference."

"The only reference I need to get a job in the stable I am going to is no reference at all."

"Whose stable?"

"Hedley Humber's."

"Humber!" He was somberly incredulous. "But why? He's a very poor trainer and he didn't train any of the doped horses. What's the point of going there?"

"He didn't train any of the horses when they won," I agreed, "but he had three of them through his hands earlier in their careers. There is also a man called P. J. Adams who at one time or another owned six more of them. Adams lives, according to the map, less than ten miles from Humber. Humber lives at Posset, in Durham, and Adams at Tellbridge, just over the Northumberland border. That means that nine of the eleven horses spent some time in that one small area of the British Isles. None of them stayed long. The dossiers of Transistor and Rudyard are much less detailed than the others on the subject of their earlier life, and I have now no doubt that checking would show that they, too, for a short while, came under the care of either Adams or Humber."

"But how could the horses' having spent some time with Adams or Humber possibly affect their speeds months or years later?"

"I don't know," I said. "But I'll go and find out."

There was a pause.

"Very well," he said heavily. "I'll tell Inskip that you are to be dismissed. And I'll tell him it is because you pestered Patricia."

"Right."

He looked at me coldly. "You can write me reports. I don't want to see you again."

I watched him walk away strongly up the gully. I didn't know whether or not he really believed any more that I had done what Patty said; but I did know that he needed to believe it. The alternative, the truth, was so much worse. What father wants to discover that his beautiful eighteen-year-old daughter is a lying slut?

And as for me, I thought that on the whole I had got off lightly; if I had found that anyone had assaulted Belinda or Helen, I'd have half killed him.

After the second exercise the following day, Inskip told me exactly what he thought of me, and I didn't particularly enjoy it.

After giving me a public dressing down in the center of the tarmac (with the lads grinning in sly amusement as they carried their buckets and hay nets, with both ears flapping), he handed back the insurance card and income tax form—there was still a useful muddle going on over the illegible Cornish address on the one October had originally provided me with—and told me to pack my bags and get out of the yard at once. It would be no use giving his name as a reference, he said, because Lord October had expressly forbidden him to vouch for my character, and it was a decision with which he thoroughly agreed. He gave me a week's wages in lieu of notice, less Mrs. Alnutt's share, and that was that.

I packed my things in the little dormitory, patted good-bye to the bed I had slept in for six weeks, and went down to the kitchen, where the lads were having their midday meal. Eleven pairs of eyes swiveled in my direction. Some were contemptuous, some were surprised, one or two thought it funny. None of them looked sorry to see me go. Mrs. Alnutt gave me a thick cheese sandwich, and I ate it walking down the hill to Slaw to catch the two-o'clock bus to Harrogate.

And from Harrogate, where?

No lad in his senses would go straight from a prosperous place like Inskip's to ask for a job at Humber's, however abruptly he had been thrown out; there had to be a period of some gentle sliding downhill if it was to look unsuspicious. In fact, I decided, it would be altogether much better if it was Humber's head traveling lad who offered me work, and not I who asked for it. It should not be too difficult. I could turn up at every course where Humber had a runner, looking seedier and seedier and more and more ready to take any job at all, and one day the lad-hungry stable would take the bait.

97

Meanwhile I needed somewhere to live. The bus trundled down to Harrogate while I thought it out. Somewhere in the northeast, to be near Humber's local meetings. A big town, so that I could be anonymous in it. An alive town, so that I could find ways of passing the time between race meetings. With the help of maps and guidebooks in Harrogate public library, I settled on Newcastle, and with the help of a couple of tolerant truck drivers, I arrived there late that afternoon and found myself a room in a back-street hotel.

It was a terrible room with peeling, coffee-colored walls, tatty printed linoleum wearing out on the floor, a narrow, hard divan bed, and some scratched furniture made out of stained plywood. Only its unexpected cleanliness and a shiny new washbasin in one corner made it bearable, but it did, I had to admit, suit my appearance and purpose admirably.

I dined in a fish-and-chip shop for three and six, and went to a cinema, and enjoyed not having to groom three horses or think twice about every word I said. My spirits rose several points at being free again and I succeeded in forgetting the trouble I was in with October.

In the morning I sent off to him in a registered package the second seventy-five pounds, which I had not given him in the gully on Sunday, together with a short formal note explaining why there would have to be a delay before I engaged myself to Humber.

From the post office I went to a betting shop and from their calendar copied down all the racing fixtures for the next month. It was the beginning of December, and I found there were very few meetings in the north before the first week in January; which was, from my point of view, a waste of time and a nuisance. After the following Saturday's program at Newcastle itself there was no racing north of Nottinghamshire until Boxing Day, more than a fortnight later.

Pondering this setback, I next went in search of a serviceable secondhand motorcycle. It took me until late afternoon to find exactly what I wanted, a souped-up 500-cc Norton, four years old and the ex-property of

98

a now one-legged young man who had done the ton once too often on the Great North Road. The salesman gave me these details with relish as he took my money and assured me that the bike would still do a hundred at a push. I thanked him politely and left the machine with him to have a new silencer fitted, along with some new hand grips, brake cables, and tires.

Lack of private transport at Slaw had not been a tremendous drawback, and I would not have been concerned about my mobility at Posset were it not for the one obtrusive thought that I might at some time find is advisable to depart in a hurry. I could not forget the journalist, Tommy Stapleton. Between Hexham and Yorkshire he had lost eight hours, and turned up dead. Between Hexham and Yorkshire lay Posset.

The first person I saw at Newcastle races four days later was the man with the black mustache who had offered me steady employment as a stable spy. He was standing in an unobtrusive corner near the entrance, talking to a big-eared boy whom I later saw leading around a horse from one of the best-known gambling stables in the country.

From some distance away I watched him pass to the boy a white envelope and receive a brown envelope in return. Money for information, I thought, and so openly done as to appear innocent.

I strolled along behind Black Mustache when he finished his transaction and made his way to the bookmakers' stands in Tattersall's. As before, he appeared to be doing nothing but examining the prices offered on the first race; and as before I staked a few shillings on the favorite in case I should be seen to be following him. In spite of his survey, he placed no bets at all, but strolled down to the rails that separated the enclosure from the course itself. There he came to an unplanned-looking halt beside an artificial redhead wearing a yellowish leopard-skin jacket over a dark-gray skirt.

She turned her head toward him, and they spoke. Presently he took the brown envelope from his breast pocket and slipped it into his race card; and after a

99

few moments he and the woman unobtrusively exchanged race cards. He wandered away from the rails, while she put the card containing the envelope into a large, shiny black handbag and snapped it shut. From the shelter of the last row of bookies I watched her walk to the entrance into the club and pass through onto the members' lawn. I could not follow her there, but I went up onto the stands and watched her walk across the nextdoor enclosure. She appeared to be well known. She stopped and spoke to several people—a bent old man with a big floppy hat, an obese young man who patted her arm repeatedly, a pair of women in mink cocoons, a group of three men who laughed loudly and hid her from my view so I could not see if she had given any of them the envelope from her handbag.

The horses cantered down the course and the crowds moved up onto the stands to watch the race. The redhead disappeared among the throng on the members' stand, leaving me frustrated at losing her. The race was run, and the favorite cantered in by ten lengths. The crowd roared with approval. While people around me flowed down from the stands, I stood where I was, waiting without too much hope to see if the leopard-skin redhead would reappear.

Obligingly, she did. She was carrying her handbag in one hand and her race card in the other. Pausing to talk again, this time to a very short fat man, she eventually made her way over to the bookmakers who stood along the rails separating Tattersall's from the club and stopped in front of one nearest the stands, and nearest to me. For the first time I could see her face clearly: she was younger than I had thought and plainer of feature, with gaps between her top teeth.

She said in a piercing, tinny voice, "I'll settle my account, Bimmo dear," and opening her handbag, took out a brown envelope and gave it to a small man in spectacles, who stood on a box beside a board bearing the words: BIMMO BOGNOR (EST. 1920), MANCHESTER AND LONDON.

Mr. Bimmo Bognor took the envelope and put it in

his jacket pocket, and his hearty "Ta, love" floated up to my attentive ears.

I went down from the stands and collected my small winnings, thinking that while the brown envelope that the redhead had given to Bimmo Bognor *looked* like the envelope that the big-eared lad had given to Black Mustache, I could not be a hundred percent sure of it. She might have given the lad's envelope to any one of the people I had watched her talk to, or to anyone on the stands while she was out of my sight; and she might then have gone quite honestly to pay her bookmaker.

If I wanted to be certain of the chain, perhaps I could send an urgent message along it, a message so urgent that there would be no wandering among the crowds, but an unconcealed direct line between a and b, and b and c. The urgent message, since Sparking Plug was a runner in the fifth race, presented no difficulty at all; but being able to locate Black Mustache at exactly the right moment entailed keeping him in sight all the afternoon.

He was a creature of habit, which helped. He always watched the races from the same corner of the stand, patronized the same bar between times, and stood inconspicuously near the gate onto the course when the horses were led out of the parade ring. He did not bet.

Humber had two horses at the meeting, one in the third race and one in the last; and although it meant leaving my main purpose untouched until late in the afternoon, I let the third race go by without making any attempt to find his head traveling lad. I padded slowly along behind Black Mustache instead.

After the fourth race I followed him into the bar and jogged his arm violently as he began to drink. Half of his beer splashed over his hand and ran down his sleeve, and he swung around cursing, to find my face nine inches from his own.

"Sorry," I said. "Oh, it's you." I put as much surprise into my voice as I could.

His eyes narrowed. "What are you doing here? Sparking Plug runs in this race."

I scowled. "I've left Inskip's."

"Have you got one of the jobs I suggested? Good."

"Not yet. There might be a bit of a delay there, like."

"Why? No vacancies?"

"They don't seem all that keen to have me since I got chucked out of Inskip's."

"You got what?" he said sharply.

"Chucked out of Inskip's," I repeated.

"Why?"

"They said something about Sparking Plug losing last week on the day you spoke to me . . . said they could prove nothing but they didn't want me around no more, and to get out."

"That's too bad," he said, edging away.

"But I got the last laugh," I said, sniggering and holding onto his arm. "I'll tell you straight, I got the bloody last laugh."

"What do you mean?" He didn't try to keep the contempt out of his voice, but there was interest in his eyes.

"Sparking Plug won't win today neither," I stated. "He won't win because he'll feel bad in his stomach."

"How do you know?'

"I soaked his salt lick with liquid paraffin," I said. "Every day since I left on Monday he's been rubbing his tongue on a laxative. He won't be feeling like racing. He won't bloody win, he won't." I laughed.

Black Mustache gave me a sickened look, pried my fingers off his arm, and hurried out of the bar. I followed him carefully. He almost ran down into Tattersalls, and began frantically looking around. The redheaded woman was nowhere to be seen, but she must have been watching, because presently I saw her walking briskly down the rails, to the same spot where they had met before. And there, with a rush, she was joined by Black Mustache. He talked vehemently. She listened and nodded. He then turned away more calmly, and walked away out of Tattersall's and back to the parade ring. The woman waited until he was out of sight; then she walked firmly into the members' enclosure and along the rails until she came to Bimmo Bognor. The little man leaned forward over the rails as she spoke earnestly into his ear. He nodded several times and she began to smile, and when he turned around to talk to his clerks, I saw that he was smiling broadly, too.

Unhurriedly I walked along the rows of bookmakers, studying the odds they offered. Sparking Plug was not favorite, owing to his waterlogged defeat last time out, but no one would chance more than five to one. At that price I staked forty pounds—my entire earnings at Inskip's—on my old charge, choosing a prosperous, jolly-looking bookmaker in the back row.

Hovering within earshot of Mr. Bimmo Bognor a few minutes later, I heard him offer seven to one against Sparking Plug to a stream of clients, and watched him rake in their money, confident that he would not have to pay them out.

Smiling contentedly, I climbed to the top of the stands and watched Sparking Plug make mincemeat of his opponents over the fences and streak insultingly home by twenty lengths. It was a pity, I reflected, that I was too far away to hear Mr. Bognor's opinion of the result.

My jolly bookmaker handed me 240 pounds in fivers without a second glance. To avoid Black Mustache and any reprisals he might be thinking of organizing, I then went over to the cheap enclosure in the center of the course for twenty boring minutes; returning through the horse gate when the runners were down at the start for the last race, and slipping up the stairs to the stand used by the lads.

Humber's head traveling lad was standing near the top of the stands. I pushed roughly past him and tripped heavily over his feet.

"Look where you're bloody going," he said crossly, focusing a pair of shoebutton eyes on my face.

"Sorry, mate. Got corns, have you?"

"None of your bloody business," he said, looking at me sourly. He would know me again, I thought.

I bit my thumbnail. "Do you know which of this lot is Martin Davies' head traveling lad?" I asked.

He said, "That chap over there with the red scarf. Why?"

"I need a job," I said, and before he could say anything, I left him and pushed along the row to the man in the red scarf. His stable had one horse in the race; I asked him quietly if they ran two, and he shook his head and said no.

Out of the corner of my eye I noticed that this negative answer had not been wasted on Humber's head lad. He probably thought, or so I hoped, that I had asked for work, and had been refused. Satisfied that the seed was planted, I watched the race (Humber's horse finished last) and slipped quietly away from the racecourse via the paddock rails and the members' car park, without any interception of Black Mustache or a vengeful Bimmo Bognor.

A Sunday endured half in my dreary room and half walking around the empty streets was enough to convince me that I could not drag through the next fortnight in Newcastle doing nothing, and the thought of a solitary Christmas spent staring at coffee-colored peeling paint was unattractive. Moreover, I had two hundred pounds of bookmakers' money packed into my belt alongside what was left of October's; and Humber had no horses entered before the Stafford meeting on Boxing Day. It took me only ten minutes to decide what to do with the time between.

On Sunday evening I wrote to October a report on Bimmo Bognor's intelligence service, and at one in the morning I caught the express to London.

Monday I spent shopping. I sent off gifts to Belinda and Helen and Philip and wrote to them apologizing in advance for the very few letters they would receive from me during the next weeks. I called at the Bank of Australia and asked them to keep all incoming mail for me until I collected it personally. News from home had been a slight risk and slow. At Posset it would be a dangerous luxury I would have to do without.

On Tuesday evening, looking civilized in some decent new clothes and equipped with an extravagant pair of Kastle skis, I signed the register of a comfortable, bright little hotel in a snow-covered village in the Dolomites.

The fortnight I spent in Italy made no difference one way or another to the result of my work for October, but it made a great deal of difference to me. It was the first real holiday I had had since my parents died, the first utterly carefree, purposeless, self-indulgent break for nine years.

I grew younger. Fast, strenuous days on the snow slopes and a succession of evenings dancing with my skiing companions peeled away the years of responsibility like skins, until at last I felt twenty-seven instead of fifty, a young man instead of a father; until the unburdening process, begun when I left Australia and slowly fermenting through the weeks at Inskip's suddenly seemed complete.

There was also a bonus in the shape of one of the receptionists, a rounded, glowing girl whose dark eyes lit up the minute she saw me and who, after a minimum of persuasion, uninhibitedly spent a proportion of her nights in my bed. She called me her Christmas box of chocolates. She said I was the happiest lover she had had for a long time, and that I pleased her. She was probably doubly as promiscuous as Patty but she was much more wholesome; and she made me feel terrific instead of ashamed.

On the day I left, when I gave her a gold bracelet, she kissed me and told me not to come back, as things were never as good the second time. She was God's gift to bachelors, that girl.

I flew back to England on Christmas night feeling as physically and mentally fit as I had ever been in my life, and ready to take on the worst that Humber could dish out. Which, as it happened, was just as well.

8

At Stafford on Boxing Day one of the runners in the first race, the selling chase, threw off his jockey a stride after landing in fourth place over the last fence, crashed through the rails, and bolted away across the rough grass in the center of the course.

A lad standing near me on the drafty steps behind the weighing room ran off cursing to catch him; but as the horse galloped crazily from one end of the course to the other, it took the lad, the trainer, and about ten assorted helpers a quarter of an hour to lay their hands on his bridle. I watched them as with worried faces they led the horse, an undistinguished bay, off the course and past me toward the racecourse stables.

The wretched animal was white and dripping with sweat and in obvious distress; foam covered his nostrils and muzzle, and his eyes rolled wildly in their sockets. His flesh was quivering, his ears lay flat back on his head, and he was inclined to lash out at anyone who came near him.

His name, I saw from the race card, was Superman. He was not one of the eleven horses I had been investigating: but his hotted-up appearance and frantic behavior, coupled with the fact that he had met trouble at Stafford in a selling chase, convinced me that he was the twelfth of the series. The twelfth; and he had come unstuck. There was, as Beckett had said, no mistaking the effect of whatever had pepped him up. I had never before seen a horse in such a state, which seemed to me much worse than the descriptions of "excited winners" I had read in the press cuttings; and I came to the conclusion that Superman was either suffering from an overdose, or had reacted excessively to whatever the others had been given.

Neither October nor Beckett nor Macclesfield had come to Stafford. I could only hope that the precautions October had promised had been put into operation in spite of its being Boxing Day, because I could not, without blowing open my role, ask any of the officials if the pre-race dope tests had been made or other precautions taken, nor insist that the jockey be asked at once for his impressions, that unusual bets should be investigated, and that the horse be thoroughly examined for punctures.

The fact the Superman had safely negotiated all the fences inclined me more and more to believe that he could not have been affected by the stimulant until he was approaching, crossing, or landing over the last. It was there that he had gone wild and, instead of winning, thrown his jockey and decamped. It was there that he had been given the power to sprint the four hundred yards, that long run-in which gave him the time and room to overhaul the leading horses.

The only person on the racecourse to whom I could safely talk was Superman's lad, but because of the state of his horse it was bound to be some time before he came out of the stables. Meanwhile there were more steps to be taken toward getting myself a job with Humber.

I had gone to the meeting with my hair unbrushed, pointed shoes unpolished, leather collar turned up, hands in pockets, sullen expression in place. I looked, and felt, a disgrace.

Changing back that morning into stable-lad clothes had not been a pleasant experience. The sweaters stank of horses, the narrow, cheap trousers looked scruffy, the underclothes were gray from insufficient washing, and the jeans were still filthy with mud and muck. Because of the difficulty of getting them back on Christmas night, I had decided against sending the whole lot to the laundry while I was away, and in spite of my distaste in putting them on again, I didn't regret it. I looked all the more on the way to being down and out.

I had changed and shaved in the cloakroom at the

107

West Kensington Air Terminal, parked my skis and grip of ski clothes in the Left Luggage department on Euston Station, slept uneasily on a hard seat for an hour or two, breakfasted on sandwiches and coffee from the cafeteria, and caught the race train to Stafford. At this rate, I thought wryly, I would have bundles of belongings scattered all over London; because neither on the outward nor on the return journeys had I cared to go to October's London house to make use of the clothes I had left with Terence. I did not want to meet October. I liked him, and saw no joy in facing his bitter resentment again unless I absolutely had to.

Humber had only one runner on Boxing Day, a weedy-looking hurdler in the fourth race. I hung over the rails by the saddling boxes and watched his head traveling lad saddle up, while Humber himself leaned on his knobbed walking stick and gave directions. I had come for a good close look at him, and what I saw was both encouraging from the angle that one could believe him capable of any evil, and discouraging from the angle that I was going to have to obey him.

His large body was encased in a beautifully cut short camel's hair overcoat, below which protruded dark trousers and impeccable shoes. On his head he wore a bowler, set very straight, and on his hands some pale unsoiled pigskin gloves. His face was large, not fat, but hard. Unsmiling eyes, a grim trap of a mouth, and deep lines running from the corners of his nose to his chin gave his expression a look of cold willfulness.

He stood quite still, making no unnecessary fussy movements, the complete opposite of Inskip, who was forever walking busily from side to side of his horse, checking straps and buckles, patting and pulling at the saddle, running his hand down legs, nervously making sure over and over that everything was in order.

In Humber's case it was the boy who held the horse's head who was nervous. Frightened, I thought, was hardly too strong a word for it. He kept giving wary, startled-animal glances at Humber, and staying out of his sight on the far side of the horse as much as possible. He was a thin, ragged-looking boy of about sixteen, and not far, I judged, from being mentally deficient.

The head traveling lad, middle-aged, with a big nose and an unfriendly air, unhurriedly adjusted the saddle and nodded to the lad to lead the horse off into the parade ring. Humber followed. He walked with a slight limp, more or less disguised by the use of the walking stick, and he proceeded in a straight line like a tank, expecting everyone else to get out of his way.

I transferred myself to the parade-ring rails in his wake and watched him give instructions to his jockey, an allowance-claimer who regarded his mount with justified disillusion. It was the head traveling-lad, not Humber, who gave the jockey a leg up, and who picked up and carried off with him the horse's rug.

Around the lads' stand, I carefully stood directly in front of the head traveling lad, and in the lull before the race started, I turned sideways and tried to borrow some money from the lad standing next to me, whom I didn't know. Not unexpectedly, but to my relief, the lad refused indignantly and more than loudly enough for Humber's head lad to hear. I hunched my shoulders and resisted the temptation to look around and see if the message had reached its destination.

Humber's horse ran out of energy in the straight and finished second to last. No one was surprised.

After that I stationed myself outside the stable gate to wait for Superman's lad, but he didn't come out for another half hour, until after the fifth race. I fell into step beside him as if by accident, saying, "Rather you than me, chum, with one like that to look after." He asked me who I worked for; I said Inskip, and he loosened up and agreed that a cup of char and a wad would go down a treat, after all that caper.

"Is he always that het up after a race?" I said, halfway through the cheese sandwiches.

"No. Usually he's dog tired. There's been all hell breaking loose this time, I can tell you."

"How do you mean?"

"Well, first they came and took some tests on all the runners before the race. Now I ask you, why before? It's not the thing, is it? Not before. You ever had one done before?"

I shook my head.

"Then, see, old Super, he was putting up the same sort of job he always does, looking as if he is going to come on to a place at least and then packing it in going into the last. Stupid basket. No guts, I reckon. They had his heart tested, but it ticks O.K. So it's no guts, sure enough. Anyway, then at the last he suddenly kicks up his heels and bolts off as if the devil was after him. I don't suppose you saw him? He's a nervy customer always, really, but he was climbing the wall when we finally caught him. The old man was dead worried. Well, the horse looked as though he had been got at, and he wanted to stick his oar in first and get a dope test done so that the Stewards shouldn't accuse him of using a booster and take away his ruddy license. They had a couple of vets fussing over him taking things to be analyzed—dead funny it was, because old Super was trying to pitch them over the stable walls—and in the end they gave him a jab of something to quieten him down. But how we're going to get him home I don't know."

"Have you looked after him long?" I asked sympathetically.

"Since the beginning of the season. About four months, I suppose. He's a jumpy customer, as I said, but before this I had just about got him to like me. Gawd, I hope he calms down proper before the jab wears off, I do straight."

"Who had him before you?" I asked casually.

"Last year he was in a little stable in Devon with a private trainer called Beaney, I think. Yes, Beaney, that's where he started, but he didn't do any good there."

"I expect they made him nervous there, breaking him in," I said.

"No, now that's a funny thing. I said to one of Beaney's lads when we were down in Devon for one of the August meetings, and he said I must be talking about the wrong horse because Superman was a placid old thing and no trouble. He said if Superman was nervous, it must have been on account of something that had happened

110

during the summer after he left their place and before he came to us."

"Where did he go for the summer?" I asked, picking up the cup of orange-colored tea.

"Search me. The old man bought him at Ascot sales, I think, for a cheap horse. I should think he will shuffle him off again after this if he can get more than knacker's price for him. Poor old Super. Silly nit." The lad stared gloomily into his tea.

"You don't think he went off is rocker today because he was doped, then?"

"I think he just went bonkers," he said. "Stark, staring, raving bonkers. I mean, no one had a chance to dope him, except me and the old man and Chalky, and I didn't, and the old man didn't, because he's not that sort, and you wouldn't think Chalky would either, he's so darn proud being promoted head traveling lad only last month . . ."

We finished our tea and went around to watch the sixth race, still talking about Superman, but his lad knew nothing else which was of help to me.

After the race I walked the half mile into the center of Stafford, and from a telephone booth sent two identical telegrams to October, one to London and one to Slaw, as I did not know where he was. They read: "Request urgent information re Superman, specifically where did he go from Beaney, permit holder, Devon, last May approximately. Answer care Post Restante, Newcastle on Tyne."

I spent the evening, incredibly distant from the gaiety of the day before, watching a dreary musical on a three-quarters-empty cinema, and slept that night in a dingy bed-and-breakfast hotel where they looked me up and down and asked for their money in advance. I paid, wondering if I would ever get used to being treated like dirt. I felt a fresh shock every time. I suppose I had been too accustomed to the respect I was offered in Australia even to notice it, far less appreciate it. I would appreciate some of it now, I ruefully thought, following the landlady into an unwelcoming little room and listen-

111

ing to her suspicious lecture on no cooking, no hot water after eleven, and no girls.

The following afternoon I conspicuously mooched around in front of Humber's head traveling lad with a hangdog and worried expression, and after the races went back by bus and train to Newcastle for the night. In the morning I collected the motorcycle, fitted with the new silencer and other parts, and called at the post office to see if there was a reply from October.

The clerk handed me a letter. Inside, without salutation or signature, there was a single sheet of typescript, which read:

Superman was born and bred in Ireland. Changed hands twice before reaching John Beaney in Devon. He was then sold by Beaney to H. Humber, Esq., of Posset, Co. Durham, on May 3. Humber sent him to Ascot sales in July, where he was bought by his present trainer for 260 guineas.

Investigations re Superman at Stafford yesterday are all so far uninformative; dope analyses have still to be completed but there is little hope they will show anything. The veterinary surgeon at the course was as convinced as you apparently were that this is another "joker," and made a thorough examination of the horse's skin. There were no visible punctures except the ones he made himself giving the horse sedation.

Superman was apparently in a normal condition before the race. His jockey reports all normal until the last fence, when the horse seemed to suffer a sort of convulsion, and ejected him from the saddle.

Further inquiries re Rudyard revealed he was bought four winters ago by P. J. Adams of Tellbridge, Northumberland, and sold again within a short time at Ascot. Transistor was bought by Adams at Doncaster three years ago, sold Newmarket Dispersal Sales three months later.

Inquiries re thirty consecutive five-pound notes reveal they were issued by Barclays Bank, Birmingham New Street branch, to a man called Lewis Greenfield, who corresponds exactly to your description of the man who approached you in Slaw. Proceedings against Greenfield and T. N. Tarleton

112

are in hand, but will be held in abeyance until after your main task is completed.

Your report on Bimmo Bognor is noted, but as you say, the buying of stable information is not a punishable offense in law. No proceedings are at presest contemplated, but warning that a spy system is in operation will be given privately to certain trainers.

I tore the page up and scattered it in the litter basket, then went back to the motorcycle and put it through its paces down the A1 to Catterick. It handled well, and I enjoyed the speed and found it quite true that it would still do a hundred.

At Catterick that Saturday Humber's head traveling lad rose like a trout to the fly.

Inskip had sent two runners, one of which was looked after by Paddy; and up on the lad's stand before the second race I saw the sharp little Irishman and Humber's head lad talking earnestly together. I was afraid that Paddy might relent toward me enough to say something in my favor, but I needn't have worried. He put my mind at rest himself.

"You're a bloody young fool," he said, looking me over from my unkempt head to my grubby toes. "And you've only got what you deserve. That man of Humber's was asking me about you, why you got the kick from Inskip's, and I told him the real reason, not all that eyewash about messing about with his nibs' daughter."

"What real reason?" I asked, surprised.

His mouth twisted in contempt. "People talk, you know. You don't think they keep their traps shut, when there's a good bit of gossip going around? You don't think that Grits didn't tell me how you got drunk at Cheltenham and blew your mouth off about Inskip's? And what you said at Bristol about being willing to put the finger on the horse's box in the yard . . . well, that got around to me, too. And thick as thieves with that crook Soupy you were, as well. And there was that time when we all put our wages on Sparking Plug and he didn't go a yard . . . I'd lay any money that was your doing. So I told Humber's man he would be a

113

fool to take you on. You're poison, Dan, and I reckon any stable is better off without you, and I told him so."

"Thanks."

"You can ride," said Paddy disgustedly, "I'll say that for you. And it's an utter bloody waste. You'll never get a job with a decent stable again. It would be like putting a rotten apple into a box of good ones."

"Did you say all that to Humber's man?"

"I told him no decent stable would take you on," he said, nodding. "And if you ask me, it bloody well serves you right." He turned his back on me and walked away.

I sighed, and told myself I should be pleased that Paddy believed me such a black character.

Humber's head traveling lad spoke to me in the pad dock between the last two races.

"Hey, you," he said, catching my arm. "I hear you're looking for a job."

"That's right."

"I might be able to put you in the way of something. Good pay, better than most."

"Whose stable?" I asked. "And how much?"

"Sixteen quid a week."

"Sounds good," I admitted. "Where?"

"Where I work. For Mr. Humber. Up in Durham."

"Humber," I repeated sourly.

"Well, you want a job, don't you? Of course, if you are so well off you can do without a job, that's different." He sneered at my unprosperous appearance.

"I need a job," I muttered.

"Well, then?"

"He might not have me," I said bitterly. "Like some others I could mention."

"He will if I put in a word for you. We're short a lad just now. There's another meeting here next Wednesday. I'll put in a word for you before that and if it is OK, you can see Mr. Humber on Wednesday and he'll tell you whether he'll have you or not."

"Why not ask him now?" I said.

"No. You wait till Wednesday."

"All right," I said grudgingly. "If I've got to."

114

I could almost see him thinking that by Wednesday I would be just that much hungrier, just that much more anxious to take any job that was offered, and less likely to be frightened off by rumors of bad conditions.

I had spent all the bookmaker's two hundred, as well as half of the money I had earned at Inskip's, on my Italian jaunt (of which I regretted not one penny), and after paying for the motorcycle and the succession of dingy lodgings, I had almost nothing left of October's original two hundred. He had not suggested giving me any more for expenses, and I was not going to ask him for any; but I judged that the other half of my Inskip pay could be spent how I liked, and I dispatched nearly all of it in the following three days on a motorcycle trip to Edinburgh, walking around and enjoying the city and thinking myself the oddest tourist in Scotland.

On Tuesday evening, when hogmanay was in full swing, I braved the headwaiter of L'Aperitif, who to his eternal credit treated me with beautifully self-controlled politeness, but quite reasonably checked, before he gave me a little table in a corner, that I had enough money to pay the bill. Impervious to scandalized looks from better dressed diners, I slowly ate, with Humber's establishment in mind, a perfect and enormous dinner of lobster, duck bigarade, lemon soufflé, and Brie, and drank most of a bottle of Chateau Leoville Lescases 1959.

With which extravagant farewell to being my own master, I rode down the A1 to Catterick on New Year's Day and in good spirits engaged myself to the worst stable in the country.

9

Rumor had hardly done Hedley Humber justice. The discomfort in which the lads were expected to live was so methodically devised that I had been there only one day before I came to the conclusion that its sole purpose was to discourage anyone from staying too long. I discovered that only the head lad and the head traveling lad, who both lived out in Posset, had worked in the yard for more than three months, and that the average time it took for an ordinary lad to decide that sixteen pounds a week was not enough was eight to ten weeks.

This meant that none of the stable hands except the two head lads knew what had happened to Superman the previous summer, because none of them had been there at the time. And caution told me that the only reason the two top men stayed was because they knew what was going on, and that if I asked *them* about Superman, I might find myself following smartly in Tommy Stapleton's footsteps.

I had heard all about the squalor of the living quarters at some stables, and I was aware also that some lads deserved no better—some I knew of had broken up and burned their chairs rather than go outside and fetch coal, and others had stacked their dirty dishes in the lavatory and pulled the chain to do the washing up. But even granted that Humber only employed the dregs, his arrangements were very nearly inhuman.

The dormitory was a narrow hayloft over the horses. One could hear every bang of their hoofs and the rattle of chains, and through cracks in the plank floor one could see straight down into the boxes. Upward through the cracks rose a smell of dirty straw and an icy draft. There was no ceiling to the hayloft except the rafters and the tiles of the roof, and no way up into it except a ladder through a hole in the floor. In the one small window a broken pane of glass had been pasted over with brown paper, which shut out the light and let in the cold.

The seven beds, which were all the hayloft held in the way of furniture, were stark, basic affairs made of a piece of canvas stretched tautly onto a tubular metal frame. On each bed there were supposed to be one pillow and two gray blankets, but I had to struggle to get mine back because they had been appropriated by others as soon as my predecessor left. The pillow had no cover, there were no sheets, and there were no mattresses. Everyone went to bed fully dressed to keep warm, and on my third day there it started snowing.

The kitchen at the bottom of the ladder, the only other room available to the lads, was nothing more than the last loose box along one side of the yard. So little had been done to make it habitable as to leave a powerful suggestion that its inmates were to be thought of, and treated, as animals. The bars were still in place over the small window, and there were still bolts on the outside of the split stable door. The floor was still of bare concrete crisscrossed with drainage grooves; one side wall was of rough boards with kick marks still in them and the other three were of bare bricks. The room was chronically cold and damp and dirty; and although it may have been big enough as a home for one horse, it was uncomfortably cramped for seven men.

The minimal furniture consisted of rough benches around two walls, a wooden table, a badly chipped electric cooker, a shelf for crockery, and an old marble washstand bearing a metal jug and a metal basin, which was all there was in the way of a bathroom. Other needs were catered to in a wooden hut beside the muck heap.

The food, prepared by a slatternly woman perpetually in curlers, was not up to the standard of the accommodation.

Humber, who had engaged me with an indifferent glance and a nod, directed me with equal lack of interest, when I arrived in the yard, to look after four horses, and told me the numbers of their boxes. Neither he nor anyone else told me their names. The head lad, who did one horse himself, appeared to have very little authority, contrary to the practice in most other training stables, and it was Humber himself who gave the orders and who made sure they were carried out.

He was a tyrant, not so much in the quality of the work he demanded as in the quantity. There were some thirty horses in the yard. The head lad cared for one horse, and the head traveling lad, who also drove the horse box, did none at all. That left twenty-nine horses for seven lads, who were also expected to keep the gallops in order and do all the cleaning and maintenance work of the whole place. On racing days, when one or two lads were away, those remaining often had six horses to see to. It made my stint at Inskip's seem like a rest cure.

At the slightest sign of shirking, Humber would dish out irritating little punishments and roar in an acid voice that he paid extra wages for extra work, and anyone who didn't like it could leave. As everyone was there because better stables would not risk employing them, leaving Humber's automatically meant leaving racing altogether. And taking whatever they knew about the place with them. It was very, very neat.

My companions in this hellhole were neither friendly nor likable. The best of them was the nearly half-witted boy I had seen at Stafford on Boxing Day. His name was Jerry, and he came in for a lot of physical abuse because he was slower and more stupid than anyone else.

Two of the others had been to prison and their outlook on life made Soupy Tarleton look like a Sunday-school favorite. It was from one of these, Jimmy, that I had had to wrench my blanket, and from the other, a thickset tough called Charlie, my pillow. They were the two bullies of the bunch, and in addition to the free use they made of their boots, they could always be relied upon to tell lying tales and wriggle themselves out of trouble, seeing to it that someone else was punished in their stead.

Reggie was a food stealer. Thin, white faced, and with a twitch in his left eyelid, he had long prehensile hands which could whisk the bread off your plate faster than the eye could follow. I lost a lot of my meager rations to him before I caught him at it, and it always remained a mystery why, when he managed to eat more than anyone else, he stayed the thinnest.

One of the lads was deaf. He told me phlegmatically in a toneless mumble that his dad had done it when he was little, giving him a few clips too many over the ear holes. His name was Bert, and as he occasionally wet himself in bed, he smelled appalling.

The seventh, Geoff, had been there longest, and even after ten weeks never spoke of leaving. He had a habit of looking furtively over his shoulder, and any mention by Jimmy or Charlie about their prison experiences brought him close to tears, so that I came to the conclusion that he had committed some crime and was terrified of being found out. I supposed ten weeks at Humber's might be preferable to jail, but it was debatable.

They knew all about me from the head traveling lad, Jud Wilson. My general dishonesty they took entirely for granted, but they thought I was lucky to have got off without going inside if it was true about October's daughter, and they sniggered about it unendingly, and made merciless obscene jibes that hit their target all too often.

I found their constant closeness a trial, the food disgusting, the work exhausting, the beds relentless, and the cold unspeakable. All of which rather roughly taught me that my life in Australia had been soft and easy, even when I thought it most demanding.

Before I went to Humber's I had wondered why anyone should be foolish enough to pay training fees to a patently unsuccessful trainer, but I gradually found out. The yard itself, for one thing, was a surprise. From the appearance of the horses at race meetings one would have expected their home surroundings to be weedy gravel, broken-hinged boxes, and flaked-off paint; but in fact the yard was trim and prosperous looking, and was kept that way by the lads, who never had time off in the afternoons. This glossy window dressing cost Humber nothing but an occasional gallon of paint and a certain amount of slave driving.

His manner with the owners who sometimes arrived for a look around was authoritative and persuasive, and his fees, I later discovered, were lower than anyone else's, which attracted more custom than he would otherwise have had. In addition, some of the horses in the yard were not racehorses at all, but hunters at livery, for whose board, lodging, and exercise he received substantial sums without the responsibility of having to train them.

I learned from the other lads that only seven of the stable's inmates had raced at all that season, but that those seven had been hard worked, with an average of a race each every ten days. There had been one winner, two seconds, and a third among them.

None of those seven was in my care. I had been allotted a quartet consisting of two racehorses that belonged, as far as I could make out, to Humber himself, and two hunters. The two racehorses were bays, about seven years old; one of them had a sweet mouth and no speed and the other a useful sprint over schooling fences but a churlish nature. I pressed Cass, the head lad, to tell me their names, and he said they were Dobbin and Sooty. These unraceman-like names were not to be found in the form book, nor in Humber's list in *Horses in Training;* and it seemed to me highly probably that Rudyard, Superman, Charcoal, and the rest had all spent their short periods in the yard under similar uninformative pseudonyms.

A lad who had gone out of racing would never connect the Dobbin or Sooty he had once looked after with the Rudyard who won a race for another trainer two years later.

But why, *why* did he win two years later? About that I was as ignorant as ever.

The cold weather came and gripped, and stayed. But nothing, the other lads said, could be as bad as the fearsome winter before; and I reflected that in that January and February I had been sweltering under the

120

midsummer sun. I wondered how Belinda and Helen and Philip were enjoying their long vacation, and what they would think if they could see me in my dirty, downtrodden sub-existence, and what the men would think, to see their employer brought so low. It amused me a good deal to imagine it; and it not only helped the tedious hours to pass more quickly, but kept me from losing my own inner identity.

As the days of drudgery mounted up, I began to wonder if anyone who embarked on so radical a masquerade really knew what he was doing.

Expression, speech, and movement had to be unremittingly schooled into a convincing show of uncouth dullness. I worked in a slovenly fashion and rode, with a pang, like a mutton-fisted clod; but as time passed all these deceptions became easier. If one pretended long enough to be a wreck, did one finally become one? I wondered. And if one stripped oneself continuously of all human dignity, would one in the end be unaware of its absence? I hoped the question would remain academic; and as long as I could have a quiet laugh at myself now and then, I supposed I was safe enough.

My belief that after three months in the yard a lad was given every encouragement to leave was amply borne out by what happened to Geoff Smith.

Humber never rode out to exercise with his horses, but drove in a van to the gallops to watch them work, and returned to the yard while they were still walking back to have a poke around to see what had been done and not done.

One morning, when we went in with the second lot, Humber was standing in the center of the yard radiating his frequent displeasure.

"You, Smith, and you, Roke, put those horses in their boxes and come here."

We did so.

"Roke."

"Sir?"

"The mangers of all your four horses are in a disgusting state. Clean them up."

"Yes, sir."

"And to teach you to be more thorough in future, you will get up at five-thirty for the next week."

"Sir."

I sighed inwardly, but this was to me one of his more acceptable forms of pinprick punishment, since I didn't particularly mind getting up early. It entailed merely standing in the middle of the yard for over an hour, doing nothing. Dark, cold, and boring. I don't think he slept much himself. His bedroom window faced down the yard, and he always knew if one was not standing outside by twenty to six, and shining a torch to prove it.

"And as for you." He looked at Geoff with caluculation. "The floor of number seven is caked with dirt. You'll clean out the straw and scrub the floor with disinfectant before you get your dinner."

"But, sir," protested Geoff incautiously, "if I don't go in for dinner with the others, they won't leave me any."

"You should have thought of that before, and done your work properly in the first place. I pay half as much again as any other trainer would, and I expect value for it. You will do as you are told."

"But, sir," whined Geoff, knowing that if he missed his main meal he would go very hungry, "Can't I do it this afternoon?"

Humber casually slid his walking stick through his hand until he was holding it at the bottom. Then he swung his arm and savagely cracked the knobbed handle across Geoff's thigh.

Geoff yelped and rubbed his leg.

"Before dinner," remarked Humber, and walked away, leaning on his stick.

Geoff missed his share of the watery, half-stewed lumps of mutton, and came in panting to see the last of the bread-and-suet pudding spooned into Charlie's traplike mouth.

"You bloody sods," he yelled miserably. "You bloody lot of sods!"

He stuck it for a whole week. He stood six more heavy blows on various parts of his body, and missed his dinner three more times, and his breakfast twice, and his supper once. Long before the end of it he was in tears, but he didn't want to leave.

After five days Cass came into the kitchen at breakfast and told Geoff, "The boss has taken against you, I'm afraid. You won't ever do anything right for him again from now on. Best thing you can do—and I'm telling you for your own good, mind—is to find a job somewhere else. The boss gets these fits now and then when one of the lads can't do anything right, and no one can change him when he gets going. You can work until you're blue in the face, but he won't take to you anymore. You don't want to get yourself bashed up anymore, now, do you? All I'm telling you is that if you stay here you'll find that what has happened so far is only the beginning. See? I'm only telling you for your own good."

Even so, it was two more days before Geoff painfully packed his old army kit bag and sniffed his way off the premises.

A weedy boy arrived the next morning as a replacement, but he only stayed three days, as Jimmy stole his blankets before he came and he was not strong enough to get them back. He moaned piteously through two freezing nights, and was gone before the third.

The next morning, before breakfast, it was Jimmy himself who collected a crack from the stick.

He came in late and cursing and snatched a chunk of bread out of Jerry's hand.

"Where's my bloody breakfast?"

We had eaten it, of course.

"Well," he said, glaring at us, "you can do my ruddy horses, as well. I'm off. I'm not bloody well staying here. This is worse than doing bird. You won't catch me staying here to be swiped at, I'll tell you that."

Reggie said, "Why don't you complain?"

"Who to?"

"Well . . . the bluebottles."

"Are you out of your mind?" said Jimmy in amazement. "You're a bloody nit, that's what you are. Can you see me, with my form, going into the cop house

123

and saying I got a complaint to make about my employer, he hit me with his walking stick? For a start, they'd laugh. They'd laugh their bleeding heads off. And then what? Supposing they come here and asked Cass if he's seen anyone getting the rough end of it? Well, I'll tell you, that Cass wants to keep his cushy job. Oh, no, he'd say, I ain't seen nothing. Mr. Humber, he's a nice, kind gentleman with a heart of gold, and what can you expect from an ex-con but a pack of bull? Don't ruddy well make me laugh. I'm off, and if the rest of you've got any sense, you'll be out of it, too."

No one, however, took his advice.

I found out from Charlie that Jimmy had been there two weeks longer than he, which made it, he thought about eleven weeks.

As Jimmy strode defiantly out of the yard, I went rather thoughtfully about my business. Eleven weeks, twelve at the most, before Humber's arm started swinging. I had already been there three, which left me a maximum of nine more in which to discover how he managed the doping. It wasn't that I couldn't probably last out as long as Geoff if it came to the point, but that if I hadn't uncovered Humber's method before he focused his attention on getting rid of me, I had very little chance of doing it afterward.

Three weeks, I thought, and I had found out nothing at all except that I wanted to leave as soon as possible.

Two lads came to take Geoff's and Jimmy's places, a tall boy called Lenny, who had been to Borstal and was proud of it, and Cecil, a far-gone alcoholic of about thirty-five. He had, he told us, been kicked out of half the stables in England because he couldn't keep his hands off the bottle. I don't know where he got the liquor from or how he managed to hide it, but he was certainly three parts drunk every day by four o'clock, and snored in a paralytic stupor every night.

Life, if you could call it that, went on.

All the lads seemed to have a good reason for having to earn the extra wages Humber paid. Lenny was repaying some money he had stolen from another employer, Charlie had a wife somewhere drawing maintenance,

Cecil drank, Reggie was a compulsive saver, and Humber sent Jerry's money straight off to his parents. Jerry was proud of being able to help them.

I had let Jud Wilson and Cass know that I badly needed to earn sixteen pounds a week because I had fallen behind on installment payments on the motorcycle, and this also gave me an obvious reason for needing to spend some time in the Posset post office on Saturday afternoons.

Public transport from the stables to Posset, a large village a mile and a half away, did not exist. Cass and Jud Wilson both had cars, but would give no lifts. My motorcycle was the only other transport available, but to the lads' fluently expressed disgust, I refused to use it on the frosty, snow-strewn roads for trips down to the pub in the evenings. As a result, we hardly ever went to Posset except on the two hours we had off on Saturday afternoons, and also on Sunday evenings, when after a slightly less relentless day's work everyone had enough energy left to walk for their beer.

On Saturdays I unwrapped the motorcycle from its thick plastic cocoon and set off to Posset with Jerry perched ecstatically on the pillion. I always took poor simpleminded Jerry because he got the worst of everything throughout the week; and we quickly fell into a routine. First we went to the post office for me to mail my imaginary installment. Instead, leaning on the shelf among the telegram forms and scraps of pink blotting paper, I wrote each week a report to October, making sure that no one from the stables looked over my shoulder. Replies, if any, I collected, read, and tore up over the litter basket.

Jerry accepted without question that I would be at least a quarter of an hour in the post office, and spent the time unsuspiciously at the other end of the shop inspecting the stock in the toy department. Twice he bought a big friction-drive car and played with it, until it broke, on the dormitory floor; and every week he bought a children's fourpenny comic, over whose picture strips he giggled contentedly for the next few days. He couldn't read a word, and often asked me to explain

125

the captions, so that I became intimately acquainted with the doings of Mickey the Monkey and Flip McCoy.

Leaving the post office, we climbed back onto the motorcycle and rode two hundred yards down the street to have tea. This ritual took place in a square, bare café with margarine-colored walls, cold lighting, and messy tabletops. For decoration there were Pepsi-Cola advertisements, and for service a bored-looking girl with no stockings and mousy hair piled into a matted, wispy mountain on top of her head.

None of this mattered. Jerry and I ordered and ate with indescribable enjoyment a heap of lamb chops, fried eggs, flabby chips, and bright-green peas. Charlie and the others were to be seen doing the same at adjoining tables. The girl knew where we came from, and looked down on us, as her father owned the café.

One our way out, Jerry and I packed our pockets with bars of chocolate to supplement Humber's food, a hoard which lasted each week exactly as long as it took Reggie to find it.

By four o'clock we were back in the yard, the motorcycle wrapped up again, the week's highlight nothing but a memory and a belch, the next seven days stretching drearily ahead.

There were hours, in that life, in which to think. Hours of trotting the horses around and around a straw track in a frozen field, hours brushing the dust out of their coats, hours of cleaning the muck out of their boxes and carrying their water and hay, hours of lying awake at night listening to the stamp of the horses below and the snores and mumblings from the row of beds.

Over and over again I thought my way through all I had seen or read or heard since I came to England; and what emerged as most significant was the performance of Superman at Stafford. He had been doped; he was the twelfth of the series; but he had not won.

Eventually I changed the order of these thoughts. He had been doped, and he had not won; but was he, after all, the twelfth of the series? He might be the thirteenth, the fourteenth; there might have been others who had come to grief.

126

On my third Saturday, when I had been at Humber's just over a fortnight, I wrote asking October to look up the newspaper cutting which Tommy Stapleton had kept, about a horse going berserk and killing a woman in the paddock at Cartmel races. I asked him to check the horse's history.

A week later I read his typewritten reply.

Old Etonian, destroyed at Cartmel, Lancashire, at Whitsun this year, spent the previous November and December in Humber's yard. Humber claimed him in a selling race, and sold him again at Leicester sales seven weeks later.

But: Old Etonian went berserk in the parade ring *before* the race; he was due to run in a handicap, not a seller; and the run-in at Cartmel is short. None of these facts conform to the pattern of the others.

Dope tests were made on Old Etonian, but proved negative.

No one could explain why he behaved as he did.

Tommy Stapleton, I thought, must have had an idea, or he would not have cut out the report, yet he could not have been sure enough to act on it without checking up. And checking up had killed him. There could be no more doubt of it.

I tore up the paper and took Jerry along to the café, more conscious than usual of the danger breathing down my neck. It didn't, however, spoil my appetite for the only edible meal of the week.

At supper a few days later, in the lull before Charlie turned on his transistor radio for the usual evening of pops from Luxembourg (which I had grown to enjoy), I steered the conversation around to Cartmel races. What, I wanted to know, were they like?

Only Cecil, the drunk, had ever been there.

"It's not like it used to be in the old days," he said owlishly, not noticing Reggie filch a hunk of his bread and margarine.

Cecil's eyes had a glazed, liquid look, but I had luckily asked my question at exactly the right moment, in the loquacious half hour between the silent bleariness of

127

the afternoon's liquor and his disappearance to tank up for the night.

"What was it like in the old days?" I prompted.

"They had a fair there." He hiccuped. "A fair with roundabouts and swings and sideshows and all. Bank holiday, see? Whitsun and all that. Only place outside the Derby you could go on the swings at the races. Course, they stopped it now. Don't like no one to have a good time, they don't. It weren't doing no harm, it weren't, the fair."

"Fairs," said Reggie scornfully, his eyes flicking to the crust Jerry held loosely in his hand.

"Good for dipping," commented Lenny, with superiority.

"Yeah," agreed Charlie, who hadn't yet decided if Borstal qualified Lenny as a fit companion for one from the higher school.

"Eh?" said Cecil, lost.

"Dipping. Working the pockets," Lenny said.

"Oh. Well, it can't have been that with the hound trails, and they stopped them, too. They were good sport, they were. Bloody good day out, it used to be, at Cartmel, but now it's the same at any other ruddy place. You might as well be at Newton Abbot or somewhere. Nothing but ordinary racing like any other day of the week." He belched.

"What were the hound trails?" I asked.

"Dog races," he said, smiling foolishly. "Bloody dog races. They used to have one before the horse races, and one afterward, but they've ruddy well stopped it now. Bloody killjoys, that's all they are. Still"—he leered triumphantly—"if you know what's what you can still have a bet on the dogs. They have a hound trail in the morning now, on the other side of the village from the racetrack, but if you get your horse bedded down quick enough you can get there in time for a bet."

"Dog races?" said Lenny disbelievingly. "Dogs won't race around no horse track. There ain't no bloody electric hare, for a start."

Cecil swiveled his head unsteadily in Lenny's direction.

"You don't have a track for hound trails," he said earnestly, in his slurred voice. "It's a *trail,* see? Some bloke sets off with a bagful of aniseed and paraffin, or something like that, and drags it for miles and miles around the hills and such. Then they let all the dogs loose and the first one to follow all around the train and get back quickest is the winner. Year before last, someone shot at the bloody favorite half a mile from home and there was a bleeding riot. They missed him, though. They hit the one just behind, some ruddy outsider with no chance."

"Reggie's ate my crust," said Jerry sadly.

"Did you go to Cartmel this year, too?" I asked.

"No," Cecil said regretfully. "Can't say I did. A woman got killed there, and all."

"How?" asked Lenny, looking avid.

"Some bloody horse bolted in the paddock, and jumped the rails of the parade ring and landed on some poor bloody woman who was just having a nice day out. She backed a loser all right, she did that day. I heard she was cut to bits, time that crazy animal trampled all over her trying to get out through the crowd. He didn't get far, but he kicked out all over the place and broke another man's leg before they got the vet to him and shot him. Mad, they said he was. A mate of mine was there, see, leading one around in the same race, and he said it was something awful, that poor woman all cut up and bleeding to death in front of his eyes."

The others looked suitably impressed at this horrific story, all except Bert, who couldn't hear it.

"Well," said Cecil, getting up, "it's time for my little walk."

He went out for his little walk, which was presumably to wherever he had hidden his alcohol, because as usual he came reeling back less than an hour later and stumbled up the ladder to his customary oblivion.

10

Toward the end of my fourth week Reggie left (complaining of hunger) and in a day or two was duly replaced by a boy with a soft face who said in a high-pitched voice that his name was Kenneth.

To Humber I clearly remained one insignficant face in this endless procession of human flotsam; and as I could safely operate only as long as that state of affairs continued, I did as little as possible to attract his attention. He gave me orders, and I obeyed them; and he cursed me and punished me—but not more than anyone else—for the things I left undone.

I grew to recognize his moods at a glance. There were days when he glowered silently all through first and second exercise and turned out again to make sure that no one skimped the third, and on these occasions even Cass walked warily and only spoke if he was spoken to. There were days when he talked a great deal but always in sarcasm, and his tongue was so rough that everyone preferred the silence. There were occasional days when he wore an abstract air and overlooked our faults, and even rarer days when he looked fairly pleased with life.

At all times he was impeccably turned out, as if to emphasize the difference between his state and ours. His clothes, I judged, were his main personal vanity, but his wealth was also evident in his car, the latest type of Cunard-size Bentley. It was fitted with back-seat television, plush carpets, radio-telephone, fur rugs, air-conditioning, and a built-in drinks cabinet holding in racks six bottles, twelve glasses, and a glittering array of chromiumed corkscrews, ice picks, and miscellaneous objects like swizzle sticks.

I knew the car well, because I had to clean it every

Monday afternoon. Bert had to clean it on Fridays. Humber was proud of his car.

He was chauffeured on long journeys in this above-his-status symbol by Jud Wilson's sister Grace, a hard-faced amazon of a woman who handled the huge car with practiced ease but was not expected to maintain it. I never once spoke to her; she bicycled in from wherever she lived, drove as necessary, and bicycled away again. Frequently the car had not been cleaned to her satisfaction, but her remarks were relayed to Bert and me by Jud.

I looked into every cranny every time while cleaning the inside, but Humber was neither so obliging nor so careless as to leave hypodermic syringes or phials of stimulants lying about in the glove compartments.

All through my first month there, the freezing weather was not only a discomfort but also a tiresome delay. While racing was suspended, Humber could dope no horses, and there was no opprtunity for me to see what difference it made to his routine when the racing was scheduled for any of the five courses with long run-ins.

On top of that, he and Jud Wilson and Cass were always about in the stables. I wanted to have a look around inside Humber's office, a brick hut standing across the top end of the yard, but I could not risk a search when any one of them might come in and find me at it. With Humber and Jud Wilson away at the races, though, and with Cass gone home to his midday meal, I reckoned I could go into the office to search while the rest of the lads were eating.

Cass had a key to the office, and it was he who unlocked the door in the morning and locked it again at night. As far as I could see, he did not bother to lock up when he went home for lunch, and the office was normally left open all day, except on Sunday. This might mean, I thought, that Humber kept nothing there which could possibly be incriminating; but on the other hand, he could perhaps keep something there which was apparently innocent but would be incriminating if one understood its significance.

However, the likelihood of solving the whole mystery

by a quick look around in an unlocked stable office was so doubtful that it was not worth risking discovery, and I judged it better to wait with what patience I could until the odds were in my favor.

There was also Humber's house, a whitewashed converted farmhouse adjoining the yard. A couple of stealthy surveys, made on afternoons when I was bidden to sweep snow from his garden path, showed that this was an ultra-neat soulless establishment like a series of rooms in shop windows, impersonal and unlived in. Humber was not married, and downstairs at least there seemed to be nowhere at all snug for him to spend his evenings.

Through the windows I saw no desk to investigate and no safe in which to lock away secrets; all the same I decided it would be less than fair to ignore his home, and if I both drew a blank and got away with an entry into the office, I would pay the house a visit at the first opportunity.

At last it began to thaw on a Wednesday night and continued fast all day Thursday and Friday, so that by Saturday morning the thin slush was disintegrating into puddles, and the stables stirred with the reawakening of hunting and racing.

Cass told me on Friday night that the man who owned the hunters I looked after required them both to be ready for him on Saturday, and after second exercise I led them out and loaded them into the horse box which had come for them.

Their owner stood leaning against the front wing of a well-polished Jaguar. His hunting boots shone like glass, his cream breeches were perfection, his pink coat fitted without a wrinkle, his stock was smooth and snowy. He held a sensible leather-covered riding stick in his hand and snapped it against his boot. He was tall, broad, and bareheaded, about forty years old, and, from across the yard, handsome. It was only when one was close to him that one could see the dissatisfied look on his face and the evidences of dissipation on his skin.

"You," he said, pointing at me with his stick. "Come here."

I went. He had heavy-lidded eyes and a few purple

thread veins on his nose and cheeks. He looked at me with superior bored disdain. I am five feet nine inches tall; he was four inches taller, and he made the most of it.

"You'll pay for it if those horses of mine don't last the day. I ride them hard. They need to be fit."

His voice had the same expensive timbre as October's.

"They're as fit as the snow would allow," I said calmly.

He raised his eyebrows.

"Sir," I added.

"Insolence," he said, "will get you nowhere."

"I am sorry, sir. I didn't mean to be insolent."

He laughed unpleasantly. "I'll bet you didn't. It's not so easy to get another job, is it? You'll watch your tongue when you speak to me in the future, if you know what's good for you."

"Yes, sir."

"And if those horses of mine aren't fit, you'll wish you'd never been born."

Cass appeared at my left elbow, looking anxious.

"Is everything all right, sir?" he asked. "Has Roke done anything wrong, Mr. Adams?"

How I managed not to jump out of my skin I am not quite sure. Mr. Adams. Paul James Adams, sometime owner of seven subsequently doped horses?

"Is this bloody gypsy doing my horses any good?" said Adams offensively.

"He's not worse than any of the other lads," said Cass soothingly.

"And that's saying precious little." He gave me a mean stare. "You've had it easy during the freeze. Too damned easy. You'll have to wake your ideas up now hunting has started again. You won't find me as soft as your master, I can tell you that."

I said nothing. He slapped his stick sharply against his boot.

"Do you hear what I say? You'll find me harder to please."

"Yes, sir," I muttered.

He opened his fingers and let the stick fall at his feet.

"Pick it up," he said.

As I bent to pick it up, he put his booted foot on my shoulder and gave me a heavy, overbalancing shove, so that I fell sprawling onto the soaking, muddy ground.

He smiled with malicious enjoyment.

"Get up, you clumsy lout, and do as you are told. Pick up my stick."

I got to my feet, picked up his stick, and held it out to him. He twitched it out of my hand, and looking at Cass, said, "You've got to show them you won't stand any nonsense. Stamp on them whenever you can. This one"—he looked me coldly up and down—"needs to be taught a lesson. What do you suggest?"

Cass looked at me doubtfully. I glanced at Adams. This, I thought, was not funny. His grayish-blue eyes were curiously opaque, as if he were drunk; but he was plainly sober. I had seen that look before, in the eyes of a stable hand I had once for a short time employed, and I knew what it could mean. I had to guess at once, and guess right, whether he preferred bullying the weak or the strong. From instinct, perhaps because of his size and evident worldliness, I guessed that crushing the weak would be too tame for him. In which case it was definitely not the moment for any show of strength. I drooped in as cowed and unresisting a manner as I could devise.

"God," said Adams in disgust. "Just look at him. Scared out of his bloody wits." He shrugged impatiently. "Well, Cass, just find him some stinking useless occupation like scrubbing the paths and put him to work. There's no sport for me here. No backbone for me to break. Give me a fox any day; at least they've got some cunning and some guts."

His gaze strayed sideways to where Humber was crossing the far end of the yard. He said to Cass, "Tell Mr. Humber I'd like to have a word with him," and when Cass had gone he turned back to me.

"Where did you work before this?"

"At Mr. Inskip's, sir."

"And he kicked you out?"

"Yes, sir."

"Why?"

"I . . . er . . ." I stuck. It was incredibly galling to have to lay oneself open to such a man; but if I gave him answers he could check in small things, he might believe the whopping lies without question.

"When I ask a question, you will answer it," said Adams coldly. "Why did Mr. Inskip get rid of you?"

I swallowed. "I got the sack for . . . er . . . for messing about with the boss's daughter."

"For messing about . . ." he repeated. "Good God." With lewd pleasure he said something which was utterly obscene. He saw me wince and laughed at my discomfiture. Cass and Humber returned. Adams turned to Humber, still laughing, and said, "Do you know why this cockerel got chucked out of Inskip's?"

"Yes," said Humber flatly. "He seduced October's daughter." He wasn't interested. "And there was also the matter of a favorite that came in last. He looked after it."

"October's daughter!" said Adams, surprised, his eyes narrowing. "I thought he meant Inskip's daughter." He casually dealt me a sharp clip on the ear. "Don't try lying to me."

"Mr. Inskip hasn't got a daughter," I protested.

"And don't answer back." His hand flicked out again. He was rather adept at it. He must have indulged in a lot of practice.

"Hedley," he said to Humber, who had impassively watched this one-sided exchange, "I'll give you a lift to Nottingham races on Monday if you like. I'll pick you up at ten."

"Right," agreed Humber.

Adams turned to Cass. "Don't forget that lesson for this lily-livered Romeo. Cool his ardor a bit."

Cass sniggered sycophantically and raised goose pimples on my neck.

Adams climbed coolly into his Jaguar, started it up, and followed the horse box containing his two hunters out of the yard.

135

Humber said, "I don't want Roke out of action, Cass. You've got to leave him fit to work. Use some sense this time." He limped away to continue his inspection of the boxes.

Cass looked at me, and I looked steadily down at my damp, muddy clothes, very conscious that the head lad counted among the enemy, and not wanting to risk his seeing that there was anything but submissiveness in my face.

He said, "Mr. Adams don't like to be crossed."

"I didn't cross him."

"Nor he don't like to be answered back to. You mind your lip."

"Has he anymore horses here?" I asked.

"Yes," said Cass, "and it's none of your business. Now he told me to punish you, and he won't forget. He'll check up later."

"I've done nothing wrong," I said sullenly, still looking down. What on earth would my foreman say about this, I thought; and nearly smiled at the picture.

"You don't need to have done nothing wrong," said Cass. "With Mr. Adams it's a case of punish first so that you won't do nothing wrong after. Sense, in a way." He gave a snort of laughter. "Saves trouble, see?"

"Are his horses all hunters?" I asked.

"No," said Cass, "but the two you've got are, and don't you forget it. He rides those himself, and he'll notice how you look after every hair on their hides."

"Does he treat the lads who look after his other horses so shocking unfair?"

"I never heard Jerry complaining. Mr. Adams won't treat you too bad if you mind your p's and q's. Now that lesson he suggested . . ."

I had hoped he had forgotten it.

"You can get down on your knees and scrub the concrete paths around the yard. Start now. You can break for dinner, and then go on until evening stables."

I went on standing in a rag-doll attitude of dejectedness, looking at the ground, but fighting an unexpectedly strong feeling of rebellion. What the hell, I thought, did October expect of me? Just how much was I to take?

136

Was there any point at which, if he went there, he would say, "Stop; all right; that's enough. That's too much. Give it up"? But remembering how he felt about me, I supposed not.

Cass said, "There's a scrubbing brush in the cupboard in the tack room. Get on with it." He walked away.

The concrete paths were six feet wide and ran around all sides of the yard in front of the boxes. They had been scraped clear of snow throughout the month I had been there so that the feed trolley could make its usual smooth journey from horse to horse, and as in most modern stables, including Inskip's and my own, they would always be kept clean of straw and excessive dust. But scrubbing them on one's knees for nearly four hours on a slushy day at the end of January was a miserable, back-breaking, insane waste of time. Ludicrous besides, and unheroic.

I had a clear choice of scrubbing the paths or getting on the motorcycle and going. Thinking firmly that I was being paid at least ten thousand pounds for doing it, I scrubbed; and Cass hung around the yard all day to watch that I didn't rest.

The lads, who had spent much of the afternoon amusing themselves by jeering at my plight as they set off for and returned from the café in Posset, made quite sure during evening stables that the concrete paths ended the day even dirtier than they had begun. I didn't care a damn about that; but Adams had sent his hunters back caked with mud and sweat and it took me two hours to clean them, because by the end of that day many of my muscles were trembling with fatigue.

Then, to crown it all, Adams came back. He drove his Jaguar into the yard, climbed out, and after having talked to Cass, who nodded and gestured around the paths, he walked without haste toward the box where I was still struggling with his black horse.

He stood in the doorway and looked down his nose at me; and I looked back. He was superbly elegant in a dark-blue pin-striped suit with a white shirt and a silver-gray tie. His skin looked fresh, his hair well brushed, his hands clean and pale. I imagined he had gone home after hunting and enjoyed a deep hot bath, a change of clothes, a drink. . . . I hadn't had a bath for a month and was unlikely to get one as long as I stayed at Humber's. I was filthy and hungry and extremely tired. I wished he would go away and leave me alone.

No such luck.

He took a step into the box and surveyed the mud still caked solid on the horse's hind legs.

"You're slow," he remarked.

"Sorry, sir."

"This horse must have been back here three hours ago. What have you been doing?"

"My three other horses, sir."

"You should do mine first."

"I had to wait for the mud to dry, sir. You can't brush it out while it's still wet."

"I told you this morning not to answer back." His hand lashed out across the ear he had hit before. He was smiling slightly. Enjoying himself. Which was more than could be said for me.

Having, so to speak, tasted blood, he suddenly took hold of the front of my jersey, pushed me back against the wall, and slapped me twice in the face, forehand and backhand. Still smiling.

What I wanted to do was to jab my knee into his groin and my fist into his stomach; and refraining wasn't easy. For the sake of realism I knew I should have cried out loudly and begged him to stop, but when it came to the point I couldn't do it. However, one could act what one couldn't say, so I lifted both arms and folded them defensively around my head.

He laughed and let go, and I slid down onto one knee and cowered against the wall.

"You're a proper little rabbit, aren't you, for all your fancy looks."

I stayed where I was, in silence. As suddenly as he had begun, he lost interest in ill-treating me.

"Get up, get up," he said irritably. "I didn't hurt you. You're not worth hurting. Get up and finish this

138

horse. And make sure it is done properly or you'll find yourself scrubbing again."

He walked out of the box and away across the yard. I stood up, leaned against the doorpost, and with uncharitable feelings watched him go up the path to Humber's house. To a good dinner, no doubt. An armchair. A fire. A glass of brandy. A friend to talk to. Sighing in depression, I went back to the tiresome job of brushing off the mud.

Shortly after a supper of dry bread and cheese, eaten to the accompaniment of crude jokes about my day's occupation and detailed descriptions of the meals which had been enjoyed in Posset, I had had quite enough of my fellow workers. I climbed the ladder and sat on my bed. It was cold upstairs. I had had quite enough of Humber's yard. I had had more than enough of being kicked around. All I had to do, as I had been tempted to do that morning, was to go outside, unwrap the motorcycle, and make tracks for civilization. I could stifle my conscience by paying most of the money back to October and pointing out that I had done at least half of the job.

I went on sitting on the bed and thinking about riding away on the motor bike. I went on sitting on the bed. And not riding away on the motor bike.

Presently I found myself sighing. I knew very well I had never had any real doubts about staying, even if it meant scrubbing those dreadful paths every day of the week. Quite apart from not finding myself good company in future if I ran away because of a little bit of eccentric charring, there was the certainty that it was specifically in Mr. P. J. Adams' ruthless hands that the good repute of British racing was in danger of being cracked to bits. It was him that I had come to defeat. It was no good decamping because the first taste of him was unpleasant.

His name typed on paper had come alive as a worse menace than Humber himself had ever seemed. Humber was merely harsh, greedy, bad-tempered, and vain, and he beat his lads for the sole purpose of making them leave. But Adams seemed to enjoy hurting for its own sake. Beneath that glossy crust of sophistication, and not far beneath, one glimpsed an irresponsible savage. Humber was forceful; but Adams, it now seemed to me, was the brains of the partnership. He was a more complex man and a far more fearsome adversary. I had felt equal to Humber. Adams dismayed me.

Someone started to come up the ladder. I thought it would be Cecil, reeling from his Saturday-night orgy, but it was Jerry. He came and sat on the bed next to mine. He looked downcast.

"Dan?"

"Yes."

"It weren't . . . it weren't no good in Posset today, without you being there."

"Wasn't it?"

"No." He brightened. "I bought my comic, though. Will you read it to me?"

"Tomorrow," I said tiredly.

There was a short silence while he struggled to organize his thoughts.

"Dan."

"Mm?"

"I'm sorry, like."

"What for?"

"Well, for laughing at you, like, this afternoon. It wasn't right . . . not when you've took me on your motor bike and all. I do ever so like going on your bike."

"It's all right, Jerry."

"The others were ribbing you, see, and it seemed the thing, like, to do what they done. So they would . . . would let me go with them, see?"

"Yes, Jerry, I see. It doesn't matter, really it doesn't."

"You never ribbed me when I done wrong."

"Forget it."

"I've been thinking," he said, wrinkling his forehead, "about me mam. She tried scrubbing some floors once. In some offices, it was. She came home fair whacked, she did. She said scrubbing floors was wicked. It made your back ache something chronic, she said, as I remember."

140

"Did she?"

"Does your back ache, Dan?"

"Yes, a bit."

He nodded, pleased. "She knows a thing or two, does my mam." He lapsed into one of his mindless silences, rocking himself gently backward and forward on the creaking bed.

I was touched by his apology.

"I'll read your comic for you," I said.

"You ain't too whacked?" he asked eagerly.

I shook my head.

He fetched the comic from the cardboard box in which he kept his few belongings and sat beside me while I read him the captions of Mickey the Monkey, Beryl and Peril, Julius Cheeser, The Bustom Boys, and all the rest. We went through the whole thing at least twice, with him laughing contentedly and repeating the words after me. By the end of the week he would know most of them by heart.

At length I took the comic out of his hands and put it down on the bed.

"Jerry," I said, "which of the horses you look after belongs to Mr. Adams?"

"Mr. Adams?"

"The man whose hunters I've got. The man who was here this morning, with a gray Jaguar, and a scarlet coat."

"Oh, that Mr. Adams."

"Why, is there another one?"

"No, that's Mr. Adams, all right." Jerry shuddered.

"What do you know about him?" I asked.

"The chap what was here before you came—Dennis, his name was—Mr. Adams didn't like him, see? He cheeked Mr. Adams, he did."

"Oh," I said. I wasn't sure I wanted to hear what had happened to Dennis.

"He weren't here above three weeks," said Jerry reflectively. "The last couple of days, he kept on falling down. Funny, it was, really."

I cut him short. "Which of your horses belongs to Mr. Adams?" I repeated.

141

"None of them do," he said positively.

"Cass said so."

He looked surprised, and also scared. "No, Dan, I don't want none of Mr. Adams' horses."

"Well, who do your horses belong to?"

"I don't rightly know. Except of course Pageant. He belongs to Mr. Byrd."

"That's the one you take to the races?"

"Uh huh, that's the one."

"How about the others?"

"Well, Mickey . . ." His brow furrowed.

"Mickey is the horse in the box next to Mr. Adams' black hunter, which I do?"

"Yeah." He smiled brilliantly, as if I had made a point.

"Who does Mickey belong to?"

"I dunno."

"Hasn't his owner ever been to see him?"

He shook his head doubtfully. I wasn't sure whether or not he would remember if an owner had in fact called.

"How about your other horse?" Jerry had only three horses to do, as he was slower than everyone else.

"That's Champ," said Jerry triumphantly.

"Who owns him?"

"He's a hunter."

"Yes, but who owns him?"

"Some fellow." He was trying hard. "A fat fellow. With sort of sticking-out ears." He pulled his own ears forward to show me.

"You know him well?"

He smiled widely. "He gave me ten bob for Christmas."

So it was Mickey, I thought, who belonged to Adams, but neither Adams nor Humber nor Cass had let Jerry know it. It looked as though Cass had let it slip out by mistake.

I said, "How long have you worked here, Jerry?"

"How long?" he echoed vaguely.

"How many weeks were you here before Christmas?"

He put his head on one side and thought. He brightened. "I came on the day after the Rovers beat the Gunners. My Dad took me to the match, see? Near our house, the Rovers' ground is."

I asked him more questions, but he had no clearer idea than that about when he had come to Humber's.

"Well," I said, "was Mickey here already, when you came?"

"I've never done no other horses since I've been here," he said. When I asked him no more questions, he placidly picked up the comic again and began to look at the pictures. Watching him, I wondered what it was like to have a mind like his, a brain like cotton wool upon which the accumulated learning of the work could make no dent, in which reason, memory, and awareness were blanketed almost out of existence.

He smiled happily at the comic strips. He was, I reflected, none the worse off for being simpleminded. He was good at heart, and what he did not understand could not hurt him. There was a lot to be said for life on that level. If one didn't realize one was an object of calculated humiliations, there would be no need to try to make oneself be insensitive to them. If I had his simplicity, I thought, I would find life at Humber's very much easier.

He looked up suddenly and saw me watching him, and gave me a warm, contented, trusting smile.

"I like you," he said, and turned his attention back to the paper.

There was a raucous noise from downstairs and the other lads erupted up the ladder, pushing Cecil among them, as he was practically unable to walk. Jerry scuttled back to his own bed and put his comic away carefully; and I, like all the rest, wrapped myself in two gray blankets and lay down, boots and all, on the inhospitable canvas. I tried to find a comfortable position for my excessively weary limbs, but unfortunately failed.

11

The office was as cold and unwelcoming as Humber's personality, with none of the ostentation of his car. It consisted of a long, narrow room with the door and the single smallish window both in the long wall facing down the yard. At the far end, away to the left as one entered, there was a door which opened into a washroom; this was whitewashed and lit by three slitlike frosted-glass windows, and led through an inner door into a lavatory. In the washroom itself there was a sink, a plastic-top table, a refrigerator, and two wall cupboards. The first of these on investigation proved to hold all the bandages, liniments, and medicines in common use with horses.

Careful not to move anything from its original position, I looked at every bottle, packet, and tin. As far as I could see, there was nothing of a stimulating nature among them.

The second cupboard, however, held plenty of stimulant in the shape of alcohol for human consumption, an impressive collection of bottles with a well-stocked shelf of glasses above them. For the entertainment of owners, not the quickening of their horses. I shut the door.

There was nothing in the refrigerator except four bottles of beer, some milk, and a couple of trays of ice cubes.

I went back into the office.

Humber's desk stood under the window, so that when he was sitting at it he could look straight out down the yard. It was a heavy, flat-topped kneehole desk with drawers at each side, and it was almost aggressively tidy. Granted Humber was away at Nottingham races and had not spent long in the office in the morning, but the tidiness was basic, not temporary. None of the

144

drawers was locked, and their contents (stationery, tax tables, and so on) could be seen at a glance. On top of the desk there was only a telephone, an adjustable reading lamp, a tray of pens and pencils, and a green glass paperweight the size of a cricket ball. Trapped air bubbles rose in a frozen spray in its depths.

The single sheet of paper which it held down bore only a list of duties for the day and had clearly been drawn up for Cass to work from. I saw disconsolately that I would be cleaning tack that afternoon with baby-voiced Kenneth, who never stopped talking, and doing five horses at evening stables, this last because the horses normally done by Bert, who had gone racing, had to be shared out among those left behind.

Apart from the desk, the office contained a large floor-to-ceiling cupboard in which form books and racing colors were kept; too few of those for the space available. Three dark-green filing cabinets, two leather armchairs, and an upright wooden chair with a leather seat stood around the walls.

I opened the unlocked drawers of the filing cabinets one by one and searched quickly through the contents. They contained racing calendars, old accounts, receipts, press cuttings, photographs, papers to do with the horse currently in training, analyses of form, letters from owners, records of saddlery and fodder transactions; everything that could be found in the office of nearly every trainer in the country.

I looked at my watch. Cass usually took an hour off for lunch. I had waited five minutes after he had driven out of the yard, and I intended to be out of the office ten minutes before he could be expected back. This had given me a working time of three-quarters of an hour, of which nearly half had already gone.

Borrowing a pencil from the desk and taking a sheet of writing paper from a drawer, I applied myself to the drawer full of current accounts. For each of seventeen racehorses there was a separate hard-covered blue ledger, in which was listed every major and minor expense incurred in its training. I wrote a list of their names, few of which were familiar to me, together with their owners and the dates when they had come into the yard. Some had been there for years, but three had arrived during the past three months, and it was only these, I thought, which were of any real interest. None of the horses which had been doped had stayed at Humber's longer than four months.

The names of the three newest horses were Chin-Chin, Kandersteg, and Starlamp. The first was owned by Humber himself and the other two by Adams.

I put the account books back where I had found them and looked at my watch. Seventeen minutes left. Putting the pencil back on the desk, I folded the list of horses and stowed it away in my money belt. The webbing pockets were filling up again with fivers, as I had spent little of my pay, but the belt still lay flat and invisible below my waist under my jeans: and I had been careful not to let any of the lads know it was there, so as not to be robbed.

I riffled quickly through the drawers of press cuttings and photographs, but found no reference to the eleven horses or their successes. The racing calendars bore more fruit in the shape of a penciled cross against the name of Superman in the Boxing Day selling chase, but there was no mark against the selling chase scheduled for a coming meeting at Sedgefield.

It was at the back of the receipts drawer that I struck most gold. There was another blue accounts ledger there, with a double page devoted to each of the eleven horses. Among these eleven were interspersed nine others who had in various ways failed in their purpose. One of these was Superman and another Old Etonian.

On the left-hand page of each double spread had been recorded the entire racing career of the horse in question, and on the right-hand pages of my eleven old friends were details of the race they each won with assistance. Beneath were sums of money which I judged must be Humber's winnings on them. His winnings had run into thousands on every successful race. On Superman's page he had written: "Lost: three hundred pounds." On Old Etonian's right-hand page there was no race record: only the single word "Destroyed."

A crossing-out line had been drawn diagonally across all the pages except those concerning a horse called Six-Ply; and two new double pages had been prepared at the end, one for Kandersteg, and one for Starlamp. The left-hand pages for these three horses were written up: the right-hand pages were blank.

I shut the book and put it back. It was high time to go, and with a last look around to make sure that everything was exactly as it had been when I came in, I let myself quietly, unnoticed, out of the door, and went back to the kitchen to see if by some miracle the lads had left me any crumbs of lunch. Naturally, they had not.

The next morning Jerry's horse Mickey disappeared from the yard while we were out at second exercise, but Cass told him Jud had run him down to a friend of Humber's on the coast, for Mickey to paddle in the sea water to strengthen his legs, and that he would be back that evening. But the evening came, and Mickey did not.

On Wednesday Humber ran another horse, and I missed my lunch to have a look inside his house while he was away. Entry was easy through an open ventilator, but I could find nothing whatever to give me any clue as to how the doping was carried out.

All day Thursday I fretted about Mickey being still away at the coast. It sounded perfectly reasonable. It was what a trainer about twelve miles from the sea could be expected to arrange. Sea water was good for horses' legs. But something happened to horses sometimes at Humber's which made it possible for them to be doped later, and I had a deeply disturbing suspicion that whatever it was was happening to Mickey at this moment, and that I was missing my only chance of finding it out.

According to the accounts books, Adams owned four of the racehorses in the yard, in addition to his two hunters. None of his racehorses was known in the yard by its real name: therefore Mickey could be any one of the four. He could in fact be Kandersteg or Starlamp.

It was an even chance that he was one or the other, and was due to follow in Superman's footsteps. So I fretted.

On Friday morning a hired box took the stable runner to Haydock races, and Jud and Humber's own box remained in the yard until lunchtime. This was a definite departure from normal; and I took the opportunity of noting the mileage on the speedometer.

Jud drove the box out of the yard while we were still eating the midday sludge, and we didn't see him come back, as we were all out on the gallop farthest away from the stables sticking back into place the divots kicked out of the soft earth that week by the various training activities; but when we returned for evening stables at four, Mickey was back in his own quarters.

I climbed up into the cab of the horse box and looked at the mileage indicator. Jud had driven exactly sixteen and a half miles. He had not, in fact, been as far as the coast. I thought some very bitter thoughts.

When I had finished doing my two racehorses, I carried the brushes and pitchforks along to see to Adams' black hunter, and found Jerry leaning against the wall outside Mickey's next-door box with tears running down his cheeks.

"What's the matter?" I said, putting down my stuff.

"Mickey . . . bit me," he said. He was shaking with pain and fright.

"Let's see."

I helped him slide his left arm out of his jersey, and took a look at the damage. There was a fierce red-and-purple circular weal on the fleshy part of his upper arm near the shoulder. It had been a hard, savage bite.

Cass came over.

"What's going on here?"

But he saw Jerry's arm, and didn't need to be told. He looked over the bottom half of the door into Mickey's box, then turned to Jerry and said, "His legs were too far gone for the sea water to cure them. The vet said he would have to put on a blister, and he did it this afternoon when Mickey got back. That's what's the matter with him. Feels a bit off color, he does, and so would

148

you if someone slapped a flaming plaster on your legs. Now you just stop this stupid blubbing and get right back in there and see to him. And you, Dan, get on with that hunter and mind your own bloody business." He went off along the row.

"I can't," whispered Jerry, more to himself than to me.

"You'll manage it," I said cheerfully.

He turned to me a stricken face. "He'll bite me again."

"I'm sure he won't."

"He tried lots of times. And he's kicking out something terrible. I daren't go into his box. . . ." He stood stiffly, shivering with fright, and I realized that it really was beyond him to go back.

"All right," I said, "I'll do Mickey and you do my hunter. Only do him well, Jerry, very well. Mr. Adams is coming to ride him again tomorrow and I don't want to spend another Saturday on my knees."

He looked dazed. "Ain't no one done nothing like that for me before."

"It's a swap," I said brusquely. "You mess up my hunter and I'll bite you worse than Mickey did."

He stopped shivering and began to grin, which I had intended, and slipping his arm painfully back inside his jersey, he picked up my brushes and opened the hunter's door.

"You won't tell Cass?" he asked anxiously.

"No," I reassured him, and unbolted Mickey's box door.

The horse was tied up safely enough, and wore on his neck a long wooden barred collar called a cradle which prevented his bending his head down to bite the bandages off his forelegs. Under the bandages, according to Cass, Mickey's legs were plastered with "blister," a sort of caustic paste used to contract and strengthen the tendons. Blistering was a normal treatment for dickey tendons. The only trouble was that Mickey's legs had not needed treatment. They had been, to my eyes, as sound as rocks. But now, however, they were definitely paining him; at least as much as with a blister, and possibly more.

As Jerry had indicated, Mickey was distinctly upset. He could not be soothed by hand or voice, but lashed forward with his hind feet whenever he thought I was in range, and made equal use of his teeth. I was careful not to walk behind him, though he did his best to turn his quarters in my direction while I was banking up his straw bed around the back of the box. I fetched him hay and water, but he was not interested, and changed his rug, as the one he wore was soaked with sweat and would give him a chill during the night. Changing his rug was a bit of an obstacle race, but by warding off his attacks with the pitchfork, I got it done unscathed.

I took Jerry with me to the feed bins, where Cass was doling out the right food for each horse, and when we got back to the boxes we solemnly exchanged bowls. Jerry grinned happily. It was infectious. I grinned back.

Mickey didn't want food either, not, that is, except lumps of me. He didn't get any. I left him tied up for the night and took myself and Jerry's sack of brushes to safety on the far side of the door. Mickey would, I hoped, have calmed down considerably by the morning.

Jerry was grooming the black hunter practically hair by hair, humming tonelessly under his breath.

"Are you done?" I said.

"Is he all right?" he asked anxiously.

I went in to have a look.

"Perfect," I said truthfully. Jerry was better at strapping a horse than at most things; and the next day, to my considerable relief, Adams passed both hunters without remark and spoke hardly a word to me. He was in a hurry to be off to a distant meet, but all the same it seemed I had succeeded in appearing too spineless to be worth tormenting.

Mickey was a good deal worse that morning. When Adams had gone, I stood with Jerry looking over the half door of Mickey's box. The poor animal had managed to rip one of the bandages off in spite of the cradle, and we could see a big raw area over his tendon.

Mickey looked around at us with baleful eyes and

150

flat ears, his neck stretched forward aggressively. Muscles quivered violently in his shoulders and hindquarters. I had never seen a horse behave like that except when fighting; and he was, I thought, dangerous.

"He's off his head," whispered Jerry, awestruck.

"Poor thing."

"You ain't going in?" he said. "He looks like he'd kill you."

"Go and get Cass," I said. "No, I'm not going in, not without Cass knowing how things are, and Humber, too. You go and tell Cass that Mickey's gone mad; that ought to fetch him to have a look."

Jerry trotted off and returned with Cass, who seemed to be alternating between anxiety and scorn as he came within earshot. At the sight of Mickey, anxiety abruptly took over, and he went to fetch Humber, telling Jerry on no account to open Mickey's door.

Humber came unhurriedly across the yard leaning on his stick, with Cass, who was a short man, trotting along at his side. Humber looked at Mickey for a good long time. Then he shifted his gaze to Jerry, who was standing there shaking again at the thought of having to deal with a horse in such a state, and then farther along to me, where I stood at the door of the next box.

"That's Mr. Adams' hunter's box," he said to me.

"Yes, sir; he went with Mr. Adams just now, sir."

He looked me up and down, and then Jerry the same, and finally said to Cass, "Roke and Webber had better change horses. I know they haven't an ounce of guts between them, but Roke is much bigger, stronger, and older." And also, I thought with a flash of insight, Jerry has a father and mother to make a fuss if he gets hurt, whereas against Roke in the next-of-kin file was the single word "None."

"I'm not going in there alone, sir," I said. "Cass will have to hold off with a pitchfork while I muck him out." And even then, I thought, we'd both be lucky to get out without being kicked.

Cass, to my amusement, hurriedly started telling Humber that if I was too scared to do it on my own, he would get one of the other lads to help me. Humber, however, took no notice of either of us, but went back to staring somberly at Mickey.

Finally he turned to me and said, "Fetch a bucket and come over to the office."

"An empty bucket, sir?"

"Yes," he said impatiently, "an empty bucket." He turned and gently limped over to the long brick hut. I took the bucket out of the hunter's box, followed him, and waited by the door.

He came out with a small labeled glass-stoppered chemist's jar in one hand and a teaspoon in the other. The jar was three-quarters full of white powder. He gestured to me to hold out the bucket, then he put half a teaspoonful of the powder into it.

"Fill the bucket only a third full of water," he said. "And put it in Mickey's manger, so that he can't kick it over. It will quieten him down, once he drinks it."

He took the jar and spoon back inside the office, and I picked a good pinch of the white powder out of the bottom of the bucket and dropped it down inside the lists of Humber's horses in my money belt. I licked my fingers and thumb afterward; the particles of powder clinging there had a faintly bitter taste. The jar, which I had seen in the cupboard in the washroom, was labeled "Soluble Phenobarbitone," and the only surprising factor was the amount of it that Humber kept available.

I ran water into the bucket, stirred it with my hand, and went back to Mickey's box. Cass had vanished. Jerry was across the yard seeing to his third horse. I looked around for someone to ask for help, but everyone was carefully keeping out of sight. I cursed. I was not going in to Mickey alone; it was just plain stupid to try it.

Humber came back across the yard.

"Get on in," he said.

"I'd spill the water dodging him, sir."

"Huh."

Mickey's hoofs thudded viciously against the wall.

"You mean you haven't got the guts."

"You'd need to be a bloody fool to go in there alone, sir," I said sullenly.

He glared at me, but he must have seen it was no use insisting. He suddenly picked up the pitchfork from where it stood against the wall and transferred it to his right hand and the walking stick to his left.

"Get on with it then," he said harshly. "And don't waste time."

He looked incongruous, brandishing his two unconventional weapons while dressed like an advertisement for *Country Life*. I hoped he was going to be as resolute as he sounded.

I unbolted Mickey's door and we went in. It had been an injustice to think Humber might turn tail and leave me there alone: he behaved as coldly as ever, as if fear was quite beyond his imagination. Efficiently he kept Mickey penned first to one side of the box and then to the other while I mucked out and put down fresh straw; he remained steadfastly at his post while I cleaned the uneaten food out of the manger and wedged the bucket of doped water in place. Mickey didn't make it easy for him, either. The teeth and hoofs were busier and more dangerous than the night before.

It was especially aggravating in the face of Humber's coolness to have to remember to behave like a bit of a coward myself, though I minded less than if he had been Adams.

When I had finished the jobs, Humber told me to go out first, and he retreated in good order after me, his well-pressed suit scarcely rumpled from his exertions.

I shut the door and bolted it, and did my best to look thoroughly frightened. Humber looked me over with disgust.

"Roke," he said sarcastically, "I hope you will feel capable of dealing with Mickey when he is half asleep with drugs?"

"Yes, sir," I muttered.

"Then in order not to strain your feeble stock of courage, I suggest we keep him drugged for some days. Every time you fetch him a bucket of water, you can get Cass or me to put some sedative in it. Understand?"

"Yes, sir."

"Right." He dismissed me with a chop of his hand.

153

I carried the sack of dirty straw around to the muck heap, and there took a close look at the bandage which Mickey had dislodged. Blister is a red paste. I had looked in vain for red paste on Mickey's raw leg; and there was not a smear of it on the bandage. Yet from the size and severity of the wound, there should have been half a cupful.

I took Jerry down to Posset on the motorcycle again that afternoon and watched him start to browse contentedly in the toy department of the post office.

There was a letter for me from October.

Why did we receive no report from you last week? It is your duty to keep us informed of the position.

I tore the page up, my mouth twisting. Duty. That was just about enough to make me lose my temper. It was not from any sense of duty that I stayed at Humber's to endure a minor version of slavery. It was because I was obstinate, and liked to finish what I started, and although it sounded a bit grandiose, it was because I really wanted, if I could, to remove British steeplechasing from Adams' clutches. If it had been only a matter of duty I would have repaid October his money and cleared out.

"It is your duty to keep us informed of the position."

He was still angry with me about Patty, I thought morosely, and he wrote that sentence only because he knew I wouldn't like it.

I composed my report.

Your humble and obedient servant regrets that he was unable to carry out his duty last week by keeping you informed of the position.

The position is still far from clear, but a useful fact has been ascertained. None of the original eleven horses will be doped again; but a horse called Six-Ply is lined up to be the next winner. He is now owned by a Mr. Henry Waddington, of Lewes, Sussex.

154

May I please have the answers to the following questions:

1. Is the powder in the enclosed twist of paper soluble Phenobarbitone?
2. What are in detail the registered physical characteristics of the race-horses Chin-Chin, Kandersteg, and Starlamp?
3. On what date did Blackburn, playing at home, beat Arsenal?

And that, I thought, sticking down the envelope and grinning to myself, that will fix him and his duty.

Jerry and I gorged ourselves at the café. I had been at Humber's for five weeks and two days, and my clothes were getting looser.

When we could eat no more, I went back to the post office and bought a large-scale hiker's map of the surrounding district, and a cheap pair of compasses. Jerry spent fifteen shillings on a toy tank which he had resisted before, and after checking to see if my good-will extended so far, a second comic for me to read to him. And we went back to Humber's.

Days passed. Mickey's drugged water acted satisfactorily, and I was able to clean his box and look after him without much trouble. Cass took the second bandage off, revealing an equal absence of red paste. However, the wounds gradually started healing.

As Mickey could not be ridden and showed great distress if one tried to lead him out along the road, he had to be walked around the yard for an hour each day, which exercised me more than him, but gave me time to think some very fruitful thoughts.

Humber's stick landed with a resounding thump across Charlie's shoulders on Tuesday morning, and for a second it looked as though Charlie would hit him back. But Humber coldly stared him down, and the next morning, delivered an even harder blow in the same place. Charlie's bed was empty that night. He was the fourth lad to leave in the six weeks I had been there (not counting the boy who stayed only three days) and of my original half-dozen dormitory companions, only Bert and Jerry remained. The time was getting perceptibly closer when

I would find myself at the top of the queue for walking the plank.

Adams came with Humber when he made his usual rounds on Thursday evening. They stopped outside Mickey's box but contented themselves with looking over the half door.

"Don't go in, Paul," said Humber warningly. "He's still very unpredictable, in spite of the drugs."

Adams looked at me where I stood by Mickey's head.

"Why is that gypsy doing this horse? I thought it was the moron's job." He sounded angry and alarmed.

Humber explained that as Mickey had bitten Jerry, he had made me change places with him. Adams still didn't like it, but looked as if he would save his comments until he wouldn't be overheard.

He said, "What is the gypsy's name?"

"Roke," said Humber.

"Well, Roke, come here, out of that box."

Humber said anxiously, "Paul, don't forget we're one lad short already."

These were not particularly reassuring words to hear. I walked across the box, keeping a wary eye on Mickey, let myself out through the door, and stood beside it, drooping and looking at the ground.

"Roke," said Adams in a pleasant-sounding voice, "what do you spend your wages on?"

"The never-never on my motor bike, sir."

"The never-never? Oh, yes. And how many installments have you still to pay?"

"About . . . er . . . fifteen, sir."

"And you don't want to leave here until you've finished paying them off."

"No, sir."

"Will they take your motorcycle away if you stop paying?"

"Yes, sir, they might do."

"So Mr. Humber doesn't need to worry about you leaving him?"

I said slowly, unwillingly, but as it happened truthfully, "No, sir."

"Good," he said briskly. "Then that clears the air,

doesn't it? And now you can tell me where you find the guts to deal with an unstable, half-mad horse?"

"He's drugged, sir."

"You and I both know, Roke, that a drugged horse is not necessarily a safe horse."

I said nothing. If there was ever a time when I needed an inspiration, this was it; and my mind was a blank.

"I don't think, Roke," he said softly, "that you are as feeble as you make out. I think there is a lot more stuffing in you than you would have us believe."

"No, sir," I said helplessly.

"Let's find out, shall we?"

He stretched out his hand to Humber, and Humber gave him his walking stick. Adams drew back his arm and hit me fairly smartly across the thigh.

If I was to stay in the yard, I had to stop him. This time the begging simply had to be done. I slid down the door, gasping, and sat on the ground.

"No, sir, don't," I shouted. "I got some pills. I was dead scared of Mickey, and I asked the chemist in Posset on Saturday if he had any pills to make me brave, and he sold me some, and I've been taking them regular ever since."

"What pills?" said Adams disbelievingly.

"Tranquil-something, he said. I didn't rightly catch the word."

"Tranquilizers."

"Yes, that's it, tranquilizers. Don't hit me anymore, sir, please, sir. It was just that I was so dead scared of Mickey. Don't hit me anymore, sir."

"Well, I'm damned." Adams began to laugh. "Well, I'm damned. What will they think of next?" He gave the stick back to Humber, and the two of them walked casually away along to the next box.

"Take tranquilizers to help you out of a blue funk. Well, why not?" Still laughing, they went in to see the next horse.

I got up slowly and brushed the dirt off the seat of my pants. Damn it, I thought miserably, what else could I have done? Why was pride so important, and abandoning it so bitter?

It was more clear than every that weakness was my only asset. Adams had this fearful kink of seeing any show of spirit as a personal challenge to his ability to crush it. He dominated Humber, and exacted instant obedience from Cass, and they were his allies. If I stood up to him even mildly, I would get nothing but a lot of bruises and he would start wondering why I stayed to collect still more. The more tenaciously I stayed, the more incredible he would find it. Hire purchase on the motor bike wouldn't convince him for long. He was quick. He knew, if he began to think about it, that I had come from October's stables. He must know that October was a Steward and therefore his natural enemy. He would remember Tommy Stapleton. The hypersensitivity of the hunted to danger would stir the roots of his hair. He could check and find out from the post office that I did not send money away each week, and discover that the chemist had sold me no tranquilizers. He was in too deep to risk my being a follow-up to Stapleton; and at the very least, once he was suspicious of me, my detecting days would be over.

Whereas if he continued to be sure of my utter spinelessness, he wouldn't bother about me, and I could if necessary stay in the yard up to five or six weeks more. And heaven forbid, I thought, that I would have to.

Adams, although it had been instinct with him, not reason, was quite right to be alarmed that it was I and not Jerry who was now looking after Mickey.

In the hours I had spent close to the horse, I had come to understand what was really the matter with him, and all my accumulated knowledge about the affected horses, and about all horses in general, had gradually shaken into place. I did by that day know in outline how Adams and Humber had made their winners win.

I knew in outline, but not in detail. A theory, but no proof. For detail and proof I still needed more time, and if the only way I could buy time was to sit on the ground and implore Adams not to beat me, then it had to be done. But it was pretty awful, just the same.

12

October's reply was unrelenting.

Six-Ply, according to his present owner, is not going to be entered in any selling races. Does this mean that he will not be doped?

The answers to your questions are as follows:

1. The powder is soluble Phenobarbitone.
2. The physical characteristics of Chin-Chin are: bay gelding, white blaze down nose, white sock, off fore. Kandersteg: gelding, washy chestnut, three white socks, both forelegs and near hind. Starlamp: brown gelding, left hind white heel.
3. Blackburn beat Arsenal on November 30.

I do not appreciate your flippancy. Does your irresponsibility now extend to the investigation?

Irresponsibility. Duty. He could really pick his words.

I read the descriptions of the horses again. They told me that Starlamp was Mickey. Chin-Chin was Dobbin, one of the two racehorses I did which belonged to Humber. Kandersteg was a pale, shambling creature looked after by Bert, and known in the yard as Flash.

If Blackburn beat Arsenal on November 30, Jerry had been at Humber's eleven weeks already.

I tore up October's letter and wrote back:

Six-Ply may now be vulnerable whatever race he runs in, as he is the only shot left in the locker since Old Etonian and Superman both misfired.

In case I fall on my nut out riding, or get knocked over by a passing car, I think I had better tell you that I had this week realized how the scheme works, even though I am as yet ignorant of most of the details.

I told October that the stimulant Adams and Humber used was in fact adrenalin; and I told him how I believed it was introduced into the bloodstream.

As you can see, there are two prime facts which must be established before Adams and Humber can be prosecuted. I will do my best to finish the job properly, but I can't guarantee it, as the time factor is a nuisance.

Then, because I felt very alone, I added impulsively, jerkily, a postscript:

Believe me. Please believe me. I did nothing to Patty.

When I had written it, I looked at this *cri de coeur* in disgust. I am getting as soft as I pretend, I thought. I tore the bottom off the sheet of paper and threw the pitiful words away, and posted my letter in the box.

Thinking it wise actually to buy some tranquilizers in case anyone checked, I stopped at the chemist's and asked for some. The chemist absolutely refused to sell me any, as they could only be had on a doctor's or dentist's prescription. How long would it be, I wondered ruefully, before Adams or Humber discovered this awkward fact.

Jerry was disappointed when I ate my meal in the café very fast, and left him alone to finish and walk back from Posset, but I assured him that I had jobs to do. It was high time I took a look at the surrounding countryside.

I rode out of Posset and, stopping the motorcycle in a lay-by, got out the map over which I had pored intermittently during the week. I had drawn on it with pencil and compasses two concentric circles: the outer circle had a radius of eight miles from Humber's stables, and the inner circle a radius of five miles. If Jud had driven straight there and back when he had gone to fetch Mickey, the place he had fetched him from would lie in the area between the circles.

Some directions from Humber's were unsuitable because of open-cast coal mines; and eight miles to the southeast lay the outskirts of the sprawling mining town called Clavering. All around the north and west sides, however, there was little but moorland interspersed with small valleys like the one in which Humber's stable lay, small fertile pockets in miles and miles of stark, windswept heath.

Tellbridge, the village where Adams lived, lay outside the outer circle by two miles, and because of this I did not think Mickey could have been lodged there during his absence from Humber's. But all the same, the area on a line from Humber's yard to Adams' village seemed the most sensible to take a look at first.

As I did not wish Adams to find me spying out the land around his house, I fastened on my crash helmet, which I had not worn since the trip to Edinburgh, and pulled up over my eyes a large pair of goggles, under which even my sisters wouldn't have recognized me. I didn't, as it happened, see Adams on my travels; but I did see his house, which was a square, cream-colored Georgian pile with gargoyle heads adorning the gateposts. It was the largest, most imposing building in the tiny group of a church, a shop, two pubs, and a gaggle of cottages which made up Tellbridge.

I talked about Adams to the boy who filled my petrol tank in the Tellbridge garage.

"Mr. Adams? Yes, he bought old Sir Lucas' place three, four years ago. After the old man died. There weren't no family to keep it on."

"And Mrs. Adams?" I suggested.

"Blimy, there isn't any Mrs. Adams," he said, laughing and pushing his fair hair out of his eyes with the back of his wrist. "But a lot of birds he has there sometimes. Often got a houseful there, he has. Nobs, now, don't get me wrong—never has anyone but nobs in his house, doesn't Mr. Adams. And anything he wants, he gets, and quick. Never mind anyone else. He woke the whole village up at two in the morning last Friday because he got into his head that he'd like to ring the church bells. He smashed a window to get in. . . . I ask you! Of course, no one says much, because he spends such

161

a lot of money in the village. Food and drink and wages, and so on. Everyone's better off since he came."

"Does he often do things like that—ringing the church bells?"

"Well, not that exactly, but other things, yes. I shouldn't think you could believe all you hear. But they say he pays up handsome if he does any damage, and everyone just puts up with it. High spirits, that's what they say it is."

But Adams was too old for high spirits of that sort.

"Does he buy his petrol here?" I asked idly, fishing in my pocket for some money.

"Not often he doesn't; he has his own tank." The smile died out of the boy's open face. "In fact, I only served him once, when his supplies had run out."

"What happened?"

"Well, he trod on my foot. In his hunting boots, too. I couldn't make out if he did it on purpose, because it seemed like that really, but why would he do something like that?"

"I can't imagine."

He shook his head, wondering. "He must have thought I'd moved out of his way, I suppose. Put his heel right on top of my foot, he did, and leaned back. I only had sneakers on. Darn nearly broke my bones, he did. He must weigh getting on for sixteen stone, I shouldn't wonder." He sighed and counted my change into my palm, and I thanked him and went on my way, thinking that it was extraordinary how much a psychopath could get away with if he was big enough and clever and well born.

It was a cold afternoon, and cloudy, but I enjoyed it. Stopping on the highest point of a shoulder of moorland, I sat straddling the bike and looking around at rolling distances of bare, bleak hills and at the tall chimneys of Clavering pointing up on the horizon. I took off my helmet and goggles and pushed my fingers through my hair to let the cold wind in to my scalp. It was invigorating.

There was almost no chance, I knew, of my finding where Mickey had been kept. It could be anywhere, in any barn, outhouse, or shed. It didn't have to be a stable, and quite likely was not a stable; and indeed, all I was sure of was that it would be somewhere tucked away out of sight and sound of any neighbors. The trouble was that in that part of Durham, with its widely scattered villages, its sudden valleys, and its miles of open heath, I found there were dozens of places tucked away out of sight and sound of neighbors.

Shrugging, I put my helmet and goggles on again, and spent what little was left of my free time finding two vantage points on high ground, from one of which one could see straight down the valley into Humber's yard, and from the other a main crossroad on the way from Humber's to Tellbridge, together with good stretches of road in all directions from it.

Kandersteg's name being entered in Humber's special hidden ledger, it was all Durham to a doughnut that one day he would take the same trail that Mickey-Starlamp had done. It was quite likely that I would still be unable to find out where he went, but there was no harm in getting the lie of the land clear in my head.

At four o'clock, I rolled back into Humber's yard with the usual lack of enthusiasm, and began my evening's work.

Sunday passed, and Monday. Mickey got no better; the wounds on his legs were healing but he was still a risky prospect, in spite of the drugs, and he was beginning to lose flesh. Although I had never seen or had to deal with a horse in this state before, I gradually grew certain that he would not recover, and that Adams and Humber had another misfire on their hands.

Neither Humber nor Cass liked the look of him, either, though Humber seemed more annoyed than anxious, as time went on. Adams came one morning, and from across the yard in Dobbin's box I watched the three of them standing looking in at Mickey. Presently Cass went into the box for a moment or two, and came out shaking his head. Adams looked furious. He took Humber by the arm and the two of them walked across to the office in what looked like an argument. I would have

163

given much to have overheard them. A pity I couldn't lip-read, I thought, and that I hadn't come equipped with one of those long-range listening devices. As a spy, I was really a dead loss.

On Tuesday morning at breakfast there was a letter for me, postmarked Durham, and I looked at it curiously because there were so few people who either knew where I was or would bother to write to me. I put it in my pocket until I could open it in private and I was glad I had, for to my astonishment it was from October's elder daughter.

She had written from her university address, and said briefly:

Dear Daniel Roke,
    I would be glad if you could call to see me for a few moments sometime this week. There is a matter I must discuss with you.

                                    Yours sincerely,
                                    Elinor Tarren

October, I thought, must have given her a message for me, or something he wanted me to see, or perhaps he intended to be there to meet me himself, and had not risked writing to me direct. Puzzled, I asked Cass for an afternoon off, and was refused. Only Saturday, he said, and Saturday only if I behaved myself.

I thought Saturday might be too late, or that she would have gone to Yorkshire for the weekend, but I wrote to her that I could come only on that day, and walked into Posset after the evening meal on Tuesday to post the letter.

Her reply came on Friday, brief again and to the point, with still no hint of why I was to go.

Saturday afternoon will do very well. I will tell the porter you are coming. Go to the side door of the College (this is the door used by students and their visitors) and ask to be shown to my room.

She enclosed a penciled sketch to show me where to find the College, and that was all.

On Saturday morning I had six horses to do, because there was still no replacement for Charlie, and Jerry had gone with Pageant to the races. Adams came as usual to talk to Humber and to supervise the loading up of his hunters, but wasted no attention or energy on me, for which I was thankful. He spent half of the twenty minutes he was in the yard looking into Mickey's box with a scowl on his handsome face.

Cass himself was not always unkind, and because he knew I particularly wanted the afternoon free, he even went so far as to help me get finished before the midday meal. I thanked him, surprised, and he remarked that he knew there had been a lot extra for everyone (except himself, incidentally) to do, as we were still a lad short, and that I hadn't complained about it as much as most of the others. And that, I thought, was a mistake I would not have to make too often.

I washed as well as the conditions would allow; one had to heat all washing water in a kettle on the stove and pour it into the basin on the marble washstand; and shaved more carefully than usual, looking into the six-by-eight-inch fly-blown bit of looking glass, jostled by the other lads who wanted to be on their way to Posset.

None of the clothes I had were fit for visiting a women's college. With a sigh I settled for the black sweater, which had a high collar, the charcoal drainpipe trousers, and the black leather jacket. No shirt, because I had no tie. I eyed the sharp-pointed shoes, but I had not been able to overcome my loathing for them, so I scrubbed my jodhpur boots under the tap in the yard, and wore those. Everything else I was wearing needed cleaning, and I supposed I smelled of horses, though I was too used to it to notice.

I shrugged. There was nothing to be done about it. I unwrapped the motor bike and made tracks for Durham.

13

Elinor's college stood in a tree-lined road along with other sturdy and learned-looking buildings. It had an imposing front entrance and a less imposing tarmacked drive entrance along to the right. I wheeled the motorcycle down there and parked it beside a long row of bicycles. Beyond the bicycles stood six or seven small cars, one of which was Elinor's little scarlet two-seater.

Two steps led up to a large oak door embellished with the single word "Students." I went in. There was a porter's desk just inside on the right, with a mournful-looking middle-aged man sitting behind it, looking at a list.

"Excuse me," I said. "Could you tell me where to find Lady Elinor Tarren?"

He looked up and said, "You visiting? You expected?"

"I think so," I said.

He asked my name, and thumbed down the list painstakingly. "Daniel Roke to visit Miss Tarren, please show him her room. Yes, that's right. Come on, then." He got down off his stool, came around from behind his desk, and breathing noisily, began to lead me deeper into the building.

There were several twists in the corridors and I could see why it was necessary to have a guide. On every hand were doors with their occupant or purpose written up on small cards set into metal slots. After going up two flights of stairs and around a few more corners, the porter halted outside one more door just like the rest.

"Here you are," he said unemotionally. "This is Miss

166

Tarren's room." He turned away and started to shuffle back to his post.

The card on the door said Miss E. C. Tarren. I knocked. Miss E. C. Tarren opened it.

"Come in," she said. No smile.

I went in. She shut the door behind me. I stood still, looking at her room. I was so accustomed to the starkness of the accommodation at Humber's that it was an odd, strange sensation to find myself again in a room with curtains, carpet, sprung chairs, cushions, and flowers. The colors were mostly blues and greens, mixed and blending, with a bowl of daffodils and red tulips blazing against them.

There was a big desk with books and papers scattered on it; a bookshelf, a bed with a blue cover, a wardrobe, a tall built-in cupboard, and two easy chairs. It looked warm and friendly. A very good room for working in. If I had had more than a moment to stand and think about it, I knew I would be envious; this was what my father and mother's death had robbed me of, the time and liberty to study.

"Please sit down." She indicated one of the easy chairs.

"Thank you." I sat, and she sat down opposite me, but looking at the floor, not at me. She was solemn and frowning, and I rather gloomily wondered if what October wanted her to say to me meant more trouble.

"I asked you to come here . . ." she started. "I asked you to come here because . . ." She stopped and stood up abruptly, and walked around behind me and tried again.

"I asked you to come," she said to the back of my head, "because I have got to apologize to you, and I'm not finding it very easy."

"Apologize?" I said, astonished. "What for?"

"For my sister."

I stood up and turned toward her. "Don't," I said vehemently. I had been too much humbled myself in the past weeks to want to see anyone else in the same position.

She shook her head. "I'm afraid"—she swallowed—

"I'm afraid that my family has treated you very badly."

The silver-blond hair shimmered like a halo against the pale sunshine which slanted sideways through the window behind her. She was wearing a scarlet jersey under a sleeveless dark-green dress. The whole effect was colorful and gorgeous, but it was clearly not going to help her if I went on looking at her. I sat down again in the chair and said with some lightheartedness, as it appeared October had not after all dispatched a dressing-down, "Please don't worry about it."

"Worry!" she exclaimed. "What else can I do? I knew, of course, why you were dismissed, and I've said several times to Father that he ought to have had you sent to prison, and now I find none of it is true at all. How can you say there is nothing to worry about when everyone thinks you are guilty of some dreadful crime, and you aren't?"

Her voice was full of concern. She really minded that anyone in her family should have behaved as unfairly as Patty had. She felt guilty just because she was her sister. I liked her for it; but then I already knew she was a thoroughly nice girl.

"How did you find out?" I asked.

"Patty told me last weekend. We were just gossiping together, as we often do. She had always refused to talk about you, but this time she laughed, and told me quite casually, as if it didn't matter anymore. Of course I know she's . . . well . . . used to men. She's just built that way. But this . . . I was so shocked. I couldn't believe her at first."

"What exactly did she tell you?"

There was a pause behind me, then her voice went on, a little shakily. "She said she tried to make you make love to her, but you wouldn't. She said . . . she said she showed you her body, and all you did was to tell her to cover herself up. She said she was so flamingly angry about that that she thought all next day about what revenge she would have on you, and on Sunday morning she worked herself up into floods of tears, and went and told Father . . . told Father . . ."

"Well," I said good-humoredly, "yes, that is, I suppose,

168

a slightly more accurate picture of what took place."
I laughed.

"It isn't funny," she protested.

"No. It's a relief."

She came around in front of me and sat down and looked at me.

"You did mind, then, didn't you?"

My distaste must have shown. "Yes. I minded."

"I told Father she had lied about you. I've never told him before about her love affairs, but this was different. . . . Anyway, I told him on Sunday after lunch." She stopped, hesitating. I waited. At last she went on, "It was very odd. He didn't seem surprised, really. Not utterly overthrown, like I was. He just seemed to get very tired, suddenly, as if he had heard bad news. As if a friend had died after a long illness, that sort of sadness. I didn't understand it. And when I said that of course the only fair thing to do would be to offer you your job back, he utterly refused. I argued, but I'm afraid he is adamant. He also refuses to tell Mr. Inskip that you shouldn't have had to leave, and he made me promise not to repeat to him or anyone what Patty had said. It is so unfair," she concluded passionately, "and I felt that even if no one else is to know, at least you should. I don't suppose it makes it any better for you that my father and I have at last found out what really happened, but I wanted you to know that I am sorry, very, very sorry for what my sister did."

I smiled at her. It wasn't difficult. Her coloring was so blazingly fair that it didn't matter if her nose wasn't entirely straight. Her direct gray eyes were full of genuine, earnest regret, and I knew she felt Patty's misbehavior all the more keenly because she thought it had affected a stable lad who had no means of defending himself. This also made it difficult to know what to say in reply.

I understood, of course, that October couldn't declare me an injured innocent, even if he wanted to, which I doubted, without a risk of its reaching Humber's ears, and that the last thing that either of us wanted was for him to have to offer to take me back at Inskip's.

No one in his right mind would stay at Humber's if he could go to Inskip's.

"If you knew," I said slowly, "how much I have wanted your father to believe that I didn't harm your sister, you would realize that what you have just said is worth a dozen jobs to me. I like your father. I respect him. And he is quite right. He cannot possibly give me my old job back, because it would be as good as saying publicly that his daughter is at least a liar, if not more. You can't ask him to do that. You can't expect it. I don't. Things are best left as they are."

She looked at me for some time without speaking. It seemed to me that there was relief in her expression, and surprise, and finally puzzlement.

"Don't you want *any* compensation?"

"No."

"I don't understand you."

"Look," I said, getting up, away from her inquiring gaze. "I'm not as blameless as the snow. I did kiss your sister. I suppose I led her on a bit. And then I was ashamed of myself and backed out, and that's the truth of it. It wasn't her fault. I did behave very badly. So please . . . please don't feel so much guilt on my account." I reached the window and looked out.

"People shouldn't be hung for murders they decide not to commit," she said dryly. "You are being very generous, and I didn't expect it."

"Then you shouldn't have asked me here," I said idly. "You were taking too big a risk." The window looked down onto a quadrangle, a neat square of grass surrounded by broad paths, peaceful and empty in the pale winter sunshine.

"Risk . . . of what?" she said.

"Risk that I would raise a stink. Dishonor to the family. Tarnish to the Tarrens. That sort of thing. Lots of dirty linen and Sunday newspapers and your father losing face among his business associates."

She looked startled, but also determined. "All the same, a wrong had been done, and it had to be put right."

"And damn the consequences?"

170

"And damn the consequences," she repeated faintly.

I grinned. She was a girl after my own heart. I had been damning a few consequences, too.

"Well," I said reluctantly, "I'd better be off. Thank you for asking me to come. I do understand that you have had a horrible week screwing yourself up for this, and I appreciate it more than I can possibly say."

She looked at her watch, and hesitated. "I know it's an odd time of day, but would you like some coffee? I mean, you've come quite a long way . . ."

"I'd like some very much," I said.

"Well . . . sit down, and I'll get it."

I sat down. She opened the built-in cupboard, which proved to hold a washbasin and mirror on one side and a gas ring and shelves for crockery on the other. She filled a kettle, lit the gas, and put some cups and saucers on the low table between the two chairs, moving economically and gracefully. Unself-conscious, I thought. Sure enough of herself to drop her title where brains mattered more than birth. Sure enough of herself to have a man who looked like I did brought to her bed-sitting room, and to ask him to stay for coffee when it was not necessary, but only polite.

I asked her what subject she was studying, and she said English. She assembled some milk, sugar, and biscuits on the table.

"May I look at your books?" I asked.

"Go ahead," she said amiably.

I got up and looked along her bookshelves. There were the language textbooks—Ancient Icelandic, Anglo-Saxon, and Middle English— and a comprehensive sweep of English writings from Alfred the Great's *Chronicles* to John Betjeman's unattainable amazons.

"What do you think of my books?" she asked curiously.

I didn't know how to answer. The masquerade was damnably unfair to her.

"Very learned," I said lamely.

I turned away from the bookshelves, and came suddenly face to face with my full-length reflection in the mirror door of her wardrobe.

171

I looked at myself moodily. It was the first comprehensive view of Roke the stable lad that I had had since leaving October's London house months before, and time had not improved things.

My hair was too long, and the sideburns flourished nearly down to the lobes of my ears. My skin was a sort of pale yellow now that the suntan had all faded. There was a tautness in the face and a wary expression in the eyes which had not been there before; and in my black clothes I looked disreputable and a menace to society.

Her reflection moved behind mine in the mirror, and I met her eyes and found her watching me.

"You look as if you don't like what you see," she said.

I turned around. "No," I said wryly. "Would anyone?"

"Well . . ." Incredibly she smiled mischievously. "I wouldn't like to set you loose in this college, for instance. If you don't realize, though, the effect which you . . . You may have a few rough edges, but I do now see why Patty tried . . . er . . . I mean . . ." Her voice trailed off in the first confusion she had shown.

"The kettle's boiling," I said helpfully.

Relieved, she turned her back on me and made the coffee. I went to the window and looked down into the deserted quad, resting my forehead on the cold glass.

It still happened, I thought. In spite of those terrible clothes, in spite of the aura of shadiness, it could still happen. What accident, I wondered for the thousandth time in my life, decided that one should be born with bones of a certain design? I couldn't help the shape of my face and head. They were a legacy from a pair of neat-featured parents: their doing, not mine. Like Elinor's hair, I thought. Born in you. Nothing to be proud of. An accident, like a birthmark or a squint. Something I habitually forgot, and found disconcerting when anyone mentioned it. And it had been expensive, moreover. I had lost at least two prospective customers

172

because they hadn't liked the way their wives looked at me instead of my horses.

With Elinor, I thought, it was a momentary attraction which wouldn't last. She was surely too sensible to allow herself to get tangled up with one of her father's ex-stable lads. And as for me, it was strickly hands off the Tarren sisters, both of them. If I was out of the frying pan with one, I was not jumping into the fire with the other. It was a pity, all the same. I liked Elinor rather a lot.

"The coffee's ready," she said.

I turned and went back to the table. She had herself very well controlled again. There was no mischievous revealing light in her face anymore, and she looked almost severe, as if she very much regretted what she had said and was going to make quite certain I didn't take advantage of it.

She handed me a cup and offered the biscuits, which I ate because the lunch at Humber's had consisted of bread, margarine, and hard, tasteless cheese, and the supper would be the same. It nearly always was, on Saturdays, because Humber knew we ate in Posset.

We talked sedately about her father's horses. I asked how Sparking Plug was getting on, and she told me, "Very well, thank you. I've a newspaper clipping about him, if you'd like to see it?" she said.

"Yes, I'd like to."

I followed her to the desk while she looked for it. She shifted some papers to search underneath, and the top one fell onto the floor. I picked it up, put it back on the desk, and looked down at it. It seemed to be some sort of quiz.

"Thank you," she said. "I mustn't lose that, it's the Literary Society's competition, and I've only one more answer to find. Now where did I put that clipping?"

The competition consisted of a number of quotations to which one had to ascribe the author. I picked up the paper and began reading.

"That top one's a brute," she said over her shoulder. "No one's got it yet, I don't think."

"How do you win the competition?" I asked.

173

"Get a complete, correct set of answers in first."

"And what's the prize?"

"A book. But prestige, mostly. We only have one competition a term, and it's difficult." She opened a drawer full of papers and oddments. "I know I put that clipping somewhere." She began shoveling things out onto the top of the desk.

"Please don't bother anymore," I said politely.

"No, I want to find it." A handful of small objects clattered onto the desk.

Among them was a small chromium-plated tube about three inches long with a loop of chain running from one end to the other. I had seen something like it before, I thought idly. I had seen it quite often. It had something to do with drinks.

"What's that?" I asked, pointing.

"That? Oh, that's a silent whistle." She went on rummaging. "For dogs," she explained.

I picked it up. A silent dog whistle. Why then did I think it was connected with bottle and glasses and— The world stopped.

With an almost physical sensation, my mind leaped toward its prey. I held Adams and Humber in my hand at last. I could feel my pulse racing.

So simple. So very simple. The tube pulled apart in the middle to reveal that one end was a thin whistle, and the other its cap. A whistle joined to its cap by a little length of chain. I put the tiny mouthpiece to my lips and blew. Only a thread of sound came out.

"You can't hear it very well," Elinor said, "but of course a dog can. And you can adjust the whistle to make it sound louder to human ears, too." She took it out of my hand and unscrewed part of the whistle itself. "Now blow." She gave it back.

I blew again. It sounded much more like an ordinary whistle.

"Do you think I could possibly borrow this for a little while?" I asked. "If you're not using it? I . . . I want to try an experiment."

"Yes, I should thnk so. My dear old sheepdog had to be put down last spring, and I haven't used it since.

174

But you will let me have it back? I am getting a puppy in the long vac, and I want to use it for his training."

"Yes, of course."

"All right, then. Oh, here's that clipping, at last."

I took the strip of newsprint, but I couldn't concentrate on it. All I could see was the drinks compartment in Humber's monster car, with the racks of ice picks, tongs, and little miscellaneous chromium-plated objects. I had never given them more than a cursory glance; but one of them was a small tube with a loop of chain from end to end. One of them was a silent whistle for dogs.

I made an effort, and read about Sparking Plug, and thanked her for finding the clipping.

I stowed her whistle in my money belt and looked at my watch. It was already after half-past three. I was going to be somewhat late back at work.

She had cleared me with October and shown me the whistle: two enormous favors. I wanted to repay her, and could think of only one way of doing it.

" 'Nowhere either with more quiet or more freedom from trouble does a man retire than into his own soul . . .' " I quoted.

She looked up at me, startled. "That's the beginning of the competition."

"Yes. Are you allowed help?"

"Yes. Anything. But . . ."

"It's Marcus Aurelius."

"*Who?*" She was staggered.

"Marcus Aurelius Antonius. Roman emperor, 121 to 180 A.D."

"The *Meditations?*"

I nodded.

"What language was it originally written in? We have to put that, too. Latin, I suppose."

"Greek."

"This is fantastic. . . . Just where did you go to school?"

"I went to a village school in Oxfordshire." So I had, for two years, until I was eight. "And we had a master who perpetually crammed Marcus Aurelius down our throats." But that master had been at Geelong.

175

I had been tempted to tell her the truth about myself all afternoon, but never more than at that moment. I found it impossible to be anything but my own self in her company, and even at Slaw I had spoken to her more or less in my natural accent. I hated having to pretend to her at all. But I didn't tell her where I had come from and why, because October hadn't, and I thought he ought to know his daughter better than I did. There were her cozy chats with Patty . . . whose tongue could not be relied on; and perhaps he thought it was a risk to his investigations. I didn't know. And I didn't tell her.

"Are you really sure it's Marcus Aurelius?" she said doubtfully. "We only get one shot. If it's wrong, you don't get another."

"I should check it then. It comes in a section about learning to be content with your lot. I suppose I remember it because it is good advice and I've seldom been able to follow it." I grinned.

"You know," she said tentatively, "it's none of my business, but I would have thought you could have got on a bit in the world. You seem . . . you seem decidedly intelligent. Why do you work in a stable?"

"I work in a stable," I told her with perfect, ironic truth, "because it's the only thing I know how to do."

"Will you do it for the rest of your life?"

"I expect so."

"And will it content you?"

"It will have to."

"I didn't expect this afternoon to turn out like this at all," she said. "To be frank, I was dreading it. And you have made it easy."

"That's all right, then," I said cheerfully.

She smiled. I went to the door and opened it, and she said, "I'd better see you out. This building must have been the work of a maze-crazy architect. Visitors have been found wandering about the upper reaches dying of thirst days after they were supposed to have left."

I laughed. She walked beside me back along the twisting corridors, down the stairs, and right back to the outside

176

door, talking easily about her life in college, talking to me freely, as an equal. She told me that Durham was the oldest English university after Oxford and Cambridge, and that it was the only place in Britain which offered a course in geophysics. She was, indeed, a very nice girl.

She shook hands with me on the step.

"Good-bye," she said. "I'm sorry Patty was so beastly."

"I'm not. If she hadn't been, I wouldn't have been here this afternoon."

She laughed. "But what a price to pay."

"Worth it."

Her gray eyes had darker gray flecks in them, I noticed. She watched me go over and sit on the motorcycle and fasten on the helmet. Then she waved her hand briefly, and went back through the door. It closed with finality behind her.

14

I stopped in Posset on the return journey to see if there was any comment from October on the theory I had sent him the previous week, but there was no letter for me at all.

Although I was already late for evening stables, I stopped longer to write to him. I couldn't get Tommy Stapleton out of my head; he had died without passing on what he knew. I didn't want to make the same mistake. Or to die, either, if it came to that. I scribbled fast.

I think the trigger is a silent whistle, the sort used for dogs. Humber keeps one in the drinks compartment of his car. Remember Old Etonian? They hold hound trails at Cartmel, on the morning of the races.

Having posted that, I bought a large slab of chocolate for food, and also Jerry's comic, and slid as quietly as I could back into the yard. Cass caught me, however, and said sourly that I'd be lucky to get Saturday off next week, as he would be reporting me to Humber. I sighed resignedly, started the load of evening chores, and felt the cold, dingy, subviolent atmosphere of the place seep back into my bones.

But there was a difference now. The whistle lay like a bomb in my money belt. A death sentence, if they found me with it. Or so I believed. There remained the matter of making sure I had not leaped to the wrong conclusion.

Tommy Stapleton had probably suspected what was going on and had walked straight into Humber's yard to tax him with it. He couldn't have known that the men he was dealing with were prepared to kill. But because he had died, I did know. I had lived under their noses for seven weeks, and I had been careful; and because I intended to remain undetected to the end, I spent a long time on Sunday wondering how I could conduct my experiment and get away with it.

On Sunday evening, at about five o'clock, Adams drove into the yard in his shining gray Jaguar. As usual at the sight of him, my heart sank. He walked around the yard with Humber when he made his normal tour of inspection, and stopped for a long time looking over the door at Mickey. Neither he nor Humber came in. Humber had been into Mickey's box several times since the day he helped me take in the first lot of drugged water, but Adams had not been in at all.

Adams said, "What do you think, Hedley?"

Humber shrugged. "There's no change."

"Write him off?"

"I suppose so." Humber sounded depressed.

"It's a bloody nuisance," said Adams violently. He looked at me. "Still bolstering yourself up with tranquilizers?"

"Yes, sir."

He laughed rudely. He thought it very funny. Then his face changed to a scowl, and he said savagely to Humber, "It's useless, I can see that. Give him the chop, then."

178

Humber turned away, said, "Right, I'll get it done tomorrow."

Their footsteps moved off to the next box. I looked at Mickey. I had done my best for him, but he was too far gone, and had been from the beginning. After a fortnight, what with his mental chaos, his continual state of druggedness, and his persistent refusal to eat, Mickey's condition was pitiable, and anyone less stony than Humber would have had him put down long ago.

I made him comfortable for his last night and evaded yet another slash from his teeth. I couldn't say I was sorry not to have to deal with him anymore, as a fortnight of looking after an unhinged horse would be enough for anyone; but the fact that he was to be put down the next day meant that I would have to perform my experiment without delay.

I didn't feel ready to do it. Thinking about it, as I put away my brushes for the night and walked across the yard toward the kitchen, I tried to find one good reason for putting it off.

The alacrity with which a good excuse for not doing it presented itself led me to the unwelcome, overwhelming realization that for the first time since my childhood, I was thoroughly afraid.

I could get October to make the experiment, I thought, on Six-Ply. Or on any of the other horses. I didn't have to do it myself. It would definitely be more prudent not to do it myself. October could do it with absolute safety, but if Humber found me out, I was as good as dead; therefore I should leave it to October.

It was then that I knew I was afraid, and I didn't like it.

It took me most of the evening to decide to do the experiment myself. On Mickey. The next morning. Shuffling it off onto October doubtless would have been more prudent, but I had myself to live with afterward. What had I really wanted to leave home for, if not to find out what I could or couldn't do?

When I took the bucket to the office door in the morning for Mickey's last dose of Phenobarbitone, there was only a little left in the jar. Cass tipped the

179

glass container upside down and tapped it on the bucket so that the last grains of white powder should not be wasted.

"That's his lot, poor bastard," he observed, putting the stopper back in the empty jar. "Pity there isn't a bit more left; we could have given him a double dose, just this once. Well, get on with it," he added sharply. "Don't hang about looking mournful. It's not you that's going to be shot this afternoon."

Well, I hoped not.

I turned away, went along to the tap, splashed in a little water, swilled around in it the instantly dissolved Phenobarbitone, and poured it away down the drain. Then I filled the bucket with clean water and took it along for Mickey to drink.

He was dying on his feet. The bones stuck out more sharply under his skin and his head hung down below his shoulders. There was still a disorientated wildness in his eye, but he was going downhill so fast that he had little strength left for attacking anyone. For once he made no attempt to bite me when I put the bucket down at his head, but lowered his mouth into it and took a few half-hearted swallows.

Leaving him, I went along to the tack room and took a new head collar out of the basket of stores. This was strictly against the rules: only Cass was supposed to issue new tack. I took the head collar along to Mickey's box and fitted it onto him, removing the one he had weakened by constant fretting during his fortnight's illness, and hiding it under a pile of straw. I unclipped the tethering chain from the old collar and clipped it onto the ring of the new one. I patted Mickey's neck, which he didn't like, walked out of his box, and shut and bolted only the bottom half of the door.

We rode out first lot, and second lot; and by then, I judged, Mickey's brain, without its morning dose, would be coming out of its sedation.

Leading Dobbin, the horse I had just returned on, I went to look at Mickey over the stable door. His head was weaving weakly from side to side, and he seemed very restless. Poor creature, I thought. Poor creature.

And for a few seconds I was going to make him suffer more.

Humber stood at his office door, talking to Cass. The lads were bustling in and out looking after their horses, buckets were clattering, voices calling to each other: routine stable noise. I was never going to have a better opportunity.

I began to lead Dobbin across the yard to his box. Halfway there I took the whistle out of my belt and pulled off its cap; then, looking around to make sure that no one was watching, I turned my head over my shoulder, put the tiny mouthpiece to my lips, and blew hard. Only a thread of sound came out, so high that I could hardly hear it above the clatter of Dobbin's feet on the ground.

The result was instantaneous and hideous.

Mickey screamed with terror.

His hoofs threshed wildly against the floor and walls, and the chain that held him rattled as he jerked against it.

I walked Dobbin quickly the few remaining yards into his stall, clipped his chain on, zipped the whistle back into my belt, and ran across toward Mickey's box. Everyone else was doing the same. Humber was limping swiftly down the yard.

Mickey was still screaming and crashing his hoofs against the wall as I looked into his box over the shoulders of Cecil and Lenny. The poor animal was on his hind legs, seemingly trying to beat his way through the bricks in front of him. Then suddenly, with all his ebbing stength, he dropped his forelegs to the ground and charged backward.

"Look out," shouted Cecil, instinctively retreating from the frantically bunching hindquarters, although he was safely outside a solid door.

Mickey's tethering chain was not very long. There was a sickening snap as he reached the end of it and his backward momentum was joltingly, appallingly stopped. His hind legs slid forward under his belly and he fell with a crash onto his side. His legs jerked stiffly. His head, still secured in the strong new head collar,

181

was held awkwardly off the ground by the taut chain, and by its unnatural angle told its own tale. He had broken his neck. As indeed, to put him quickly out of his frenzy, I had hoped he might.

Everyone in the yard had gathered outside Mickey's box. Humber, having glanced perfunctorily over the door at the dead horse, turned and looked broodingly at his six ragged stable lads. The narrow-eyed harshness of his expression stopped anyone from asking him questions. There was a short silence.

"Stand in a line," he said suddenly.

The lads looked surprised, but did as he said.

"Turn out your pockets," said Humber.

Mystified, the lads obeyed. Cass went down the line looking at what was produced and pulling the pockets out like wings to make sure they were empty. When he came to me I showed him a dirty handkerchief, a penknife, a few coins, and pulled my pockets inside out. He took the handkerchief from my hand, shook it out, and gave it back. The whistle at my waist was only an inch from his fingers.

I felt Humber's searching gaze on me from six feet away, but as I studied to keep my face vacantly relaxed and vaguely puzzled, I was astonished to find that I was neither sweating nor tensing my muscles to make a run for it. In an odd way the nearness of the danger made me cool and clearheaded. I didn't understand it, but it certainly helped.

"Back pocket?" asked Cass.

"Nothing in it," I said casually, turning half around to show him.

"All right. Now you, Kenneth."

I pushed my pockets in again, and replaced their contents. My hands were steady. Extraordinary, I thought.

Humber watched and waited until Kenneth's pockets had been innocently emptied; then he looked at Cass and jerked his head toward the loose boxes. Cass rooted around in the boxes of the horses we had just exercised. He finished the last, came back, and shook his head. Humber pointed silently toward the garage which shel-

182

tered his Bentley. Cass disappeared, reappeared, and again unexcitedly shook his head. In silence Humber limped away to his office, leaning on his heavy stick.

He couldn't have heard the whistle, and he didn't suspect that any of us had blown one for the sole purpose of watching its effect on Mickey, because if he had, he would have had us stripped and searched from head to foot. He was still thinking along the lines of Mickey's death being an accident; and having found no whistle in any of the lads' pockets or in their horses' boxes, he would conclude, I hoped, that it was none of that downtrodden bunch who had caused Mickey's brainstorm. If only Adams would agree with him, I was clear.

It was my afternoon for washing the car. Humber's own whistle was still there, tucked neatly into a leather retaining strap between a corkscrew and a pair of ice tongs. I looked, and left it where it was.

Adams came the next day.

Mickey had gone to the dog-meat man, who had grumbled about his thinness, and I had unobtrusively returned the new head collar to the store basket, leaving the old one dangling as usual from the tethering chain. Even Cass had not noticed the substitution.

Adams and Humber strolled along to Mickey's empty box and leaned on the half door, talking. Jerry poked his head out of the box next door, saw them standing there, and hurriedly disappeared again. I went normally about my business, fetching hay and water for Dobbin and carting away the muck sack.

"Roke," shouted Humber, "come here. At the double."

I hurried over. "Sir?"

"You haven't cleaned out this box."

"I'm sorry, sir. I'll do it this afternoon."

"You will do it," he said deliberately, "before you have your dinner."

He knew very well that this meant having no dinner at all. I glanced at his face. He was looking at me with calculation, his eyes narrowed and his lips pursed.

I looked down. "Yes, sir." I said meekly. Damn it,

I thought furiously; this was too soon. I had been there not quite eight weeks, and I ought to have been able to count on at least three more. If he was already intent on making me leave, I was not going to be able to finish the job.

"For a start," said Adams, "you can fetch out that bucket and put it away."

I looked into the box. Mickey's bucket still stood by the manger. I opened the door, walked over, picked it up, turned around to go back, and stopped dead.

Adams had come into the box after me. He held Humber's walking stick in his hand, and he was smiling.

I dropped the bucket and backed into a corner. He laughed.

"No tranquilizers today, eh, Roke?"

I didn't answer.

He swung his arm and the knobbed end of the stick landed on my ribs. It was hard enough, in all conscience. When he lifted his arm again, I ducked under it and bolted out through the door. His roar of laughter floated after me.

I went on running until I was out of sight, and then walked and rubbed my chest. It was going to be a fair-sized bruise, and I wasn't too keen on collecting many more. I supposed I should be thankful at least that they proposed to rid themselves of me in the ordinary way, and not over a hillside in a burning car.

All through that long, hungry afternoon I tried to decide what was best to do. To go at once, resigned to the fact that I couldn't finish the job, or to stay the few days I safely could without arousing Adams' suspicions. But what, I depressedly wondered, could I discover in three or four days that I had been unable to discover in eight weeks.

It was Jerry, of all people, who decided for me.

After supper (baked beans on bread, but not enough of it) we sat at the table with Jerry's comic spread open. Since Charlie had left, no one had a radio, and the evenings were more boring than ever. Lenny and Kenneth were playing dice on the floor. Cecil was out getting drunk. Bert sat in his silent world on the bench

184

on the other side of Jerry, watching the dice roll across the concrete.

The oven door was open, and all the switches on the electric stove were turned on as high as they would go. This was Lenny's bright idea for supplementing the small heat thrown out by the paraffin stove Humber had grudgingly provided. It wouldn't last longer than the arrival of the electricity bill, but it was warm meanwhile.

The dirty dishes were stacked in the sink. Cobwebs hung like a cornice where the walls met the ceiling. A naked light bulb lit the brick-walled room. Someone had spilled tea on the table, and the corner of Jerry's comic had soaked it up.

I sighed. To think that I wasn't happy to be about to leave this squalid existence, now that I was being given no choice!

Jerry looked up from his comic, keeping his place with his finger.

"Dan?"

"Mmm?"

"Did Mr. Adams bash you?"

"Yes."

"I thought he did." He nodded several times, and went back to his comic.

I suddenly remembered his having looked out of the box next to Mickey's before Adams and Humber had called me over.

"Jerry," I said slowly, "did you hear Mr. Adams and Mr. Humber talking, while you were in the box with Mr. Adams' black hunter?"

"Yes." he said, without looking up.

"What did they say?"

"When you ran away, Mr. Adams laughed and told the boss you wouldn't stand it long. Stand it long," he repeated vaguely, like a refrain, "stand it long."

"Did you hear what they said before that? When they first got there, and you looked out and saw them?"

This troubled him. He sat up and forgot to keep his place.

"I didn't want the boss to know I was still there,

185

see? I ought to have to finished that hunter a good bit before then."

"Yes. Well, you're all right. They didn't catch you."

He grinned and shook his head.

"What did they say?" I prompted.

"They were cross about Mickey. They said they would get on with the next one at once."

"The next what?"

"I don't know."

"Did they say anything else?"

He screwed up his thin little face. He wanted to please me, and I knew this expression meant he was thinking his hardest.

"Mr. Adams said you had been with Mickey too long, and the boss said yes, it was a bad . . . a bad . . . um . . . oh, yes . . . risk, and you had better leave, and Mr. Adams said yes, get on with that as quick as you can and we'll do the next one as soon as he's gone." He opened his eyes wide in triumph at this sustained effort.

"Say that again," I said. "The last bit, that's all."

One thing Jerry could do, from long practice with the comics, was to learn by heart through his ears.

Obediently he repeated, "Mr. Adams said get on with that as quick as you can and we'll do the next one as soon as he's gone."

"What do you want most on earth?" I asked.

He looked surprised and then thoughtful, and finally a dreamy look spread over his face.

"Well?"

"A train," he said. "One you wind up. You know. And rails and things. And a signal." He fell silent in rapture.

"You shall have them," I said. "As soon as I can get them."

His mouth opened.

I said, "Jerry, I'm leaving here. You can't stay when Mr. Adams starts bashing you, can you? So I'll have to go. But I'll send you the train. I won't forget, I promise."

The evening dragged away as so many others had

done, and we climbed the ladder to our unyielding beds, where I lay on my back in the dark with my hands laced behind my head and thought about Humber's stick crashing down somewhere on my body in the morning. Rather like going to the dentist for a drilling, I thought ruefully: the anticipation was worse than the event. I sighed, and went to sleep.

Operation Eviction continued much as expected the next day.

When I was unsaddling Dobbin after the second exercise, Humber walked into the box behind me and his stick landed with a thud across my back.

I let go of the saddle—which fell on a pile of fresh droppings—and swung around.

"What did I do wrong, sir?" I said, in an aggrieved voice. I thought I might as well make it difficult for him, but he had an answer ready.

"Cass tells me you were late back at work last Saturday afternoon. And pick up that saddle. What do you think you're doing, dropping it in that dirt?"

He stood with his legs planted firmly apart, his eyes judging his distance.

Well, all right, I thought. One more, and that's enough.

I turned around and picked up the saddle. I already had it in my arms and was straightening up when he hit me again, more or less in the same place, but much harder. The breath hissed through my teeth.

I threw the saddle down again in the dirt and shouted at him. "I'm leaving. I'm off. Right now."

"Very well," he said coldly, with perceptible satisfaction. "Go and pack. Your cards will be waiting for you in the office." He turned on his heel and slowly limped away, his purpose successfully concluded.

How frigid he was, I thought. Unemotional, sexless, and calculating. Impossible to think of him loving, or being loved, or feeling pity, or grief, or any sort of fear.

I arched my back, grimacing, and decided to leave Dobbin's saddle where it was, in the dirt. A nice touch, I thought. In character, to the bitter end.

15

I took the polythene sheeting off the motorcycle and coasted gently out of the yard. All the lads were out exercising the third lot, with yet more to be ridden when they got back; and even while I was wondering how five of them were possibly going to cope with thirty horses, I met a shifty-looking boy trudging slowly up the road to Humber's with a kit bag slung over his shoulder. More flotsam. If he had known what he was going to, he would have walked more slowly still.

I biked to Clavering, a dreary mining town of mean back-to-back terraced streets jazzed up with chromium and glass in the shopping center, and telephoned to October's London house.

Terence answered. Lord October, he said, was in Germany, where his firm was opening a new factory.

"When will he be back?"

"Saturday morning, I think. He went last Sunday, for a week."

"Is he going to Slaw for the weekend?"

"I think so. He said something about flying back to Manchester, and he's given me no instructions for anything here."

"Can you find the addresses and telephone numbers of Colonel Beckett and Sir Stuart Macclesfield for me?"

"Hang on a moment." There was a fluttering of pages, and Terence told me the numbers and addresses. I wrote them down and thanked him.

"Your clothes are still here, sir," he said.

"I know." I grinned. "I'll be along to fetch them quite soon, I think."

We rang off, and I tried Beckett's number. A dry, precise voice told me that Colonel Beckett was out, but that he would be dining at his club at nine, and could be reached then. Sir Stuart Macclesfield, it transpired, was in a nursing home recovering from pneumonia. I had hoped to be able to summon some help in keeping a watch on Humber's yard so that when the horse box left with Kandersteg on board it could be followed. It looked, however, as though I would have to do it myself, as I could visualize the local police neither believing my story nor providing anyone to assist me.

Armed with a rug and a pair of good binoculars bought in a pawnshop, and also with a pork pie, slabs of nut chocolate, a bottle of vichy water, and some sheets of foolscap paper, I rode the motorcycle back through Posset and out along the road that crossed the top of the valley in which Humber's stables lay. Stopping at the point I had marked on my previous excursion, I wheeled the cycle a few yards down into the scrubby heathland, and found a position where I was off the skyline, more or less out of sight from passing cars, and also able to look down into Humber's yard through the binoculars. It was one o'clock, and there was nothing happening there.

I unbuckled the suitcase from the carrier and used it as a seat, settling myself to stay there for a long time. Even if I could reach Beckett on the telephone at nine, he wouldn't be able to rustle up reinforcements much before the next morning.

There was, meanwhile, a report to make, a fuller, more formal, more explanatory affair than the notes scribbled in Posset's post office. I took out the foolscap paper and wrote, on and off, for most of the afternoon, punctuating my work by frequent glances through the binoculars. But nothing took place down at Humber's except the normal routine of the stable.

I began:

To The Earl of October
    Sir Stuart Macclesfield
    Colonel Roderick Beckett
Sirs,

The following is a summary of the facts which have so far come to light during my investigations on your behalf, together with some deductions which it seems reasonable to make from them.

Paul James Adams and Hedley Humber started collaborating in a scheme for ensuring winners about four years ago, when Adams bought the Manor House and came to live at Tellbridge, Northumberland.

Adams (in my admittedly untrained opinion) has a psychopathic personality, in that he impulsively gives himself pleasure and pursues his own ends without any consideration for other people or much apparent anxiety about the consequences to himself. His intelligence seems to be above average, and it is he who gives the orders. I believe it is fairly common for psychopaths to be aggressive swindlers; it might be enlightening to dig up his life history.

Humber, though dominated by Adams, is not as irresponsible. He is cold and controlled at all times. I have never seen him genuinely angry (he uses anger as a weapon) and everything he does seems to be thought out and calculated. Whereas Adams may be mentally abnormal, Humber seems to be simply wicked. His comparative sanity may act as a brake on Adams, and have prevented their discovery before this.

Jud Wilson, the head traveling lad, and Cass, the head lad, are both involved, but only to the extent of being hired subordinates. Neither of them does as much stable work as their jobs would normally entail, but they are well paid. Both own big cars of less than a year old.

Adams' and Humber's scheme is based on the fact that horses learn by association and connect noises to events. Like Pavlov's dogs who would come to the sound of a bell because they had been taught it meant feeding time, horses hearing the feed trolley rattling across a stable yard know very well that their food is on the way.

If a horse is accustomed to a certain consequence following closely upon a certain noise, he automatically *expects* the consequence whenever he hears the noise. He reacts to the noise in anticipation of what is to come.

If something frightening were substituted—if, for instance, the rattle of the feed trolley were followed always

190

by a thrashing and no food—the horse would soon begin to fear the noise, because of what it portended.

Fear is the stimulant which Adams and Humber have used. The appearance of all the apparently "doped" horses after they had won—the staring, rolling eyes and the heavy sweat—was consistent with their having been in a state of terror.

Fear strongly stimulates the adrenal glands, so that they flood the bloodstream with adrenalin; and the effect of extra adrenalin, as of course you know, is to release the upsurge of energy needed to deal with the situation, either by fighting back or by running away. Running, in this case. At top speed, in panic.

The laboratory reports stated that the samples taken from all the original eleven horses showed a high adrenalin content, but that this was not significant because horses vary enormously, some always producing more adrenalin than others. I, however, think that it *was* significant that the adrenalin counts of those eleven horses were uniformly higher than average.

The noise which triggered off their fear is the high note of the sort of silent whistle normally used for training dogs. Horses can hear it well, though to human ears it is faint; this fact makes it ideal for the purpose, as a more obtrusive sound (a football rattle, for instance) would soon have been spotted. Humber keeps a dog whistle in the drinks compartment of his Bentley.

I do not yet know for sure how Adams and Humber frighten the horses, but I can make a guess.

For a fortnight I looked after a horse known in the yard as Mickey (registered name, Starlamp), who had been given the treatment. In Mickey's case, it was a disaster. He returned from three days' absence with large raw patches on his forelegs and in a completely unhinged mental state.

The wounds on his legs were explained by the head lad as having been caused by the application of a blister. But there was no blister paste to be seen, and I think they were ordinary burns caused by some sort of naked flame. Horses are more afraid of fire than of anything else, and it seems probable to me that it is expectation of being burnt that Adams and Humber have harnessed to the sound of a dog whistle.

I blew a dog whistle to discover its effect on Mickey. It was less than three weeks after the association had been planted, and he reacted violently and unmistakably. If you care to, you can repeat this trial on Six-Ply; but give him room to bolt in safety.

Adams and Humber chose horses that looked promising throughout their racing careers but had never won on account of running out of steam or guts at the last fence; and there are of course any number of horses like this. They bought them cheaply one at a time from auction sales or out of selling races, instilled into them a noise-fear association, and quietly sold them again. Often, far from losing on the deal, they made a profit (*cf.* past histories of horses collected by officer cadets).

Having sold a horse with such a built-in accelerator, Adams and Humber then waited for it to run in a selling chase at one of five courses: Sedgefield, Haydock, Ludlow, Kelso, and Stafford. They seem to have been prepared to wait indefinitely for this combination of place and event to occur, and in fact it has only occurred twelve times (eleven winners and Superman) since the first case twenty months ago.

These courses were chosen, I imagine, because their extra-long run-in gave the most room for the panic to take effect. The horses were often lying fourth or fifth when landing over the last fence, and needed time to overhaul the leaders. If a horse was too hopelessly behind, Adams and Humber could just have left the whistle unblown, forfeited their stake money, and waited for another day.

Selling chases were preferred, I think, because horses are less likely to fall in them, and because of the good possibility of the winners changing hands yet again immediately afterward.

At first sight it looks as if it would have been safer to have applied this scheme to flat racing; but flat racers do not seem to change hands so often, which would lessen the confusion. Then again, Humber has never held a flat license, and probably can't get one.

None of the horses has been galvanized twice, the reason

probably being that having once discovered they were not burned after hearing the whistle, they would be less likely to expect to be again. Their reaction would no longer be reliable enough to gamble on.

All the eleven horses won at very long odds, varying from 10–1 to 50–1, and Adams and Humber must have spread their bets thinly enough to raise no comment. I do not know how much Adams won on each race, but the least Humber made was 1,700 pounds, and the most was 4,500.

Details of all the processed horses, successful and unsuccessful, are recorded in a blue ledger at present to be found at the back of the third drawer down in the center one of three green filing cabinets in Humber's stable office.

Basically, as you see, it is a simple plan. All they do is make a horse associate fire with a dog whistle, and then blow a whistle as he lands over the last fence.

No drugs, no mechanical contrivances, no help needed from owner, trainer, or jockey. There was only a slight risk of Adams and Humber being found out, because their connections with the horses was so obscure and distant.

Stapleton, however, suspected them and I am certain in my own mind that they killed him, although there is no supporting evidence.

They believe now that they are safe and undetected; and they intend during the next few days, to plant fear in a horse called Kandersteg. I have left Humber's employ, and am writing this while keeping a watch on the yard. I propose to follow the horse box when Kandersteg leaves in it, and discover where and how the heat is applied.

I stopped writing and picked up the binoculars. The lads were bustling about doing evening stables and I stretched myself luxuriously and enjoyed not being down there among them.

It was too soon, I thought, to expect Humber to start on Kandersteg, however much of a hurry he and Adams were in. They couldn't have known for certain that I would depart before lunch, or even that day, and they were bound to let my dust settle before making a move. On the other hand, I couldn't risk missing them. Even the two miles to the telephone in Posset made ringing up Beckett a worrying prospect. It would take no longer for Kandersteg to be loaded up and carted off than for me to locate Beckett in his club. Mickey-Starlamp had been both removed and brought back in daylight, and it might be that Humber never moved any horses about by night. But I couldn't be sure. I bit the end of my pen in indecision. Finally, deciding not to telephone, I added a postscript to the report.

I would very much appreciate some help in this watch, because if it continues for several days I could easily miss the horse box through falling asleep. I can be found two miles out of Posset on the Hexham road, at the head of the valley which Humber's stables lie in.

I added the time, the date, and signed my name. Then I folded the report into an envelope, and addressed it to Colonel Beckett.

I raced down to Posset to put the letter in the box outside the post office. Four miles. I was away for just under six minutes. It was lucky, I think, that I met no traffic on either part of the trip. I skidded to a worried halt at the top of the hill, but all appeared normal down in the stables. I wheeled the motorcycle off the road again, down to where I had been before, and took a long took through the binoculars.

It was beginning to get dark and lights were on in nearly all the boxes, shining out into the yard. The dark, looming bulk of Humber's house, which lay nearest to me, shut off from my sight his brick office and all the top end of the yard, but I had a sideways view of the closed doors of the horse-box garage, and I could see straight into the far-end row of boxes, of which the fourth from the left was occupied by Kandersteg.

And there he was, a pale, washy chestnut, moving across and catching the light as Bert tossed his straw to make him comfortable for the night. I sighed with relief, and sat down again to watch.

The routine work went on, untroubled, unchanged. I watched Humber, leaning on his stick, make his slow inspection around the yard, and absentmindedly rubbed

194

the bruises he had given me that morning. One by one the doors were shut and the lights went out until only a single window glowed yellow, the last window along the right-hand row of boxes, the window of the lads' kitchen. I put down the binoculars, and got to my feet and stretched.

As always on the moors, the air was on the move. It wasn't a wind, scarcely a breeze, more like cold current flowing around whatever it found in its path. To break its chilling persistence on my back I constructed a rough barricade of the motorcycle with a bank of brushwood on its roadward, moorward side. In the lee of this shelter I sat on the suitcase, wrapped myself in the rug, and was tolerably warm and comfortable.

I looked at my watch. Almost eight o'clock. It was a fine, clear night, and the sky was luminous with the white blaze of the stars. I still hadn't learned the northern-hemisphere patterns except for the Great Bear and Pole Star. And there was Venus dazzling away to the west-southwest. A pity that I hadn't thought of buying an astral map to pass the time.

Down in the yard the kitchen door opened, spilling out an oblong of light. Cecil's figure stayed there for a few seconds silhouetted; then he came out and shut the door, and I couldn't see him in the dark. Off to his bottle, no doubt.

I ate some pie, and a while later, a bar of chocolate.

Time passed. Nothing happened down in Humber's yard. Occasionally a car sped along the road behind me, but none stopped. Nine o'clock came and went. Colonel Beckett would be dining at his club, and I could after all have gone safely down to ring him up. I shrugged in the darkness. He would get my letter in the morning, anyway.

The kitchen door opened again, and two or three lads came out, picking their way with a torch around to the elementary sanitation. Upstairs in the hayloft a light showed dimly through that half of the window not pasted over with brown paper. Bedtime. Cecil reeled in, clutching the doorpost to stop himself from falling.

The downstairs light went out, and finally the upper one as well.

The night deepened. The hours passed. The moon rose and shone brightly. I gazed out over the primeval rolling moors and thought some unoriginal thought, such as how beautiful the earth was, and how vicious the ape creature who inhabited it. Greedy, destructive, unkind, power-hungry old homo sapiens. Sapiens, meaning wise, discreet, judicious. What a laugh. So fair a planet should have evolved a sweeter-natured, saner race. Nothing that produced people like Adams and Humber could be termed a roaring success.

At four o'clock I ate some more chocolate and drank some water, and for some time thought about my stud farm sweltering in the afternoon sun twelve thousand miles away. A sensible, orderly life waiting for me when I had finished sitting on wintry hillsides in the middle of the night.

Cold crept through the blanket as time wore on, but it was no worse than the temperature in Humber's dormitory. I yawned and rubbed my eyes, and began to work out how many seconds had to pass before dawn. If the sun rose (as expected) at ten to seven, that would be a hundred and thirteen times sixty seconds, which made it 6,780 ticks to Thursday. And how many to Friday? I gave up. It was quite likely I would still be sitting on the hillside, but with a little luck, there would be a Beckett-sent companion to give me a pinch when things started moving.

At six-fifteen the light went on again in the lads' quarters, and the stable woke up. Half an hour later, the first string of six horses wound its way out of the yard and down the road to Posset. No gallops on the moors on Thursday. Road-work day.

Almost before they were out of sight, Jud Wilson drove into the yard in his substantial Ford and parked it beside the horse-box shed. Cass walked across the yard to meet him, and the two of them stood talking together for a few minutes. Then through the binoculars I watched Jud Wilson go back to the shed and open its big double doors, while Cass made straight for Kandersteg's box, the fourth door from the end.

196

They were off.

And they were off very slickly. Jud Wilson backed the box into the center of the yard and let down the ramp. Cass led the horse straight across and into the horse box, and within a minute was out helping to raise and fasten the ramp again. There was then a fractional pause while they stood looking toward the house, from where almost instantly the limping back view of Humber appeared.

Cass stood watching while Humber and Jud Wilson climbed up into the cab. The horse box rolled forward out of the yard. The loading-up had taken barely five minutes from start to finish.

During this time I dropped the rug over the suitcase and kicked the brushwood away from the bike. The binoculars I slung around my neck and zipped inside the leather jacket. I put on my crash helmet, goggles, and gloves.

In spite of my belief that it would be to the north or the west that Kandersteg would be taken, I was relieved when this proved to be the case. The horse box turned sharply west and trundled up the far side of the valley along the road which crossed the one I was stationed on.

I wheeled the bike onto the road, started it, and abandoning (this time with pleasure) my third clump of clothes, rode with some dispatch toward the crossroads. There, from a safe quarter of a mile away, I watched the horse box slow down, turn right, northward, and accelerate.

16

I crouched in a ditch all day and watched Adams, Humber, and Jud Wilson scare Kandersteg into a lathering frenzy.

It was wicked.

The means they used were as simple in essence as

the scheme, and consisted mainly in the special layout of a small, two-acre field.

The thin, high hedge around the whole field was laced with wire to about shoulder height, strong but without barbs. About fifteen feet inside this there was a second fence, solidly made of posts and rails which had weathered to a pleasant grayish brown.

At first glance it looked like the arrangement found at many stud farms, where young stock are kept from damaging themselves on wire by a wooden protective inner fence. But the corners of this inner ring had been rounded, so that what in effect had been formed was a miniature race track between the outer and inner fences.

It all looked harmless. A field for young stock, a training place for racehorses, a show ring—take your pick. With a shed for storing equipment, just outside the gate at one corner. Sensible. Ordinary.

I half-knelt, half-lay in the drainage ditch which ran along behind the hedge, near the end of one long side of the field, with the shed little more than a hundred yards away in the far opposite corner, to my left. The bottom of the hedge had been cut and laid, which afforded good camouflage for my head, but from about a foot above the ground the leafless hawthorn grew straight up, tall and weedy; as concealing as a sieve. But as long as I kept absolutely still, I judged I was unlikely to be spotted. At any rate, although I was really too close for safety, too close even to need to use the binoculars, there was nowhere else that gave much cover at all.

Bare hillsides sloped up beyond the far fence and along the end of the field to my right; behind me lay a large open pasture of at least thirty acres; and the top end, which was screened from the road by a wedge of conifers, was directly under Adams' and Humber's eyes.

Getting to the ditch had entailed leaving the inadequate shelter of the last flattening shoulder of hillside and crossing fifteen yards of bare turf when none of the men was in sight. But retreating was going to be less pulse-quickening, since I had only to wait for the dark.

The horse box was parked beside the shed, and almost as soon as I had worked my way around the hill to my present position, there was a clattering of hoofs on the ramp as Kandersteg was unloaded. Jud Wilson led him around through the gate and onto the grassy track. Adams, following, shut the gate and then unlatched a swinging section of the inner fence and fastened it across the track, making a barrier. Walking past Jud and the horse, he did the same with another section a few yards farther on, with the result that Jud and Kandersteg were now standing in a small pen in the corner. A pen with three ways out: the gate out of the field, and the rails which swung across like level crossing gates on either side.

Jud let go of the horse, which quietly began to eat the grass, and he and Adams let themselves out and disappeared into the shed to join Humber. The shed, made of weathered wood, was built like a single loose box, with a window and a split door, and I imagined it was there that Mickey had spent much of the three days he had been away.

There was a certain amount of clattering and banging in the shed, which went on for some time, but as I had only a sideways view of the door, I could see nothing of what was happening.

Presently all three of them came out. Adams walked around behind the shed and reappeared beyond the field, walking up the hillside. He went at a good pace right to the top, and stood gazing about him at the countryside.

Humber and Wilson came through the gate into the field, carrying between them an apparatus which looked like a vacuum cleaner, a cylindrical tank with a hose attached to one end. They put the tank down in the corner, and Wilson held the hose. Kandersteg, quietly cropping the grass close beside them, lifted his head and looked at them, incurious and trusting. He bent down again to eat.

Humber walked the few steps along to where the

swinging rail was fastened to the hedge, seemed to be checking something, and then went back to stand beside Wilson, who was looking up toward Adams.

On top of the hill, Adams casually waved his hand.

Down in the corner of the field, Humber had his hand to his mouth; I was too far away to see with the naked eye if what he held there was a whistle, and too close to risk getting out the glasses for a better look. But even though, try as I might, I could hear no noise, there wasn't much room for doubt. Kandersteg raised his head, pricked his ears, and looked at Humber.

Flame suddenly roared from the hose in Wilson's hand. It was directed behind the horse, but it frightened him badly, all the same. He sat back on his haunches, his ears flattening. Then Humber's arm moved, and the swinging barrier, released by some sort of catch, sprang back to let the horse out onto the track. He needed no telling.

He stampeded around the field, skidding at the corners, lurching against the inner wooden rail, thundering past ten feet from my head. Wilson opened the second barrier, and he and Humber retired through the gate. Kandersteg made two complete circuits at high speed before his stretched neck relaxed to a more normal angle and his wildly thrusting hindquarters settled down to a more natural gallop.

Humber and Wilson stood and watched him, and Adams strolled down the hill to join them at the gate.

They let the horse slow down and stop of his own accord, which he did away to my right, after about three and a half circuits. Then Jud Wilson unhurriedly swung one of the barriers back across the track, and waving a stick in one hand and a hunting whip in the other, began to walk around to drive the horse in front of him along into the corner. Kandersteg trotted warily ahead, unsettled, sweating, not wanting to be caught.

Jud Wilson swung his stick and his whip and trudged steadily on. Kandersteg trotted softly past where I lay, his hoofs swishing through the short grass; but I was no longer watching. My face was buried in the roots

200

of the hedge, and I ached with the effort of keeping still. Seconds passed like hours.

There was a rustle of trouser leg brushing against trouser leg, a faint clump of boots on turf, a crack of the long thong of the whip . . . and no outraged yell of discovery. He went past, and on up the field.

The muscles that had been ready to expel me out of the ditch and away toward the hidden motorcycle gradually relaxed. I opened my eyes and looked at leaf mold close to my face, and worked some saliva into my mouth. Cautiously, inch by inch, I raised my head and looked across the field.

The horse had reached the barrier and Wilson was unhooking and swinging the other one shut behind him, so that he was again penned into the small enclosure. There, for about half an hour, the three men left him. They themselves walked back into the shed, where I could do nothing but wait for them to appear again.

It was a fine, clear, quiet morning, but a bit cold for lying in ditches, especially damp ones. Exercise, however, beyond curling and uncurling my toes and fingers, was a bigger risk than pneumonia; so I lay still, taking heart from the thought that I was dressed from head to foot in black, and had a mop of black hair as well, and was crouched in blackish-brown rotting dead leaves. It was because of the protective coloring it offered that I had chosen the ditch in preference to a shallow dip in the hillside, and I was glad I had, because it was fairly certain that Adams from his lookout point would at once have spotted a dark intruder on the pale-green hill.

I didn't notice Jud Wilson walk out of the shed, but I heard the click of the gate, and there he was, going into the little enclosure and laying his hand on Kandersteg's bridle, for all the world as if he was consoling him. But how could anyone who liked horses set about them with a flamethrower? And Jud, it was clear, was going to do it again. He left the horse, went over to the corner, picked up the hose, and stood adjusting its nozzle.

Presently Adams appeared and climbed the hill, and

then Humber, limping on his stick, joined Jud in the field.

There was a long wait before Adams waved his hand, during which three cars passed along the lonely moorland road. Eventually Adams was satisfied. His arm languidly rose and fell.

Humber's hand went immediately to his mouth.

Kandersteg already knew what it meant. He was running back on his haunches in fear before the flame shot out behind him and stopped him dead.

This time there was a fiercer, longer, closer burst of fire, and Kandersteg erupted in greater terror. He came scorching around the track . . . and around again; it was like waiting for the ball to settle in roulette with too much staked. But he stopped this time at the top end of the field, well away from my hiding place.

Jud walked across the middle of the field to come up behind him, not around the whole track. I sighed deeply with heartfelt relief.

I had folded my limbs originally into comfortable angles, but they were beginning to ache with inactivity, and I had a cramp in the calf of my right leg, but I still didn't dare move while all three men were in my sight and I in theirs.

They shut Kandersteg into his little pen and strolled away into the shed, and cautiously, as quietly as I could in the rotting leaves, I flexed my arms and legs, got rid of the cramp, and discovered pins and needles instead. Ah, well . . . it couldn't go on forever.

They were, however, plainly going to repeat the process yet again. The flamethrower still lay by the hedge.

The sun was high in the sky by this time, and I looked at the gleam it raised on the leather sleeve of my left arm, close to my head. It was too shiny. Hedges and ditches held nothing as light-reflecting as black leather. Could Wilson possibly, *possibly* walk a second time within feet of me without coming close enough to the hedge to see a shimmer which shouldn't be there?

Adams and Humber came out of the shed and leaned over the gate, looking at Kandersteg. Presently they lit cigarettes and were clearly talking. They were in no hurry. They finished the cigarettes, threw them away, and stayed where they were for another ten minutes. Then Adams walked over to his car and returned with a bottle and some glasses. Wilson came out of the shed to join them and the three of them stood there in the sun, quietly drinking and gossiping in the most commonplace way.

What they were doing was, of course, routine to them. They had done it at least twenty times before. Their latest victim stood warily in his pen, unmoving, frightened, far too upset to eat.

Watching them drink made me thirsty, but that was among the least of my troubles. Staying still was becoming more and more difficult. Painful, almost.

At long last they broke it up. Adams put the bottle and glasses away and strolled off up the hill, Humber checked the quick release on the swinging barrier, and Jud adjusted the nozzle of the hose.

Adams waved. Humber blew.

This time the figure of Kandersteg was sharply, terrifyingly silhouetted against a sheet of flame. Wilson swayed his body, and the brilliant, spreading jet flattened and momentarily swept under the horse's belly and among his legs.

I nearly cried out, as if it were I that was being burned, not the horse. And for one sickening moment it looked as if Kandersteg was too terrified to escape.

Then, squealing, he was down the track like a meteor, fleeing from fire, from pain, from a dog whistle. . . .

He was going too fast to turn the corner. He crashed into the hedge, bounced off, stumbled and fell. Eyes starting out of his head, lips retracted from his teeth, he scrambled frantically to his feet and bolted on, past my head, up the field, around again and around again.

He came to a jolting halt barely twenty vards away from me. He stood stock still with sweat dripping from his neck and down his legs. His flesh quivered convulsively.

Jud Wilson, whip and stick in hand, started on his walk around the track. Slowly I put my face down among the roots and tried to draw some comfort from the fact that if he saw me there was still a heavily wired fence between us, and I should get some sort of start in running away. But the motorcycle was hidden on rough ground two hundred yards behind me, and the curving road lay at least as far beyond that again, and Adams' gray Jaguar was parked on the far side of the horse box. Successful flight wasn't something I'd have liked to bet on.

Kandersteg was too frightened to move. I heard Wilson shouting at him and cracking the whip, but it was a full minute before the hoofs came stumbling jerkily, in bursts and stamps, past my head.

In spite of the cold, I was sweating. Dear heavens, I thought, there was as much adrenalin pouring into my bloodstream as into the horse's; and I realized that from the time Wilson started his methodical walk around the track, I had been able to hear my own heart thudding.

Jud Wilson yelled at Kandersteg so close to my ear that it felt like a blow. The whip cracked.

"Get on, get on, get on there."

He was standing within feet of my head. Kandersteg wouldn't move. The whip cracked again. Jud shouted at the horse, stamping his boot on the ground in encouragement. The faint tremor came to me through the earth. He was a yard away, perhaps, with his eyes on the horse. He had only to turn his head . . . I began to think that anything, even discovery, was preferable to the terrible strain of keeping still.

Then, suddenly, it was over.

Kandersteg skittered away and bumped into the rails, and took a few more uneven steps back toward the top of the field. Jud Wilson moved away after him.

I continued to behave like a log, feeling exhausted. Slowly my heart subsided. I started breathing again . . . and unclamped my fingers from handfuls of leaf mold.

Step by reluctant step Jud forced Kandersteg around to the corner enclosure, where he swung the rails across and penned the horse in again. Then he picked up the flamethrower and took it with him through the gate. The job was done. Adams, Humber, and Wilson stood in a row and contemplated their handiwork.

The pale coat of the horse was blotted with huge

204

dark patches where the sweat had broken out, and he stood stiff legged, stiff necked, in the center of the small enclosure. Whenever any of the three men moved, he jumped nervously and then stood rigidly still again; and it was clearly going to be some long time before he had unwound enough to be loaded up and taken back to Posset.

Mickey had been away three days, but that, I judged, was only because his legs had been badly burned by mistake. As Kandersteg's indoctrination appeared to have gone without a hitch, he should be back in his own stable fairly soon.

It couldn't be too soon for me and my static joints. I watched the three men potter about in the sunlight, wandering between car and shed, shed and horse box, aimlessly passing the morning and managing never to be all safely out of sight at the same time. I cursed under my breath and resisted a temptation to scratch my nose.

At long last they made a move. Adams and Humber folded themselves into the Jaguar and drove off in the direction of Tellbridge. But Jud Wilson reached into the cab of the horse box, pulled out a paper bag, and proceeded to eat his lunch sitting on the gate. Kandersteg remained immobile in his little enclosure, and I did the same in my ditch.

Jud Wilson finished his lunch, rolled the paper bag into a ball, yawned, and lit a cigarette. Kandersteg continued to sweat, and I to ache. Everything was very quiet. Time passed.

Jud Wilson finished his cigarette, threw the stub away, and yawned again. Then slowly, slowly, he climbed down from the gate, picked up the flamethrower, and took it into the shed.

He was scarcely through the door before I was slithering down into the shallow ditch, lying full length along it on my side, not caring about the dampness but thankfully, slowly, painfully straightening one by one my cramped arms and legs.

The time, when I looked at my watch, was two o'clock.

I felt hungry, and regretted that I hadn't had enough sense to bring some of the chocolate.

I lay in the ditch all afternoon, hearing nothing, but waiting for the horse box to start up and drive away. After a while, in spite of the cold and the presence of Jud Wilson, I had great difficulty in keeping awake; a riduculous state of affairs which could only be remedied by action. Accordingly I rolled over onto my stomach and inch by careful inch raised my head high enough to see across to Kandersteg and the shed.

Jud Wilson was again sitting on the gate. He must have seen my movements out of the corner of his eye, because he looked away from Kandersteg, who stood in front of him, and turned his head in my direction. For a fleeting second it seemed that he was looking straight into my eyes; then his gaze swept past me, and presently, unsuspiciously, returned to Kandersteg.

I let my held breath trickle out slowly, fighting down a cough.

The horse was still sweating, the dark patches showing up starkly, but there was a less fixed look about him, and while I watched, he swished his tail and restlessly shook his neck. He was over the hump.

More cautiously still, I lowered my head and chest down again onto my folded arms, and waited some more.

Soon after four, Adams and Humber came back in the Jaguar, and again, like a rabbit out of its burrow, I edged up for a look.

They decided to take the horse home. Jud Wilson backed the horse box to the gate and let down the ramp, and Kandersteg, sticking in his feet at every step, was eventually pulled and prodded into it. The poor beast's distress was all too evident, even from across the field. I liked horses. I found I was wholly satisfied that because of me, Adams and Humber and Wilson were going to be out of business.

Gently I lay down again, and after a short while I heard both the engines—first the Jaguar's and then the horse box's—start up and drive off, back toward Posset.

When every sound of them had died away, I stood

up, stretched, brushed the leaf mold from my clothes, and walked around the field to look at the shed.

It was fastened shut with a complicated-looking padlock, but through the window I could see it held little besides the flamethrower, some cans presumably holding fuel, a large tin funnel, and three garden chairs folded and stacked against one wall. There seemed little point in breaking in, though it would have been simple enough since the padlock fittings had been screwed straight onto the surface of the door and its frame. The screwdriver blade of my penknife could have removed the whole thing, fussy padlock intact. Crooks, I reflected, could be as fantastically dim in some ways as they were imaginative in others.

I went through the gate into Kandersteg's little enclosure. The grass where he had stood was scorched. The inside surfaces of the rails had been painted white, so that they resembled racecourse rails. I stood for a while looking at them, feeling a secondhand echo of the misery the horse had endured in that harmless-looking place, and then let myself out and walked away, around past my hiding place in the ditch and off toward the motorcycle. I picked it up, hooked the crash helmet onto the handlebars, and started the engine.

So that was the lot, I thought. My job was done. Safely, quietly, satisfactorily done. As it should be. Nothing remained but to complete yesterday's report and put the final facts at the Stewards' disposal.

I coasted back to the place from where I had kept a watch on Humber's yard, but there was no one there. Either Beckett had not got my letter or he had not been able to send any help, or the help, if it had arrived, had got tired of waiting and departed. The rug, suitcase, and remains of food lay where I had left them, undisturbed.

On an impulse, before packing up and leaving the area, I unzipped my jacket and took out the binoculars to have a last look down into the yard.

What I saw demolished in one second flat my complacent feeling of safety and completion.

A scarlet sports car was turning into the yard. It

stopped beside Adams' gray Jaguar, a door opened, and a girl got out. I was too far away to distinguish her features but there was no mistaking that familiar car and that dazzling silver-blond hair. She slammed the car door and walked hesitantly toward the office, out of my sight.

I swore aloud. Of all damnable, unforeseeable, dangerous things to happen! I hadn't told Elinor anything. She thought I was an ordinary stable lad. I had borrowed a dog whistle from her. And she was October's daughter. What were the chances, I wondered numbly, to her keeping quiet on the last two counts and not giving Adams the idea that she was a threat to him.

She ought to be safe enough, I thought. Reasonably, she ought to be safe as long as she made it clear that it was I who knew the significance of dog whistles, and not she.

But supposing she didn't make it clear? Adams never behaved reasonably, to start with. His standards were not normal. He was psychopathic. He could impulsively kill a journalist who seemed to be getting too nosy. What was to stop him from killing again, if he got it into his head that it was necessary?

I would give her three minutes, I thought. If she asked for me, and was told I had left, and went straight away again, everything would be all right.

I willed her to return from the office and drive away in her car. I doubted whether in any case, if Adams was planning to harm her, I could get her out safely, since the odds against, in the shape of Adams, Humber, Wilson, and Cass, were too great for common sense. I wasn't too keen on having to try. But the three minutes went past, and the red car stood empty in the yard.

She had stayed to talk and she had no notion that there was anything that should not be said. If I had done as I had wanted and told her why I was at Humber's, she would not have come at all. It was my fault she was there. I clearly had to do my best to see she left again in mint condition. There was no choice.

I put the binoculars in the suitcase and left it and the rug where they were. Then, zipping up the jacket and fastening on the crash helmet, I restarted the bike and rode it down and around and in through Humber's gate.

I left the bike near the gate and walked across toward the yard, passing the shed where the horse box was kept. The doors were shut, and there was no sign of Jud Wilson. Perhaps he had already gone home, and I hoped so. I went into the yard at the top end beside the wall of the office, and saw Cass at the opposite end looking over the door of the fourth box from the left. Kandersteg was home.

Adams' Jaguar and Elinor's TR-4 stood side by side in the center of the yard. Lads were hustling over their evening jobs, and everything looked normal and quiet.

I opened the office door, and walked in.

17

So much for my fears, I thought. So much for my melodramatic imagination. She was perfectly safe. She held a half-empty glass of pink liquid in her hand, having a friendly drink with Adams and Humber, and she was smiling.

Humber's heavy face looked anxious, but Adams was laughing and enjoying himself. It was a picture which printed itself clearly on my mind before they all three turned and looked at me.

"Daniel!" Elinor exclaimed. "Mr. Adams said you had gone."

"Yes. I left something behind. I came back for it."

"Lady Elinor Tarren," said Adams with deliberation, coming around behind me, closing the door and leaning against it, "came to see if you had conducted the experiment she lent you her dog whistle for."

It was just as well, after all, that I had gone back.

"Oh, surely I didn't say that," she protested. "I just came to get the whistle, if Daniel had finished with it.

I mean, I was passing, and I thought I could save him the trouble of sending it. . . ."

I turned to him. "Lady Elinor Tarren," I said with equal deliberation, "does not know what I borrowed her whistle for. I didn't tell her. She knows nothing about it."

His eyes narrowed and then opened into a fixed stare. His jaw bunched. He took in the way I had spoken to him, the way I looked at him. It was not what he was used to from me. He transferred his stare to Elinor.

"Leave her alone," I said. "She doesn't know."

"What on earth are you talking about?" said Elinor, smiling. "What was this mysterious experiment, anyway?"

"It wasn't important," I said. "There's . . . er . . . there's a deaf lad here, and we wanted to know if he could hear high-pitched noises, that's all."

"Oh," she said. "And could he?"

I shook my head. "I'm afraid not."

"What a pity." She took a drink, and ice tinkled against the glass. "Well, if you've no more use for it, do you think I could have my whistle back?"

"Of course." I dug into my money belt, brought out the whistle, and gave it to her. I saw Humber's astonishment and Adams' spasm of fury that Humber's search had missed so elementary a hiding place.

"Thank you," she said, putting the whistle in her pocket. "What are your plans now? Another stable job? You know," she said to Humber, smiling. "I'm surprised you let him go. He rode better than any lad we've ever had in Father's stables. You were lucky to have him."

I had not ridden well for Humber. He began to say heavily, "He's not at all good . . ." when Adams smoothly interrupted him.

"I think we have underestimated Roke, Hedley. Lady Elinor, I am sure Mr. Humber will take him back on your recommendation, and never let him go again."

"Splendid," she said warmly.

Adams was looking at me with his hooded gaze to make sure I had appreciated his little joke. I didn't think it very funny.

"Take your helmet off," he said. "You're indoors and in front of a lady. Take it off."

"I think I'll keep it on," I said equably. And I could have done with a full suit of armor to go with it. Adams was not used to my contradicting him, and he shut his mouth with a snap.

Humber said, puzzled, "I don't understand why you bother with Roke, Lady Elinor. I thought your father got rid of him for . . . well . . . molesting you."

"Oh, no." She laughed. "That was my sister. But it wasn't true, you know. It was all made up." She swallowed the last of her drink and with the best will in the world put the finishing touches to throwing me to the wolves. "Father made me promise not to tell anyone that it was all a story, but as you're Daniel's employer, you really ought to know that he isn't anything like as bad as he lets everyone believe."

There was a short, deep silence. Then I said, smiling, "That's the nicest reference I've ever had. . . . You're very kind."

"Oh, dear," she said, laughing. "You know what I mean . . . and I can't think why you don't stick up for yourself more."

"It isn't always advisable," I said, and raised an eyebrow at Adams. He showed signs of not appreciating my jokes, either. He took Elinor's empty glass.

"Another gin and Campari?" he suggested.

"No, thank you. I must be going."

He put her glass down on the desk with his own, and said, "Do you think Roke would be sort of man who'd need to swallow tranquilizers before he found the nerve to look after a difficult horse?"

"Tranquilizers? *Tranquilizers?* Of course not. I shouldn't think he ever took a tranquilizer in his life. Did you?" she said, turning to me and beginning to look puzzled.

"No," I said. I was very anxious for her to be on her way before her puzzlement grew any deeper. Only while she suspected nothing and learned nothing was she safe enough.

"But you said . . ." began Humber, who was still unenlightened.

"It was a joke. Only a joke," I told him. "Mr. Adams laughed about it quite a lot, if you remember."

"That's true. I laughed," said Adams somberly. At least he seemed willing for her ignorance to remain undisturbed, and to let her go.

"Oh." Elinor's face cleared. "Well . . . I suppose I'd better be getting back to college. I'm going to Slaw tomorrow for the weekend. . . . Do you have any message for my father, Daniel?"

It was a casual, social remark, but I saw Adams stiffen.

I shook my head.

"Well . . . it's been very pleasant, Mr. Humber. Thank you so much for the drink. I hope I haven't taken too much of your time."

She shook Humber's hand, and Adams', and finally mine.

"How lucky you came back for something. I thought I'd missed you . . . and that I could whistle for my whistle." She grinned.

I laughed. "Yes, it was lucky."

"Good-bye then. Good-bye, Mr. Humber," she said, as Adams opened the door for her. She said good-bye to him on the doorstep, where he remained, and over Humber's shoulder I watched through the window as she walked across to her car. She climbed in, started the engine, waved gaily to Adams, and drove out of the yard. My relief at seeing her go was even greater than my anxiety about getting out myself.

Adams stepped inside, shut the door, locked it, and put the key in his pocket. Humber was surprised. He still did not understand.

He said, staring at me, "You know, Roke doesn't seem the same. And his voice is different."

"Roke, damn him to hell, is God knows what."

The only good thing in the situation that I could see was that I no longer had to cringe when he spoke to me. It was quite a relief to be able to stand up straight for a change. Even if it didn't last long.

"Do you mean it is Roke, and not Elinor Tarren, after all, who knows about the whistle?"

"Of course," said Adams impatiently. "For Christ's sake, don't you understand anything? It looks as though October planted him on us, though how in hell he knew . . ."

"But Roke is only a stable lad."

"Only," said Adams savagely. "But that doesn't make it any better. Stable lads have tongues, don't they? And eyes? And look at him. He's not the stupid worm he's always seemed."

He picked up one of the glasses and smashed it violently against the wall.

"No one would take his word against yours," said Humber.

"No one is going to take his word at all."

"What do you mean?"

"I'm going to kill him," said Adams.

"I suppose that might be more satisfactory." Humber sounded as if he were discussing putting down a horse.

"It won't help you," I said. "I've already sent a report to the Stewards."

"We were told that once before," said Humber, "but it wasn't true."

"It is, this time."

Adams said violently, "Report or no report, I'm going to kill him. There are other reasons. . . ." He broke off, glared at me, and said, "You fooled me. *Me*. How?"

I didn't reply. It hardly seemed a good time for light conversation.

"This one," said Humber reflectively, "has a motorcycle."

I remembered that the windows in the office's washroom were all too small to escape through. The door to the yard was locked, and Humber stood in front of his desk, between me and the window. Yelling could only bring Cass, not the poor rabble of lads, who didn't even know I was there, and wouldn't bother to help me in any case. Both Adams and Humber were taller and heavier than I was, Adams a good deal so. Humber had his stick and I didn't know what weapon Adams proposed

213

to use; and I had never been in a serious fight in my life. The next few minutes were not too delightful a prospect.

On the other hand I was younger than they and, thanks to the hard work they had exacted, as fit as an athlete. Also I had the crash helmet. And I could throw things. . . . Perhaps the odds weren't impossible after all.

A polished wooden chair with a leather seat stood by the wall near the door. Adams picked it up and walked toward me. Humber, remaining still, slid his stick through his hands and held it ready.

I felt appallingly vulnerable.

Adams' eyes were more opaque than I had ever seen them, and the smile which was growing on his mouth didn't reach them. He said loudly, "We might as well enjoy it. They won't look too closely at a burned-out smash."

He swung the chair. I dodged it all right but in doing so got within range of Humber, whose stick landed heavily on top of my shoulder, an inch from my ear. I stumbled and fell, and rolled; and stood up just in time to avoid the chair as Adams crashed it down. One of the legs broke off as it hit the floor, and Adams bent down and picked it up. A solid, straight, square-edged chair leg with a nasty sharp point where it had broken from the seat.

Adams smiled more, and kicked the remains of the chair into a corner.

"Now," he said, "we'll have some sport."

If you could call it sport, I suppose they had it.

Certainly after a short space of time they were still relatively unscathed, while I had added some more bruises to my collection, together with a fast-bleeding cut on the forehead from the sharp end of Adams' chair leg. But the crash helmet hampered their style considerably. and I discovered a useful talent for dodging. I also kicked.

Humber, being a slow mover, stayed at his post guarding the window and slashed at me whenever I came within his reach. As the office was not large, this happened too often. I tried from the beginning either to

214

catch hold of one of the sticks, or to pick up the broken chair, or to find something to throw, but all that happened was that my hands fared badly, and Adams guessed my intentions regarding the chair and made sure I couldn't get hold of it. As for throwing things, the only suitable objects in that bare office were on Humber's desk, behind Humber.

Because of the cold night on the hillside, I was wearing two jerseys under my jacket, and they did act as some sort of cushion; but Adams particularly hit very hard, and I literally shuddered whenever he managed to connect. I had had some idea of crashing out through the window, glass and all, but they gave me no chance to get there, and there was a limit to the time I could spend trying.

In desperation I stopped dodging and flung myself at Humber. Ignoring Adams, who promptly scored two fearful direct hits, I grasped my ex-employer by the lapels, and with one foot on the desk for leverage, swung him around and threw him across the narrow room. He landed with a crash against the filing cabinets.

There on the desk was the green glass paperweight. The size of a cricket ball. It slid smoothly into my hand, and in one unbroken movement I picked it up, pivoted on my toes, and flung it straight at Humber where he sprawled off balance barely ten feet away.

It took him centrally between the eyes. A sweet shot. It knocked him unconscious. He fell without a sound.

I was across the room before he hit the floor, my hand stretching out for the green glass ball, which was a better weapon to me than any stick or broken chair. But Adams understood too quickly. His arm went up.

I made the mistake of thinking one more blow would make no real difference and didn't draw back from trying to reach the paperweight even when I knew Adams' chair leg was on its way down. But this time, because I had my head down, the crash helmet didn't save me. Adams hit me below the rim of the helmet, behind the ear.

Dizzily twisting, I fell against the wall and ended up lying with my shoulders propped against it and one leg doubled underneath me. I tried to stand up, but there seemed to be no strength left in me anywhere. My head was floating. I couldn't see very well. There was a noise inside my ears.

Adams leaned over me, unsnapped the strap of my crash helmet, and pulled it off my head. That meant something, I thought groggily. I looked up. He was standing there smiling, swinging the chair leg. Enjoying himself.

In the last possible second my brain cleared a little and I knew that if I didn't do something about it, this blow was going to be the last. There was no time to dodge. I flung up my right arm to shield my undefended head, and the savagely descending piece of wood crashed into it.

It felt like an explosion. My hand felt numb and useless by my side.

What was left? Ten seconds. Perhaps less. I was furious. I particularly didn't want Adams to have the pleasure of killing me. He was still smiling. Watching to see how I would take it, he slowly raised his arm for the coup de grace.

No, I thought, no. There was nothing wrong with my legs. What on earth was I thinking of, lying there waiting to be blacked out when I still had two good legs? He was standing on my right. My left leg was bent under me and he took no special notice when I disentangled it and crossed it over in front of him. I lifted both my legs off the ground, one in front and one behind his ankles, then I kicked across with my right leg, locked my feet tight together, and rolled my whole body over as suddenly and strongly as I could.

Adams was taken completely by surprise. He over-balanced with wildly swinging arms and fell with a crash on his back. His own weight made the fall more effective from my point of view, because he was winded and slow to get up. I couldn't throw any longer with my numb right hand. Staggering to my feet, I picked the green glass ball up in my left hand and smashed it against Adams' head while he was still on his knees. It seemed to have no effect. He continued to get up. He was grunting.

Desperately I swung my arm and hit him again, low down on the back of the head. And this time he did go down; and stayed down.

I half fell beside him, dizzy and feeling sick, with pain waking up viciously all over my body and blood from the cut on my forehead dripping slowly onto the floor.

I don't know how long I stayed like that, gasping to get some breath back, trying to find the strength to get up and leave the place, but it can't really have been very long. And it was the thought of Cass, in the end, which got me to my feet. By that stage I would have been a pushover for a toddler, let alone the wiry little head lad.

Both of the men lying in heaps on the ground, not stirring. Adams was breathing very heavily; snoring, almost. Humber's chest scarcely moved.

I passed my left hand over my face and it came away covered with blood. There must be blood all over my face, I thought. I couldn't go riding along the road covered in blood. I staggered into the washroom to rinse it off.

There were some half-melted ice cubes in the sink. Ice. I looked at it dizzily. Ice in the refrigerator. Ice clicking in the drinks. Ice in the sink. Good for stopping bleeding. I picked up a lump of it and looked in the mirror. A gory sight. I held the lump of ice on the cut and tried, in the classic phrase, to pull myself together. With little success.

After a while I splashed some water into the sink and rinsed all the blood off my face. The cut was then revealed as being only a couple of inches long and not serious, though still obstinately oozing. I looked around vaguely for a towel.

On the table by the medicine cupboard stood a glass jar with the stopper off and a teaspoon beside it. My glance flickered over it, looking for a towel, and then back, puzzled. I took three shaky steps across the room. There was something the jar should be telling me, I thought, but I wasn't grasping things very clearly.

A bottle of Phenobarbitone, in powder form, like the stuff I'd given Mickey every day for a fortnight. Only Phenobarbitone, that was all. I sighed.

Then it struck me that Mickey had had the last dose in the bottle. The bottle should be empty. Tipped out. Not full. Not a new bottle full to the bottom of the neck, with the pieces of wax from the seal still lying in crumbs on the table beside it. Someone had just opened a new bottle of soluble Phenobarbitone and used a couple of spoonfuls.

Of course. For Kandersteg.

I found a towel and wiped my face. Then I went back into the office and knelt down beside Adams to get the door key out of his pocket. He had stopped snoring.

I rolled him over.

There isn't a pretty way of saying it. He was dead.

Small trickles of blood had seeped out of his ears, eyes, nose, and mouth. I felt his head where I had hit him, and the dented bones moved under my fingers.

Aghast and shaking, I searched in his pockets and found the key. Then I stood up and went slowly over to the desk to telephone to the police.

The telephone had been knocked onto the floor, where it lay with the receiver off. I bent down and picked it up, clumsily left-handed, and my head swam with dizziness. I wished I didn't feel so ill. Straightening up with an effort, I put the telephone back on the desk. Blood started trickling down past my elbow. I hadn't the energy to wash it off again.

Out in the yard one or two lights were on, including the one in Kandersteg's box. His door was wide open and the horse himself, tied up by the head, was lashing out furiously in a series of kicks. He didn't look in the least sedated.

I stopped with my finger in the dial of the telephone, and felt myself go cold. My brain cleared with a click.

Kandersteg was not sedated. They wouldn't want his memory lulled. The opposite, in fact. Mickey had not been given any Phenobarbitone until he was clearly deranged.

I didn't want to believe what my mind told me: that one or more teaspoonfuls of soluble Phenobarbitone in a large gin and Campari would be almost certainly fatal.

Sharply I remembered the scene I had found in the office, the drinks, the anxiety on Humber's face, the enjoyment on Adams'. It matched the enjoyment I had seen when he thought he was killing me. He enjoyed killing. He had thought from what she had said that Elinor had guessed the purpose of the whistle, and he had wasted no time in getting rid of her.

No wonder he had raised no objections to her leaving. She would drive back to college and die in her room miles away, a silly girl who had taken an overdose. No possible connection with Adams or Humber.

And no wonder he had been so determined to kill me: not only because of what I knew about his horses, or because I had fooled him, but because I had seen Elinor drink her gin.

It didn't need too much imagination to picture the scene before I had arrived. Adams saying smoothly, "So you came to see if Roke had used the whistle?"

"Yes."

"And does your father know you're here? Does he know about the whistle?"

"Oh, no, I only came on impulse. Of course he doesn't know."

He must have thought her a fool, blundering in like that; but probably he was the sort of man who thought all women were fools, anyway.

"You'd like some ice in your drink? I'll get some. No bother. Just next door. Here you are, my dear, a strong gin and Phenobarbitone and a quick trip to heaven."

He had taken the same reckless risk of killing Stapleton, and it had worked. And who was to say that if I had been found in the next county over some precipice, smashed up in the ruins of a motor bike, and Elinor died in her college, he wouldn't have gotten away with two more murders?

If Elinor died.

My finger was still in the telephone dial. I turned it three times—nine, nine, nine. There was no answer. I rattled the button, and tried again. Nothing. It was dead, the whole telephone was dead. Everything was dead. Mickey was dead, Stapleton was dead, Adams was dead, Elinor . . . Stop it, stop it. I dragged my scattering wits together. If the telephone wouldn't work, someone would have to go to Elinor's college and prevent her from dying.

My first thought was that I couldn't do it. But who else? If I was right, she needed a doctor urgently, and any time I wasted on bumbling about finding another telephone or another person to go in my stead was just diminishing her chances. I could reach her in less than twenty minutes. By telephoning in Posset I could hardly get help for her any quicker.

It took me three shots to get the key in the keyhole. I couldn't hold the key at all in my right hand, and the left one was shaking. I took a deep breath, unlocked the door, walked out, and shut it behind me.

No one noticed me as I went out of the yard the way I had come and went back to the motor bike. But it didn't fire properly the first time I kicked the starter, and Cass came around the end of the row of boxes to investigate.

"Who's that?" he called. "Is that you, Dan? What are you doing back here?" He began to come toward me.

I stamped on the starter fiercely. The engine sputtered, coughed, and roared. I squeezed the clutch and kicked the bike into gear.

"Come back," yelled Cass. But I turned away from his hurrying figure, out of the gate and down the road to Posset, with gravel spurting under the tires.

The throttle was incorporated into the hand grip of the right-hand handlebar. One merely twisted it toward one to accelerate and away to slow down. Twisting the hand grip was normally easy. It was not easy that evening because once I had managed to grip it hard enough to turn it, the numbness disappeared from my arm with a vengeance. I damned nearly fell off before I was through the gate.

It was ten miles northeast to Durham. One and a half downhill to Posset, seven and a half across the moors on a fairly straight and unfrequented secondary road, one mile through the outskirts of the city. The last part, with turns and traffic and too much change of pace, would be the most difficult.

Only the knowledge that Elinor would probably die if I came off kept me on the motor bike at all, and altogether it was a ride I would not care to repeat. I didn't know how many times I had been hit, but I didn't think a carpet had too much to tell me. I tried to ignore it and concentrate on the matter in hand.

Elinor, if she had driven straight back to college, could not have been there long before she began to feel sleepy. As far as I could remember, never having taken much notice, barbiturates took anything up to an hour to work. But barbiturate dissolved in alcohol was a different matter. Quicker. Twenty minutes to a half hour, perhaps. I didn't know. Twenty minutes from the time she had left the yard was easily enough for her to drive back safely. Then what? She would go up to her room; feel tired; lie down; and go to sleep.

During the time I had been fighting with Adams and Humber, she had been on her way to Durham. I wasn't sure how long I had wasted dithering about in the washroom in a daze, but she couldn't have been back in college much before I started after her. I wondered whether she would have felt ill enough to tell a friend, to ask for help; but even if she had, neither she nor anyone else would know what was the matter with her.

I reached Durham; made the turns; even stopped briefly for a red traffic light in a busy street; and fought down an inclination to go the last half mile at walking pace in order to avoid having to hold the throttle anymore. But my ignorance of the time it would take the poison to do irreparable damage added wings to my anxiety.

18

It was getting dark when I swung into the College entrance, switched off the engine, and hurried up the steps to the door. There was no one at the porter's desk and the whole place was very quiet. I ran down the corridors, trying to remember the turns, found the stairs, went up two flights. And it was then that I got lost. I had suddenly no idea which way to turn to find Elinor's room.

A thin, elderly woman with pince-nez was walking toward me carrying a sheaf of papers and a thick book on her arm. One of the staff, I thought.

"Please," I said, "which is Miss Tarren's room?"

She came close to me and looked at me. She did not approve of what she saw. What would I give, I thought, for a respectable appearance at this moment.

"Please," I repeated. "She may be ill. Which is her room?"

"You have blood on your face," she observed.

"It's only a cut . . . please tell me . . ." I gripped her arm. "Look, show me her room, then if she's all right and perfectly healthy I will go away without any trouble. But I think she may need help very badly. Please believe me . . ."

"Very well," she said reluctantly. "We will go and see. It is just around here . . . and around here."

We arrived at Elinor's door. I knocked hard. There was no answer. I bent down low to the keyhole. The key was in the lock on her side, and I could not see in.

"Open it," I urged the woman, who was still eyeing me dubiously. "Open it, and see if she's all right."

She put her hand on the knob and turned it. But the door didn't budge. It was locked.

I banged on the door again. There was no reply.

"Now please listen," I said urgently. "As the door is locked on the inside, Elinor Tarren is in there. She doesn't answer because she can't. She needs a doctor very urgently indeed. Can you get hold of one at once?"

The woman nodded, looking at me gravely through the pince-nez. I wasn't sure that she believed me, but apparently she did.

"Tell the doctor she has been poisoned with Pheno-barbitone and gin. About forty minutes ago. And please, please hurry. Are there anymore keys to this door?"

"You can't push out the key that's already there. We've tried on other doors, on other occasions. You will have to break the lock. I will go and telephone." She retreated sedately along the corridor, still breathtakingly calm in the face of a wild-looking man with blood on his forehead and the news that one of her students was halfway to the coroner. A tough-minded university lecturer.

The Victorians who had built the place had not intended importunate men friends to batter down the girls' doors. They were a solid job. But in view of the thin woman's calm assumption that breaking in was within my powers, I didn't care to fail. I broke the lock with my heel, in the end. The wood gave way on the jamb inside the room, and the door opened with a crash.

In spite of the noise I had made, no students had appeared in the corridor. There was still no one about. I went into Elinor's room, switched on the light, and swung the door back into its frame behind me.

She was lying sprawled on top of her blue bedspread fast asleep, the silver hair falling in a smooth swath beside her head. She looked peaceful and beautiful. She had begun to undress, which was why, I supposed, she had locked her door, and she was wearing only a bra and briefs under a simple slip. All these garments were white with pink rosebuds and ribbons. Pretty. Belinda would have liked them. But in these circumstances they were too poignant, too defenseless. They increased my grinding worry.

The suit that Elinor had worn at Humber's had been dropped in two places on the floor. One stocking hung over the back of a chair; the other was on the floor just beneath her slack hand. A clean pair of stockings lay on the dressing table, and a blue woolen dress on a hanger was hooked onto the outside of the wardrobe. She had been changing for the evening.

If she hadn't heard me kicking the door in, she wouldn't wake by being touched, but I tried. I shook her arm. She didn't stir. Her pulse was normal, her breathing regular, her face as delicately colored as normal. Nothing looked wrong with her. I found it frightening.

How much longer, I wondered anxiously, was the doctor going to be? The door had been stubborn—or I had been weak, whichever way you looked at it—and it must have been more than ten minutes since the thin woman had gone to telephone.

As if on cue, the door swung open and a tidy, solid-looking middle-aged man in a gray suit stood there taking in the scene. He was alone. He carried a suitcase in one hand and a fire hatchet in the other. Coming in, he looked at the splintered wood, pushed the door shut, and put the ax down on Elinor's desk.

"That saved time, anyway," he said briskly. He looked me up and down without enthusiasm and gestured to me to get out of the way. Then he cast a closer glance at Elinor with her rucked-up slip and her long, bare legs, and said to me sharply, suspiciously, "Did you touch her clothes?"

"No," I said bitterly. "I shook her arm. And felt her pulse. She was lying like that when I came in."

Something, perhaps it was only my obvious weariness, made him give me a suddenly professional, impartial survey. "All right," he said, and bent down to Elinor.

I waited behind him while he examined her, and when he turned around I noticed he had decorously pulled down her rumpled slip so that it reached smoothly to her knees.

"Phenobarbitone and gin," he said. "Are you sure?"

"Yes."

"Self-administered?" He started opening his case.

"No. Definitely not."

"This place is usually teeming with women," he said

224

inconsequentially. "But apparently they're all at some meeting or another." He gave me another intent look. "Are you fit to help?"

"Yes."

He hesitated. "Are you sure?"

"Tell me what to do."

"Very well. Find me a good-sized jug and a bucket or large basin. I'll get her started first, and you can tell me how this happened later."

He took a hypodermic syringe from his case, filled it, and gave Elinor an injection into the vein on the inside of the elbow. I found a jug and a basin in the built-in cupboard.

"You've been here before," he observed, eyes again suspicious.

"Once," I said; and for Elinor's sake added, "I am employed by her father. It's nothing personal."

"Oh. All right, then." He withdrew the needle, dismantled the syringe, and quickly washed his hands.

"How many tablets did she take, do you know?"

"It wasn't tablets. Powder. A teaspoonful, at least. Maybe more."

He looked alarmed, but said, "That much would be bitter. She'd taste it."

"Gin and Campari . . . it's bitter anyway."

"Yes. All right. I'm going to wash out her stomach. Most of the drug must have been absorbed already, but if she had as much as that . . . well, it's still worth trying."

He directed me to fill the jug with tepid water, while he carefully slid a thickish tube down inside Elinor's throat. He surprised me by putting his ear to the long protruding end of it when it was in position, and he explained briefly that with an unconscious patient who couldn't swallow, one had to make sure the tube had gone into the stomach and not into the lungs. "If you can hear them breathe, you're in the wrong place," he said.

He put a funnel into the end of the tube, held out his hand for the jug, and carefully poured in the water. When what seemed to me a fantastic amount had disap-

225

peared down the tube, he stopped pouring, passed me the jug to put down, and directed me to push the basin near his foot. Then, removing the funnel, he suddenly lowered the end of the tube over the side of the bed and into the basin. The water flowed out again, together with all the contents of Elinor's stomach.

"Hm," he said calmly. "She had something to eat first. Cake, I should say. That helps."

I couldn't match his detachment.

"Will she be all right?" My voice sounded strained.

He looked at me briefly and slid the tube out.

"She drank the stuff less than an hour before I got here?"

"About fifty minutes, I think."

"And she'd eaten. . . . Yes, she'll be all right. Healthy girl. The injection I gave her—Megimide—is an effective antidote. She'll probably wake up in an hour or so. A night in the hospital, and it will be out of her system. She'll be as good as new."

I rubbed my hand over my face.

"Time makes a lot of difference," he said calmly. "If she'd lain here many hours . . . A teaspoonful; that must be twelve grains or more." He shook his head. "She would have died."

He took a sample of the contents of the basin for analysis, and covered the rest with a hand towel.

"How did you cut your head?" he said suddenly.

"In a fight."

"It needs stitching. Do you want me to do it?"

"Yes. Thank you."

"I'll do it after Miss Tarren has gone to the hospital. Dr. Pritchard said she would ring for an ambulance. They should be here soon."

"Dr. Pritchard?"

"The lecturer who fetched me in. My office is only around the corner. She telephoned and said a violent, bloodstained youth was insisting that Miss Tarren was poisoned, and that I'd better come and see." He smiled briefly. "You haven't told me how all this happened."

"Oh . . . it's such a long story," I said tiredly.

"You'll have to tell the police," he pointed out.

I nodded. There was too much I would have to tell the police. I wasn't looking forward to it. The doctor took out pen and paper and wrote a letter to go with Elinor to the hospital.

There was a sudden eruption of girls' voices down the passage, and a tramp of many scholarly feet, and the opening and shutting of doors. The students were back from their meeting; from Elinor's point of view, too soon, as they would now see her being carried out.

Heavier footsteps came right up to her room and knuckles rapped. Two men in ambulance uniform had arrived with a stretcher, and with economy of movement and time, they lifted Elinor between them, tucked her into blankets, and bore her away. She left a wake of pretty voices raised in sympathy and speculation.

The doctor swung the door shut behind the ambulance men and without more ado, took from his case a needle and thread to sew up my forehead. I sat on Elinor's bed while he fiddled around with disinfectant and the stitching.

"What did you fight about?" he asked, tying knots.

"Because I was attacked," I said.

"Oh?" He shifted his feet to sew from a different angle, and put his hand on my shoulder to steady himself. He felt me withdraw from the pressure and looked at me quizzically.

"So you got the worst of it?"

"No," I said slowly. "I won."

He finished the stitching and gave a final snip with the scissors.

"There you are, then. It won't leave much of a scar."

"Thank you." It sounded a bit weak.

"Do you feel all right?" he said abruptly. "Or is pale fawn tinged with gray your normal coloring?"

"Pale fawn is normal. Gray just about describes how I feel." I smiled faintly. "I got a bang on the back of the head, too."

He explored the bump behind my ear and said I would live. He was asking me how many other tender spots I had about me, when another heavy tramp of footsteps

227

could be heard coming up the corridor, and presently the door was pushed open with a crash.

Two broad-shouldered, businesslike policemen stepped into the room.

They knew the doctor. It appeared that he did a good deal of police work in Durham. They greeted each other politely and the doctor started to say that Miss Tarren was on her way to the hospital. They interrupted him.

"We've come for him, sir," said the taller of them, pointing at me. "Stable lad, name of Daniel Roke."

"Yes, he reported Miss Tarren's illness . . ."

"No, sir, it's nothing to do with a Miss Tarren or her illness. We want him for questioning on another matter."

The doctor said, "He's not in very good shape. I think you had better go easy. Can't you leave it until later?"

"I'm afraid that's impossible, sir."

They both came purposefully over to where I sat. The one who had done the talking was a redheaded man about my own age with an unsmiling, wary face. His companion was slightly shorter, brown eyed, and just as much on guard. They looked as if they were afraid I was going to leap up and strangle them.

With precision, they leaned down and clamped hard hands around my forearms. The redhead, who was on my right, dragged a pair of handcuffs from his pocket, and between them they fastened them on my wrists.

"Better take it quietly, chum," advised the redhead, evidently mistaking my attempt to wrench my arm free of his agonizing grip as a desire to escape in general.

"Let . . . go," I said. "I'm not . . . running anywhere."

They did let go, and stepped back a pace, looking down at me. Most of the wariness had faded from their faces, and I gathered that they really had been afraid I would attack them. It was unnerving. I took two deep breaths to control the soreness of my arm.

"He won't give us much trouble," said the dark one. "He looks like death."

"He was in a fight," remarked the doctor.

"Is that what he told you, sir?" The dark one laughed.

I looked down at the handcuffs locked around my

228

wrists; they were, I discovered, as uncomfortable as they were humiliating.

"What did he do?" asked the doctor.

The redhead answered. "He . . . er . . . he'll be helping in inquiries into an attack on a racehorse trainer he worked for and who is still unconscious, and on another man who had his skull bust right in."

"Dead?"

"So we are told, sir. We haven't actually been to the stables, though they say it's a shambles. We two were sent up from Clavering to fetch him in, and that's where we're taking him back to, the stables being in our area, you see."

"You caught up with him very quickly," commented the doctor.

"Yes," said the redhead with satisfaction. "It was a nice bit of work by some of the lads. A lady here telephoned to the police in Durham about half an hour ago and described *him*, and when they got the general call from Clavering about the job at the stables, someone connected the two descriptions and told us about it. So we were sent up to see, and bingo . . . there was his motor bike, right number plate and all, standing outside the College door."

I lifted my head. The doctor looked down at me. He was disillusioned, disenchanted. He shrugged his shoulders and said in a tired voice, "You never know with them, do you? He seemed . . . well . . . not quite the usual sort of tearaway. And now this." He turned away and picked up his bag.

It was suddenly too much. I had let too many people despise me and done nothing about it. This was one too many.

"I fought because they attacked me," I said.

The doctor half turned around. I didn't know why I thought it was important to convince him, but it seemed so at the time.

The dark policeman raised an eyebrow and said to the doctor, "The trainer was his employer, sir, and I understand the man who died is a rich gentleman whose horses were trained there. The head lad reported the killing. He saw Roke belting off on his motor bike and thought it was strange, because Roke had been sacked the day before, and he went to tell the trainer about it, and found him unconscious and the other man dead."

The doctor had heard enough. He walked out of the room without looking back. What was the use of trying? Better just do what the redhead said, and take it quietly, bitterness and all.

"Let's be going, chum," said the dark one. They stood there, tense again, with watchful eyes and hostile faces.

I got slowly to my feet. Slowly, because I was perilously near to not being able to stand up at all, and I didn't want to seem to be asking for a sympathy I was clearly not going to get. But it was all right; once upright I felt better, which was psychological as much as physical, because they were then not two huge threatening police-men but two quite ordinary young men of my own height doing their duty, and very concerned not to make any mistakes.

It worked the other way with them, of course. I think they had subconsciously expected a stable lad to be very short, and they were taken aback to discover I wasn't. They became visibly more aggressive; and I real-ized that in the circumstances, and in those black clothes, I probably seemed to them, as Terence had once put it, a bit dangerous and hard to handle.

I didn't see any sense in getting roughed up anymore, especially by the law, if it could be avoided.

"Look," I sighed. "Like you said, I won't give you any trouble."

But I suppose they had been told to bring in someone who had gone berserk and smashed a man's head in, and they were taking no chances. Redhead took a fierce grip of my right arm above the elbow and shoved me over to the door, and once outside in the passage, the dark one took a similar grip on the left.

The corridor was lined with girls standing in little gossiping groups. I stopped dead. The two policemen pushed me on. And the girls stared.

That old saying about wishing the floor would open and swallow one up suddenly took on a fresh personal

230

meaning. What little was left of my sense of dignity revolted totally against being exhibited as a prisoner in front of so many intelligent and personable young women. They were the wrong age. The wrong sex. I could have stood it better if they had been men.

But there was no easy exit. It was a good long way from Elinor's room the the outside door, along those twisting corridors and down two flights of stairs, and every single step was watched by interested female eyes.

This was the sort of thing one wouldn't be able to forget. It went too deep. Or perhaps, I thought miserably, one could even get accustomed to being hauled around in handcuffs if it happened often enough. If one were used to it, perhaps one wouldn't care . . . which would be peaceful.

I did at least manage not to stumble, not even on the stairs, so to that extent something was saved from the wreck. The police car, however, into which I was presently thrust seemed a perfect haven in contrast.

I sat in front, between them. The dark one drove.

"Phew," he said, pushing his cap back an inch. "All those girls." He had blushed under their scrutiny and there was a dew of sweat on his forehead.

"He's a tough boy, is this," said Redhead, mopping his neck with a white handkerchief as he sat sideways against the door and stared at me. "He didn't turn a hair."

I looked straight ahead through the windshield as the lights of Durham began to slide past, and thought how little could be told from a face. That walk had been a torture. If I hadn't shown it, it was probably only because I had by then had months of practice of hiding my feelings and thoughts, and the habit was strong. I guessed—correctly—that it was a habit I would find strength in clinging to for some time to come.

I spent the rest of the journey reflecting that I had got myself into a proper mess and that I was going to have a very unpleasant time getting out. I had indeed killed Adams. There was no denying or ducking that. And I was not going to be listened to as a respectable solid citizen but as a murdering villain trying every dodge to escape the consequences. I was going to be taken at face value, which was very low indeed. That couldn't be helped. I had, after all, survived eight weeks at Humber's only because I looked like dregs. The appearance which had deceived Adams was going to be just as convincing to the police, and proof that in fact it already was sat on either side of me in the car, watchful and antagonistic.

Redhead's eyes never left my face.

"He doesn't talk much," he observed, after a long silence.

"Got a lot on his mind," agreed the dark one, with sarcasm.

The damage Adams and Humber had done gave me no respite. I shifted uncomfortably in my seat, and the handcuffs clinked. The lightheartedness with which I had gone in my new clothes to Slaw seemed a long, long time ago.

The lights of Clavering lay ahead. The dark one gave me a look of subtle enjoyment. A capture made. His purpose fulfilled. Redhead broke another long silence, his voice full of the same sort of satisfaction.

"He'll be a lot older when he gets out," he said.

I emphatically hoped not; but I was all too aware that the length of time I remained in custody depended solely on how conclusively I could show that I had killed in self-defense. I wasn't a lawyer's son for nothing.

The next hours were abysmal. The Clavering police force were collectively a hardened, cynical bunch suppressing as best they could a vigorous crime wave in a mining area with a high unemployment percentage. Kid gloves did not figure in their book. Individually they may have loved their wives and been nice to their children. but if so, they kept their humor and humanity strictly for leisure.

They were busy. The building was full of bustle and hurrying voices. They shoved me. still handcuffed, from room to room under escort and barked out intermittent questions. "Later," they said. "Deal with that one later. We've got all night for him."

232

I thought with longing of a hot bath, a soft bed, and a handful of aspirins. I didn't get any of them.

At some point late in the evening they gave me a chair in a bare, brightly lit little room, and I told them what I had been doing at Humber's and how I had come to kill Adams. I told them everything that had happened that day. They didn't believe me, for which one couldn't blame them. They immediately, as a matter of form, charged me with murder. I protested. Uselessly.

They asked me a lot of questions. I answered them. They asked them again. I answered. They asked the questions like a relay team, one of them taking over presently from another, so that they all appeared to remain full of fresh energy while I grew more and more tired. I was glad I did not have to maintain a series of lies in that state of continuing discomfort and growing fatigue, as it was hard to keep a clear head, even for the truth, and they were waiting for me to make a mistake.

"Now tell us what really happened."

"I've told you."

"Not all that cloak-and-dagger stuff."

"Cable to Australia for a copy of the contract I signed when I took on the job." For the fourth time I repeated my solicitor's address, and for the fourth time they didn't write it down.

"Who did you say engaged you?"

"The Earl of October."

"And no doubt we can check with him, too?"

"He's in Germany until Saturday."

"Too bad." They smiled nastily. They knew from Cass that I had worked in October's stable. Cass had told them I was a slovenly stable lad, dishonest, easily frightened, and not very bright. As he had believed what he said, he had carried conviction.

"You got into trouble with his lordship's daughter, didn't you?"

Damn Cass, I thought bitterly, damn Cass and his chattering tongue.

"Getting your own back on him for sacking you, aren't you, by dragging his name into this?"

233

"Like you got your own back on Mr. Humber for sacking you yesterday."

"No. I left because I had finished my job there."

"For beating you, then?"

"No."

"The head lad said you deserved it."

"Adams and Humber were running a crooked racing scheme. I found them out, and they tried to kill me." It seemed to me it was the tenth time that I had said that without making the slightest impression.

"You resented being beaten. You went back to get even. . . . It's a common enough pattern."

"No."

"You brooded over it and went back and attacked them. It was a shambles. Blood all over the place."

"It was my blood."

"We can group it."

"Do that. It's my blood."

"From that little cut? Don't be so stupid."

"It's been stitched."

"Ah, yes, that brings us back to Lady Elinor Tarren. Lord October's daughter. Got her into trouble, did you?"

"No."

"In the family way . . ."

"No. Check with the doctor."

"So she took sleeping pills . . ."

"No. Adams poisoned her." I had told them twice about the bottle of Phenobarbitone, and they must have found it when they had been at the stables, but they wouldn't admit it.

"You got the sack from her father for seducing her. She couldn't stand the disgrace. She took sleeping pills."

"She had no reason to feel disgraced. It was not she, but her sister, Patricia, who accused me of seducing her. Adams poisoned Elinor in gin and Campari. There are gin and Campari and Phenobarbitone in the office and also in the sample from her stomach."

They took no notice. "She found you had deserted her on top of everything else. Mr. Humber consoled

234

her with a drink, but she went back to college and took sleeping pills."

"No."

They were skeptical, to put it mildly, about Adams' use of the flamethrower.

"You'll find it in the shed."

"This shed, yes. Where did you say it was?"

I told them again, exactly. "The field probably belongs to Adams. You could find out."

"It only exists in your imagination."

"Look and you'll find it, and the flamethrower."

"That's likely to be used to burning off the heath. Lots of farmers have them, around here."

They had let me make two telephone calls to try to find Colonel Beckett. His manservant in London said he had gone to stay with friends in Berkshire for Newbury races. The little local exchange in Berkshire was out of action, the operator said, because a water main had burst and flooded a cable. Engineers were working on it.

Didn't my wanting to talk to one of the top brass of steeplechasing convince them, I wanted to know?

"Remember that chap we had in here once who'd strangled his wife? Nutty as a fruitcake. Insisted on ringing up Lord Bertrand Russell, didn't he, to tell him he'd struck a blow for peace."

At around midnight one of them pointed out that even if—and, mind you, he didn't himself believe it—even if all I had said about being employed to find out about Adams and Humber was, against all probability, true, that still didn't give me the right to kill them.

"Humber isn't dead," I said.

"Not yet."

My heart lurched. Dear God, I thought, not Humber, too. Not Humber, too.

"You clubbed Adams with the walking stick, then?"

"No. I told you, with a green glass ball. I had it in my left hand and I hit him as hard as I could. I didn't mean to kill him, just to knock him out. I'm right-handed. . . . I couldn't judge very well how hard I was hitting with my left."

235

"Why did you use your left hand, then?"

"I told you."

"Tell us again."

I told them again.

"And after your right arm was put out of action, you got on a motorcycle and rode ten miles to Durham? What sort of fools do you take us for?"

"The fingerprints of both my hands are on that paperweight. The right ones from when I threw it at Humber, and the left ones on top, from where I hit Adams. You have only to check."

"Fingerprints now," they said sarcastically.

"And while you're on the subject, you'll also find the fingerprints of my left hand on the telephone. I tried to call you from the office. My left-hand prints are on the top in the washroom . . . and on the key, and on the door handle, both inside and out. Or at least, they were. . . ."

"All the same, you rode that motor bike."

"The numbness had gone by then."

"And now?"

"It isn't numb now, either."

One of them came around beside me, picked up my right wrist, and pulled my arm up high. The handcuffs jerked and lifted my left arm as well. The bruises had all stiffened and were very sore. The policeman put my arm down again. There was a short silence.

"That hurt," one of them said at last, grudgingly.

"He's putting it on."

"Maybe . . ."

They had been drinking endless cups of tea all evening and had not given me any. I asked if I could have some then, and got it; only to find that the difficulty I had in lifting the cup was hardly worth it.

They began again.

"Granted Adams struck your arm, but he did it in self-defense. He saw you throw the paperweight at your employer and realized you were going to attack him next. He was warding you off."

"He had already cut my forehead open . . . and hit me several times on the body, and once on the head."

236

"Most of that was yesterday, according to the head lad. That's why you went back and attacked Mr. Humber."

"Humber hit me only twice yesterday. I didn't particularly resent it. The rest was today, and it was mostly done by Adams." I remembered something. "He took my crash helmet off when he had knocked me dizzy. His fingerprints must be on it."

"Fingerprints again."

"They spell it out," I said.

"Let's begin again at the beginning. How can we believe a yob like you?"

Yob. One of the leather boys. Tearaway. Rocker. I knew all the words. I knew what I looked like. What a millstone of a handicap.

I said despairingly, "There's no point in pretending to be a disreputable, dishonest stable lad if you don't look the part."

"You look the part all right," they said offensively. "Born to it, you were."

I looked at their stony faces, their hard, unimpressed eyes. Tough, efficient policemen who were not going to be conned. I could read their thoughts like glass: if I convinced them and they later found out it was all a pack of lies, they'd never live it down. Their instincts were all dead against having to believe. My bad luck.

The room grew stuffy and full of cigarette smoke and I became too hot in my jerseys and jacket. I knew they took the sweat on my forehead to be guilt, not heat, not pain.

I went on answering all their questions. They covered the ground twice more with undiminished zeal, setting traps, sometimes shouting, walking around me, never touching me again, but springing the questions from all directions. I was really much too tired for that sort of thing, because apart from the wearing-out effect of the injuries, I had not slept for the whole of the previous night. Toward two o'clock I could hardly speak from exhaustion, and after they had woken me from a sort of dazed sleep three time in half an hour, they gave it up.

237

From the beginning I had known that there was only one logical end to that evening, and I had tried to shut it out of my mind, because I dreaded it. But there you are . . . you set off on a primrose path and if it leads to hell that's just too bad.

Two uniformed policemen, a sergeant and a constable, were detailed to put me away for the night, which I found involved a form of accommodation to make Humber's dormitory seem a paradise.

The cell was cubic, eight feet by eight by eight, built of glazed bricks, brown to shoulder height and white above that. There was a small barred window too high to see out of, a narrow slab of concrete for a bed, a bucket with a lid on it in a corner, and a printed list of regulations on one wall. Nothing else. Bleak enough to shrink the guts; and I had never much cared for small enclosed spaces.

The two policemen brusquely told me to sit on the concrete. The removed my boots and the belt from my jeans, and also found and unbuckled the money belt underneath. They took off the handcuffs. Then they went out, shut the door with a clang, and locked me in.

The rest of that night was in every way rock bottom.

19

It was cool and quiet in the corridors of Whitehall. A superbly mannered young man deferentially showed me the way and opened a mahogany door into an empty office.

"Colonel Beckett will not be long, sir. He has just gone to consult a colleague. He said I was to apologize if you arrived before he came back, and to ask if you would like a drink. And cigarettes are in this box, sir."

"Thank you." I smiled. "Would coffee be a nuisance?"

"By no means. I'll have some sent in straight away. If you'll excuse me?" He went out and quietly closed the door.

It rather amused me to be called "sir" again, especially by smooth civil servants barely younger than myself. Grinning, I sat down in the leather chair facing Beckett's desk, crossed my elegantly trousered legs, and lazily settled to wait for him.

I was in no hurry. It was eleven o'clock on Tuesday morning, and I had all day and nothing to do but buy a clockwork train for Jerry and book an air ticket back to Australia.

No noise filtered into Beckett's office. The room was square and high, and was painted a restful pale-greenish-gray color, walls, door, and ceiling alike. I supposed that here the furnishings went with rank; but if one were an outsider, one would not know how much to be impressed by a large but threadbare carpet, an obviously personal lampshade, or leather, brass-studded chairs. One had to belong, for these things to matter.

I wondered about Colonel Beckett's job. He had given me the impression that he was retired, probably on a full disability pension since he looked so frail in health, yet here he was with a well-established niche at the Ministry of Defense.

October had told me that in the war Beckett had been the sort of supply officer who never sent all left boots or the wrong ammunition. Supply officer. He had supplied me with Sparking Plug and the raw material containing the pointers to Adams and Humber. He'd had enough pull with the Army to dispatch in a hurry eleven young officer cadets to dig up the past history of obscure steeplechasers. What, I wondered, did he supply nowadays, in the normal course of events?

I suddenly remembered October's saying, "We thought of planting a stable lad. . . ." Not "I thought," but "We." And for some reason I was now sure that it had been Beckett, not October, who had originally suggested the plan; and that explained why October

239

had been relieved when Beckett approved me at our first meeting.

Unexcitedly turning these random thoughts over in my mind, I watched two pigeons fluttering around the windowsill and tranquilly waited to say good-bye to the man whose staff work had ensured the success of the idea.

A pretty young woman knocked and came in with a tray on which stood a coffeepot, cream jug, and pale-green cup and saucer. She smiled, asked if I needed anything else, and when I said not, gracefully went away.

I was getting quite good at left-handedness. I poured the coffee and drank it black, and enjoyed the taste.

Snatches of the past few days drifted idly in and out of my thoughts. . . .

Four nights and three days in a police cell trying to come to terms with the fact that I had killed Adams. It was odd, but although I had often considered the possibility of being killed, I had never once thought that I myself might kill. For that, as for so much else, I had been utterly unprepared; and to have caused another man's death, however much he might have asked for it, needed a bit of getting over.

Four nights and three days of gradually finding that even the various ignominies of being locked up were bearable if one took them quietly, and feeling almost like thanking Redhead for his advice.

On the first morning, after a magistrate had agreed that I should stay where I was for seven days, a police doctor came and told me to strip. I couldn't, and he had to help. He looked impassively at Adams' and Humber's widespread handiwork, asked a few questions, and examined my right arm, which was black from the wrist to well above the elbow. In spite of the protection of two jerseys and a leather jacket, the skin was broken where the chair leg had landed. The doctor helped me dress again and impersonally departed. I didn't ask him for his opinion, and he didn't give it.

For most of the four nights and three days I just waited, hour after silent hour. Thinking about Adams:

Adams alive and Adams dead. Worrying about Humber. Thinking of how I could have done things differently. Facing the thought that I might not get out without a trial . . . or not get out at all. Waiting for the soreness to fade from the bruises and failing to find a comfortable way of sleeping on concrete. Counting the number of bricks from the floor to the ceiling and multiplying by the length of the walls (subtract the door and window). Thinking about my stud farm and my sisters and brother, and about the rest of my life.

On Monday morning there was the by then familiar scrape of the door being unlocked, but when it opened it was not as usual a policeman in uniform, but October.

I was standing up, leaning against the wall. I had not seen him for three months. He stared at me for a long minute, taking in with obvious shock my extremely disheveled appearance.

"Daniel," he said. His voice was low and thick.

I didn't think I needed any sympathy. I hooked my left thumb into my pocket, struck a faint attitude, and raised a grin.

"Hullo, Edward."

His face lightened, and he laughed.

"You're so bloody tough," he said. Well . . . let him think so.

I said, "Could you possibly use your influence to get me a bath?"

"You can have whatever you like as soon as you are out."

"Out? For good?"

"For good." He nodded. "They are dropping the charge."

I couldn't disguise my relief.

He smiled sardonically. "They don't think it would be worth wasting public funds on trying you. You'd be certain of getting an absolute discharge. Justifiable homicide, quite legitimate."

"I didn't think they believed me."

"They've done a lot of checking up. Everything you told them on Thursday is now the official version."

"Is Humber . . . all right?"

241

"He regained consciousness yesterday, I believe. But I understand he isn't lucid enough yet to answer questions. Didn't the police tell you that he was out of danger?"

I shook my head. "They aren't a very chatty lot here. How is Elinor?"

"She's well. A bit weak, that's all."

"I'm sorry she got caught up in things. It was my fault."

"My dear chap, it was her own," he protested. "And Daniel . . . about Patty . . . and the things I said . . ."

"Oh, nuts to that," I interrupted. "It was a long time ago. When you said 'Out,' did you mean out now, this minute?"

He nodded. "That's right."

"Then let's not hang around in here anymore, shall we? If you don't mind?"

He looked about him and involuntarily shivered. Meeting my eyes, he said apologetically, "I didn't foresee anything like this."

I grinned faintly. "Nor did I."

We went to London, by car up to Newcastle and then by train. Owing to some delay at the police station discussing the details of my return to attend Adams' inquest, any cleaning-up processes would have meant our missing the seats October had reserved on the nonstop Flying Scotsman, so I caught it as I was.

October led the way into the dining car, but as I was about to sit down opposite him, a waiter caught hold of my elbow.

"Here, you," he said roughly. "Clear out. This is first class only."

"I've got a first-class ticket," I said mildly.

"Oh, yes? Let's see it, then."

I produced from my pocket the piece of white cardboard.

He sniffed and gestured with his head toward the seat opposite October. "All right, then." To October he said, "If he makes a nuisance of himself, just tell me, sir, and I'll have him chucked out, ticket or no ticket." He went off, swaying to the motion of the accelerating train.

Needless to say, everyone in the dining car had turned around to have a good view of the rumpus.

Grinning, I sat down opposite October. He looked exceedingly embarrassed.

"Don't worry on my account," I said. "I'm used to it." And I realized that I was indeed used to it at last and that no amount of such treatment would ever trouble me again. "But if you would rather pretend you don't know me, go ahead." I picked up the menu.

"You are insulting."

I smiled at him over the menu. "Good."

"For deviousness, Daniel, you are unsurpassed. Except possibly by Roddy Beckett."

"My dear Edward . . . have some bread."

He laughed, and we traveled amicably to London together, as ill-assorted-looking a pair as ever rested heads on British Railways' starched white antimacassars.

I poured some more coffee and looked at my watch. Colonel Beckett was twenty minutes late. The pigeons sat peacefully on the windowsill and I shifted gently in my chair, but with patience, not boredom, and thought about my visit to October's barber, and the pleasure with which I had had my hair cut short and sideburns shaved off. The barber himself (who had asked me to pay in advance) was surprised, he said, at the results.

"We look a lot more like a gentleman, don't we? But might I suggest . . . a shampoo?"

Grinning, I agreed to the shampoo, which left a high-water mark of cleanliness about midway down my neck. Then, at October's house, there was the fantastic luxury of stepping out of my filthy disguise into a deep hot bath, and the strangeness with which I afterward put on my own clothes. When I had finished dressing, I took another look in the same long mirror. There was the man who had come from Australia four months ago, a man in a good dark-gray suit, a white shirt, and a navy-blue silk tie; there was his shell, anyway. Inside I wasn't the same man, nor ever would be again.

I went down to the crimson drawing room, where October walked solemnly all around me, gave me a

glass of bone-dry sherry, and said, "It is utterly unbelievable that you are the young tyke who just came down
with me on the train."

"I am," I said dryly, and he laughed.

He gave me a chair with its back to the door, where
I drank some sherry and listened to him making social
chitchat about his horses. He was hovering around the
fireplace, not entirely at ease, and I wondered what
he was up to.

I soon found out. The door opened and he looked
over my shoulder and smiled.

"I want you both to meet someone," he said.

I stood up and turned around.

Patty and Elinor were there, side by side.

They didn't know me at first. Patty held out her hand
politely and said, "How do you do?" clearly waiting
for her father to introduce us.

I took her hand in my left one and guided her to
a chair.

"Sit down," I suggested. "You're in for a shock."

She hadn't seen me for three months, but it was only
four days since Elinor had made her disastrous visit
to Humber's. She said hesitantly, "You don't look the
same . . . but you're Daniel." I nodded, and she blushed
painfully.

Patty's bright eyes looked straight into mine, and
her pink mouth parted.

"You . . . are you really? Danny boy?"

"Yes."

"Oh." A blush as deep as her sister's spread up from
her neck, and for Patty that was shame indeed.

October watched their discomfiture. "It serves them
right," he said, "for all the trouble they have caused."

"Oh, no," I exclaimed. "It's too hard on them . . .
and you still haven't told them anything about me, have
you?"

"No," he agreed uncertainly, beginning to suspect
there was more for his daughters to blush over than
he knew, and that his surprise meeting was not an unqual-
ified success.

"Then tell them now, while I go and talk to Terence

. . . and Patty . . . Elinor . . ." They looked surprised at my use of their first names and I smiled briefly. "I have a very short and defective memory."

They both looked subdued when I went back, and October was watching them uneasily. Fathers, I reflected, could be very unkind to their daughters without intending it.

"Cheer up," I said. "I'd have had a dull time in England without you two."

"You were a beast," said Patty emphatically, sticking to her guns.

"Yes . . . I'm sorry."

"You might have told us," said Elinor in a low voice.

"Nonsense," said October. "He couldn't trust Patty's tongue."

"I see," said Elinor slowly. She looked at me tentatively. "I haven't thanked you for . . . for saving me. The doctor told me . . . all about it." She blushed again.

"Sleeping beauty." I smiled. "You looked like my sister."

"You have a sister?"

"Two," I said. "Sixteen and seventeen."

"Oh," she said, and looked comforted.

October flicked me a glance. "You are far too kind to them, Daniel. One of them made me loathe you and the other nearly killed you, and you don't seem to care."

I smiled at him. "No. I don't. I really don't. Let's just forget it."

So in spite of a most unpromising start, it developed into a good evening, the girls gradually losing their embarrassment and even, by the end, being able to meet my eyes without blushing.

When they had gone to bed, October put two fingers into an inner pocket, drew out a slip of paper, and handed it to me without a word. I unfolded it. It was a check for ten thousand pounds. A lot of noughts. I looked at them in silence. Then, slowly, I tore the fortune in half and put the pieces in the ashtray.

"Thank you very much," I said. "But I can't take it."

"You did the job. Why not accept the pay?"

"Because . . ." I stopped. Because what? I was not sure I could put it into words. It had something to do with having learned more than I had bargained for. With diving too deep. With having killed. All I was sure of was that I could no longer bear the thought of receiving money for it.

"You must have a reason," said October, with a touch of irritation.

"Well, I didn't really do it for the money, to start with, and I can't take that sort of sum from you. In fact, when I get back I am going to repay you all that is left of the first ten thousand."

"No," he protested. "You've earned it. Keep it. You need it for your family."

"What I need for my family, I'll earn by selling horses."

He stubbed out his cigar. "You're so infuriatingly independent that I don't know now how you could face being a stable lad. If it wasn't for the money, why did you did it?"

I moved in my chair. The bruises still felt like bruises. I smiled faintly, enjoying the pun.

"For kicks, I suppose."

The door of the office opened, and Beckett unhurriedly came in. I stood up. He held out his hand, and remembering the weakness of his grasp, I put out my own. He squeezed gently and let go.

"It's been a long time, Mr. Roke."

"More than three months," I agreed.

"And you completed the course."

I shook my head, smiling. "Fell at the last fence, I'm afraid."

He took off his overcoat and hung it on a knobbed hat rack, and unwound a gray woolen scarf from his neck. His suit was nearly black, a color which only enhanced his extreme pallor and emphasized his thinness; but his eyes were as alive as ever in the gaunt, shadowed sockets. He gave me a long, observant scrutiny.

"Sit down," he said. "I am sorry to have kept you waiting. I see they've looked after you all right."

"Yes, thank you." I sat down again in the leather

chair, and he walked around and sank carefully into the one behind his desk. His chair had a high back and arms, and he used them to support his head and elbows.

"I didn't get your report until I came back to London from Newbury on Sunday morning," he said. "It took two days to come from Posset and didn't reach my house until Friday. When I had read it, I telephoned to Edward at Slaw and found he had just been rung up by the police at Clavering. I then telephoned to Clavering myself. I spent a good chunk of Sunday hurrying things up for you in various conversations with ever higher ranks, and early on Monday it was decided finally in the office of the Director of Public Prosecutions that there was no charge for you to answer."

"Thank you very much," I said.

He paused, considering me. "You did more toward extricating yourself than Edward or I did. We only confirmed what you had said and had you freed a day or two sooner than you might have been. But it appeared that the Clavering police had already discovered from a thorough examination of the stable office that everything you had told them was borne out by the facts. They had also talked to the doctor who had attended Elinor, and to Elinor herself, and taken a look at the shed with the flamethrower, and cabled to your solicitor for a summary of the contract you signed with Edward. By the time I spoke of them, they were taking the truth of your story for granted, and were agreeing that you had undoubtedly killed Adams in self-defense.

"Their own doctor—the one who examined you—had told them straight away that the amount of crushing your right forearm had sustained was entirely consistent with its having been struck by a force strong enough to have smashed in your skull. He was of the opinion that the blow had landed more or less along the inside of your arm, not straight across it, thus causing extensive damage to muscles and blood vessels, but no bone fracture; and he told them that it was perfectly possible for you to have ridden a motor bike a quarter of an hour later if you had wanted to enough."

"You know," I said, "I didn't think they had taken any notice of a single word I said."

"Mmm. Well, I spoke to one of the C.I.D. men who questioned you last Thursday evening. He said they brought you in as a foregone conclusion, and that you looked terrible. You told them a rigmarole which they thought was nonsense, so they asked a lot of questions to trip you up. They thought it would be easy. The C.I.D. man said it was like trying to dig a hole in a rock with your fingernails. They all ended up by believing you, much to their own surprise."

"I wish they'd told me," I sighed.

"Not their way. They sounded a tough bunch."

"They seemed it, too."

"However, you survived."

"Oh, yes."

Beckett looked at his watch. "Are you in a hurry?"

"No." I shook my head.

"Good . . . I've rather a lot to say to you. Can you lunch?"

"Yes. I'd like to."

"Fine. Now, this report of yours." He dug the handwritten foolscap pages out of his inside breast pocket and laid them on the table. "What I'd like you to do now is to lop off the bit asking for reinforcements and substitute a description of the flamethrower operation. Right? There's a table and chair over there. Get to work, and when it's done I'll have it typed."

When I had finished the report, he spent some time outlining and discussing the proceedings which were to be taken against Humber, Cass, and Jud Wilson, and also against Soupy Tarleton and his friend Lewis Greenfield. He then looked at his watch again and decided it was time to go out for lunch. He took me to his club, which seemed to me to be dark brown throughout, and we ate steak, kidney, and mushroom pie, which I chose because I could manage it unobtrusively with a fork. He noticed, though.

"That arm still troubling you?"

"It's much better."

He nodded and made no further comment. Instead

he told me of a visit he had paid the day before to an elderly uncle of Adams', whom he had discovered living in bachelor splendor in Piccadilly.

"Young Paul Adams, according to his uncle, was the sort of child who would have been sent to a reform school if he hadn't had rich parents. He was sacked from Eton for forging checks and from his next school for persistent gambling. His parents bought him out of scrape after scrape and were told by a psychiatrist that he would never change, or at least not until late middle age. He was their only child. It must have been terrible for them. The father died when Adams was twenty-five, and his mother struggled on, trying to keep him out of too disastrous trouble. About five years ago she had to pay out a fortune to hush up a scandal in which Adams had apparently broken a youth's arm for no reason at all, and she threatened to have him certified if he did anything like that again. And a few days later she fell out of her bedroom window and died. The uncle, her brother, says he has always thought that Adams pushed her."

"Very likely, I should think," I agreed.

"So you were right about his being psychopathic."

"Well, it was pretty obvious."

"From the way he behaved to you personally?"

"Yes."

We had finished the pie and were on to cheese. Beckett looked at me curiously and said, "What sort of life did you really have at Humber's stable?"

"Oh"—I grinned—"you could hardly call it a holiday camp."

He waited for me to go on and when I didn't, he said, "Is that all you've got to say about it?"

"Yes, I think so. This is very good cheese."

We drank coffee and a glass of brandy out of a bottle with Beckett's name on it, and eventually walked back slowly to his office.

As before, he sank gratefully into his chair and rested his head and arms, and I as before sat down opposite him on the other side of his desk.

"You are going back to Australia soon, I believe?" he said.

"Yes." ·

"I expect you are looking forward to getting back into harness."

I looked at him. His eyes stared straight back, steady and grave. He waited for an answer.

"Not altogether."

"Why not?"

I shrugged, grinned. "Who likes harness?" There was no point, I thought, in making too much of it.

"You are going back to prosperity, good food, sunshine, your family, a beautiful house, and a job you do well . . . isn't that right?"

I nodded. It wasn't reasonable not to want to go to all that.

"Tell me the truth," he said abruptly. "The unvarnished, honest truth. What is wrong?"

"I'm a discontented idiot, that's all," I said lightly.

"Mr. Roke." He sat up slightly in the chair. "I have a good reason for asking these questions. Please give me truthful answers. What is wrong with your life in Australia?"

There was a pause, while I thought and he waited. When at last I answered, I was aware that whatever his good reason was, it would do no harm to speak plainly.

"I do a job which I ought to find satisfying, and it leaves me bored and empty."

"A diet of milk and honey, when you have teeth," he observed.

I laughed. "A taste for salt, perhaps."

"What would you have been had your parents not died and left you with three children to bring up?"

"A lawyer, I think, though possibly . . ." I hesitated.

"Possibly what?"

"Well . . . it sounds a bit odd, especially after the last few days . . . A policeman."

"Ah," he said softly. "That figures." He leaned his head back again and smiled.

"Marriage might help you feel more settled," he suggested.

"More ties," I said. "Another family to provide for. The rut forever."

"So that's how you look at it. How about Elinor?"

"She's a nice girl."

"But not for keeps?"

I shook my head.

"You went to a great deal of trouble to save her life," he pointed out.

"It was only because of me that she got into danger at all."

"You couldn't know that she would be so strongly attracted to you and find you so . . . er . . . irresistible that she would drive out to take another look at you. When you went back to Humber's to extricate her, you had already finished the investigation, tidily, quietly, and undiscovered. Isn't that right?"

"I suppose so. Yes."

"Did you enjoy it?"

"Enjoy it?" I repeated, surprised.

"Oh, I don't mean the fracas at the end, or the hours of honest toil you had to put in." He smiled briefly. "But the . . . shall we say, the chase?"

"Am I, in fact, a hunter by nature?"

"Are you?"

"Yes."

There was a silence. My unadorned affirmative hung in the air, bald and revealing.

"Were you afraid at all?" His voice was matter-of-fact.

"Yes."

"To the point of incapacity?"

I shook my head.

"You knew Adams and Humber would kill you if they found you out. What effect did living in perpetual danger have on you?" His voice was so clinical that I answered with similar detachment.

"It made me careful."

"Is that all?"

251

"Well, if you mean was I in a constant state of nervous tension, then no, I wasn't."

"I see." Another of his small pauses. Then he said, "What did you find hardest to do?"

I blinked, grinned, and lied. "Wearing those loathsome pointed shoes."

He nodded as if I had told him a satisfying truth. I probably had. The pointed shoes had hurt my pride, not my toes.

And pride had got the better of me properly when I visited Elinor in her college and hadn't been strong enough to play an oaf in her company. All that stuff about Marcus Aurelius was sheer showing off, and the consequences had been appalling. It didn't bear thinking of, let alone confessing.

Beckett said idly, "Would you ever consider doing something similar again?"

"I should think so. Yes. But not like that."

"How do you mean?"

"Well . . . I didn't know enough, for one thing. For example, it was just luck that Humber always left his office unlocked, because I couldn't have got in if he hadn't. I don't know how to open doors without keys. I would have found a camera useful; I could have taken films of the blue ledger in Humber's office, and so on, but my knowledge of photography is almost nil. I'd have got the exposures wrong. Then I had never fought anyone in my life before. If I'd known anything at all about unarmed combat, I probably wouldn't have killed Adams or been so much battered myself. Apart from all that, there was nowhere where I could send you or Edward a message and be sure you would receive it quickly. Communications, in fact, were pretty hopeless."

"Yes. I see. All the same, you did finish the job in spite of those disadvantages."

"It was luck. You couldn't count on being lucky twice."

"I suppose not." He smiled. "What do you plan to do with you twenty thousand pounds?"

"I . . . er . . . plan to let Edward keep most of it."

"What do you mean?"

"I can't take that sort of money. All I ever wanted was to get away for a bit. It was he who suggested such a large sum, not me. I don't think he thought I would take on the job for less, but he was wrong. . . . I'd have done it for nothing if I could. All I'll accept is the amount it has cost for me to be away. He knows; I told him last night."

There was a long pause. Finally Beckett sat up and picked up a telephone. He dialed and waited.

"This is Beckett," he said. "It's about Daniel Roke. . . . Yes, he's here." He took a postcard out of an inner pocket. "Those points we were discussing this morning . . . I have had a talk with him. You have your card?"

He listened for a moment, and leaned back again in his chair. His eyes were steady on my face.

"Right?" He spoke into the telephone. "Numbers one to four can all have an affirmative. Number five is satisfactory. Number six, his weakest spot . . . he didn't maintain his role in front of Elinor Tarren. She said he was good mannered and intelligent. No one else thought so. . . . Yes, I should say so, sexual pride . . . apparently only because Elinor is clever as well as pretty, since he kept it up all right with her younger sister. . . . Yes . . . oh, undoubtedly it was his intellect as much as his physical appearance which attracted her. . . . Yes, very good looking; I believe you sometimes find that useful. . . . No, he doesn't. He didn't look in the mirror in the washroom at the club or in the one on the wall here. . . . No, he didn't admit it today, but I'd say he is well aware he failed on that point. . . . Yes, rather a harsh lesson. It may still be a risk, or it may have been sheer unprofessionalism. . . . Your Miss Jones could find out, yes."

I didn't particularly care for this dispassionate vivisection, but short of walking out, there seemed to be no way of avoiding it. His eyes still looked at me expressionlessly.

"Number seven . . . normal reaction. Eight, slightly obsessive, but that's all the better from your point of view." He glanced momentarily down at the card he

253

held in his hand. "Nine . . . well, although he is British by birth and spent his childhood here, he is Australian by inclination, and I doubt whether subservience comes easily. . . . I don't know, he wouldn't talk about it. . . . No, I wouldn't say he had a vestige of a martyr complex, he's clear on that. . . . Of course you never get a perfect one. . . . It's entirely up to you. . . . Number ten? The three *b*'s. I should say definitely not to the first two, much too proud. As for the third, he's the type to shout for help. Yes, he's still here. Hasn't moved a muscle. . . . Yes, I do think so. . . . All right . . ." I'll ring you again later."

He put down the receiver. I waited. He took his time, and I refrained consciously from fidgeting under his gaze.

"Well?" he said at last.

"If you're going to ask what I think, the answer is no."

"Because you don't want to, or because of your sisters and brother?"

"Philip is still only thirteen."

"I see." He made a weak-looking gesture with his hand. "All the same, I'd better make sure you know what you are turning down. The colleague who kept me late this morning, and to whom I was talking just now, runs one of the counterespionage departments—not only political but scientific and industrial, and anything else which crops up. His section is rather good at doing what you have done—becoming an inconspicuous part of the background. It's amazing how little notice even agents take of servants and workmen . . . and his lot have had some spectacular results. They are often used to check on suspected immigrants and political refugees who may not be all they seem, not by watching from afar, but by working for or near them day by day. And recently, for instance, several of the section have been employed as laborers on top-secret construction sites. . . . There have been some disturbing leaks of security —complete site plans of secret installations have been sold abroad—and it was found that a commercial espionage firm was getting information through operatives actually putting brick on brick and photographing the building at each stage."

"Philip," I said, "is only thirteen."

"You wouldn't be expected to plunge straight into such a life. As you yourself pointed out, you are untrained. There would be at least a year's instruction in various techniques before you were given a job."

"I can't," I said.

"Between jobs all his people are given leave. If a job takes as long as four months, like the one you have just done, they get about six weeks off. They never work more than nine months in a year, if it can be helped. You could often be home in the school holidays."

"If I am not there all the time, there won't be enough money for fees and there won't be any home."

"It is true that the British Government wouldn't pay you as much as you earn now," he said mildly, "but there are such things as full-time stud managers."

I opened my mouth and shut it again.

"Think about it," he said gently. "I've another colleague to see . . . . I'll be back in an hour."

He levered himself out of the chair and slowly walked out of the room.

The pigeons fluttered peaceably on the windowsill. I thought of the years I had spent building up the stud farm, and what I had achieved there. In spite of my comparative youth, the business was a solid success, and by the time I was fifty, I could with a bit of luck put it among the top studs in Australia and enjoy a respected, comfortably off, influential middle age.

What Beckett was offering was a lonely life of unprivileged jobs and dreary lodgings, a life of perpetual risk which could very well end with a bullet in the head.

Rationally there was no choice. Belinda and Helen and Philip still needed a secure home with the best I could do for them as a father substitute. And no sensible person would hand over to a manager a prosperous business and become instead a sort of sweeper-up of some of the world's smaller messes . . . one couldn't put the job any higher than that.

But irrationally . . . with very little persuasion I had

255

already left my family to fend for themselves, for as Beckett said, I wasn't of the stuff of martyrs; and the prosperous business had already driven me once into a pit of depression.

I knew now clearly what I was, and what I could do.

I remembered the times when I had been tempted to give up, and hadn't. I rememberd the moment when I held Elinor's dog whistle in my hand and my mind made an almost muscular leap at the truth. I remembered the satisfaction I felt in Kandersteg's scorched enclosure, knowing I had finally uncovered and defeated Adams and Humber. No sale of any horse had ever brought so quiet and complete a fulfillment.

The hour passed. The pigeons defecated on the window and flew away. Colonel Beckett came back.

"Well?" he said. "Yes or no?"

"Yes."

He laughed aloud. "Just like that? No questions or reservations?"

"No reservations. But I will need time to arrange things at home."

"Of course." He picked up the telephone receiver. "My colleague will wish you to see him before you go back." He rested his fingers on the dial. "I'll make an appointment."

"And one question."

"Yes?"

"What are the three *b*'s of number ten?"

He smiled secretly, and I knew he had intended that I should ask: which meant that he wanted me to know the answer. Devious, indeed. My nostrils twitched as if at the scent of a whole new world. A world where I belonged.

"Whether you could be bribed or bludgeoned or blackmailed," he said casually, "into changing sides."

He dialed the number, and altered my life.